Beautiful writing ... from an exceptionally gifted new talent. I look forward to more from Aaron Michael Ritchey.

—Jeanne C. Stein, bestselling author of the Anna Strong Chronicles

Aaron Michael Ritchey writes with a poetic grace that reminds me of a young Ray Bradbury.

—Bonnie Ramthun, author of *The White Gates*, a Truman Award Finalist

... richly drawn, beautifully complex characters ...

—Kirkus Reviews

Ritchey's voice is authentic and engaging.

—Chris Mandeville, author of *Seeds*, an Amazon Bestseller

THE JUNIPER WARS

DANDELION IRON

BOOK ONE

THE JUNIPER WARS
DANDELION IRON

BOOK ONE

AARON MICHAEL
RITCHEY

WordFire Press
Colorado Springs, Colorado

ISBN: 978-1-61475-349-0

Cover design by Julie Duong

Art Director Kevin J. Anderson

Book Design by RuneWright, LLC
www.RuneWright.com

Published by
WordFire Press, an imprint of
WordFire, Inc.
PO Box 1840
Monument CO 80132

Kevin J. Anderson & Rebecca Moesta, Publishers

WordFire Press Trade Paperback Edition March, 2016
Printed in the USA
wordfirepress.com

DEDICATION

For my dad, one of the good guys. No, I ain't yella.

MAGNIFICAT

The Sino wasn't a war. It only looked like that to the casual observer. Really, the Sino was an Armageddon.

—Former President Jack Kanton
48th President of the United States
On the 29th Anniversary of the start of the
Sino-American War
July 28, 2057

(i)

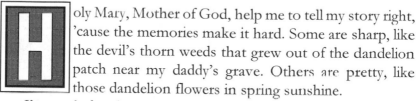oly Mary, Mother of God, help me to tell my story right, 'cause the memories make it hard. Some are sharp, like the devil's thorn weeds that grew out of the dandelion patch near my daddy's grave. Others are pretty, like those dandelion flowers in spring sunshine.

I've read a lot about the tragedies of the first half of the twenty-first century. Lots of history books about the Sino-American war, and the Sino is a hard bit of bacon for anyone to chew, Chinese and Americans alike. Lots of novels and videos about the Yellowstone Knockout and the five states it plunged into darkness: New Mexico, Colorado, Utah, Wyoming, and Montana. Otherwise known as the Juniper.

My story is about what happened after all that—after the city people left the Juniper, after the salvage operators took everything that wasn't nailed down and folks started ranching and farming. A story about how my love for a boy almost got my family killed when everything we ever loved was in dire jeopardy and our only hope was on a gamble; bad cards in an impossible poker game with the Devil grinning us down. A love story, an adventure, but also a family drama about three sisters who loved each other as much as they hated each other as much as they wanted to be like one another.

When I was sixteen, I was living in Cleveland, Ohio, going to the Sally Browne Burke Academy for the Moral and Literate. A bright future lay ahead of me. That all changed forever on the Ash Wednesday of 2058, a holy day of obligation that broke my heart.

Like always, my sister Wren did the heartbreaking. She was good at that.

CHAPTER ONE

I truly believe in boy meets girl. I have no doubt romantic love is Divine will. Even though our men are waning, we must trust in the wisdom of romantic love and not let money, fear, or force interfere with God's perfect plan.

—Sally Browne Burke
Founder of the New Morality Movement
February 14, 2058

(i)

Wren was on her way to my boarding school with bad news and a gun in her hand. She'd been living wild in Amarillo.

If I'd known my sister was coming, I'd have run.

My best friend, Anjushri Rawat, and I were ditching history by hiding out in an empty classroom—just the two of us surrounded by school desks and wood polished to a shine. Dust motes floated in the sunshine streaming through the tall windows. Made the room smell musty, but in a good way. Between the windows were RSD screens embedded in the wall, each showing a different bit of video. Some were of famous alumni from the Sally Browne Burke Academy for the Moral and Literate in Cleveland, Ohio, women doing important things, flashes of their biographies. Others showed nature scenes, which supposedly were meant to soothe us, but no one paid much attention to them. I didn't.

Right then, all I cared about was making sure Anju went to the Sammy Hawkins dance with Billy Finn, so true love could win the day. Well, true love was going to need a lot of help. Anju didn't have a chance at all with Billy.

Her ethnicity wasn't the issue, nor was her religion, since she was a Catholic from Goa, a particularly Christian part of India. Anju and I went to Mass together.

No, the problem was Billy's parents, who were drooling over the wealth Becca Olson brought to the table.

Boys were rare, and I knew I'd never get one. I wasn't rich or pretty enough. My body betrayed me at every turn—too big, too tall, my face too round. My eyes were reddish-brown like Colorado mud, my hair as strawed and yellowed as Juniper grass in January.

Only about fifty boys attended the Academy, roughly ten percent of the student population. For some girls, the competition for a date could be brutal, but not for me. Most days, I accepted the fact that my true treasures were my dedication to the New Morality and Anju's friendship. I had my fantasies about boys like any sixteen-year-old girl, but I figured I'd die unmarried. There were worse things.

I'd grown up in the Colorado territory and I'd witnessed such worse things firsthand. Not that Mama sent me away to boarding school to keep me safe. She'd made it clear—safety was an illusion and God loved the bold. At twelve, I packed my gear and climbed aboard a train, eastbound. I'd only gone home once 'cause it's a long way from Cleveland to the Juniper, a long trip, dangerous and expensive.

No electricity in the Juniper. None at all. During the early years of the Sino-American War, the Chinese nuked Yellowstone and killed the buzz in five western states. Nearly thirty years after the Yellowstone Knockout and still no power. President Jack tried to govern those states, but it wasn't long before America was sewing flags with only forty-five stars.

In that classroom with Anju, I figured I was done with my home in the Colorado territory forever. Sure, I might visit the ranch now and again, to see Mama and my older sister Sharlotte, but I was learning electrical engineering and looking at fat jobs in big corporations.

Besides, could I live without the Internet and video? Not hardly.

But first, true love, Anju and Billy Finn, forever and ever, Amen. That was the only reason I would sin by ditching class. Anju, however, wasn't impressed with my plan.

"I know you're trying to be all heroic, but it's not going to work," she said. "Billy and I can still be friends, I guess, but we both know Becca Olson is going to get him in the end."

Everything she said was the truth, but my plan popped all hot and greasy in my head. Regardless of the odds, I'd win the day for love and get revenge on that no-good, stuck-up Becca Olson. "Come on, Anju, throw it in gear and think happy thoughts. How many seasons of *Lonely Moon* have you and Billy watched together?"

"All of them," she admitted.

"All of them. And do you think Becca Olson ever watched even a single episode?"

Anju shook her head. Her hands were wrapped up in her New Morality dress, lots of gray fabric from throat to ankles. I'd seen her in a sari, all that brightly colored fabric contrasted beautifully with her dark features and darker hair, but she was New Morality, like me.

"You get to class," I said. "I'll be the hero. Just you watch."

"Okay." Anju moved to the door then turned around. "You know, odds are, we'll both die alone."

I rolled my eyes. "Thank you, oh voice of doom. I woke up with a little headache. Prolly brain cancer, huh?"

Anju dropped her eyes. She wasn't laughing.

I laughed for both of us. I was used to doing it. "It's gonna be okay."

"Thank you, Cavatica. Thank you for being my friend."

Anju disappeared out the door, leaving me alone with my Hayao 5 electric slate and my plan, two things I loved as much as any girl ever loved a cute boy or the season premiere of their favorite show. The first thing I did was text Becca Olson to invite her to come chat with me, face to face. Kept it vague and real mysterious so she'd come. Then I checked the audio cables plugged into my slate, checked the server connection, checked the microphone. Everything was ready.

A flicker on one of the RSDs caught my eye and I had a moment of wonder. One screen showed Canadian geese on the wing flying in a *V* during migration. Outside the window, I caught a glimpse of the same species of geese, flying through a sky blackened by clouds. The downy white of their breast feathers gleamed in contrast to the gray storm, both on the video and outside the window. For a moment, strong memories of the ranch took me away—feet in stirrups, a restless horse under me, listening to the honking racket of geese on the wing.

I didn't feel nostalgic, only grateful. If I wanted to hear geese, all I had to do was Google the noise. Reality is oftentimes overrated. Case in point, *Lonely Moon*, the Juniper-based TV drama Anju and Billy loved. That show was a whole lot easier to understand than the reality of those states turned territories.

Since my trap was ready for Becca, I had a chance to pray. Eyes closed, I asked for forgiveness for ditching class. Next, I prayed God would shine His all-powerful light upon my righteous cause— true love.

(ii)

Before all my adventures, Becca Olson was my favorite villain—rich, pretty, and mean. On the first day I met her, four-and-half years prior, I hadn't bowed before her royalty. She took it as a snub, since I was just some Juniper girl, about as precious as a rusted penny, and she was an Olson, of the Shaker Heights Olsons, don't you know?

Becca was a young woman on a mission—to conquer every bit of the world she could. Starting with Billy Finn. She'd dismissed both Anju and me as immigrants from foreign lands and adversaries not worth her time.

Becca flounced through the door along with three of her flouncy friends, petticoated up. All that fabric rubbing together sounded like a rainstorm had entered the room.

Officially, New Morality dresses were supposed to be of a neutral color and cover as much skin as possible to let the natural beauty of a young woman's soul shine. The New Morality wardrobe guidelines also opposed any sort of accessories—bracelets, rings, necklaces, headbands proclaimed a woman not only frivolous but also vain. Vanity shadowed pride, one of the seven deadly sins.

Bangles layered the wrists of Becca and her friends. Every finger sported jewelry except their left ring fingers. The neon colors of their dresses gleamed bright enough to hurt. Only their hands and faces were visible, which was good enough for the dress code. However, the colors let everyone know they were only paying lip service to the New Morality.

I felt sorry for them. Such clothing and rebelliousness displayed a lack of moral character. But wealth and privilege often inflicted spiritual damage of that sort. The staff frowned on Becca and her entourage, and the administration did too, only the huge donations prolly softened their outrage.

"What do you want?" Becca demanded right off.

I eyed all the faces. It felt like a gunfight, like the ones my sister Wren was always getting into. Wren used semi-automatic pistols. My weapons were far different, but just as powerful.

"It's about Billy Finn," I said. Hand in the pocket of my gray dress, I pressed the execute button on the remote control of my slate.

The overhead speakers out in the hall popped and hissed for a second, but I was confident Becca and her crew weren't bright enough to pay attention to such a small detail. I had patched into the audio cables in the wall. I could've hacked into the router and transmitted the signal wirelessly, but the IT department would've shut off my broadcast right away. This way, they couldn't stop me until they got to the server room. I had five minutes easy.

"What about Billy?" Becca's face radiated contempt. "He asked me to the Sammy Hawkins dance. I accepted. End of story."

I cleared my throat. I wanted everyone in the school to hear me real well. "Well, Becca, everybody knows Anju and Billy are in love. I was thinking you should be a darling and step aside and let them be together. Remember what Sally Browne Burke said about—"

"Oh, please." She scoffed. "Billy Finn is viable, which makes him a commodity, which means only those who have the money will get him. Anju doesn't have the cash. I do. Where do you think he got his new frictionless car? Who do you think is going to pay for his college? Why else do you think he asked me to the stupid dance? Don't be naïve."

Becca Olson was doing exactly what I needed her to do—turning up skank cards at the poker table. Aces high.

I played stupid. "Oh well, you know, I was just trying—"

"I know what you're doing. You're just trying to butt into my business. Well, I can't believe Anju is in love with Billy. I mean, he's such a fat little toad, but then again, he's viable, and we all know what that means in this day and age. The boy could have hooves and a tail and we'd all still be falling over ourselves to get to him—every one of us. It's a competition I'll win."

I should've stopped there. I really should've. But I was sixteen, I had my enemy in my gun sights, and Becca's sneer made me want to empty the clip on her.

"As I was saying," I said so innocently, "Sally Browne Burke declares that now more than ever, romantic love is required for the betterment of our species. It's an idea that our own Mrs. Justice embraces. Natural romantic attraction will bring together boys and girls whom God has destined for each other, which will result in strong, God-fearing children. Why, just the other day, Mrs. Justice—"

Becca erupted. "Mrs. Justice is probably *gillian*."

Gillian, as in *tong xing lian*, as in same sex love.

I gasped, and though I couldn't believe how well my plan was coming together, part of me felt bad for both Becca and Mrs. Justice. Such an accusation could kill a career, especially at a school like the Sally Browne Burke Academy. That year we'd lost two students and a teacher 'cause of gossip. The New Morality insisted homosexuality was a sin. Liberals disagreed. I felt caught in the middle.

"You don't mean that," I said, a little out of breath.

Becca seemed to enjoy my shock. "But I do. I mean, she wants us to call her Mrs. Justice. How old fashioned is that? And there's no Mr. Justice, never was, which makes me think she has some girl on the side. *Gillian* or not, she's just a parrot, and not a very pretty one at that. Sally Browne Burke says something and Mrs. Justice repeats it. Whatever. Romantic love is dead and gone. Now it's all about money. Are we done?"

Standing by the door, Marcy Bauer, one of Becca's friends, cocked her head and knit her brows. She was the closest to the overhead speakers in the hall, which had just broadcast our entire conversation to every room in the school, including Billy Finn's classroom. Including Mrs. Justice's office.

"Becca, I think everyone can hear you," Marcy said with awe in her voice.

I let my smile shine.

The truth hit Becca like a punch. "You filthy piece of trash!"

I thought to run, but Becca and her friends blocked the door. Dang. Hadn't thought of an escape route. Silly me.

(iii)

I scooped up my electric slate, yanked out the audio cords, and got ready to run that petticoat gauntlet.

"I'm going to make you pay!" Becca clattered toward me. She hooked her fingers into claws.

"You really don't wanna do that," I warned her, but she wasn't going to listen. She threw herself at me, telegraphing her attack.

I dodged her. Four years in civilization had civilized a little of the dodge out of me, but twelve years of growing up with two cowgirl-tough older sisters had left my reflexes spring-loaded.

Becca sped past me, but the other girls rushed forward.

Marcy Bauer grabbed my dress, and I stomped her foot. She screamed. I socked Ethel Walters in the stomach, bending her over. Priscilla Carrington reached for me, but I swung a hip and knocked her flat. Becca, had turned and rejoined the fight. She caught my face with her nails, blazing a scratch across my cheek. The pain raised my *shakti*. I punched Becca right in the nose, prolly breaking it. Dropped her to the floor like a bag full of rags.

I felt a little bad, but only a little—she could afford the plastic surgery. And it gave me an escape route. Rich girls in Ohio generally don't get punched in the nose. Shocked them all as still as stone.

I strode through the perfume and sniffling like Moses through the Red Sea.

"Don't you walk away from me, you filthy piece of Juniper trash," Becca snarled.

I stopped at the door. I felt proud to have grown up in a house my mama had fought to build and bled to keep. Before I knew it, I had turned back around. Two princesses lay on the floor of the classroom and two girls stood frozen.

"You don't know how ridiculous you are, with your country talk and bumpkin manners." Becca's face was tearful and bloody and every ounce of pretty was gone, swallowed up by her cruel, mercenary heart. Her neon dress swirled across the floor and her thin arms shook, holding her weight. "Only stupid people live in the Juniper. Stupid or criminally insane. Which one are you?"

I grinned, letting her know nothing she said could hurt me. "Well, I'm criminal enough to have knocked you down. Stupid enough to stand here listening to your nonsense. If you come after me, well, I'll show you my crazy." Dang, that was something my sister Wren might've said.

"Do you know who I am? Do you know how much money my family gives to this school? You'll be sorry, Cavatica Weller. You and that Anju, you'll both pay! Billy Finn is mine. I bought him."

"You can't buy people," I said. "Billy and Anju are meant to be together."

Becca lowered her head. Blood from her nose dripped onto the floor. She laughed hard, cried harder. "You're so stupid. You're so jacking stupid."

"Prolly," I said, "but I'd rather be stupid than heartless."

Overhead through the speakers, Mrs. Justice called out, "Cavatica Weller, please report to my office immediately." She sounded bitten. Like something was chewing on her. Which would've been my sister Wren at that moment.

"See," Becca said, "you're in trouble. Not me."

I was in trouble, but I had no idea how bad it was going to get. If I had, I would've called the Cleveland police myself.

CHAPTER TWO

The New Morality is a mother's voice, calling her children home. It is late. We are alone. Night is coming. But if we listen, we can hear our mother calling us to dinner because the kitchen is warm and there is hope, always hope, for those who listen.

—Sally Browne Burke
From the Eighth Annual International
New Morality Conference
June 21, 2057

(i)

Like I said, my sister was coming with hard news.

But then Wren was hard.

How she got that way was a mystery we didn't talk about much, but we thought about all the time.

Maybe it was 'cause Wren was the middle sister in a time of trouble. Maybe it was 'cause she liked beer more than milk growing up, or maybe it was simple genetics. Either way, Wren courted the Devil when he didn't come calling on his own accord.

I figured Wren prolly got a calloused heart by growing up on the hip of a woman who had to fight every day to put food on the table. With a sick husband and a big Burlington ranch falling to pieces, Mama didn't have much time to give Wren what she needed. Heck, I'm not sure anybody could have given her what she needed.

Wren's real name was Irene, but after five seconds, Mama knew she had named her wrong—Irene was a Wren, a soul that had to fly 'cause sitting still hurt too much.

She was late-night gorgeous, black hair, black eyes, and skin like desert-bleached bone. She walked as if the earth was bowing down before her beauty.

My oldest sister Sharlotte was Wren's complete opposite in everything including how much of Mama's affection she got. Mama held Sharlotte close to her heart, especially after Elwyn died as a baby. That was when Mama still worked salvage, living hand to mouth and under fire. She hadn't counted on meeting Charles Weller, hadn't counted on getting pregnant, though God built our species to be fruitful and multiply. Or so we'd been taught.

My sister Shar and Mama were cut from the same stiff cloth. Both were upright, hardworking and concrete-corset stubborn.

Sharlotte was the oldest, born near the end of Mama's salvaging days. Four years later came Wren, and four years after that came me. By the time I was born, Mama had mellowed some, but then I wasn't a problem. By then I had a passel of mothers around on the ranch, so I couldn't walk two steps into trouble without getting caught and thrown back onto the straight and narrow.

We should've had a big family full of girls, but that wasn't meant to be. Lots of embroidered blankets for the baby girls who died—Elwyn, Fern, Willa, and Avery. Mama would've thrown the blankets out, but Sharlotte kept them in her bedroom, folded on her bed.

My classmates at the Academy couldn't understand why Juniper folks wanted big ol' families, and it wasn't 'cause we were Catholic. No, down on the farm, it boiled down to simple economics—the more kids, the more free labor.

And if you struck it rich with a viable boy? Even better.

But women having babies without proper healthcare, too much work, and iffy nutrition added up to more dead babies and dead mothers than most Yankees liked to consider.

Yankees. That was what the Juniper folks called other Americans. Even Southerners. It was ironic, but Juniper folks grew up on beefsteak and irony.

After all the death, only three Weller girls remained—Sharlotte, Wren, and me. We all boiled over with what the Hindus call *shakti*, raw female power.

Maybe that was what had poisoned Wren against the world. All that death.

No, something happened between Wren and Mama early on, something bad. Or maybe I just wanted an easy explanation. In this life, easy answers generally aren't worth a rotting haystack left out in the rain.

(ii)

Mrs. Justice's office smelled like books, money, and the Nyco floor polish. Everything shined—the floor, the bookshelves, the wainscoting, and her big desk. Mrs. Justice was just as shiny, ramrod straight behind the desk. Wren lounged in a chair in front of it. A lacy yellow dress covered her, but it was far too short to be New Morality. No, it was a party girl's dress, and I immediately colored with embarrassment.

Wren smiled at me. Lips curled. Eyes cold. She then hitched up the right side of her skirt and yanked out a Springfield XD Subcompact 9mm pistol from a holster Velcroed to her upper thigh.

Truth be told, her evil smile scared me more than the handgun.

Mrs. Justice gasped. The white washed out of her face even as red flushed her neck. "What are you doing?"

"Well, Mrs. Justice," Wren said slowly, "like I told you, I ain't leavin' without our money."

With my heart pounding, I gripped my slate like it was a shield. "Wren, no." Not sure what I was saying no to, but it seemed like the logical thing to say. What money was she talking about?

"Well, Cavvy, Mrs. Justice says that if you leave early she won't reimburse us your tuition. I don't think that's fair, do you?" Wren popped the magazine out, snapped back the action, and then with practiced speed caught the bullet that ejected out the side. She regarded my principal. "Our conversation was making me tense. Firearms generally calm my nerves, but now that my little pistol ain't loaded, there's no reason for you to be scared." She placed the pistol, magazine, and bullet on the desk.

Same old Wren. I hadn't seen her in four years, not since she was sixteen, growing into her talons and fangs. Watching her, though, it seemed like yesterday.

Mrs. Justice didn't say a word—too pale to talk. Guns do that to law-abiding people outside in the World. Inside, the Juniper was the Juniper, outside, for us, was the World, where electricity worked and there were actual laws.

"Why would I be leaving early?" I asked.

My sister shrugged, then, with that evil smile still on her face, she said, "Mama's dead."

A sharp shock swept through me, too big for me to feel. So I studied my sister's smile, would've taken a picture of it, just to figure it out. The words my sister said were hard, but her smile was harder.

Mrs. Justice finally found her voice. "My condolences, Cavatica, for your mother. I know you two must both be grieving. However, that doesn't excuse your sister for bursting into my office and demanding the rest of this year's tuition. Moreover, I refuse to be intimidated. I know you both grew up in chaos, but Ohio has strict gun control laws, and our Academy has a policy of zero tolerance ..."

Her voice became a drone. I couldn't stop looking at Wren, wondering if she was telling the truth. Mama dead? Couldn't be. Women like my mama didn't die. There were too many chores to do. Too much money to chase. Death didn't dare touch a woman like my mama.

"I'm calling security and the police." Mrs. Justice got up and walked out. Wren and I didn't move.

"How'd she die?" It was a dumb question 'cause of course she was alive.

"Heart attack. She got herself into big money problems, and then dropped dead. Now the ranch is in trouble, and Sharlotte ..." Wren closed her eyes, shook her head, and grinned with hate. "Sharlotte said if I didn't come and fetch you, she'd hire killers on me. But I wanted to come. It's been a long time, Princess, and I was curious to see how you've grown. By the way, I for one appreciated your little display. That Becca Olson sounded like a real rich priss."

Standing there, I tried not to believe her, but my denial was draining away like sand under my feet.

Then it hit me what Wren's smile meant. Wren had issues with inappropriate emotional reactions, something we studied in my psychology class, but this was something more. Wren wanted to see my reaction, wanted to see what I looked like gutted and laid open by the news. For her, it was entertainment.

Fury filled me. But anger is what psychologists call an iceberg emotion. Underneath the rage, icy sorrow and colder despair gushed and swirled. If I had to swim in that freezing water, I'd pull Wren down with me. And I hated when she called me princess. So I reared back to slap that evil smile off her face.

Even sitting, Wren ducked it easily. "Oh, hell no, girl. What they been teachin' you here? Not how to fight. I saw that comin' a kilometer away."

Rattler-quick, Wren was on her feet. With her free hand, she tweaked my nose.

The sour smell of liquor oozed from her pores. No surprise there.

Mrs. Justice's office was not a place to fight—too crowded with furniture, books, and whatnot, but still, I tried to wrestle my sister down. Even half-drunk, Wren was stronger and meaner. She kneed me in the thigh and shoved me to the hardwood floor.

"Back in the day, you'd have dodged that," Wren said. "Your time with these Yankees done slowed you down. Let me help you up." She put out a hand, fingernails painted a bright cherry-red.

I knocked her hand away. "I don't want to go home. I want to graduate. I've already started looking at colleges." That was true, even though I was only a junior.

"I don't care what you want." Wren retrieved the magazine and slammed it back into the pistol. She chambered a round, then ejected the magazine, and pressed the spare bullet in on top of the others. She slid the magazine home into the butt of the 9mm. Once more fully loaded. "Sharlotte wants you, and what Sharlotte wants Sharlotte gets. You can argue with her."

I couldn't match Wren in a fistfight, but I had other weapons, nasty bombs with my sister's name stamped on them in big black letters.

I stood up and wiped some sweat off my forehead, then started pushing red buttons, launching missiles, going to war. Fire one. "You drunk? Well, you are weak-willed, or that's what Mama always used to say."

A little of that self-satisfied smirk faded from Wren's face. "What Mama said don't matter no more. She's dead. And yeah, I had a few beers on the train, but I'm far from drunk."

"Sure Mama died of a heart attack. Worrying over you finally broke her heart." Fire two.

Wren laughed, jiggling the Springfield 9 in my general direction. "Oh, you're good. I see what you're doing, and it won't work."

Fire three. "Sharlotte really did threaten to kill you, didn't she? How does that feel? Your own sister wanting you dead? Just goes to show, you really don't belong in our family—not when Mama was alive, and definitely not now that she's ... gone."

My voice tripped on that last word, but still, it was a direct hit. This time, I saw Wren's attack coming and ran behind Mrs. Justice's desk. I didn't think Wren would shoot me. At least I hoped she wouldn't. Sisters shouldn't kill each other, even if they want to much of the time.

"Let's just go," Wren said, smile gone. I had won, but it felt empty, which is why fighting with family is so useless. Every time you hit 'em good, it feels like hitting yourself.

"I'm sorry." I breathed it out. "For what I said. But I ain't going home. I'll call Sharlotte on her next run to Hays."

Wren's pretty eyes were distant and that pretty mouth curled up in a chew. "Ain't gonna be no more runs to Hays. When Mama died, she left us a whole stack of bills and no money, but Sharlotte has this crazy plan to save the ranch. We have to get home, right away. Funeral is Saturday."

What Wren said, it was as if she was speaking Mandarin. No more cattle runs to Hays? Sharlotte having a crazy plan? Sharlotte Weller was Sunday-straight, a clear-thinking responsible woman. She made Sally Browne Burke look like a whiskey-headed party girl.

And it was Wednesday. No way could we get to Burlington in three days.

Since Wren was talking crazy, I figured I might as well join her. "I'm not going back, Wren. Never. I'm through with the Juniper.

And if I have to have a sister like you, I'm through with family." Yeah, I clung to my denial, but I was so comfortable at my fancy Academy, with electricity and gun laws and mostly nice girls, that I couldn't imagine going back home. And I didn't really want to believe Mama was dead. If I stayed in school, it meant Mama would still be alive and everything would be normal.

Right then, Mrs. Justice burst into the room. Behind her was campus security, two big women, scowling, dressed in gray.

Behind the security women, Ohio policewomen jogged over, carrying Armalite Thor stunners. They looked like silver guns without barrels, but fully charged, the stunners could throw electrical charges as far as ten meters, knock you down and leave you gnawing on your tongue. Non-lethal. Gun laws went into effect for everyone in the U.S., civilians and the police alike.

Mrs. Justice was yelling. "See! She has a gun! Arrest her. Arrest them both!"

"Ah, hell, here we go," Wren whispered. I heard the danger-quiet in my sister's voice.

"No, Wren!"

Her Springfield 9 coughed thunder.

I had completely forgotten how loud a gun was, and how much trouble one could cause in the hands of my gunslinger sister.

(iii)

Being in a gunfight is not like riding a bicycle. My glands had forgotten how to handle the spitfire of my adrenaline.

Back when I was a kid growing up in the Juniper, I got used to firearms and killed my fair share of deer and antelope. Even before June Mai Angel, we had Outlaw Warlords in the Juniper, and I grew up reloading Mama's rifle during gun battles. I guess that made me tough. Gave me awful dreams, I'll tell you what. Noise, blood, and bullets. Dreams about Queenie, the Outlaw Warlord my mama killed dead.

But that had been a long time ago, so when Wren started shooting, I didn't react like I should've. Wren's years of hard living had given her a tolerance for grit and gunfire. I'd grown as soft as the rest of the Yankees.

The security guards and policewomen didn't realize that Wren was aiming high. All they knew was that a pretty girl in a yellow dress was shooting at them. One of the cops raised a stunner, and Wren shot it out of her hand.

"Out the window, Cavvy," Wren yelled.

"No, Wren, we gotta give ourselves up. You can't kill those women! They're just doing their job!"

"Saturday, Cavvy, that's the funeral. Can't get there if we're in prison. I got priors and they'll get you for accessory."

I was too blind from the violence to think her argument through, and I was right next to the window. Part of me figured if we could get out of there, Wren wouldn't kill anyone. For one mad moment, I thought about trying to take her down myself, but how could I ever hope to stand up to Wren? She'd taken me in every fight we'd ever had. And it was clear God Himself had trouble keeping her in line. What chance did I have? So I followed along.

I threw open the window, punched through the screen, and jumped out into rose bushes. Thorns tore my dress and ripped my skin. Wren dashed out after me, her gun smoking in the February cold. The rotten-egg smell of gunpowder brought back too many memories.

Stunners zapped the grass around us. The sparkling blue of the energy bolts raised the hair on my arms. Wren turned and fired into the brick, keeping the cops and security guards inside.

"Okay, Wren, now that you got me expelled and on the run, what's your big plan to get us out of here?"

Wren smirked. "Didn't reckon on a shootout."

Great, she didn't have an exit strategy. Just like me. I'd have to save us.

More stunner beams flashed from other policewomen hustling toward us across the lawn.

Wren and I ran into the faculty parking lot filled with old elm trees and polished cars. We ducked behind a Dodge Imaginos resting on its hydraulic landing pads. I dashed my fingers across my slate, leaving sweat marks, and speed-dialed Anju.

She answered and her face filled my screen. I was about to tell her I needed help when I heard a policewoman's voice close by.

"Backup is on its way. Approach with caution. They are armed and dangerous."

"Not as armed as I'd like to be," Wren murmured. "But more dangerous than you could ever imagine."

"Wren, it's wrong to kill. Sixth commandment. We're Catholic, remember?"

"Where are your ashes, Miss Mary?" Wren asked it in a laugh.

"Mass was tonight," I said, then …

"Cavatica? Is that you? I can't see your face." Anju's voice blasted out of my slate's speakers. Dang it all. I thumbed down the volume and centered my face in the camera.

"Anju, where are you?" I whispered.

"In Billy's car. In the student parking lot. He found me right away, once he heard your broadcast. What's up?"

"Over here!" a policewoman yelled. "I think they're over here!"

Didn't have much time. The cavalry needed to come before Wren killed anybody.

Footsteps echoed. "I'll cut them off on this side!"

"Amateurs," Wren grunted.

She was right. Yelling and running gave away their positions. America had been so peaceful since the Sino ended that police training was bound to suffer.

I kept my voice low. "Anju, I need you and Billy to come get me in the faculty parking lot. And, um, there's gonna be some shooting."

"At least four shots," Wren whispered.

"You didn't bring an extra magazine? Who's the amateur now?"

Wren twisted a lip. "Didn't reckon on a shootout."

"Cavatica, what's happening?" Anju licked her lips nervously. "Shooting?"

Wren popped up and fired. A car alarm went off. She sank back down, nodding. "Just two of them cops are close by. Other four are hanging back, waiting on more firepower."

Sirens wailed in the distance. More firepower on the way.

"Come and fetch us, Anju, please," I pleaded.

"I don't know. Gunshots?" Sweat beaded on her forehead. It was a lot to ask, but I was desperate. My heart felt like it was trying to crawl out of my throat.

"Please, Anju." I paused, then knew the perfect thing to say. "You said you always wondered what it would be like to live out an episode of *Lonely Moon*, right? Well, here is your chance."

She took in a deep breath. "Okay, we'll come." She glanced over at Billy and smiled. "I owe you everything. Billy knows I love him for him."

"Wonderful. Now come get us, girl. Fast."

A shoe slid over the asphalt. A policewoman whirled around the car, stunner in her fist.

Wren grabbed her hand, twisted her backward, and used the woman's own stunner on her. The woman toppled over and shook like sizzling bacon on the asphalt. Wren looked at the silver half-gun. "Prolly better than killing 'em."

Up again, she stunned the other policewoman who was creeping up on us.

Billy's car swooshed into the parking lot, a sweet Ford Pegasus, frictionless and as red as Wren's fingernails.

Suddenly, a Chevy Landspeeder next to us exploded as if struck by lightning. I could smell the air cooking.

I froze up like a rabbit on the road. What in the heck could do something like that?

Wren grabbed me by the hair and threw me into the cramped back seat of Billy's Pegasus. She tossed the stunner into my lap, raised up her Springfield 9 to pop off another shot, then slid in next to me. Billy took off, pedal to the metal.

I glanced back and saw a woman in black with a big silver rifle in her hands. She aimed that monstrosity at us, and I was trying to get a word out, when Wren flung herself between the front seats and grabbed the wheel, cranking it to the right. Floating on air, we rocked to the side just as a crackling lightning bolt seared past us and hit a tree, blowing through its roots, bark, and branches like the wrath of God. The tree creaked over, falling toward us. Wren slammed the wheel left and we careened under it.

Billy was a short, chubby boy with bad acne, and you could see every zit stand up tall on his pale face. "Excuse me, ma'am, but I think—"

"Sure thing, Johnson." Wren sat back down in the backseat. "You can be the big man and drive. I just didn't want us hit by that charge gun back there."

"That was a charge gun?" I didn't know the Armalite Zeus 2 had become standard issue for the Cleveland Police Department. The charge guns could be dialed back to a mere stunner, but when on full power, they could disintegrate flesh. I had no idea what setting the policewoman had her rifle set to, but it seemed pretty dang lethal.

Speaking of stunners, I slid the one Wren threw me into my pocket. Hoped she'd forget about it. I thought about using it on her right then, but like it or not, Wren was my best hope for getting home. Going back to school was impossible now.

Wren tapped Billy on the shoulder. "Okay, Johnson, this is what we're going to do. Next gas station, you and your girlfriend get out. We'll call and let you know where we stashed your car. You won't report your car stolen, will you?"

"No, of course not," Billy said. His forehead crinkled in confusion. "But my name is not Johnson. And what's a gas station?"

"Juice plug," I mumbled.

Wren shrugged at the words. Didn't mean a thing to her. "All you boys are johnsons. That's all you're good for now."

"Wren! Where are your manners?" Stupid for me to be so shocked, but my world had cracked apart and was currently on fire. My body trembled from the adrenaline of the gunfight, and my brain felt shredded from Wren's horrible news about our mama, our poor dead mama.

Anju sat speechless in front of us. I felt bad for her 'cause not only had I gotten her into trouble, I was going to have to tell her goodbye forever.

If we weren't arrested first.

CHAPTER THREE

The Sterility Epidemic is the black plague of our times. Luckily, instead of superstitious priests mumbling chants, we have the American Reproduction Knowledge Initiative. Let the churches and morality movements save your souls. The ARK is here to save our species.

—Tiberius "Tibbs" Hoyt
President and CEO of the ARK
January 1, 2058

(i)

Sitting in the backseat with Wren, I listened to the sirens wailing in the distance. If one of the policewomen had scanned Billy's license plate, they'd find us easy.

I had to get home. I had to touch Mama one more time before we buried her.

If the police did find us, I knew what would happen—Wren had two bullets left. While I was worrying about Mama and those two bullets, Billy, for some odd reason, was worrying about Wren calling him johnson.

"Excuse me, ma'am, my name is Billy Finn."

Wren had one hand on Anju's headrest. "Don't care who you are." She pointed with her Springfield 9. "There, at that gas station, you and your girlfriend get out. And thanks for the ride."

Billy was wise enough not to argue. He drove his frictionless car over to the juice plug.

Becca Olson sure had given him a nice present. The Pegasus had an Eggdrop-class Eterna battery so it didn't need the juice plugs like the Mushus did. Eggdrops could easily get a thousand kilometers without any trouble. I had a little hero-worship for Maggie Jankowski of the GE Corporation, even though she named her batteries after Chinese food. That took a lot of gall after the horrors of the Sino.

We all piled out. Wren got into the driver's seat, while I tried to figure out a way to say goodbye to Anju and Billy. I wished I was like Wren, ice-cold inside, or Sharlotte, who had a horseshoe for a heart.

Instead, I was all squish and tears. My life in Cleveland was over, and all the emotions finally caught up with me. I ran over and hugged Anju. "I gotta go, Anju, and I prolly ain't never comin' back."

"What? Cavatica, you don't mean—"

Wren yelled from behind the wheel, "Enough of that girly 'strogen huggin'. We gotta go!"

I cried full-on as I rambled, "Anju, my mama's dead and the ranch is in trouble, and my sisters both are crazy, and we don't have no money for tuition for next year. Coming back would be so hard and expensive. I just love you so much."

Anju held me while she sobbed. "Oh, Cavatica, I'll write to you about Billy and me. We're going steady, and it's all because of you. Your plan worked!"

We hugged, cried buckets, and I worried that Wren might think I was *gillian*, but another part of me didn't care 'cause I loved Anju so much. Friends like that were worth more than all of the money Maggie Jankowski and Tibbs Hoyt had put together and gathering interest.

I got in and held Anju's hand through the passenger's window until Wren cursed us and drove off.

Wren *tsked*. "What a display, Cavatica Jeanne Weller. I don't think I could live with myself after all that."

I didn't realize my hands were trembling until I wiped the tears from my face.

Couldn't believe I was on the run from the cops. Couldn't believe I'd pinned all my hopes for getting home on Wren. Couldn't believe I had to go back to the Juniper without a mother there to protect me. Couldn't believe any of it.

(ii)

I tried to calm myself by focusing on my breath, something I'd learned from Anju. Breathe in through my nose and out through my mouth. At the same time, I said a Hail Mary, every phrase either an inhale or an exhale.

Slowly, I got to feeling a little better. Staring out the window also helped. The streets became prettier and richer with every kilometer. Immaculate gardens and pristine flower beds lined perfectly maintained streets. Being from the Juniper, I could appreciate unblemished asphalt, but then they had road crews constantly laying down blacktop.

Everyone was working. Unemployment was close to zero percent due to the low population after the Sino and the Sterility Epidemic. I know it might sound sexist, but with fewer boys we had less crime and less violence. I'd done a research paper on prison populations during the last half of the twentieth century, and the ratio of incarcerated men to women did make one pause. Now, America was closing down women's prisons. We just didn't need as many anymore.

Out in the World, America prospered with unlimited energy, a strong economy, flying cars, and sunshine. Pretty much a paradise, and I was Eve, disgraced and exiled back to the Juniper.

Wren drove slowly, so we wouldn't draw attention to ourselves. Still, it seemed every street had a police cruiser on it. From the window of one cruiser, the flash of a scanner hit the ID chips in our vehicle, but they'd just show a car registered to Billy Finn, an upstanding member of society. If they called him, Billy would cover for me.

Part of me wished the police would find us, but another part knew I had to leave Eden to go home and bury Mama. Her funeral was just three days away. No Ash Wednesday smudges for me.

My lungs felt heavy, and I prayed to God for forgiveness and strength.

We drove past the ARK clinic in Shaker Heights, and like always, guards stood out front to escort people in and keep protestors out. I watched as a teenage boy and his parents swagger up the steps. He wasn't going in there to test his viability, no, he was going in there to sell.

Some viable boys strutted around like stallions, others, like Billy Finn, were far more bashful. For them, going to an ARK clinic meant humiliation regardless of the paycheck. Everyone knew what they did in the little rooms. I'd have died of embarrassment if I'd been a viable boy.

The ARK, otherwise known as the American Reproduction Knowledge Initiative, was a company run by Tibbs Hoyt, the richest man in the world. The ARK's business was researching our boy problem and selling Male Product. Since the boy was viable, he and his parents were making a bundle selling what he was lucky enough to have.

So few boys were around. The Sino-American War had decimated whole generations of men, and to make matters worse, at the very height of the casualties, fewer and fewer boys were born until it got to the point that only one out of every ten babies was male. Of those boys, only one in ten was viable, meaning they weren't sterile. Most people thought it was Chinese bio-warfare gone wrong 'cause it affected the whole world. Religious folk thought it was the wrath of God punishing us for our many sins.

And some blamed the Sterility Epidemic on the Yellowstone Knockout. It made a certain amount of sense—this huge cataclysm created the Juniper and started the Sterility Epidemic all at the same time, but part of me didn't like how convenient it all seemed.

I glanced over at Wren. She was driving tight-fisted and tight-jawed. "Hey, Cavvy, look up the Amtrak schedule on your computer thingy. I can't remember when the train to Chicago leaves."

Hands shaking, I was about to thumb on my slate when I realized the police would be scanning for my MAC address. I had to register my slate with the school to get on their satellite network, and the minute I popped on, the police would use it to track me.

But I could get around that. I had downloaded some pirated *Lonely Moon* episodes for Anju until the guilt got to me. I went to confession and Father Stein was clear, no more pirating. Still, I had batch files to re-route my connection to servers in Finland, so I started up my slate in safe mode, tweaked some settings, then rebooted and like magic, my connection was re-routed through Helsinki, complete with a phony MAC address.

Right away, there, on my homepage, news alerts, video all about Cleveland and all about us. Roadblocks, street teams sweeping the avenues, and our pictures, both terrible and unflattering. Eyewitness accounts of the gunfight said it was as vicious as the O.K. Corral.

Wren glanced over and smirked. "Nobody even got killed. But yeah, the Yankees would blow this all out of proportion." Her smirk turned frowny. "This is the wrong car to be in, way too conspicuous. We can't drive outta town. And even if we could afford it, the airport would be suicide. Train is our only hope. Gotta be in McCook, Nebraska, Friday morning, or we'll miss the funeral. Sharlotte'll kill me." A pause. "Well, she'll try."

"Why McCook? Ain't nothin' there. We can pick up the thruway rail in Sterling and that will take us to Burlington. That's what I did when I came home for Christmas a couple years ago. You weren't around."

Wren didn't respond. She just drove, her brow pinched.

On my slate, I found the Capital Limited train bound for Chicago leaving the Amtrak station at 12:58 PM. Even with a long layover in Chicago, we would make it to McCook early Friday morning. If we could get out of Cleveland at all.

Like Wren said, going to the airport would've gotten us caught, and regardless, we couldn't fly into the Juniper. No electricity. We could've gotten close though. Back in 2044, I had flown into Omaha and then took a train to Sterling. But that was when we had money.

Wren was dangerous, sure, and I could've used the stunner on her and took off on my own, but then I'd never make the funeral on Saturday. I needed Wren, but I couldn't figure out her plan. If we got into McCook on Friday morning, we still couldn't get to Burlington in a day. It was a 142 kilometers by the old highways.

Even with a fast stage, it was a two-day journey. A full two days driving the horses into a sweat.

"Tell me, Wren. Why McCook? And why Saturday for Mama's funeral? Why so quick?"

"You'll see," was all the answer I got.

We parked in a parking garage downtown next to a Chevy Landspeeder, named after the old *Star Wars* video. 'Speeders were one of the first frictionless cars to hit the market, thanks to American ingenuity.

I was on my slate, about to message Anju, when Wren stopped me. "Don't tell them where the car is yet. Not until we're safe."

"But Wren—"

Her stare stopped me from saying more.

We had to walk a bit, but we finally made it through the doors of the train station, a tiny place, just a couple of benches, a place for luggage, and the ticket counter. Wren bought our tickets with lots of wrinkled-up money. I didn't have a dime. I guess I could've sold my electric slate 'cause once we hit Buzzkill, Nebraska, my slate would be as useless as a soggy paper plate. The Juniper's electromagnetic field wiped hard drives clean. It chewed up computers and spit out the parts—only good for the gold in the motherboards.

Still, I couldn't part with my slate, not right then.

Wren went to the baggage counter with tickets to exchange for luggage. The clerk brought Wren's old army duffle as well as a brand new backpack. My sister shouldered both bags and turned. That was when the three policewomen came through the front door.

Three women, searching faces, searching for us.

My mouth went open, my feet iced up solid to the floor, but Wren pulled me into the men's bathroom quick, before they saw us and before I could argue.

All my concerns faded right away when I realized we were trapped. No windows. Only way out was through the police outside.

(iii)

Even though us being in the men's room wasn't proper, Wren was smart—not a lot of men to use the men's room. We hurried to the handicap stall at the very end. My knees hardly held me upright, I was shaking so bad.

"Now for disguises, right quick and in a hurry," Wren said. "Hopefully it'll take them girls a bit before they check the men's room."

From her army duffle, she took out two pairs of jeans, her jeans, way too small for me. And two frilly blouses, again, her size.

"Wren! I can't—"

"Shut up." She threw the jeans at me then pulled little bottles and square containers out of her army duffle and balanced them on the toilet. Lipsticks, rouge, and whatnot. She took off her dress in a big swoop of fabric and dropped it to the floor.

I couldn't help but notice her lacy underwear and curvy, muscled body. She moved and flexed like a million-dollar racing pony. Not like me. I was built like a draft horse after a week in an ugly pen.

She tugged on the jeans, then the frilly white top, which she only half-buttoned, showing skin, not caring. Her Springfield 9 went into the back of her skin-tight jeans, covered by the blouse.

Wren turned to me. "Put on them clothes. I'll do up your face. And then we'll play it like I say."

Fear jumbled my insides. We had to hurry, but I could guess what her plan was, and I couldn't do it—not even for a disguise. Not even to make Mama's funeral.

"You want us to dress like ladies of the night," I said.

She rolled her eyes. "Ladies of the night? Jesus, am I absconding with Sally Browne Burke?"

"Good word, absconding. Figured you'd be limited to two syllable words."

Her mouth got small. "We don't have a choice. This'll work. Them Yankee cops are looking for a schoolgirl from your fancy Academy, so if we go out there as party girls, it'll trick 'em. Yankees think everybody from the Juniper is the same. To them, we're all just party girl harlots, dumb as dirt. Well, we'll give them what they want, and you won't have to do anything unseemly. Trust me, I'll get those jeans on you, even if I have to bloody you to do it."

"Fine. Just don't look."

Through the wall, we heard a stall door slam open. It was the cops, checking the ladies' room next door. We were running out of time.

"Cavvy, this is not the time for modesty. They're coming. We have to hurry."

"Turn around anyhow."

She did, grumbling, "Hell, this is so stupid, we both got the same parts. And we're sisters."

Yeah, sisters, and she'd make fun of every mole just to be mean.

Putting on those jeans was torture, skin-peeling, fat-pinching, embarrassing torture. I got them over my hips, but I couldn't get them buttoned. The blouse was skintight. Even so, I buttoned it up to my chin.

Wren sighed and started undoing buttons. "For this to work, Cavvy, you gotta show 'em what the Lord gave you, but the Devil wants you to use."

She really had done those dirty things in Amarillo that Sharlotte had wrote me about. Which made me kind of feel sorry for her—my sister, doing those desperate things 'cause she couldn't tolerate our family. Sure, the non-viable boys made money that way, but so did girls brought low by our troubled times, and they made a quarter of what the parlor boys made. Sad. All of it so sad and tragic.

Another stall slammed next door in the ladies' room. Bang.

Wren moved like lightning. She hair sprayed and teased both of our hair until we had halos of frizz, then she painted herself, painted me, and did it quick and good and in a flash. When she powdered my face, the scratches Becca Olson gave me burned, but I hardly felt the pain. Too nervous.

The door to the men's room opened. Wren and I froze, staring into each other's eyes. We heard the footsteps on the floor. Then a zipper. Then, I won't say what we heard, but it wasn't the police.

The bathroom door creaked opened again. A woman's voice called in, "Excuse me, is the men's room clear?"

The guy answered, "No, ma'am."

The guy would smell the hairspray and know we were girls. Would he tell the police?

The guy washed his hands and left, but we could hear him, "Yes, officer, someone is still in there. They're almost done I think."

Good. Gave us a minute. And the guy didn't mention the hairspray smell.

Wren and I packed up our dresses, hers in her army duffle and mine in the new backpack. But not before I saw what was inside— clothes, brand new, high-quality North Face polypropylene long underwear, Nferno synthetic wool hat and scarf, Secondskin gloves, and a big Mortex parka, brown and sagebrush green.

I zipped up the backpack and asked, "Is all that stuff for me? It must have cost a fortune."

"Maybe, but I didn't buy it."

"Wren, it's wrong to steal. Eighth commandment. You wanna burn in hell forever?"

Wren hit us both with eye-blistering perfume. "Don't get scary on me, Princess. What I done already is gonna make me burn, so one more little sin isn't gonna do much. I'll deal with hell once I get there. For now, I have a passel of other demons to fight. Might as well start with those cops outside."

We left the handicap stall and my reflection in the mirror above the sink showed a stranger, mostly harlot, but a little bit pretty, too. I almost looked good, as long as I kept my eyes on my face. Once they wandered over to Wren, I felt like a grease-painted clown. Wren was goddess-hot—any viable boy for kilometers around would kill to be with her but not me.

I had my dignity, chastity, and womanly modesty. Sally Browne Burke said those were more important than beauty. I wanted to believe that was true. Standing next to Wren, though, the words felt hollow.

She examined me. "Good. You're young, and the young in you will sell this.

Anyone looks at you, you wink and smile like you wanna party, and it'll shock 'em back. If you gotta talk, twang up your language to show them how country-stupid you are, and they'll never know how smart you are."

I was too shook up to appreciate the compliment.

I figured we'd go out to face them right away, but Wren had another surprise for me. She went to the sink and not only brushed her teeth, but flossed them as well.

Instead of asking why the dental hygiene at a time like that, I took the Mortex parka out of the backpack and slipped it on—kept my hands in my pockets, one holding the stunner. If Wren drew her gun, I'd zap her. There'd be no killing if I could help it.

Wren turned, noticed the coat, and nodded. "Good. The coat makes you look like you're ashamed, and the cops might like that. I'll do the talking, and you just smile at them like you love them. Can you do that?"

I nodded, though I doubted I could ever do such a thing.

"What are you going to do?" I asked.

Wren gave me a long look, her black eyes cool and completely inscrutable. You'd need a gosh darn Rosetta stone to figure out some of the looks she gave me. But just when I thought to give up, I noticed how tired her eyes were, and not just tired, but like she was defeated, deep down in some dark place inside.

I followed Wren out of the bathroom and right into the scorching gaze of the three policewomen, Cleveland's finest, two with Thor stunners and one lugging a Zeus 2 charge gun.

"There they are," one said, pointing at us.

CHAPTER FOUR

The liberals want to confuse the issue by calling the women gillian, which comes from a Chinese phrase, both disgusting and un-American. Use whatever word you want, but God created women to give themselves to men. Better a woman lose her life than to let go of her honor, for the Lord will never forgive the unrepentant sinner. Not in these impossible times. Not ever.

—Reverend Kip Parson
General Secretary of the New Morality Movement
April 2, 2057

(i)

With the policewomen staring at us, Wren burst out laughing, suddenly as silly and dumb as a puppy. "Gosh, Elly May, we were in the men's room? Goodness gracious, what a dumb thing for us to do!"

I thought we were going to try to sneak by the police, but instead Wren was making a spectacle of herself. I had no idea what was going on, only that she was calling me Elly May and my hand was sweating on the handle of the stunner in my coat pocket. My hammering heart sucked the spit from my mouth.

One of the policewomen stepped up to us. Her nametag read Officer Dee Kane, and she was an unimpressed, long-haired woman in a starched and ironed dress, New Morality for sure. She stopped Wren. "Excuse me, ma'am, can we have a word with you?"

"Sure, Officer, but we're not in trouble for being in the men's room, are we? I hope not."

My sister had gone from warrior to wanton flirt, all girly 'strogen, friendly, kissy. The transformation was unnerving.

"Can we see some identification?" Officer Dee asked.

"Sure, sure," Wren said. "Hey, Elly May, you got your ID, right?"

My face collapsed into slack-jawed stupid. "I ain't got none." Which was the Lord's truth. My wallet with my Territory ID was back in my room at the Academy.

Wren touched my arm. "Ah, Elly, I told you to remember to pack it. Well, you always were a little slow, but you're still pretty as a picture. We're both a little flustered on account of my mother dying." Her smile faded. Her eyes misted. "My mother, Elly's auntie, dead. It was all so sudden. Heart attack." A tear tracked down her cheek.

Officer Kane put out a hand to Wren. "Can I see *your* ID then?"

Wren reached back.

My fingers tightened on the stunner, ready, if my sister went for her pistol.

Instead, she pulled a Territory ID card out of her back pocket. Didn't need a driver's license in the territories 'cause we drove horses, buggies, bicycles, and only rarely a truck or minivan fitted with an ASI steam attachment.

"Sure thing, my ID, Officer, sure." Wren handed it over sweetly, like her spit was honey.

Officer Kane studied the plastic card. "So you're Willimina Carson from Amarillo? When does your train leave?"

Of course Wren would have a fake Territory ID.

"Oh, you can call me Willie," Wren grinned with tears still in her eyes—flirting and somehow meaning it. "We're on the Capital Limited to Chicago, 12:58 PM. Is there a problem?"

Officer Kane shrugged. "Just looking for some girls, sisters. We think you might be them." She gave the ID back to Wren.

Wren nodded real seriously and shoved the card in her back pocket with a ridiculous little wiggle. "Well, we're girls, Officer. Are you sure we're not the ones you're looking for?"

I was dying inside. Why was she pushing our luck?

"I'm not sure yet. Would you allow us to do a retinal scan?"

"Sure," Wren said. "Anything you want to do to us you can."

I blushed at what she said. Shameless.

"What about you, Elly May?" Officer Kane asked.

"Okay."

After the SISBI laws were passed, the police were allowed to scan eyes for identification purposes. Most everyone at my Academy had had their eyes mapped and put in the big federal database, but of course that meant a signed parental consent form. Not sure Mama ever got the letter asking for permission 'cause no permission ever came back.

Officer Kane took out her slate and inserted a scanner in the USP3 slot. She held it up to Wren's eyes, and a light flashed, followed by an ugly beep. I could picture the dialogue message: *Eyescan not found.*

One of the other policewomen talked to Wren while Kane moved over to scan me. Officer Betty Pell's short hair and short-sleeved dress proved she wasn't New Morality. The third officer held her charge gun loosely and a look of boredom sat squarely on her face. A jumpsuit covered her, but nothing covered her scalp— she had a buzz cut. Girls at school would've called her *gillian*, but I tried hard not to stereotype people.

"Where in the Juniper are you girls from exactly?" Officer Pell asked.

"Lamar," Wren replied. "In the Colorado territory."

"What did your mama do before she died?"

"Ran cattle on her own for a long time," Wren said, "before Dob Howerter bought our ranch, and then she worked for him."

"She squat for land?"

"Yes, ma'am, got a big stake. Held it for as long as she could. I never liked cattle work none so I went to Amarillo. Took Elly May with me on account of all the girls in our family. Not a single a boy. Like most folks."

Officer Kane brought the scanner up to my face. I opened my eyes wide. The light flashed, leaving dots that blurred my vision.

Another ugly beep. Nope. Not in their system.

"What were you doing in Ohio?" Kane asked me.

Wren answered her instead. "Came for a big party, danced for lots of rich women, and I bet you even would know some, though I won't say who was there. Me and Elly May need to be discreet."

Officer Pell and Kane exchanged a glance. A big scandal had rocked Philadelphia not a month before—politicians caught with party girls and parlor boys.

Officer Kane pulled Officer Pell away. "Excuse us for a moment."

The two talked, and I couldn't hear much, only that Kane wanted to take us in and Pell didn't want the trouble. They went back and forth, and then dang me if Officer Kane didn't wave us away. "You're free to go."

"Thank you, officer," Wren said. "Good luck catchin' those sisters. Come on, Elly."

Casually, we headed toward the door to the platform. Wren wasn't smiley, girly 'strogen, flirty anymore. Her face was cellblock stone, and weary, as if all that play acting had cost her everything she was inside.

"Walk slow, Cavvy, but trust me, we're not out of this yet. That old gal Kane is trying to outthink her instincts, but her instincts are prolly too true to ignore."

We hit the empty platform and waited for the train. Not a lot of security for train travel, not like airlines, so we didn't have to worry about metal detectors. Lake Erie's wet stench mingled with the oily smell of the tracks—like a fish crawling through mud. Many of the wood planks of the platform had been replaced with Trex boards, composites synthesized from recycled materials. Across the tracks rose the gray wall of Cleveland's skyscrapers.

As we waited, my insides turned into cold mash.

We're safe.

We're not safe.

Wren is a genius.

Wren is crazy.

A sleek, silver train clattered in. Faces peered at us through clean plastic windows.

My heart leapt. We were going to get out of this. Somehow, Wren's disguises and acting had saved us.

The doors opened and we climbed into an empty train car. But not before I heard a voice yell out our fake names, "Willie! Elly May!"

The three policewomen marched out onto the platform, coming toward us.

We weren't safe. And Wren was most definitely crazy.

(ii)

I shuffled into a row of seats but didn't sit down. It felt like someone was trying to drown me in my own cold fear. How could Wren live like this?

My sister stood in the aisle near me. She stared out the window, her eyes sharp as razors, her jaw set. I knew she was thinking about how she could take down three women with only two bullets. I couldn't let that happen. "Wren, don't kill nobody. Let's just go to jail, okay?" My guts twisted. If we went to jail, I'd miss Mama's funeral.

Wren turned to me. "Sharlotte said to get you back to Burlington, and I will." She reached out a hand and touched my hair in a caress, then drew back. Soft words were on her lips, but she didn't say them. Instead, her voice came out hard. "I'll deal with the cops, you get yourself to McCook, then ask around for Sketchy. She'll get you to Sharlotte. You bury Mama, Cavvy. You live a good life. Tell Shar I did what I was told for once in my goddamn life."

A lump caught in my throat. I figured Wren didn't care about family, and she surely didn't care about me. She had told me our mama was dead with a smile on her face. But now she was going to make sure I got home even if it meant she spent her life in prison. I just couldn't understand her.

Kane and Pell stepped through the front entrance of the train car. The woman with the charge gun came in through the back door, cutting off our escape.

"We need you to come with us," Officer Kane said.

"Hey, officer." Wren grinned. Mask back on. "What's the problem? You ain't still mad about us being in the men's room, are you?"

"Since Elly May doesn't have any ID, we'd like to bring her downtown to confirm her identity."

I trembled behind Wren. Her arm curled behind her back, fingers on her gun. I blocked the view of the policewoman behind me, so she couldn't see Wren's hand. And she couldn't see me ease the stunner out of my pocket.

My heart fluttered frantic in my chest.

"Please, officers," Wren pleaded. "If we miss this train, we'll miss the funeral. Ain't nobody in Cleveland who can ID my sister."

"Sorry," Kane said, "but we need to take Elly May in."

"Okay," Wren whispered, "if that's the way you want it." She went to pull the gun, but I was faster. I slammed the stunner into her back and hit my sister with three million volts of Eterna goodness.

Twisting, shaking, Wren crumbled into a seat, right down on her own pistol. I dropped the stunner under her as well. Her mouth churned as she shook from the zap. Looked like a seizure, and suddenly I had a plan.

"Willie!" I wailed.

"What happened to her?" Officer Kane asked.

I leashed my extensive vocabulary and kept my voice dull. "She has spells. She's sad about her mama. And my auntie. Her mama is dead. Which is to also say my auntie is dead."

Officer Kane's eyes showed her doubt.

Pell sighed and shook her head. "This is great. Just great."

I rolled up a cast-off *Modern Society* magazine and shoved it into Wren's mouth to keep her from biting off her tongue.

Meanwhile, I plucked the fake ID from Wren's back pocket and held it out to Kane. "Here, ma'am. This made things okay before, didn't it?"

Officer Kane ignored the ID. Her eyes darted from her slate to Wren and me. "Are you Cavatica Weller?"

I shook my head ardently. "I'm Elly May Wallach, Willie's cousin. Please don't take us away. Please."

Wren moaned and chewed on the magazine.

I turned to her. "Willie, you had a seizure. Should I get you your eckilepsky medicine? Or do you think you're going to puke?"

Her eyes flared open. Oh, she was going to smack me good once she got her nervous system back online.

"Do you really think either of them are from the Sally Browne Burke Academy?" Pell asked Officer Kane. "And how are we going to ID them if they really are Juniper girls?"

Hope leapt in my chest. Could this work?

"If she barfs in the car, I'm not cleaning it up," the third officer grumbled.

"And I'm not doing the paperwork for the hospital visit," Pell said.

Officer Kane glared at her comrades, then went back to studying me.

I slapped my palms together like I was praying. Heck, I *was* praying. "Please, ma'am, please don't take her away for being a party girl. She promises she'll stop. And I won't do it no more neither. Please let us go to Auntie Carson's funeral. If you take us downtown, we'll miss the whole thing."

"Come on, Dee," Pell said. "These girls aren't gunslingers."

Officer Kane sighed. "Fine. But you keep yourselves clean, okay?"

My head jerked around in a nervous nod. "Yes, ma'am, clean, like how Sally Burke Browne says to be."

"It's Sally Browne Burke." Officer Kane gestured to Wren. "Is she going to be okay?"

Wren spit out the magazine. "Yeah," she slurred, "I get spells. I got medicine."

"I have a sister who had epilepsy," Pell said, "but we could afford the surgery. Maybe once you get some money, you could look into that."

I dropped my head. "Ain't no way we could afford no surgery. But thank you for letting us go."

Through the speakers, the conductor's voice announced the train would be leaving.

Officer Pell patted my shoulder. "Take care. I can't imagine what you've been through, but things will get better."

I nodded, embarrassed.

The few seconds it took them to get off the train felt like a lifetime. Once the door slammed behind them, I could breathe again.

The train moved off and passengers threaded their way into the car. I wanted to yell out in relief, but I didn't. I thought about our sheriff back in Burlington. She would've locked us up, but then, that was in the Juniper. Out in the World, things were different, kinder. Far kinder.

Took a few minutes until Wren finally got her tongue back in her mouth, but her make-up was all over the place. She looked like she had just survived a hard night working parties for tips and kisses.

"You gonna hit me, Wren?" I asked, keeping my distance.

"Nope, Cavvy, you done real good." She reached into her pocket and came up with our tickets. I stowed the pistol and the stunner in Wren's army duffle. We walked through three cars and finally found our seats. I stuffed our bags into the overhead compartment.

We were in the clear. No more cops. Officer Kane's instincts had been undone by our Weller girl *shakti*.

(iii)

We got off the train in Chicago 'cause the California Zephyr didn't leave until the next afternoon. In the lobby of the Amtrak station, I called Anju on my slate, and told her where to find Billy's car. She said the police were still scratching their heads, wondering how we got away. Anju and I shed more tears, then said goodbye.

Wren was out of cash, but I was hungry, so I sold my slate to a Chicago girl for seventy-five dollars. She was real happy 'cause she had the Hayao 4, which didn't cache as well as the Version 5. She giggled. I felt like I'd sold my right arm.

Dinner was McDonald's. Wren ate factory-farmed burgers, which I thought was disgusting, but I was sure my yogurt hadn't come from happy Juniper cows. We took turns pretending to sleep, sitting upright on benches while janitors cleaned around us.

Once we got on the California Zephyr, I washed the make-up off my face, then changed back into my New Morality dress. I felt so much better out of those vulgar clothes. I'd grown up in a dress, and wearing jeans felt like risking hellfire. Wren, of course, stayed swathed in denim.

My sister wasn't much for casual conversation, but she obsessed over her dental hygiene. She brushed her teeth every fifteen minutes or so. And she didn't wait until we crossed into the

Juniper to dig her dual Colt .45 Terminators out of her army duffle. I watched as she strapped them smokewagons on her hips, tying off the holsters to her thighs for a quicker draw. The pistols were completely customized—cherry wood grips, extended sixteen-centimeter barrels, and double-stacked magazines giving her fourteen bullets with one in the chamber. If twenty-nine ACP hollow points weren't enough, you best run.

She couldn't have gotten her pistols out in Cleveland 'cause of the gun control laws, and her Terminators were too big to hide. I understood why she had taken a 9mm and why she hadn't had extra ammo for it. The 9mm was just a toy. Her Colts were her everything.

Until we reached Buzzkill, Nebraska, we were officially under American law, but none of the Yankees on the train dared quote statutes to my sister.

I was nervous about leaving the World, but I didn't have a choice. The police hadn't harassed us in Chicago, but we were still vulnerable until we crossed into the Juniper. Our sheriff, Lily, in Burlington often said the Juniper scared Yankee police—they wouldn't go there chasing criminals.

Wren tucked her long Betty knife into a sheath next to her right holster. All weaponed up, Wren gave me the Springfield 9. Two bullets left.

"I get outta line, Cavvy, put me down for good."

She was joking, but still, I swallowed hard and stuck the pistol in my dress pocket, hoping I wouldn't have to use it.

CHAPTER FIVE

The Sino-American War sure was a hungry thing. The Sino ate up all of our natural resources just like it ate up our sons, our fathers, our brothers. Then it chewed on all of us during the nuclear winter after the Yellowstone Knockout. It even devoured five whole states. Left nothing behind but salvage.

—Former President Jack Kanton
On the 28th Anniversary of the Yellowstone Knockout
March 30, 2057

(i)

The train rolled into Buzzkill, Nebraska after sunset on Thursday night, a day and a half after I used the stunner on Wren. The buildings of the town tumbled together, all squat and gaudy, painted in bright colors. The Hindu elephant god, Ganesha, dressed up like a cowboy, welcomed us from a neon billboard glowing brightly thanks to Eterna batteries. Across the way slumped a hotel painted an eye-biting yellow. A mural of Sita and Rama covered the side. I knew who they were 'cause my friend Satya Nayar did a report on *The Ramayana* in the fourth grade. Anju also gave me an education, though she'd see me get uncomfortable and switch topics. I'd found the stories interesting, but being Roman Catholic, learning about other gods felt blasphemous.

However, I'd studied enough European history to know religious intolerance led to mass murder, and I wasn't going to sin by letting hate and fear govern me. So I went out of my way to befriend people of other cultures, including those from a religion that didn't just have one or two other gods, but millions. Besides, I'd grown up surrounded by Hindus.

The Sino had cut the U.S. population in half, and the Sterility Epidemic didn't help things any. Employers couldn't run their businesses without employees, so President Jack relaxed immigration laws and brought over anyone who wanted to come. Mostly, East Indians had answered the call. India hadn't been pulled into the Sino, and their country was overflowing with folks. As we've seen throughout history, immigrant labor is more fluid and more desperate. A lot of Hindus ended up in the Juniper, so in the territories, we had cowgirls and two kinds of Indians, Native Americans and Hindus. Ironic.

Before the Yellowstone Knockout, that section of Nebraska had been empty except for a few ranches and farms, but once folks figured out it had become the edge of civilization, the city of Buzzkill sprang up overnight to handle the salvage work. Mama had told us stories about the early days of Buzzkill. She said it had been a shantytown, more tents than buildings, with stacks of salvage teetering in towers—stuff like used cabling, copper piping, wood, furniture, Nintendo ShockBoxes, and other electronics. It'd lie in piles until auctioneers could sell it off to salvage merchants who would take it east in trains or trucks. Billions of dollars and megatons of junk moved through there.

Now Buzzkill thrived on Juniper livestock and produce. Marketing people, hired by the likes of Dob Howerter and Mavis Meetchum, had convinced the Yankees that Juniper homegrown was healthier for them than anything factory farmed. And better tasting, I might add, though President Jack said Juniper beef tasted like sagebrush and sorrow.

Thanks to some bipartisan hijinks circumnavigating the 22nd Amendment, that man had four terms as president. It gave him ample opportunity to say a lot of clever things, but I never cared much for him. President Jack was no Franklin D. Roosevelt, and he gave up too quickly on the Juniper, in my opinion. First thing he did in office was sign the Masterson-Wayne Act, which officially set the states affected by the Yellowstone Knockout back to being dusty territories, barely governed.

The only real law was the cattle barons and the Outlaw Warlords. Some said Howerter was as bad as an outlaw, though he didn't move around as much. The Warlords scrapped over territory, trade routes, and taxes. Not that there were real taxes involved, only protection money. Give them cash or they'd burn down your farm and steal your livestock.

Even though it was late, people packed the streets of Buzzkill, Yankees and Juniper folk alike. Women in rainbow saris mixed with girls in worn cowgirl leathers. Quite a party. I could smell the spicy food, and my mouth watered. The food on the train was pretty good, but it wasn't like down-home Hindu lentils or Mexican *carnitas*.

The train stopped at the depot near the border of the Juniper, which was the part of Buzzkill I liked the best. Outside were stacks and stacks of computer monitors, TVs, every type of screen, from 25 centimeter slate ECDs to the 550 centimeter Sony Reality Simulator Displays. The screens showed all kinds of video—cooking shows, music Youtubes, old-timey Westerns, that new science fiction show, *Altered*, and, of course, *Lonely Moon*.

On the edges of the Juniper, electricity flickered. The screens would buzz out and go dead. Thirty seconds later, they would light back up and the parade of video would go on.

The train's whistle howled, letting us know the engineers were transitioning from batteries to steam. The firebox prolly burned Old Growth coal, synthesized out of old-growth forests—something about the carbon in the aged wood—but of course the environmentalists were against cutting down ancient trees to use in the Juniper. Only a matter of time before Old Growth was outlawed since most Yankees cared more about old trees than Juniper people.

The door at the front of our train car banged open, and in walked four border guards. No dresses for them. Each wore a uniform, including pants, and carried an MG21 assault rifle. A sharp-faced woman marched down the aisle, asking for tickets and ID.

I tensed, but Wren just laughed. "Don't get your *shakti* in a bunch, Cavvy. Those women don't care about people going into the Juniper. Nope. Only about people getting out. We couldn't play act our way past them if this train was pointed east, not without ID and a better story than we had in Cleveland."

Two years ago, I hadn't really thought about the border crossing 'cause I was fourteen and innocent. Now, with Wren, I was anything but.

The video screens lit up, and I noticed something I'd missed before—a chain-link fence, topped with razor wire. Living in Ohio, I hadn't really thought much about the effects of the SISBI laws. The news feeds had focused more on the privacy issues involved and less on the security fences around the Juniper.

The woman in charge woke a mother and her little girl a couple of rows down from us. She went through their papers, and then continued until she got to us. Wren gave the woman her ID and our tickets. She barely glanced at it. The guards moved on without a word. Didn't even give Wren's guns a second look.

Still, I was in a sweat. Their MG21 machine guns were American standard issue, hardcore military. Once more, assault rifles were going to be a part of my life.

The little girl's squeal startled me. Her and her mama had got on in Omaha, but the little one had been sleeping. Now, the girl was wide-awake, waving around a comic book.

"Mama, are there really mutants in the Juniper?"

Wren opened her mouth to say something, then closed it.

"Mutants? Maybe. There are all sorts of strange things in the Juniper. Watch now."

The lights in the cabin went off. Then, darkness for a moment, until the sapropel lights hissed on. A heavy oily smell followed. Sapropel was the leftovers of the leftovers of oil shale like torbanite. It was weak stuff, but I grew up under its murky amber light. Smelling it again, hearing the hiss, sent my heart thumping. The memories. Lord, the memories and the guns.

The train lurched forward down the tracks. Outside, the flickering video screens disappeared behind us, swallowed up by the darkness as we moved west through the open plain of the Juniper; Nebraska land no more.

(ii)

Ten minutes later, the little girl once again peppered her mama with questions. "And what about June Mai Angel? I heard that song about how she pulled the zeppelin out of the sky. *The Ballad of the Black Dog*, that's the song. It says she killed them all except for one girl, so she could tell the world how bad June Mai is. Does she rob trains, too?"

"I don't think so, Laura."

Wren half stood, but I put a hand on her shoulder. "No, Wren, it ain't worth it. She's only a little girl."

"And what about the savages?" the girl kept on. "In my comic book, they attack trains and kill everyone, but this train is guarded, right Mama? We saw the guards and their big guns." She meant the border guards, but no, they were long gone.

Wren shook me off and strutted away, all hips and pistols. She sat down next to a frumpy woman in a New Morality dress across the aisle from the girl and her mama.

"Hi, my name is Willie Carson, and I couldn't help but overhear you talkin'." Wren smiled, showing white teeth, which should be white, as much as she brushed them.

I sat in my seat praying Wren wouldn't cuss too much.

The mama pulled her daughter close, eyes glued to Wren's Colt .45 Terminators. "Can we help you, miss?"

Wren grinned at the mama. "Your daughter had a whole passel of questions about the Juniper, and I was born in the Colorado territory. Lived there and all over the Juniper. My mama was one of the first ones to go in for salvage work after the Yellowstone Knockout."

The girl sat up straight. "People call it the Yellowstone Knockout," she said knowingly, "but it wasn't a knockout at all. We fought the Chinese even after they nuked us. Even in the forever winter times."

The nuclear winter. For three months, the temperatures across the northern hemisphere fell to subzero, even in June. The temperature stayed low and average rainfall dropped by seventy-five percent for years after that. I'd heard lots of scary stories about that time when the sky went dark and everything not dead wanted to die. Folks didn't have fresh produce for years—meals came out of a can, and they were grateful for every bite.

The Yellowstone Knockout.

I'd grown up with that great event shadowing every part of my life. Really, it created not just the Juniper, but me, my family, a whole generation.

The Sino-American War started on July 28, 2028. Not even a year later, the Chinese nuked Yellowstone on Good Friday, 2029, which caused all sorts of evil things—darkness, disease, starvation. Could've been worse. The Chinese used a hydrogen bomb, fusion not fission, so most of the radiation was nullified in the blast. That was just the beginning though.

That intense heat so close to the surface capped off the Yellowstone caldera, one of the most active volcanic regions on Earth. Lucky it did, or it might have been the end of us all. Once the surface was sealed, things got interesting, geologically speaking. The pressure building underground finally cracked open, causing a flood basalt. As it happened, the channelized basalt flowed out of the Yellowstone's throat in just the right combination of ionized molten iron, direction, and speed that it created a massive electromagnetic field.

And the EM field didn't go away. A gigantic plume of magma under the ground kept the ionization going as it poured up and out of the ground, pushing the field of cooling lava down the Yellowstone Valley toward the Snake River in Idaho. The problem wasn't the flowing lava, which moved about thirty centimeters a day, like a slow-moving tsunami wave. The problem was the ionized molten iron coming out of the Yellowstone's throat. That kept the EM field active and relatively stable. As the video screens in Buzzkill demonstrated, at the edge of the Juniper the power fluctuated. On the border it didn't fry electronics outright, only disrupted the current. But inside the EM field, it not only killed all electricity, but due to the strong, highly variable magnetic nature of the phenomena, it wiped out any type of compact flash memory. Which was why I had to sell my slate in Chicago.

No one knew how long the EM field would last. The Deccan Traps in India, another example of a flood basalt, had erupted for a million years. We were only thirty years into it. If the lava kept flowing at the current rate it would overtake Boise in about seven thousand years. The geology gave the scientists a lot to study—how it happened and how to bring power back to the Juniper.

Why nuke Yellowstone? That was another question everyone asked, and theories drifted around like cottonwood fluff. Political scientists and military minds argued about it, just like doctors argued over what caused the Sterility Epidemic.

There were a lot of mysteries for people to ponder, but right then I had my own little conundrum far closer to home. How could my sister be so gentle and kind to this little girl? Wren's smile was so soft. "I like you, Princess. What's your name?"

The girl glanced at her mother, who nodded. "Go ahead." The woman relaxed a little, and I figured she was curious about the life of a Juniper gunslinger. From the looks of them, she and her daughter were prolly on their way to Sterling to visit relatives or some such business. A real adventure for them, though Sterling was the safest city in the Colorado territory.

"Laura Tucker," the little girl said.

"Well, Laura Tucker, you're right. We didn't give up after the Knockout. But I don't wanna talk about the Sino. I want to tell you the truth about the Juniper."

"Are there mutants?" Laura squinched up her face like she wouldn't be able to handle the truth.

"Nope. No mutants."

The frumpy woman next to Wren spoke up. "But what about the radiation from the Knockout? How can you be so certain?"

Wren's eyes narrowed and her voice got quiet. "Ain't no mutants. Like I said, I've been all over the Juniper, traveling with a circus, sometimes as a sharpshooter, sometimes as a trapeze artist, and I would've seen a mutant in a sideshow somewhere along the way."

The woman harrumphed loudly. I suppressed a desire to go over and explain to her the difference between fission and fusion.

The girl fell over herself to ask another question. "What about the savages?"

The mama shushed her. "Now, Laura, that ain't politically correct to say. Right, Miss Carson?"

Wren shrugged. "I guess. In the Juniper, we call 'em the Wind River people. We took their land away from 'em once, but the

Knockout gave it back, and they're not gonna let history repeat itself. You go up into Wyoming or Montana, well, the Wind River people'll cut your throat rather than look at you. To protect their land."

Even though the Native Americans killed to keep their borders sealed, some folks supported them. Mavis Meetchum, for example, who was the biggest rancher in the Northern Colorado territory, let loose a thousand head of buffalo into Wyoming—partly as a peace offering, partly to give the Wind River people something to eat. Mavis was as clever as she was rich, which made Sterling such a safe place.

"Trains can't go north," Wren continued, "so to get to California the Union Pacific and Amtrak have to run their trains south through New Mexico. Can't go through the Rocky Mountains, 'cause of the weather and the Outlaw Warlords."

"Like June Mai Angel."

Wren nodded. "Yep. June Mai Angel runs the central part of the Colorado territory. Up north is the Psycho Princess, who paints towns all pink. She kidnaps the girls and brainwashes them to be as crazy as she is. Believe or not, the Psycho Princess kills any boy she meets, viable or not. The Juniper has always had bad women runnin' around. Prolly where folks got the stupid idea there were mutants."

The frumpy woman shrugged and looked out the window.

Wren continued. "Why, when I was twelve or thirteen, our ranch got attacked by an Outlaw Warlord by the name of Queenie. She would raid ranches and farms for food, salvage, and boys. To sell. Big trade in boys nowadays, but you know that from school."

"Only if they're viable." Laura tumbled over that last word.

"Uh-huh," Wren agreed. "But my mama shot Queenie, right between her eyes. She and her girls were comin' at us, and my sister back there, well, she wasn't much older than you when she was reloading for Mama, and it was down to the last clip and them Outlaw Warlords were coming in for a last run, and Mama yelled out, and stood straight, and she was just so ..."

Wren's voice fell away.

I felt tears in my eyes as the memories bit me—the dirt stinging my face, the bullets in the air, electrifying my teeth, a crazy terror in my heart.

And Mama, clutching her over-under M16, which we named Tina Machinegun, yelling, "Dammit, Cavvy. You can't drop no more bullets. You keep jacking up, we're all gonna die!"

It was bad cursing, but that was what she'd said.

My hands were shaking so bad, and I was crying so much, most of the bullets didn't make it into the clips. The brass glittered around me in the trench we had dug around our house.

Then this great big woman came up, Queenie, face painted with mud. I remember the flash of her teeth, and she had this big machine gun and it was chugging away at us. Mama was out of ammunition. She'd taken a round in the arm, and her blood dripped on me. One of our ranch hands, Nikki Breeze, screamed from somewhere that she'd been shot, and I was certain we were all going to die, until at the very last minute, Mama snatched a half-load from my hand, slammed that clip into Tina Machinegun and blew Queenie off her feet.

It was dewy-wet that morning. In my young mind, I thought I could smell Queenie's brains in the mud. Now, whenever I smell that wet, muddy spring smell, I say to myself, "Smells like Queenie's brains this morning."

Laura Tucker was looking at Wren with wide-eyed hero worship as my sister told the story.

"But my mama's dead now," Wren whispered.

"Was she killed by June Mai Angel?" Laura asked.

"Nope. Heart attack. No one alive could kill my mama 'cept for God. He took her home to heaven, and left us here all alone."

Laura put a hand on Wren's hand.

"I'm sorry, miss. For your loss." She said it with such seriousness that Wren laughed and laughed.

"If the Juniper is such a bad place, why did your mama go there in the first place?" the little girl asked.

The question caught Wren off guard. She didn't say anything for a long time. Then she answered, "Family. She hated her family in Cleveland."

"Hated?" Laura asked in wonder. "How can you hate your own family?"

"It's good you don't know." Wren patted her hand. "But maybe it wasn't just family that sent Mama west and kept her here. You know, the Juniper is a hard place to live but it's also beautiful, and wild, and it's the only place left in the world you can be free. The Juniper ain't got no identity laws, no income taxes, nothing but open plains and starry skies, and a girl can make her way here. If you're tough, smart, quick with a gun, you can live here, really live.

"I ain't never gonna leave." Wren grinned and changed gears. "Well, Laura Tucker, I hope you feel better. With all them questions you asked, I reckon you were a little scared. Well, until we hit McCook, you ain't got nothin' to be scared of. Yeah, they have guards on this train, but they ain't seen what I've seen, or done what I done, so until I get off, you got me and my Colt Terminators to protect you, and I ain't never lost a fight yet. Well, except when my little sister shot me in the back." Wren paused. "You know, you kinda remind me of Cavvy when she was little and sweet, like my own little baby doll." Her voice fell away.

For a long a time, it was quiet, Wren staring off. Then she cleared her throat, leaned in, and kissed the little girl's cheek.

"Now look at my sister!" My sister stood, talking loud and waking everybody up. "Cavatica Jeanne Weller, all grown up. Mark my words, Laura Tucker, I won't never be killed by anyone that's not family."

Wren strutted back to our seat, smiling at all the stares, murmurs, and hate. "Mutants!" My sister half-yelled the word. "Ain't no mutants in the Juniper. Just a buncha scaredy-cat lies."

"Quiet down, Wren," I said, embarrassed.

I didn't believe in mutants either, not really, but I'll tell you what, growing up driving cattle to Hays, Kansas, there were some nights I heard things and saw things that made me think rough beasts slouched through the Juniper—creatures that God never meant to walk the earth.

Wren pulled her hat down and was asleep in seconds. I should've slept, but I hurt from the trauma of going to war at eight years old. And I missed my mama even though I hadn't seen her in a long time. Two years.

And now she was gone, and I didn't want to go back to the violence of the Juniper. I missed my slate, my bed at the Academy, Anju, and her sighs over Billy Finn. The idea of going back to the Juniper made me want to curl up into a little ball and weep.

(iii)

Even after the memories of Queenie faded away, I couldn't sleep, and a daydream crept into my head. I was at Anju and Billy's wedding in Ohio. There was a boy there, one of Billy's cousins. Though he was surrounded by girls, his eyes never left my face.

It was a look that said some things were meant to be.

He excused himself from all the girls 'cause he was real kind and gentle, but when he approached me, I could see he was at a loss for words. I took his hand and said, "Yeah, I felt it, too." We talked all night long, danced to every song until finally we left and found a bench in a deserted park in Cleveland. I snuggled into his coat as we watched the dawn come up cold on the horizon. My own boy. I wouldn't care if he was viable or not, swear to God, just as long as he was a boy of my very own.

It was such a nice fantasy, but then I remembered a conversation I had with Sharlotte when I came home for Christmas two years before. It was just us, sitting beside the fire in the parlor. Sharlotte worked on repairing a stirrup. I talked about Robert, a fine-looking viable boy at school who never seemed to belong, viable or not. I didn't have a chance with him 'cause girls prettier and richer than me clung to him like wood ticks.

Pine burned in the fireplace, and the smoke smelled sweet. I sat on the hearth, enjoying the warmth, talking and talking, until I realized Sharlotte had fallen silent and distracted. She was in the old rocker, her face lost in the shadows. Her leather-working tools rested on her lap. After a while, she spoke. "You're lucky, Cavvy, to be at that school, to be with boys. Ain't no boys around here that ain't taken or promised or already married. If you find a boy, you know to keep him close, right?"

"Ain't gonna be no boy for me," I'd said. "Some nights that's hard to think on, and other nights I don't care at all. There's so much more to life than romance, despite what all those cheap eBooks say."

"It gets harder the longer you go," Sharlotte said quietly. "Maybe it's not so much the boys involved, maybe it's more the desire to be wanted. To have someone look at you and to see the joy on their face and to know you yourself are the source of such happiness."

In some ways, the generation before us had it easier. At least they'd grown up with the hope of marriage and men. For Sharlotte and me, we'd grown up knowing how unlikely it was we'd marry, and we were too Catholic for any sort of polygamy and too New Morality to be *gillian*.

It'd been quite the confession from Sharlotte, who generally didn't say much. She seemed to catch herself. "However, I should hope you aren't reading romances, eBooks or otherwise. You are there to learn, not to go off into fantasylands. For whatever reason, God is testing us, and as women, we will be strong, we will be chaste, and when the sinful thoughts come, we will let our duty and honor be the compass to guide us to calmer waters."

"Amen," I'd whispered.

But Sharlotte going off like that, sounding like she'd memorized a Kip Parson sermon, I knew she'd visited fantasylands of her own.

The rocking of the train finally tricked me into sleeping, until Wren jostled me awake. "We're getting off in McCook, Princess. We have people to meet and things to do. Or like we say in Amarillo, things to meet and people to do."

"Don't call me princess," I growled. I didn't want to leave my dreams. Out in the real world I was fearful, sick with sadness, and I had no idea who we had to meet or how we were going to get from McCook to Burlington in a day.

Worse than all that, I was going to leave the safety of the train for the hell and harshness of the Juniper.

My troubled homeland.

CHAPTER SIX

I come from generations of Polish scientists, but I also grew up with Pollack jokes. The Polish mind just works differently—call it visual-spatial, call it big picture, call it whatever you want, but I have the ultimate Pollack joke. How many Pollacks does it take to invent a battery that changes the world? One. Me.

—Maggie Jankowski
Today Show Interview
May 24, 2057

(i)

Wren and I got off the train and you could almost hear the other passengers sigh with relief. Before my sister left, though, she blew Laura a kiss.

I followed Wren through the little depot, down steps to the street, and into the early-morning cold and dark. My belly rumbled, but we'd eaten through our cash, and nothing was open anyway. We stopped for a moment to put on our Mortex coats.

Not a soul stirred in McCook, Nebraska. The stockyards were silent, but soon the cowgirls would be up brewing coffee and working on their account sheets, waiting for a train to take their headcount to Buzzkill. McCook was a scrubby batch of nothing buildings, and the whole place stank of cattle, front-end chewing and back-end pooping, if you'll excuse my language. That smell, mixed with the sage, carried on the winter wind, brought me back to the trauma of my childhood—I nearly ran back to the depot for an eastbound ticket.

Yet, I felt homesick as I walked through that town. The night had frozen the mud into a tangled crust, which kept tripping my boots, just like when I was six years old and walking to where the horse-drawn trailer picked me up for school. Part of me wanted to run back to Cleveland, but another part wanted to see my ranch again, pet my ponies, get long hugs from Aunt Bea.

Wren and I walked until McCook was behind us, and we headed west on what used to be US Route 34, but now was just a long stretch of dirt, narrowed by yellow grass and scrub—the asphalt long gone.

I knew I couldn't ask Wren where we were going or who we were meeting 'cause she would just ignore my questions. So, I slipped on the Secondskin gloves as well as the Nferno hat and scarf, and soon was warm again. I was grateful Wren had stolen those things, but I still asked Jesus for forgiveness.

Morning light threw tall grass-shadows onto the dead highway. I was eyeing puddles for a drink, but they were frozen into white spider webs of ice. Wren kept moving, relentless, like a robot, too pretty and tough for the cold.

In the distance, something hovered on the horizon, not quite a tree, but neither hill nor building.

"Wren, what's that in the sky?" I had an uneasy notion of what it could be.

She didn't respond.

We got closer. Oh, Lord, then I understood everything.

A huge Jonesy-class zeppelin, cabled down to the foundation of a big red barn, dwarfed both the barn and the neighboring farmhouse. The frost on the galvanized Kevlar skin of the airship glistened in the sunlight as smoke from the steam engine swirled about in black wisps. The airship turned to show me her four back fins and three idle propellers. From the tip of her nose to the back fin, she was at least 150 meters with a diameter of 50 meters—a silver warehouse drifting in the breeze, straining at her cables, bobbing, tugging, bobbing some more.

Underneath the behemoth, cowgirls, horses, and cattle moved like miniature toys on a model train set.

I stood, spellbound. I'd seen zeppelins before at the airship port in Burlington, and that was when my fascination started—with the engineering of them, not the actual experience of flying in one.

My love for guns was similar. Mama used to say I talked like an ordinance salesperson in training. I loved the makes, the models, the mechanisms, but when it came to the actual shooting, I'd mess things up—unless it was deer hunting or target practice, then I wasn't too bad.

Watching the zeppelin drift, my guts melted. Only one way to get to Burlington from McCook in a day. We were going to fly.

The lyrics of *The Ballad of the Black Dog* went through my head. Based on a true story, the song recounted the fate of a doomed zeppelin, pulled out of the sky by June Mai Angel. She left only one survivor to tell the tale. The rest. Butchered.

"Please, Wren, no."

My sister shook her head at me.

We walked up to the farm, and Wren grabbed the first person she saw. "Where's Sketchy?"

A woman in a New Morality dress pointed to a huge woman dressed in a wool skirt and a leather flight jacket. She had some kind of flying cap on her head, and what looked like cattling goggles around her neck. Leather and wool meant she was old school Juniper 'cause most folks wore the new synthetics, like Wren had stolen for me.

We got closer, and the huge woman put out a hand covered in fingerless gloves. Her fat-lipped mouth opened to reveal a scatter of teeth stuck into big, pink gums. Her dazed blue eyes were spread so far apart she looked toady. Soot covered every centimeter of her.

"I'm Sketchy, and I bet you dollars to donuts you be the Weller girls, and it's a shame about your mama and all, but my mama's dead too in the ABQ, and I miss her sorrowful. Your mama paid me all up front, quite a pretty penny, bless her, and I got Sharlotte Weller's letter from the BUE, and she has that crazy plan, and I'll do it 'cause I like her, and the money's good, and it should help my reputation as an intrepid entrepreneur long as I don't jack things up."

How could Mama have paid Sketchy up front if we were having money problems? Hiring on a zeppelin wouldn't help with that. I still had no idea what was going on. Wren sure as heck wasn't going to tell me, and it didn't feel right asking the strange woman in front of me.

"Please to meet you, Sketchy," Wren put out a hand.

Sketchy pumped it like she was hoping water would come pouring out of Wren's mouth. "Glad you found the Srikrishna ranch. As I thought, we got here late last night 'cause the wind shifted out of the west. I knew it would, but Tech doubted me, though I'm never wrong when it comes to wind, storms, and hogs."

Wren nodded, her face once again inscrutable. I had no idea what my sister thought about our odd captain who held our lives in her greasy, black fists. Butterflies invaded my belly, and I hoped I wouldn't puke them out. But then they were all I would throw up 'cause of how empty I felt.

"Hey, Sketchy, did our price include food?" Wren asked, hungry too it seemed. "We haven't eaten in a while, and I suppose we could use something to drink. Got any beer?"

"No beer. Tech is in that group for alcoholics. But yeah, food and water, but first I gotta get my money from Miss Srikrishna on account of it being her farm. I delivered her antibiotics for her sick cows, but they don't eat 'em. Miss Srikrishna and her girls don't eat the cows, I mean. Dairy farm, and Miss Srikrishna is a vegetarian. Tech's a vegetarian. Me and Peeperz like pepperoni pizza, but we never get it, like we don't get video unless we're in the ZZK or the HYS or the OKC, or—"

"Okay, Sketchy." Wren cut her off 'cause she prolly figured if she didn't step in Sketchy would keep on talking until noon. "We'll get onboard your blimp, and we'll eat once we take off. Okay?"

The big woman hissed through the last of her teeth. "Don't call my Jonesy a blimp. I was called a blimp growin' up in the ABQ, and I won't stand for it. Besides, the *Moby Dick* is a rigid dirigible, 'kay?"

I was so tired, and Sketchy talked so quickly and with such a peculiarity, I was having trouble understanding her. I closed my eyes to keep it all straight. Tech must be her partner, maybe her engineer, and there was someone else on the airship by the name of Peeperz. And instead of saying the names of the cities, Sketchy referred to them by their airport codes. ABQ for Albuquerque, ZZK for Buzzkill, BUE for Burlington, HYS for Hays, Kansas. And *Moby Dick*—that had to be the name of her zeppelin—was a Jonesy-class dirigible with a rigid skeleton covered with next-generation lightweight Kevlar. Inside the superstructure would be sixteen to twenty air-cells of low-pressure theta-helium, or what we called thelium, which was a synthetic gas since the real helium had run out decades ago. Thelium provided greater lift than the real stuff.

"Okay, Ms. Sketchy, I'm sorry," Wren said, and she put out her hand again.

That surprised me. Why didn't Wren get snotty with the captain?

Sketchy shuffled her feet side to side, like she was debating on whether she wanted to be friendly or not, then shook hands with Wren. "'Kay, Miss Weller. I accept your 'pology." Then she pushed Wren aside and grabbed my hand. "Good to meetcha, Cavatica. You're named after that spider in *Charlotte's Web*. Tech read me the story, and I cried so much 'cause that spider loved that pig so." She gave a big grunt of laughter. "Me crying over spiders and pigs. It's girly 'strogen, it is, but I'm girly 'strogen, and proud of it. It's pretty stupid, if you ask me, that girls get ashamed of acting like girls, but the world's a crazy place nowadays."

What she said surprised me, but I didn't show it. Instead, I remained polite. "It's good to meet you, but how did you know my name?"

Sketchy grinned with a tooth overlapping her lip. "I remember everything and every name, and I sure like yer sister Sharlotte. Now, we gotta go. Just yell to Tech to drop the ladder. Climb on up. And Peeperz is up there, but you won't meet him 'cause he's shy. You're our only passengers, so once I get my money, we'll go."

And then she tore past us and started shouting, "Ms. Srikrishna! Come on out and pay me! I know you will, even though you ain't a Christian."

She kept on yelling. I was latched on to Wren. "We're gonna die if we get on that zeppelin with that mad woman."

Wren *tsked.* "Cavvy, I'm shocked at you, judging a book by its cover. Sketchy is a legend, whether you know it or not."

"Please, Wren," I begged but she turned away from me in my weakness. I followed her into the barn and up to the roof. The zeppelin above us filled the entire sky with silver instead of gray clouds. Under it, I felt like an ant.

Wren yelled and a rope ladder tumbled ten meters down from the mid-bay hatch in the hull of the dirigible. No gondola on her. Everything was tucked inside the *Moby Dick's* skin.

With her army duffle on her back, Wren scurried up the ladder like a squirrel up a tree.

I didn't move. I was high enough on that barn that I could hear the hiss of gas filling the zeppelin. At least the gas wasn't hydrogen, so it wouldn't explode like the *Hindenburg*—low pressure so any minor punctures in the air cells wouldn't cause a problem. Didn't make me feel any better though.

Especially when I contemplated why the outer skin was made of Kevlar—Outlaw Warlords were shooting down zeppelins for the plunder. The *Moby Dick* could lose up to five of her sixteen air-cells, but any more would send us crashing out of the sky.

Wren scuttled back down the ladder, shouldered my backpack, and then started up. She turned around, chin on her shoulder. "Come on, scaredy cat."

Sure, she could make fun of me. She had been in the circus while I was learning the mathematics of micro-circuitry.

I shook my head.

Wren laughed. "Gonna have to grab a hold of your *shakti* to get up here. No other way."

I took off my gloves and stuffed them in my coat. I put a hand on a plastic rung.

"Help me, Mama," I said, and I got choked up. She couldn't help me no more, not on this side of the grave. She wouldn't hold me again. Not ever again.

A foot up, a hand up, and the rope ladder swayed with the zeppelin bobbing and tugging, as if the whole thing was trying to shake me off.

Wren looked down at me from between her boots where she sat in the hatch. "You can do it, Cavvy. Keep your eyes on me and do one rung at a time."

My arms shook, my legs trembled, my heart quaked. One rung at a time, but I was exhausted in minutes. We did calisthenics at the

Academy, but shame on me, I would generally ditch them to watch video with Anju. I figured growing up in the Juniper, working day and night, would've been calisthenics enough for a lifetime.

The *Moby Dick* listed to the side and I swung out past the barn until only dirt was below me. If I fell, I'd plummet all the way to the ground.

No help for it. I scrambled up the ladder until Wren could haul me into the zeppelin. I lay on the floor, wheezing but alive.

I was in another world. And if Sketchy was odd, I wondered what flavor of crazy I would find in her partner Tech.

(ii)

Still gasping on the floor, trying to get my strength, I looked around.

I had studied zeppelins in school in my free time 'cause they weren't part of the normal curriculum. Besides, zeppelins and other Juniper-type technology felt like forbidden knowledge. Mama had made it clear, I was sent to the Academy to learn about electronics and all types of Yankee engineering. I was going to be a full-fledged electrical engineer once the Juniper got its buzz back. That had been Mama's master plan, but it had failed miserably. The electricity stayed gone, and no amount of cable shielding or wireless broadcasting could withstand the flood basalt's electromagnetic field. Maggie Jankowski herself had studied the problem. Loved that Maggie Jankowski. I wrote her letters. Of course, she never answered. She was Maggie Jankowski, and I was just some Juniper girl.

Wren put out a hand. "Can I help you up, Princess?"

"Don't call me that," I said and got to my feet. It took a bit to get used to the gentle sway of the floor, but of course, Wren moved around like she'd been born flying. Not me. I fell against her a lot, but she kept me upright, sighing and smirking as she did it.

Inside, the *Moby Dick* was one big open space, a huge cargo bay. The floor, the walls, the beams crisscrossing the ceiling, all were made of shiny gray Neofiber. Engineers synthesized Neofiber from recycled plastics, and it had become the material of choice for building pretty much everything. Lightweight, flexible, its chemical bonds rivaled titanium for their strength.

Between the ceiling beams, the air-cell compartments held big translucent bladders full of thelium, keeping the whole thing afloat.

Clearly, the *Moby Dick* was made for work, not comfort. All along the walls, nylon straps lashed down empty wooden pallets. Big, plastic two-hundred-liter barrels were also tied down, lining both sides of the bay. There must have been nearly a hundred and fifty thousand liters of water all told. Not sure why they had so much water, unless they used it as ballast, but that would be a whole lot of weight. Thanks to the thelium, though, the *Moby* could handle it.

On our left lay the cockpit. The bulletproof glass windshield lit up the chairs and hammocks. Light also poured in from the portholes all along the cargo bay.

On our right, at the back of the zeppelin, a slender figure worked on an array of gray machinery and pipes next to the enormous rear cargo door, which dropped down to create a ramp for loading and unloading. They had extensions for the ramp, so if they couldn't get to an airship port, they could load directly from the ground.

"Let's go say hello," I said.

Wren shrugged, but followed me. The open bay had the musty smell of both coal and Old Growth dust.

The woman at the engine turned. Her face was clean, though dust, grease, and engine puke blackened her overalls. Striking green eyes took us in, quite a contrast to her thick, dark eyelashes and inky dark hair. She was a looker. Unlike Sketchy, who was trying to be New Morality, the woman wore tight overalls, and that made me uncomfortable. As did the ink of tattoos on her neck, fingers, and hands. Only rough, rebel girls had tattoos.

"Hi," I said. "I'm Cavatica Weller. This is my sister Wren."

The beautiful woman ignored Wren and addressed me. "I'm Tech. Where's Sketchy?"

"Getting money from Miss Srikrishna," I answered.

Tech turned and cranked a wheel. Thelium spit and hissed as it filled the air-cells above us. "Sorry, but I don't talk to passengers. Go wait up front."

Then I saw it. I stuttered and pointed at an Eterna battery bolted into a housing on the floor. Underneath the transparent plastic, I could see the coils, what Maggie Jankowski dubbed the noodles. "Hey … hey … that's a Kung Pao. Dang, Wren, do you know what that means?"

Wren yawned. "Big deal. It don't work here."

Tech burst in. "You're right, it doesn't work in the Juniper, but Cavatica should be impressed. They are monstrously expensive and powerful. You know that train you rode in on? It's powered by a Kung Pao—all that weight, hundreds of thousands of kilos, pulled by one battery. Outside of the Juniper, our battery only spins the propellers and keeps the lights on. But it can spin the propeller faster than any traditional engine."

"How'd you get it?" I asked, totally forgetting that Tech didn't talk to passengers.

Tech, though, talked to me. "Sketchy got it from someone, somehow. I don't know. She gave it to me, and I fixed it into place. When the Kung Pao works, we can get up to 200 kilometers an hour. We have the fastest Jonesy in the world."

"Dang." I stood there nodding, loving all the tech talk. "And with the Kung Pao, since you don't use it much, you wouldn't have to recharge it for years and years. Which means it's also more cost effective."

Tech smiled at me as she brushed her hair behind her ear, careful not to get any muck on her face. "Yeah, you got it. Would you like to see the steam engine?"

"Sure," I said, "but I like batteries a whole lot more."

Wren had no interest in us, so she wandered off.

Meanwhile, Tech showed me the steam engine, made from a titanium alloy, making the engine far lighter and more efficient than what people traditionally used. Even twentieth century zeppelins didn't have the lightweight tech the *Moby Dick* had. Everything was compact, from the firebox in the boiler to the piping that channeled the steam to the pistons. Her Old Growth closet was fully stocked, which must've cost a fortune.

Again, most likely, Mama had paid that particular bill.

Tech pointed at a small door next to the coal closet. "That's access to the lookouts. We have two, one on top next to the top fin, the crow's nest, and then one below, at the very bottom of the hull, the crow's basement. They're connected by a ladder. We have auxiliary lines from the steam engine to heat those places and to power the gun turrets. Both have MXP-X3 belt feed machineguns."

"Triple-Xs," I said, nodding. "That's a whole lotta firepower."

"You bet it is," Tech said. "Peeperz, our lookout, is always bugging us to let him fire one, but we wouldn't want him hurt in a firefight, and gunners are notoriously easy targets. We have a weapons locker, and it's always been enough." She pointed at a wide cabinet on the right side of the bay near the back cargo door.

Weapons locker. I didn't have the nerve to ask about any of her previous battles.

Tech finished off the tour by letting me crank the wheel to shut off the flow of thelium.

"So, it all works," she said, "but the switching is completely julie-rigged, so it can be tricky, and with just a crew of three, I keep busy. And interestingly enough, a lot of times we just ride the wind. Sketchy is good with the weather."

"Aren't you always telling her she's wrong?" I asked.

Tech shrugged, almost smiling. "Sketchy is pretty much perfect. I have to tease her about something."

That struck me as odd 'cause the woman I met looked crazy and talked even crazier. But Tech knew her stuff, and Wren had been nice to Sketchy, so maybe she was special.

I found Wren in the cockpit, sitting in the captain's chair in front of four other empty seats. Nearby were hammocks swaying over footlockers secured to the floor next to a little refrigerator. A door led to the bathroom.

Wren's fingers played idly across the steering yoke, the knobs, and the levers. All designed to work with or without electricity.

Wasn't long before Sketchy climbed up the ladder and marched over to Wren and me. "Okay, Weller girls, let's get on with it. Weather in the Juniper is a real puzzle, and it could snow on us, or rain on us, or both, or neither, or it could be real nice and sunshiny. Though today, we're gonna have to fight the wind a bit, so it'll slow us down. I'll get you in by tomorrow, I promise. As long as that goddamn June Mai Angel doesn't shoot us down."

I furrowed my brow at Sketchy's blasphemy, but I didn't say anything.

Wren and I sat in the two backseats by the hammocks.

Sketchy and Tech talked through voice tubes, and it wasn't long before the mooring cables were unhitched and cranked up. We drifted off on the wind while Tech stoked the firebox, until the steam engine started pumping the pistons. The rhythmic *womp-womp* of the engine wasn't as loud as I thought it'd be. We floated away from the Srikrishna dairy farm as easy and quiet as you please, like we were just another puffy cloud.

Every so often, the *Moby Dick* would shudder a bit when a gust of wind hit us, and my stomach would lurch. I couldn't imagine what it would be like to be inside the *Moby Dick* during a windstorm. Prolly like being inside a pillow during a pillow fight.

"You wanna tell me about Mama's money problems?" I asked Wren, to make conversation, hoping it would take my mind off my uneasiness.

She shrugged. "No. Sharlotte didn't think I could keep her secret, and so that's exactly what I'm going to do. Besides, her letter was short and sweet. Well, the parts where she wasn't threatening me. All you need to know is that the ranch is in trouble, and Sharlotte wants you home to help her save it."

"Can I read the letter?" I asked.

"Nope. Burned it."

That brought a sigh out of me. "Okay, you wanna tell me about your time in the circus?"

Another annoyed shrug. "No. You got your education, and I got mine. Despite what Mama wanted."

I didn't know what to say after that. I figured Wren had been hurt when Mama had chosen me to go away for school. But I was the logical choice. Mama knew she couldn't run the ranch without Sharlotte, and, Wren being Wren, she couldn't have sat still long enough to learn anything.

Wren left home right after I went away to school. And never went back. I heard all about that last, epic battle between Mama and Wren in a letter from Sharlotte. Happened on the day before Wren's seventeenth birthday, right before Thanksgiving. Mama and Wren had almost thrown punches, which didn't make sense since Mama never beat Wren. Sharlotte did, had to, but not Mama.

I couldn't stand the awkward silence, so I talked, trying to make it right somehow. "I sure cried when Mama told me I'd be going away for school. I loved the ranch."

"Didn't sound like it back at the Academy." Wren said it like talking to me was compounding her boredom exponentially. "You said you never wanted to go back to the Juniper."

"Well, I got used to the civilization," I murmured.

"Wasn't in Mama's plan. You were to learn electricity and come back and make us all rich once the buzz came back. You were gonna be the big hero, you knew that, right? Or did she keep it secret?"

"No, I knew. But with the power still gone, maybe Mama would've understood if I had wanted to stay in Cleveland."

Wren grunted a laugh. "For being so smart, you sure are stupid. Mama would've drug you home by the ear. Not that she would've needed to. Not you, not Miss Perfect. She'd only have to holler from the front porch, and even in Ohio, you'd have come running back."

"And what about you?" I shot back. "Mama could've had a basement full of beer kegs and all the money in the world, and you still would've run off to do God knows what in Amarillo."

"What's that old song? God don't live in Texas anymore." Wren smiled. "And you get used to the Devil's kisses. You want to hear about that particular part of my education? I learned a lot being a party girl. Sure I did."

My stomach twisted, sick. I never should've tried to talk to Wren. It was a losing proposition, always.

She wanted to fight more. "You look up our relatives in Cleveland? No, of course not. 'Cause' Mama never told you where to look, never even told us her maiden name. We were just Charles Weller's daughters and that was it. Y'all think Mama and Sharlotte were the same, but no, Mama was like me when she was young. Maybe too much, since she'd rather fight Outlaw Warlords in the Juniper than deal with her family in the World. Ha, and what did Abigail do when she first started salvaging? God knows what, but I bet you Mama knew about kissing the Devil. Prolly as much as I do."

I couldn't sit there and listen to her evil tongue wagging. I ran from her, found a porthole and looked out, trying to wipe what she had said from my mind. Mama and Wren weren't alike. Never.

Sure, Mama had left Cleveland 'cause she didn't see eye to eye with her parents, but that didn't mean she was a hollow-souled drunk like Wren.

I tried to distract myself by focusing on the scenery, but there wasn't much to see—just long stretches of flat nothing. Grass, sagebrush, and scrub. Occasionally, a farm or ranch broke up the monotony. Prettier than the ground was the sky, a heartbreaking blue.

I finally sat back down, but Wren didn't turn to talk to me. Good.

Breakfast, lunch, and dinner were protein bars, a little fruit going bad, and water from the blue plastic barrels strapped to the walls. The day passed, twilight crept into the sky, and I finally crawled into a hammock to take a nap. The *womp-womp* rhythm of the engine and the gentle sway of the deck lulled me into a deep sleep.

Until the first explosion rocked the zeppelin.

Then Sketchy really started cursing.

CHAPTER SEVEN

I don't tell my grandchildren ghost stories, and I don't show them horror video. When I want to scare 'em good, I tell 'em about June Mai Angel. We all sleep with the lights on.

—Former President Jack Kanton
48th President of the United States
February 17, 2058

(i)

I toppled out of the hammock and onto the deck. Another explosion thrashed the *Moby Dick*. Machine gun fire erupted. Bullets *thunked* into the Kevlar.

Wren slung a seatbelt over her shoulder. She was still in one of the four seats behind Sketchy. Where I should've been.

A voice, tinny and frightened, vibrated out of a voice tube above the captain's chair. "A big Johnny zeppelin is coming in fast above us. Eleven o'clock. Pirates, I'll bet. And under us on the ground, a Cargador with a grappling hook cannon." First time I heard Peeperz talk. He sounded like a ten-year-old, voice squeaky with fear.

Cargadors were vehicles built by Caterpillar Incorporated for the salvage monkeys back in the day. They were huge tractor-type rigs, bouncing around on gigantic rubber wheels, completely steam-powered.

"Goddamn June Mai Angel!" Sketchy hollered into her voice tube. "Peeperz, stay in the crow's basement, and no, you can't use the Triple-X unless I say so."

Tech's voice erupted from the tube. "They can't pierce our armor, so they're shooting high with their cannons, trying to get us low. They're missing on purpose, but for how much longer?"

"Goddamn June Mai Angel!" Sketchy cranked the steering yoke. The zeppelin swooped sideways, and I skittered across the deck to the bathroom.

"Get yourself in a chair, Cavatica!" Sketchy yelled.

The zeppelin careened to the side again, and I was thrown back against the bathroom door.

Another explosion rocked us, and for a minute, the sky outside the windshield was full daylight with the blast. I heard the plunk of the shrapnel slapping the *Moby Dick's* skin. The stink of the explosion struck my nose.

From Tech, "If they get us any lower, you know what'll happen!"

"Can't go up! That Johnny is above us!"

Fear filled their voices. My stomach shrunk up inside me. Sticky sweat broke out over my body.

Another tilt of the zeppelin sent me sliding over the floor until I caught hold of a hammock and held on tight.

Sketchy furiously worked pedals, gears, knobs, and the yoke. "We've seen her Cargadors before. June Mai Angel anchors 'em to the rocks and she can pull zeppelins down with grappling hooks and winch cables. She forces you low and then her soldiers yank you right out of the sky, like how they done the *Zoso*, which was a good ship, an old Bobby, run by my friend Elisabeth Skylar, which is a good name for a zeppelin pilot."

There was a chunking sound, one great big *chunk*, and we jerked to a stop. The zeppelin's nose rose up into the sky, which left me dangling on the hammock. The Cargador on the ground had snagged our back end with grappling hooks.

"Damn that June Mai Angel!" Sketchy howled.

"Pirates are coming!" More screaming fear from Tech.

Wren snarled as she unbuckled herself. Nothing inscrutable about her now, 'cause her eyes blazed, almost gleeful. Finally,

finally, Wren could fight as hard as she wanted, as hard as she could, as hard as her heart would let her. With a Colt .45 Terminator in each hand, she slid down the deck, boots first, until she hit a barrel strapped to the wall.

Peeperz broke through again. "Oh gosh, that big Johnny zeppelin is gonna pull up on our starboard. She has her side doors wide open. Them pirates are gonna board us."

Sketchy caterwauled. "Don't know how they think to get in, but we gotta blow up that Cargador down below to get free." Then yelling to Tech. "Keep the engines hot! Once we pull away, we'll have to clear out fast or they'll kill us all just for the fun of it."

Or most of us. June Mai Angel always left one lone survivor to tell the tale, to warn the living.

More explosions smacked us around followed by more chunking sounds, this time from the Johnny firing grappling hooks into our hull. June Mai's pirates had us hogtied, leashed down stern and starboard. I was close enough to a porthole to see the cables connecting our two airships. Pirates zip-lined down toward us. They wore a mixture of black ninja clothes and ragged cowgirl outfits, cattling goggles, and on their backs, wicked MG21 rifles straight out of the Sino, big and brutal.

I glanced down. Tech, a hundred meters away, wrestled open the weapons locker. She was arming up, and where was I? Clinging to a hammock, doing nothing. Mama would want me fighting. Still, I was paralyzed.

A voice roared from outside, "Surrender now. June Mai Angel is offering you mercy. Give us your vessel and you will live. Fight us and you will die in pain."

It all got quiet for a minute. Sketchy and I locked eyes. Her face was white. "Sorry, Cavatica, but I can't give up the *Moby Dick*. She's all I got. We gotta fight 'em off even though the odds are against us. Always bad odds for us good people."

Wren steadied herself against a barrel while she wrapped an orange extension cord around her left wrist. She answered that outlaw in a howl reserved for gut-shot cougars. "You want some pain, you goddamn skank? I'll show you pain!"

As if to answer her, we heard a hiss, a click, and the *foosh* of blowtorches. The noxious smell of burning plastic filled the air. They were cutting through Neofiber around portholes on the starboard side of the *Moby Dick* to get in. Lord in Heaven, my sister smiled.

Sketchy turned with a Saigia Streetsweeper, a drum-fed 12-gauge semi-automatic shotgun. She stuck her mouth near the voice tube. "Tech! We'll take care of the pirates. You gotta blow us free from that Cargador. And Peeperz, you stay quiet 'til I say so. Then you're gonna get your chance to use that Triple-X. Gonna have to light 'em up, but only when I say."

Everyone was getting ready to fight, and there I was, froze-up, scared solid.

Tech opened the weapons locker, and by God, she pulled out a bazooka, more precisely, a Torrent 6, and a box of T13 thermite rockets. The zeppelin shivered, fighting the cables binding us. The box skittered away from Tech.

The same voice from outside shouted orders, "Beta five, execute. Alpha two, execute."

At first, my head didn't register what they were saying. Then it hit me. It was Sino military talk and they were about to execute a plan to get inside and murder us.

"Gonna grenade us or gas us!" Sketchy shouted.

A piece of Neofiber clattered onto the floor down from Wren. They had cut through, but my sister wasn't close enough to shoot them, and besides, she had the wrong angle. But Wren had a plan. With the orange extension cord in one hand, she flung herself out across the floor of the bay, a .45 Terminator in her grip, firing steadily. She lined up perfectly with the opening and killed the pirate before she could throw anything inside.

Tech tried to walk across the back cargo door to get to the box of rockets by the port wall, but the *Moby Dick* bucked around like an unbroke stallion. She tripped and couldn't get to her feet.

"Delta three, down." More Sino military talk.

I yelled at myself, "You keep jacking up, Cavvy, we're all gonna die!" Same words my mama used during our battle with Queenie.

I let go of the hammock and slid down the deck, aiming for the box of rockets so I could help Tech.

"Come on, you dirty skanks!" Wren yowled. "Come and get me. I'm still waiting on that pain you promised!" She gripped the blue plastic barrels along the starboard wall, glancing around with wildcat eyes, looking for her next target.

I glided past her to the box on the cargo door. The *Moby Dick* calmed for a moment, and despite the panic killing me, I lugged the box over to Tech at the starboard wall.

More smoldering Neofiber pieces scattered across the floor. A woman's voice called in. "Surrender now. We outnumber you. We outgun you."

Wren laughed. "Oh, you're scarin' me. I'm just so jackin' scared."

"You will be. If we have to capture you, we'll eat you, feet first, so you can watch us do it. Alpha four, go."

Wren's Terminators thundered some more, and I prayed her aim was true. *Please God.*

Tech pushed the Torrent 6 into me. "Cavvy, I can't get to the mid-bay hatch, so I'm going to open up the cargo door. Hold on to something, and don't let that box of rockets fly out."

I looked up. On the end of the orange extension cord, Wren swung back and forth across the bay like a spider. Her left hand gripped the cord, her right held a big pistol, and it roared something fierce, cutting down pirates as they tried to squeeze through the holes blowtorched in the side of our airship.

"Come on!" Wren cackled. "Can't you do better? Can't you at least get inside, you dirty skanks? Then we can really play. I got my Betty knife, and she's real thirsty."

Her next words lost in the din of the throaty *thwock* of machine guns firing into the *Moby Dick's* bay. Tracer bullets flashed in the dim light. Wren would be killed for sure.

"Cavvy, grab hold!" Tech warned. "The cargo door is opening!"

I went to grab a handle on the wall, but couldn't get to it. The *Moby Dick* flopped to the left, and I was thrown onto the cargo door. Just as it opened.

Tech must have unhinged the hydraulics 'cause the rear cargo door snapped open and we all fell out—the bazooka, the box of rockets, and me.

(ii)

I slid down the cargo door on my back. At the last minute, the heel of my foot caught the lip at the very bottom of the door, and

I fell against the chain holding the doors at an angle. I clung there, the cold wind blasting my skin numb.

The Torrent 6 banged my shoulder, and I threw my head back to pin the bazooka to the bay door. The box of T13 rockets was long gone.

Tech must've been hanging down like a monkey 'cause she grabbed the bazooka and propped it on my shoulder. I then felt her loading the Torrent 6. Somehow, she still had a thermite rocket.

"No time to pull you up, Cavvy," she said. "Besides, you're safer out there. And you have the perfect angle to blow up the Cargador."

Sorry to say it, but I burst into tears.

Wren would have yelled at me in disgust. Tech, though, got nice and gentle. "You have to free us, Cavvy. And you can. This Torrent 6 is just a machine, and you're good with machines. I could tell that right away. Okay, you're loaded."

"Just a machine," I managed to say.

More Sino talk from somewhere. "Omega eight, execute."

I didn't need to wipe away the tears—the wind did that. The Torrent 6 now felt like a tool in my hands. I had my elbow hooked around the cargo door chain and held the two handles of the bazooka with numb hands. The tube rested heavily on my shoulder.

"Arm it," Tech said. "The switch is right by your thumb."

My thumb hit that switch. Manual, of course, no electricity, and I had to press with some force. *Click*. Armed.

"Okay, Cavvy, aim for the sapropel lamps on the Cargador. We only have one shot. You can't miss."

The pressure was unbearable, yet Tech was right. The Torrent 6 was just a tool, and I had a good angle. I looked down through the crosshairs on the bazooka's sights with just enough light left in the evening sky for me to see. Below us, I followed the straining cables, thwacking and thrumming, down to the glow of the sapropel lamps on the Cargador, a big dump truck looking thing.

Behind me, the thunder of machineguns. June Mai's pirates had overrun our zeppelin. Wren's maniacal laughter came from close by, and from the sound of it, she had commandeered a machinegun of her own. From the cockpit, Sketchy's shotgun coughed. All that noise muddied my concentration.

Until Tech tapped my head. "Okay, Cavvy, you're loaded. The rocket is armed. Gotta shoot now, Cavvy."

Aim. I knew how to aim. Mama had taught me. Suddenly, I was seven again, and Mama was teaching me to shoot my dad's lever-action Winchester .22 rifle. Her face had been warm against my cheek, her arms strong around me.

"Let it surprise you, Cavvy," she had said. "You don't jerk the trigger, you squeeze it slowly, right when a part of you knows it's a good shot, but the other part is surprised you're gonna shoot at all. You can do it." Her voice, so gentle, whispered out of the past.

Wren was far less patient. "Goddammit, Cavvy, will you jackin' shoot already!"

But Wren didn't matter. Only Tech and my mama did. I altered the angle of the bazooka 'cause the rocket would spit fire behind it when it launched. Didn't want to burn Tech with the back blast. I focused on steadying the jerk of the crosshairs on the dim glow below us.

The crosshairs lined up on the Cargador, but only for an instant. That was when I slowly squeezed the trigger. Not jerked. Squeezed.

Then the surprise   the tremendous *whoosh* of the missile firing and then the whistle of that rocket streaking through the air. The rocket struck the Cargador dead on. The explosion lit up the ground. The thermite burned like hellfire through both metal and rock, while June Mai's outlaws scurried away.

Our zeppelin tore loose, the severed cables dangling off the back. We shot up and leveled off, then hurtled to starboard. We were still connected to the Johnny.

Tech heaved me inside.

Wren was next to us, firing into the *Moby Dick's* cargo bay, and I whirled to see June Mai's pirates, shooting at us. Tech and I hit the deck while bullets whistled over our heads, making my teeth ache.

Sketchy was behind the captain seat, her shotgun sticking out, spitting fire—she wasn't going to hit anyone firing like that.

But Wren was prone on her belly with an MG21 machinegun, resting on the floor, perfect for aiming. She picked them off until the last two charged forward, both armed with big knives. Wren ducked one and kicked her out the back door where she fell, silent, to her death. The other slammed into Wren like a maniac devil.

Sketchy's voice burst from a tube near me. "Still tied to the Johnny, and she's a big one. Too big for us to pull away from." Then to the boy in the crow's basement, "Okay, Peeperz, light 'em up."

The boy didn't think twice. The .50 caliber Triple-X machine-gun started up in a thrumming rumble below. I darted over to one of the jagged holes the pirates had cut into the hull.

The Triple-X's tracers and bullets ripped through a cable. The recoil sounded like a whip crack. Not only was Peeperz keeping more pirates from zip-lining across, he was also aiming for the cables, trying to free us. Smart boy. But would it be enough?

"Cavvy," my sister grunted.

I pivoted. Wren lay sprawled on her back, the last of the pirates on top of her. Both my sister and the red-faced woman gripped the handle of a Betty knife, their hands entwined.

The tip of the blade hovered above Wren's eye.

(iii)

I stood there, stupidly watching as my sister strained to keep the Betty knife out of her skull even as the pirate pushed it down ever closer.

Tech snatched the Torrent 6 away from me and dashed over to the weapons locker, digging for more rockets.

Wren struggled, grunting. She huffed out three words. "Two ... bullets ... left."

It took me a second, but then I realized the Springfield 9 was still in my pocket. I fumbled the pistol out, tried to aim, but the *Moby Dick* jerked about, and I couldn't get close enough to fire at point blank range. My hands were shaking as much as the zeppelin.

Sweat coursed down my face. I looked down the sights of my gun, but everything was jumping, unsettled. My courage left me. Even if I had a thousand bullets, I couldn't take that shot.

The pirate glanced up at me as I held a wobbling pistol in an unsteady hand.

The fury in her eyes promised that once she finished Wren, she'd come gunning for me.

In that second, June Mai's woman lost her focus. Wren jerked her own head to the side, letting the knife blade stab into the deck. My sister kneed the pirate right in her diaphragm, which left her gasping on the deck. Wren got to her feet, grabbed the woman by the hair, and threw her right out the back.

Tech knelt at a hole in the *Moby Dick's* side with the Torrent 6 resting on her shoulder. Loaded and armed, she pulled the trigger. The rocket struck the airship across from us. The explosion ignited the thermite and torched the Johnny-class zeppelin. It sank in a wicked display of white smoke from the busted steam engine and the black smoke of melting Neofiber. Pirates leapt to their death. Wren snickered like it was all just some kind of dirty joke.

We'd done it. We'd tangled with June Mai Angel's outlaws and lived to tell the tale. Not many could say that. Not one in a hundred. All 'cause Wren had unleashed the demons inside her.

While I watched the spectacle, Wren snatched her Springfield 9 out of my hand in disgust, then marched over to the very edge of the deck.

"Hey, skank," she said to one last pirate dangling off the edge. "I got two bullets left. But you only need one."

Wren leaned over to watch the body fall. An intense fierceness lit up her face. She turned. Her eyes fell on me. In an instant, the rage was gone.

What replaced it?

Disappointment. A soft kind of hurt. The fighting was over, and I knew from growing up with her, normal life wasn't something Wren enjoyed very much.

CHAPTER EIGHT

Profanity stems from what a culture considers the unspeakable. Traditionally, such things had to do with bodily functions and the sex act. I find it interesting that the word "jack" has replaced the f-word. Have males, themselves, become profane?

—Dr. Anna M. Colton, PhD
Professor of Sociology, Princeton University
"On the Nature of Curses"
Modern Society Magazine
September 9, 2057

(i)

The *Moby Dick* chugged away, too high for any other attempts to bring her down.

I knelt by the open cargo door and watched the frenzied scatter of the people in the firelight flickering below. There weren't just a few outlaws, but lots, like a whole battalion. June Mai Angel had an army. A real army.

What if she brought that army of Sino veterans into Burlington? Could we fight them? No way. Too many, too well trained, too well armed. We'd need the U.S. Army, and they weren't particularly interested in the Juniper. President Jack made sure of that during his administration.

I thought about the razor wire fence I'd seen in Buzzkill. We weren't states, just territories, and maybe we weren't even that anymore.

Dread curled like a snake in my belly as June Mai's outlaw army disappeared behind us.

"Can I close the door, Cavatica?" Tech asked.

I nodded.

She sighed and hit the steam-powered hydraulics to raise the cargo door.

Sketchy still hooted and hollered up front. Wren's disappointment seemed gone. She strutted around the bay like the cock of the walk. "Goddamn, I love machine guns like Sally Browne Burke loves Jesus. Swear to God."

"Watch your language," I said.

"Excuse me, Miss Morality, for saving your ass while you were such a scaredy-cat. If you hadn't blown up that Cargador, I'd have to slap you."

Tech came over and hugged me. "You did great, Cavatica. You saved us."

"Yeah, but she couldn't make a simple shot to save me." Wren grinned at my hurt. "Oh, Mama would be so ashamed of you."

I hung my head. "Sorry, Wren. I just couldn't risk you. If I had accidentally shot you I never would've been able to live with myself."

Wren laughed. "Well, Princess, you were just annoying enough to distract that *kutia* so I could get her myself. You weren't completely useless." Wren marched back to the cockpit but not before checking the holes along the side of the *Moby Dick*, looking for someone else to kill. She still had one bullet left in the Springfield 9.

Tech shook her head. "I can't imagine growing up with a sister like that. You're a hero, even if Wren can't see it."

I shrugged, still feeling awful. We hugged again, and I made my way to the cockpit seats. I sat down in a seat behind the captain's chair next to Wren. This time, I seat-belted myself in.

"You okay, Peeperz?" Sketchy asked into her voice tube.

The tinny voice answered. "Yeah, I'm okay. It was fun and scary, but maybe more scary than fun. That Triple-X sure packs a wallop."

Sketchy grunted in reply.

I looked over, and Wren was sleeping. That girl amazed me. Here she had just killed a whole passel of outlaws and minutes later she was sound asleep. My heart still jumped about in my chest.

Hours went by, and the moon rose out of the east, revealing a world of silver sagebrush and blowing grasses. Snow glowed on the north sides of ridges and in gullies.

We flew over a town, or what was left of it. The moonlight glimmered down on skeleton buildings, salvaged down to the foundation. Siding littered the shadows. Junk piles glowed white, the plastic old and brittle.

Growing up on cattle drives, I'd trudged through those graveyard towns. Weeds cracked the cement into pieces. Wind slapped the fragments of curtains blowing through busted-out windows. I knew those places were haunted. I didn't think we had mutants in the Juniper, but ghosts? Sure we did. After the death and sickness of the Yellowstone Knockout's nuclear winter, those towns lost countless folks. Their ghosts would still be there, pining over the lives they never got to live.

Everyone was really quiet until Sketchy pointed down at another ghost town beneath us. Only it wasn't a ghost town. "You know where we are, Miss Cavatica?" she asked.

"No clue, Sketch," I said.

"We're over the BUE. The *Moby Dick* got you home, bless her heart."

(ii)

At first it was hard to find any landmarks, but then I saw the grain elevators and the big carousel. Once I got my bearings, it looked about how I remembered it. The fairground topped the north end of town, Main Street was due south. I had grown up eating funnel cakes and riding around on the carousel at the Kit Carson Fair, and gosh, that old carousel was nearly a hundred and fifty years old. Still going. Juniper tough.

The bright path of Interstate 70 cut across the land. The asphalt was long gone, burned in the engines of Cargadors. Cook asphalt over a fire to remove the gravel and you've got something that, when cooled, will harden into chunks like coal.

Crush Jones and other salvage monkeys had tried to cover the old I-70 with concrete 'cause they got tired of the pits and ruin of an unpaved road, but it was too many kilometers for them. They attempted to use other materials, and so I-70 looked like a patchwork quilt, some concrete, some gravel, some ground-up bits of plastic.

In between the highway and the carousel was the town. Or what was left of it. Some houses remained, some houses had been stripped, and their foundations looked like tumbled gravestones. Empty propane tanks and rusted swing sets sprinkled the landscape—playthings for the town kids to use.

Burlington had never been big, even before the Sino, but now it was just a nowhere place. No traffic on I-70. Only a few trains from Sterling or Lamar, which was the real capital of the Colorado territory. Burlington did have a zeppelin port, kind of. The little shack built on top of the grain elevator wasn't much of a port, but it was something.

As we drifted toward the grain elevator, west of the carousel and Main Street, Sketchy tugged on a cord and blasted the steam whistle. At ten o'clock at night, it'd make the town folks grumble.

It also woke up Wren, but she didn't speak. She just sat up in her chair, staring. She looked haggard, and truth be told, a little scared. Of what, I had no clue. What could possibly scare her?

"Flash 'em, Tech!" Sketchy yelled over her shoulder.

I turned around to see Tech was at the mid-bay hatch with a sapropel lantern. She used the moveable hood to flash out Morse code to Darla Patil, the Hindu woman who worked as the port operator.

I went to help Tech with the two big mooring cable wheels in the back. They had two more up front. We cranked down the cables and Darla secured us to the grain elevator.

Tech then fastened the rope ladder to the D-rings and kicked it down through the mid-bay hatch. By that time, Wren and Sketchy had joined us.

"Well, we'll stick here for repairs," Sketchy said, "and we'll be there for the funeral. We all loved Abigail."

I was tired and jumbled enough to ask, "Thank you, Ms. Sketchy, but I've been wondering. Mama couldn't have pre-paid you to pick me up 'cause she didn't know she'd pass. So what did she pay you to do?"

Sketchy looked at Wren, and Wren shook her head. "No. Not until after the funeral. Sharlotte's orders."

"What's going on?" I asked.

Sketchy smiled showing her pink gums. "We'll be talking again, Cavatica Weller, oh yes we will be. We're gonna go on a big adventure together."

Her hinting made it worse. "Just tell me a little."

Wren gave me a disgusted look. "Don't you start whining. You almost let me get killed tonight, so don't be any more of a pain in the ass than you already are.

"God, I need a drink." She sauntered away toward Darla's two-room shack.

Well, good. I knew the way home. I didn't need her anymore.

I turned to Sketchy, "Now that she's gone, maybe you can tell me?"

Sketchy shrugged. "I seen what your sister did to them outlaws. I'm gonna keep my mouth shut. And Tech, you will too, right?"

"Ridiculous," Tech muttered.

That ended that. I'd have to wait.

I started to go when Tech hugged me. "It was so great talking with you, Cavatica. You really are going to be an amazing engineer." I hugged her back, thinking it was kind of a big goodbye gesture. We'd see each other the next day, but for some reason, I was special to Tech. Despite her tattoos and overalls, she was kind, and I appreciated her gentleness towards me.

After the hug, I shook Sketchy's big paw, said goodbye, and climbed down the rope ladder. It was only about three or four meters. Not a big deal after what I'd been through.

Now that I knew where to look, I could see Peeperz crow's basement, way at the back of the zeppelin. The barrel of the Triple-X machinegun was barely visible. A sapropel lamp lit Peeperz' little clear-plastic enclosure, and I figured it was prolly really cozy in there, warmed by the steam engine through copper piping. Funny, I had only heard the boy's voice and not seen him.

The damage the *Moby Dick* had taken was as easy to see. Shredded Kevlar flapped over the cracked Neofiber underneath where the grappling hooks had caught hold. Boarding cables still dangled from her. Along the sides, pinpricks of light winked at me from the bullet holes. Nice thing about Neofiber, Tech could melt patches into the plastic. Before long, the *Moby Dick* would be better than ever.

The wind gusted sharp and cold, making the two mooring cables creak. Wren stood next to Darla's shack. I walked across the wood planks to get to my sister. It was the first time I'd ever been there, but I was familiar with Darla. Small town. She was on her way to secure the *Moby Dick's* two front mooring cables, but she stopped to welcome us. The light from her lantern flashed off her nose ring and bindi. "Why, bless me, Shiva, but if it ain't the Weller sisters, Wren and Cavatica. You both have growed up so much!"

She hugged us. Her sari was soft and silky, and she smelled like incense. "Ah, Cavvy, you're so big and pretty now. Like a Juniper Parvati."

I smiled politely. Yeah, I was big in all the wrong places, pretty in none of the right.

Darla frowned at Wren. "A Weller girl wearing jeans, it ain't proper."

"Well, my mama ain't around no more to see if I dress right." Without another word, Wren disappeared down the ladder on the side of the grain elevator.

"Sorry about my sister," I said.

Darla kept on frowning, though I was sure she wasn't surprised. Everyone in town knew Wren and her contrary nature. "Wait here just a minute," Darla said. She hurried into the shack.

In the meantime, I got my gloves, scarf, and hat out of my backpack.

Darla emerged and handed me an umbrella. "Sharlotte was here the other day and she left this. She was in a real hurry."

"Sharlotte was here? Why?" I couldn't imagine Sharlotte climbing up the ladder of the grain elevator. And besides, she had too much to do on the ranch to be making social calls.

Darla shook her head. "Your big sister had a real bad meeting with Dob Howerter. And guess who else was here? I know, you'll think I'm plumb loco, but I swear on Nandi's broad back, it was Tibbs Hoyt. They were flying north to Sterling in the fanciest, fastest Jimmy you ever saw. The Celebration Day."

I had to clap my surprised mouth closed. Tibbs Hoyt and Dob Howerter. Richest man in the world followed by the richest man in the Juniper. And Sharlotte, right there with them. Most likely, they'd talked about Sharlotte's mysterious plan.

Darla laughed at me. "That's right. I swear to you, it's the truth."

Still I couldn't speak.

She laughed some more. "We'll see you tomorrow at the funeral, and welcome home!"

Tomorrow ... the funeral ... for my mama. Didn't feel real and that was okay. Like I said, sometimes reality is overrated.

"Thanks, Miss Patil," I said. "Thanks for greetin' us so friendly. I'll give Sharlotte back her umbrella." My fancy new backpack had a slot that fit the umbrella perfectly.

"Hey Darla!" Sketchy's voice called down from above us. "You gonna secure our front end or we gonna have to do it ourselves?"

"I'm comin', Sketch. Don't get your skirts in a bunch!"

I left Darla to her work and climbed down the ladder. I got a little shaky 'cause of the heights, but then at least it was solid metal, not the like the rope ladder I'd had to scale to get into the *Moby Dick*. And I'd been hanging off the zeppelin in a battle, so climbing down was no big deal. I was getting braver. My Secondskin gloves were real thin, yet real warm. How I loved modern technology.

At the bottom, Wren was waiting for me. I was a little surprised, a little wary.

"You okay?" she asked.

"Yeah, Wren, are you?"

Wren shrugged, no smile, just slitted eyes, cool and tough. "Yeah, right as rain. But they were bad, Cavvy. Those outlaw skanks were tough. We were damn lucky we got away."

"But we beat them," I said. I couldn't quite believe it, but we did.

"Only 'cause you made that shot with the Torrent 6. If you had missed, they'd have killed us all. Then ate us, I guess. That's what they'd said they'd do. Sure were a lot of them."

And that was the only confession of fear I would get. But come to find out, that wasn't what was scaring my troubled sister.

Wren fell silent as she pulled on her own parka, then her fur-lined leather work gloves. Adjusting her cowgirl hat, she strutted off toward Main Street.

I followed until I realized she was going into the Chhaang House Hotel and Tavern. I had to stop. A girl my age couldn't go in there. But I couldn't stay out in the cold, and nothing else was open. Not Antonia's General Store and Feed Shop, not the *Colorado Courier*, which was the local newspaper. Sheriff Lily's office was also closed, but I figured if Wren went into the Chhaang House for a whiskey, the sheriff's office wouldn't be closed for long.

Main Street used to be nice, like an old town from the Old West. But after the Yellowstone Knockout, the nice had been stripped down, leaving only cinderblock structures. The town women had tried to pretty up the place, with flowerbeds and window boxes, but the buildings on Main Street still looked like a collection of two-story bomb shelters patched up with leftover siding, drywall, and plywood. The street begged for pavement, but instead it got a muddy collection of gravel and bits of ground-up plastic carted out of Denver stores.

I paced around on the sidewalk, then I laughed at myself. I'd stunned Wren to trick the police, and I'd used a bazooka to free our airship during a fight with pirates. I had enough *shakti* to go into a bar. Maybe I could be a shining example of sobriety to the women drinking inside.

Or I could walk home. The chill breeze and darkness didn't make that idea very appealing though. Besides, what was waiting for me at home? A dead mother and a scowling older sister and mountains of chores.

All my fretting suddenly didn't mean a thing, 'cause when I heard Wren yell, "Pilate!" I ran through the doors. Pilate was a carnival of a man, a close family friend, and a Catholic priest. Kind of. He'd been a chaplain in the Sino, but he said the war shot most of the holy out of him.

Folks either loved him like biscuits or hated him like flour weevils.

Including me. Love and hate—that was Pilate.

(iii)

The Chhaang House Hotel and Tavern was packed to the doors with cattle hands, travelers, and town women. The place was jumping, fireplace blazing, booze at the bar, johnnycakes and sausages on the burner, and even a three-piece band—an upright bass, violin, and guitar. Only two men were there, Old Man Singh, owner, operator, and fry cook as well as Pilate, who was hugging Wren and grinning.

When Pilate saw me, his hazel eyes took on a twinkle and his grin widened. Though he was older into middle age, his boyish face and long, dark hair made him handsome, but then he was a Roman Catholic priest, so that didn't matter. Or it shouldn't have.

He gave Wren a last squeeze and then let her go. In the flickering light of the tallow candles, I noticed something that filled me with wonder. There were tears on Wren's face. Real big tears. She caught me looking and wiped them away, quick. Why would Wren cry hugging Pilate? I'd have thought Wren's tear ducts were drier than a Wyoming oil well.

Pilate wrapped his big, strong arms around me. The way he smelled—cigars, coffee, and man—brought back memories of him coming to visit our ranch. Pilate would never stay for long. He'd pop in, wow us, and pop out, always on the move. Always a real mystery. He was part traveling priest, part soldier, part sheriff. He'd served three extended tours in the Sino as a chaplain, though he'd fought more than he'd prayed. He was born a New Yorker, yet had found a home in the Juniper.

I stepped back and took him in—cowboy tall and lean, all in black, from his polished black boots to his black suit coat. His hair was black as mountain soil, and long, more rock star than priest. A white plastic priest's collar winked from his throat. The collar was the only color on him. In a holster at his side hung a sawed-off Mossberg & Sons G203 quad cannon, otherwise known as a Beijing Homewrecker. Four barrels loaded with 20mm grenades can do all sorts of things, none of them very nice. Pilate said his Homewrecker was one confused weapon. It didn't know if it was a shotgun that wanted to be a grenade launcher, or a grenade launcher that wanted to be a shotgun. A bandolier of ammunition dangled from the back of his chair.

Pilate grinned. "Cavatica Weller, not only do you look good, but I bet you're a genius engineer by now. So sorry about your mom."

I glanced back at Wren's tear-streaked face. A flash of her eyes told me I'd better look at something else before I got smacked.

"Hey everybody," someone yelled. "Cavatica and Wren are back for their mother's funeral. Now it's a party!"

Women I'd barely met and hardly remembered rushed over to shake my hand or hug me. Some cried. Some laughed. They all said they were sorry about my mama and what a wonderful woman she'd been.

"This one's for Abigail Weller!" the bassist of the band yelled out, and they started up a completely redneck rendition of *Proud Mary*. Everyone knew Mama loved Tina Turner and that old-timey rhythm and blues music. The bassist tried to sing, but we couldn't really hear her.

Once the hubbub died down, Pilate pulled us over to a table and sat me down across from a woman in a bruised-blue dress. It was hard to tell her age. She had gray in her hair and some crow's feet around her eyes. Her skin was too gray to be called pale, and her lips too red. Despite her sallow complexion, she was pretty, but looking into her eyes was like peering into a cracked mirror.

The woman was obviously with Pilate, but I didn't know how that could be, since he was a priest. My head was spinning so much I wanted to take a step outside to catch my breath.

Pilate introduced us. "Cavatica, I'd like for you to meet Rosie Petal. Petal, this is Cavatica."

Petal's cracked-mirror eyes fell on me, and she was smiling, but no one was home. For a minute, I forgot all my manners. What was she doing with Pilate?

Pilate cleared his throat, and I shook her hand. Like shaking hands with slender strips of beef jerky.

Pilate picked up his cigar and coffee as a silence fell over us all. I hadn't seen Pilate in a couple of years, not since the Christmas two years prior. I wasn't sure when Wren saw him last, but Petal knew Wren.

She frowned at my sister like she was raw sewage. "Hello, Wren, you jackering *besharam besiya*."

My mouth dropped open. For one, the language. For two, Wren was certain to carve up that weak-looking woman with her Betty knife.

Instead, Wren said gently, "Hi, Rosie. How have you been feelin'?"

Petal didn't answer the question. "Who are you trying to impress, Wren? You wear your tight jeans and cake make-up on your face, but why? There's no one here to date, is there? No, but you just love to have people look at you. You are the poison that poisons everyone around you."

Pilate stepped in. "Hush, Petal, mind your manners."

Petal closed her eyes. "Looking at her makes me want to vomit. Will you give me my medicine and put me to bed, Pilate?" The woman stood up, and Pilate got up with her. They both disappeared up the stairs.

My guts felt twisted from seeing Pilate with that broken woman, and then what she had said to Wren. I just had to ask, "Who is she, Wren? And what's her medicine?"

My sister shrugged, hid her face as she got up, and went to the bar. She came back with two foamy-headed beers and a whiskey. She carried all three like she knew a thing or two about waitressing. She slid a beer in front of me.

I pushed it away. "No. I don't believe liquor is appropriate for ladies. And I am underage. Just 'cause we live in the Juniper doesn't mean we can flaunt the laws of the country we hope to rejoin."

"Don't you sound all cultured," Wren sneered. "Yankee laws don't apply in the Juniper. Lucky for us, and more for me." She knocked that beer back in one long gulp.

A few cowgirls elbowed each other and pointed. One woman whispered, "Yeah, that's Wren Weller all right."

"Where did you get the money to buy that?" I asked.

"Oh, I'm sure someone will step up to pay. Maybe Pilate. Maybe I'll have to do some dancin' to pay for it 'cause I'm such the party girl sinner."

I didn't know what to say to that, so I went to the bar and ordered a curried sausage from Old Man Singh.

"On the house, Cavatica," he said. "On account of your mother passin'. You have my condolences."

Well, one mystery solved. Why hadn't Wren just told me Old Man Singh gave her free drinks?

I'd chomped through the sausage by the time Pilate came down the steps. Then I noticed Betsy McNamara watching him cross the room. In her bonnet and New Morality dress, Betsy looked uncomfortable and out of place in the saloon. She was a young widow who ranched a little spread north of town. She had a few daughters, but only just recently a son. I found it odd she was in the saloon. She should've been home with her children and her headcount.

Pilate sat down and re-lit his cigar with a silver torch lighter. "Well, ladies," he started. His eyes turned hard when he saw Wren drinking. "I thought you were going to quit."

Wren threw back her shot of whiskey. "Are you gonna AA me, Pilate? Is that how you wanna spend your night?"

Pilate's smile turned smirky. "Good point." He directed his attention to me. "So, tell me about yourself, Cavatica Weller. Last time I saw you, you were fourteen and sullen. I hope you've grown out of that sullen. Both of your sisters seem to have found a home there."

My eyes kept going back and forth between Wren and Pilate, and then yeah, Betsy who continued to stare at Pilate. Part of me wished I had walked home. My heart felt too weary to try and figure it all out.

Well, I just had to start with Petal. "Who is that woman you're with, Pilate? And what is her medicine?"

Pilate tapped his cigar ashes on the floor. "Petal's an old war buddy," he said. "She came home with the Ladies in Waiting. During the Sino, she got really sick, but she got worse once we got her home. Her medicine is the only thing that keeps her upright."

The Sino-American War ended on Easter Sunday, 2045, but it wasn't until the Eterna batteries were perfected that we could bring home all the soldiers. Ladies in Waiting, that's what we called the women trapped in those horrid internment camps 'cause the world had warred itself out of all its fuel and left the shipping industry in shambles. It took ten long years to bring all our American soldiers home.

Thanks to the Vatican, Pilate was able to get out of China a year after the war ended. Maybe he felt guilty about leaving Petal behind, but he still hadn't answered my question about the medicine. Then again, it really wasn't any of my business.

He smiled cheerily. "And as you can see, she hates Wren. But then, your sister has a short list of admirers. Me, you, Sharlotte, and who was that guy you were seeing in the circus, Wren? I can never remember his name."

My sister stood up. "Only you like me, Pilate. Maybe Cavvy did once, but prolly not anymore. As for Sharlotte, well, she hates me far worse than Petal ever could."

I didn't say a word. She was right on all accounts.

Wren went to the bar and returned with a bottle of Pains whiskey, locally-distilled and guaranteed to kill any bacteria or brain cell it touched.

"Glad you're not just going to drink beer," Pilate said. "What fun would that be?"

The way he said it, as a challenge for her to destroy herself, bothered me. Had Pilate changed? Or had I?

"So, Cavatica," Pilate said with a smile, "let's talk about happier things. Tell me about your trip home. I hope it went well."

And there I was, all confused and tore up, but Pilate's smile made me smile as well. For some reason, he could always make me feel better. "No," I said, "it didn't go well at all. I had to use a stunner on Wren to get away from the Ohio police."

That made Pilate laugh. "Okay, now I have to hear the whole story! Tell me every little thing."

I talked while Wren got drunk and Pilate laughed at her. All the while, Betsy watched us. What did she want?

When I told Pilate about freezing up when Wren needed my help, I winced, afraid of what he would say.

Pilate sipped his coffee, smoked a bit on his stogie, and then said, "Well, sounds like when you had to make the shot, you did. You used the Torrent 6 to free the zeppelin. I still can't believe you survived that. I bet you're the first airship ever to escape June Mai Angel's evil clutches."

"But with Wren and that outlaw, I froze up. Couldn't even fire a single shot to help her ..." My voice fell away.

"Prolly wanted to see me dead." Wren slurred the words.

Pilate ignored that. He slid his hand into mine and shook his head and got real sad. "You hesitated because there's a goodness in you, Cavatica. Right then, you couldn't believe how horrible the world could be, or what horrible things we're forced to do to survive in it. That doesn't make you weak, it makes you good."

"Makes her weak," Wren muttered.

"And getting loaded makes you strong? If anything, it makes her untrained."

Wren threw back another shot of Pains. "I ain't never been trained."

"You've been trained, all right," Pilate said. "I've known Navy Seals who've seen less combat than you. Between me, your mother, and this cruel world, you're about as battle-grizzled and PTSD'd as you can get."

"Here's to my PTSD!" Wren toasted him and sucked down another shot.

At the time, I didn't know what PTSD was, so I looked questioningly at Pilate, who answered, "Post Traumatic Stress Disorder. It's a mental illness. Like religion and television, only with more sweat and tremors."

That's when I first started to understand how traumatized I was. Most people know about the severe cases of PTSD, but we all walk around with trauma. Life is hard. Growing up in the Juniper, life cut hard into brutal.

I was about to ask Pilate about Sharlotte's mysterious plan when Wren slipped off her chair and under the table. She'd drunk herself out cold.

Pilate breathed out cigar smoke. "And there you have it. However weak you think you are, Cavatica Weller, there are a variety of examples around you that might challenge that notion. Weakness, like bravery, comes in all different shapes, sizes, and flavors."

Suffice to say, we didn't walk home that night. I was kind of relieved, kind of frustrated. I wanted to get home, but I wanted Mama to be there. Couldn't have both.

Old Man Singh gave us a room and Pilate helped me haul Wren into bed. The room was nice, with paintings on the wall, curtains on the window, and some plastic flowers. I was closing the door when Betsy McNamara came up the steps talking to Pilate.

I shouldn't have spied, but I couldn't help myself. Betsy twisted her bonnet in discomfort. Her face glowed with sweat. Why was she so nervous? It was only Pilate.

Betsy spoke in a hushed voice. "I was saving money to go into Hays, to visit the ARK clinic there, but then I needed antibiotics for my headcount. I used up all my money, so I couldn't buy any ..." She didn't say the last word. The "S" word. Male Product. Her eyes were on the floor, hidden.

ARK, as in Noah's boat. Ironic.

Hays, Kansas, had the closest ARK clinic, but other border towns had them as well, like Buzzkill, Nebraska, and the OKC. The main corporate headquarters of the ARK was in New York City, most expensive real estate in the world, but then Tibbs Hoyt could afford it.

He and the ARK, like most of the World, ignored the Juniper, so if one of our women needed Male Product, she'd have to travel. But like we've seen, traveling was expensive and dangerous.

Then it dawned on me why Betsy was so sweaty and nervous. And how she had gotten pregnant with her son.

My heart fell into my stomach like a stone.

"You want to try again?" Pilate whispered the question with such kindness and compassion in his voice, it brought tears to my eyes. At the same time, it made my throat close up.

I shut the door without making a sound. Pilate was a Roman Catholic priest with a collar and everything. What he was doing was a sin. Or was it? Betsy couldn't afford the ARK and there weren't a lot of men around who were viable. Most likely, Betsy wanted a big family to help work her ranch, but then if she popped out a viable boy, she'd be set. A few trips to the ARK clinic in Hays and she'd be rich.

I understood Betsy's motives, but how could Pilate justify his actions? He'd taken an oath of celibacy. And if he was sleeping with women to give them babies, why keep Petal around? Was she really just a war buddy? It didn't seem like it to me.

Even with my troubled mind, I was tired enough to fall right asleep in the flouncy bed next to my sister who slept as silent as the dead. The smell wasn't too bad. Like a perfumed distillery.

(iv)

The next morning, we got up, and I couldn't look Pilate in the eye. I wondered if Betsy had taken him up on his offer, but it was too hard a thing to ponder. I'd grown up thinking Pilate was half-saint, half-magician, but right then he seemed more like the prince of sinners.

Wren and I borrowed horses from Aggie Garcia's ranch, which was near town. Pilate and Petal had horses of their own. We all rode up a crushed plastic stretch of I-70 until we saw our blue house on the hill.

Wren stopped, gazing up at our homestead, with that nothing look on her face.

We all stopped with her. The quiet felt so uncomfortable, I had to say something. "Well, Wren, you got us home in time. You did it."

She ignored me. More quiet. Just a breeze blowing over our faces.

"It won't be as bad as you think," Pilate said to her.

"No," Wren said. "It'll be worse."

I looked closely at her face. On it was an expression I'd rarely seen.

My sister was afraid to go home.

CHAPTER NINE

I've given the Juniper my children. Some made it, some didn't. I've given the Juniper my blood and buckets full of my sweat. In return, she gave me wind, riches, and wonder. I couldn't leave the Juniper. I'd land in Cleveland and fall over. No wind there. At least not the kind of wind I'm used to.

—Abigail Weller
Colorado Courier Interview
June 6, 2057

(i)

The four of us, Pilate, Petal, Wren, and I, rode up our driveway. Gravel crunched under the hooves of our horses.

Wren reined her pony to a stop. She sat in the saddle, eyes closed. Petal glared at her.

We heard the barking before we saw our three new dogs, Edward, Jacob, and Bella. Edward and Jacob were big German Shepherds, but Bella was a Norwegian Elkhound. Even though she was smaller, Bella ruled over them both, and the boys pretty much followed her everywhere.

Kind of unfair, that Bella had two boys and I'd prolly never even get one. But the Sterility Epidemic affected only humans.

I got off my horse to play with the dogs. They were big, wet, and frisky. For a minute, it made me forget the sadness I was coming home to. Then I got a big lick on my cheek, and my heart twinged, missing Brownie and Lady, the dogs from my childhood.

But then I just had to smile when a cowbell clanged in the distance. Our best Angus steer, Charles Goodnight, stood on the hillside, sniffing the air. I could hardly believe I was seeing him again.

Wren saw him, too. "That goddamn steer is gonna outlive us all."

Charles Goodnight was the smartest bovine you could ever meet. More than once, Aunt Bea said that Charles Goodnight was better than ninety percent of men who had all their parts and walked on two legs. Every year, he led our headcount to Hays, and came back to do it again and again. Other bulls were bigger and meaner, but even they would follow Charles Goodnight anywhere.

Tenisha Keys and Nikki Breeze, two of our employees, must have heard the dogs bark. On horses, they rode over a ridge to check, saw us, and waved. Both were petite, pretty African-American women and more like family than employees. Nikki Breeze had her hair all up in cornrows, unlike Keys, whose dreadlocks tangled down her back. Keys was a quiet one. From the little I'd heard, she'd had a rough time of it in East St. Louis, and things got so awful she came west. Must have been real bad if the Juniper was the better alternative.

Keys was new, but Nikki Breeze had been with us even before the Queenie attack. She was middle-aged, but looked as young as Keys, who was only a little older than Sharlotte.

Breeze and Keys charged over, both in New Morality dresses with thick leggings and dusters. "Welcome home, girls!" Breeze called. Both she and Keys dismounted, and I shook their hands.

"Sharlotte's in the house," Breeze said. "We're getting things ready for the funeral." She tripped on that last word, her throat clogged up with tears. "Your mama went quick, Cavvy, I was there."

I looked away before I started bawling. "Thanks, Nikki. Thanks for being with her at the end."

Pilate, Petal, and Wren got off their horses to shake hands, though both Keys and Breeze were cool toward them. No one liked Wren in Burlington, Petal was odd, and Pilate, well, Sharlotte hated Pilate enough for it to turn everyone against him.

Breeze and Keys took our horses and put them in the stable. Then they finished working on their ranch chores, so they could work on the funeral. The three dogs followed after, as did Charles Goodnight, swishing his tail.

We continued on foot up the gravel path and across the little bridge that covered the trench we'd dug for protection. Grass filled it, since June Mai Angel hadn't taken to raiding farms, only cattle drives. Still, up a hill, with that trench, our house was a good place to make a stand. When Queenie attacked, all of our neighbors had clustered there with us.

Right then, it was as if such violence had never happened there. The morning air was heavy with ranch smells: three thousand head of cattle, fifty horses, pigs, chickens all created quite a bouquet. A gust of wind brought the smell of dry, winter grass and drying mud—the perfume of my homeland.

I knew I had to look in on Mama, but part of me didn't want to. Being home, smelling the ranch, it made me feel like a kid again, and I just knew Mama would come bursting out of the back door, coming to hug me, and, of course, put me to work.

I dawdled away from Pilate, Petal, and Wren, taking in the ranch, taking my time, 'cause it was easier than facing the hard truth.

Our spread was so pretty. The house was a nice cotton-candy blue Victorian that perched on a little hill sticking out of the yellowed plains like a winsome smile on an ugly girl. The original house had been a ramshackle wreck, the wood too old for salvage, and the insides equally worthless. But after the territory government in Lamar gave land to squatters, Mama hired the best builders around to tear it down and rebuild it, keeping the house old-fashioned, as was the style. Yet Mama added some modern touches as well. Every window in the place could be locked tight with Neofiber shutters, turning our house into a fortress. You couldn't tell that though, not even if you looked hard.

A wide, wrap-around porch hugged the building. Fancy lace curtains showed through white-trimmed windows 'cause the defensive shutters were open wide. Three big stoves kept the place tolerable in the winter. Lots of nice rooms on ten thousand acres of fine grazing land, fertile after the Knockout and more rain than usual. Near the house, to the west, stood our big red barn and a bunkhouse where most of our employees lived—Breeze, Keys, Annabeth Burton, and Aunt Bea.

Yeah, Aunt Bea, but not like that black-and-white video with the old lady and the sheriff. Our Aunt Bea was Beatrice Maria Mercedes Gonzales, Mexican down to her tortillas. She sure felt like an aunt. Mama and Bea had hooked up early in the Juniper, both recognizing a tireless, bloody-fingered worker in each other. Workers, sisters to the grave, that was Mama and Bea.

Annabeth was new. I heard all about her from Sharlotte's letters. Annabeth came south from Mavis Meetchum's outfit and joined us to be closer to her aging mother in Burlington. Our new hire was experienced, but old, with a face like a work glove.

We had a fifth employee on the Weller ranch, and though Lucretia Macaby had only been with us a short time, Crete was young enough for Mama to feel motherly over her. She got a room in the house up in the attic. I knew Crete from elementary school, and she was too blonde, too flirty, and too silly to make it in the Juniper. Eventually, like her sisters, the family would get enough money and they'd send her into the World where she'd trick some boy into marrying her.

"Cavatica." Pilate's voice made me turn. At the top of the driveway, Pilate pointed to the icehouse, which sat in the shade of the back patio that led into the kitchen. "Your mom should still be in there. You might want to pay your respects."

It was time. I took in a big, deep breath. I wasn't ready, but I had to face her.

Wren pulled open the door to the icehouse, looked inside for a minute, shrugged, and then walked away toward the house.

Pilate shook his head at her.

"See, Pilate," Petal said in a scratchy, loud voice, "she feels so guilty, she can't even face her own dead mother. What a *besharam kutia*."

Pilate shushed her. Wren kept walking like she hadn't heard, but I knew she had.

I couldn't care about that right then. I found myself walking across the ground to the icehouse. The air inside the little shed dropped thirty degrees. Packed inside were big, solid squares of ice covered with sawdust. My mother lay on the dirt floor, wrapped in a sheet.

I bent down to unwrap her. I didn't know if I was supposed to do it or not, but I wanted to see her now. I couldn't find the edge of the sheet, and I felt too weak to turn her over. Something wet dropped on my hand. I didn't even know I was crying. It was like I was a stranger to myself. Who was this girl crying? Who was this girl kneeling down in front of her dead mother? She sure wasn't me.

This strange, crying girl talked in a strangled voice. "I wanna see her face, Pilate. Can you help me?"

"Sure, Cavatica."

We unwrapped the body until it was my mother, in her work dress, her face sunken in, her skin snowy dead.

That body, shriveled and cold, that wasn't my mama. Mama had gone away, and she would never come bursting out of the house again, or push me to work, or hug me, or sing that old R&B song with every bit of soul she had.

How much do I love you, oh, where do I start? Through the valleys of my soul, 'cross the mountains of my heart.

I fell down next to her, and I sobbed. I couldn't get all the sobs out of me—it was like I was so full of tears I would split open wide if I tried to keep a single one inside.

Sharlotte and Wren were suddenly there, and I knew they wouldn't cry.

So I cried for all three of us until they had to drag me off. 'Cause I'd never hear my mama sing again. Not ever again.

Through the valleys of my soul, 'cross the mountains of my heart.

(ii)

Around noon on that Saturday, I was in my room, looking over my old things. My bedroom was painted a light blue and the curtains were lacey and frilly. For most every birthday I ever had, Mama gave me candles. I rarely burned them, so there were pretty candles all over. Most things, though, were either too small or too childish for me to care about anymore. Still, everything was clean and pristine. Leave it to Sharlotte to dust an unused room.

I had spent most of the morning in my bedroom, only leaving to help prepare Mama's body for the funeral.

I was fingering through the ribbons I'd won at the Kit Carson County Fair when Sharlotte knocked on the door. "You ready to help, Cavvy?"

"Yeah, sure." I opened the door. Sharlotte had been so busy, we really hadn't talked.

Standing there in her cloudy gray Sally dress, which was New Morality, only a little fancier, my sister looked like she was playing dress-up, but not very well. Shar was a big woman, meaty and curvy and strong as an ox. We shared the same straw-colored hair, a round face like our mother, but Sharlotte was far prettier. Like Wren, Sharlotte's pretty was in her dark-lashed, nighttime eyes, which they both got from Daddy. Problem was, you rarely saw Sharlotte's eyes. Most of the time a cowgirl hat hid her eyes. Or she was walking away, going to work, getting things done—all you saw was her ponytail. Sharlotte would've cut her hair short if the New Morality allowed it and if people wouldn't have gossiped.

"Glad you're feeling better," Sharlotte said, which meant she was glad I had finally stopped crying. She went to turn away.

"How you doing with Mama passing?" I asked.

Sharlotte looked at me like I was crazy. Of course she didn't answer that question. Nope. She'd rather talk about her to-do list, which was her very own gospel.

"I still have some cooking to do. And Wren insisted on liquor, so she's bringing it in from town. Bet you she'll be late. I can't believe I agreed to let Crete go with her. Both put together don't have the sense of a good dog. I should've sent Charles Goodnight along to keep 'em in check. I'll need you to make sure the tables are set, and we'll need the old black pots from the cellar. Thanks for helping us get Mama in her New Morality dress, and I guess Wren did the make-up good, though I know she'd rather be drinking. That Wren. She'll never change. I'm just glad Mama isn't around to see her in jeans."

"Wren did her face pretty," I said, which was kind of a lie 'cause you can't paint the dead to look like the living.

Sharlotte went on with the last of her list. "Most things are ready. Father Vincent can't get here from Sterling, so Pilate is going to do the funeral, which pains me to no end, but there is nothing to do about it. Technically, he's still a priest, though I keep writing letters to the bishop."

I wasn't a bit surprised Sharlotte was trying to get Pilate excommunicated.

Even so, I felt like I had to protect him for some reason. "He'll do right by Mama. You know how close they were."

"I'd rather let a Bible-drunk Protestant bury Mama, but what's done is done." Sharlotte had her hand in her coat pocket, gripping something. Her voice changed. "Did Mama ever talk to you about Daddy? About his health?"

"Well, about his cancer, but that's all."

Sharlotte nodded, distracted. "I found some medical reports, going through Mama's papers. Lots of papers to go through when people die. I suppose it's all on computers back in the World."

"It is," I agreed, but right then, I didn't care a whit about medical reports or papers. Heck, the funeral didn't even seem all that important anymore. In some ways, me sobbing over Mama had already buried her. She was gone. So was Daddy. Now I wanted to know more about the living. From my backpack, I took out the umbrella and told her what Darla had said. "Did you really meet Tibbs Hoyt?" I asked.

She nodded. "He didn't even look at me. Dob was nicer. He gave me his condolences about Mama. I told him we were hurting financially, from Mama dying and from other stuff. I asked him to give us a break in Hays so we could sell our headcount there."

Dob Howerter and Mama started ranching around the same time, and Mama would go to his Colorado Territory Ranching Association meetings to give him a hard time about his organization. They'd been friends for a long time, until Dob hit it big.

"What'd he say, Sharlotte?"

My sister grimaced. "Said that he was sorry, but he wasn't going to budge. Said his plan was to own every beefsteak in the Colorado Territory, starting with ours. He's even making a play for Mavis up north."

Mavis Meetchum, second biggest cattle operation in the Colorado territory. Dob Howerter being first. We used to play with Mavis' kids and Howerter's nephews growing up. Wellers, Howerters, and Meetchums, all trying to tame a wild land, and trying to run each other out of business, with us Wellers on the losing side. Season three of *Lonely Moon* had a similar story arc.

Now was my time to get some answers. "So with prices fixed in Hays, what's your plan, Sharlotte? I keep asking and no one will tell me. Where are we going to drive our cattle to?"

Sharlotte's mouth grew small. "Let's bury Mama. Then we can talk business. It's what she would want. And in the end, it was her plan, not mine."

"I can't believe this!" My voice rose nearly to a shout.

Sharlotte's lips disappeared. "I guess your big, fancy school in Cleveland didn't teach you about patience. Or manners. Or timing." Sharlotte's voice came out cold as snow. "It's not a simple conversation, and I don't want to go into it now. Besides, we have our mother's funeral to prepare for. Don't you think that's more important than our headcount?"

I sighed. No use arguing with Sharlotte. Might as well try milking a rock. "Okay, Shar, fine. You still think I'm a little kid and I ain't got no say in the family, but you'll learn. I'm not a child anymore."

She turned away and left me with nothing but her back, strong and broad. "If you're not a child, then quit acting like it. Weeping for hours on end. What good can that do for anybody? Nothing. We have a lot to do and people are going to be here any minute. Aunt Bea needs our help in the kitchen, and that's what matters. The food has to be good. Has to be. Everything else can go to pot, but not the food. Never that."

The food was amazing, but that didn't save the funeral from being a circus with the Weller girls in all three rings of it. Let me tell you, Sally Browne Burke might be wrong on some things, but on liquor, she is absolutely right.

(iii)

That afternoon the whole town filled our house, talking, hugging, complaining about Dob Howerter and whispering about June Mai Angel. Sketchy, Tech, and Peeperz were there as well. Peeperz was a skinny ten-year-old boy with a scarred-up face that pinched his eyes almost shut—ironic, given his particular occupation. He was quiet and nice and took my hand gently, like I would break. Heck, he looked like he would break.

It'd be impolite to ask about the scars, but I was extra nice to him.

"Thanks for lookin' out for us, Peeperz."

He shrugged. Sketchy talked for 'em all anyway. Lord, could she go on about nothing at all. I got a long hug from Tech, who was wearing a dress—not New Morality, but close enough for a tough girl like her. Tattoos decorated every bit of skin showing.

Three o'clock in the afternoon, our numbers swelled from out of town visitors. Mama was pretty much a celebrity in the Juniper. Mavis Meetchum wanted to come, but couldn't. She sent a nice card and expensive flowers instead.

In a crowd, we walked to the gravesite, down the hill from our house by our east fence. It was sweaty in the sunshine, but when the wind blew off those Rocky Mountains, you could feel every snowflake that had fallen that winter. In the distance, the windmill well creaked as it spun in the breeze.

Pilate looked like he had just stepped out of the Chhaang House. Same priest collar. Same black slacks and polished black cowboy boots. But now he wore his waterproof duster, so big, stiff, and thick you could stand it up in a corner and swear it was a man. The only thing missing was his black cowboy hat that looked like it had outlived a dozen gunfights and would outlive a dozen more. His long black hair hung free.

At the sight of Pilate, Sharlotte scowled so bad I thought her face would turn blue and fall off. She was standing on my right. Wren was on my left. Keys, Breeze, Crete, and Aunt Bea walked out with a simple pine-box coffin on their shoulders and work gloves on their hands, contrasting their nice Sally dresses. They needed the gloves to hold the ropes stretched across the hole they had dug. Centimeter by centimeter, they reverently laid my mama down into her grave right next to Daddy's. Both had stone Celtic crosses as grave markers.

The dead babies were there as well. Placards set in marble dotted the ground with only their names and the year they died. Elwyn, Fern, Willa, and Avery. Not one had lived to see a dash on their markers.

I had been cryin' so much, I was numbed down to my bones. What wasn't numb, the wind took care of.

Petal stood by herself, away from everyone. She kept her head lowered, but every once in a while, she'd lower it a little too far and catch herself with a jerk. If I hadn't known better, I would've sworn she was sleeping on her feet. She sure was a strange one. Why was Pilate with her?

Speaking of which, once all eyes were on our wayward priest, he swept his hair out of his face, bent and picked up some dirt. "Y'all know what this is?" He twanged it up a little, but that was only for our benefit. He generally talked straight-up Yankee.

He let the dirt drop from his fingers. "That's dirt. They say ashes to ashes and dust to dust because we come from dirt, and we go back to dirt, and I won't get graphic because I don't want Sharlotte to shoot me." He paused as we all chuckled.

"Abigail Weller is gonna be dirt before too long, gone, back to the earth. I could read from the gospel, but I would imagine many of you would be getting your own guns out if I made my eulogy too long. I know Wren would." Another bout of laughter, this time a little more uncomfortable.

"But I always liked the story about the empty tomb. They rolled away the stone. They looked inside. It was empty because Jesus had risen from the dead. He was resurrected—checked out before noon, took off for greener pastures, gone to Texas." He let out a deep breath, like he was steadying himself. "Like all of us, Abigail had her broken places. Like many, she escaped into the Juniper because of a troubled past and a wounded heart. And some of the things she had to do in the Juniper wounded her even more. So much pain. Hard to get to the other side of it."

His voice cracked, and I couldn't believe it, but the smile was gone, and there were tears in Pilate's eyes. With him crying, I started crying, too. I glanced at Wren. She was stone faced.

Pilate talked through his tears. "With death comes sorrow, but also there comes healing. In death, Abigail has found the other side of her pain. If she had a soul, it's at rest. If there is a God, she's with Him now. However, if heaven is empty and we're nothing but our brain chemistry, well, she's gone regardless. Either way, her body will become dirt, and that dirt will grow hay to nourish her headcount. Even in death, Abigail found a way to keep working. I'm not sure about the molecular science behind death, decay, and the minerals in the dirt, but I bet you Cavatica could tell us because she's a smart one. Too smart for guns or violence."

He gave me a teary little grin. I blushed and looked away. How could he have doubts about Mama having a soul? How could he have doubts about the existence of God? What kind of a priest was he? Sharlotte frowned, just itching for Pilate to stop, but powerless to stop him. She was far too proper to make a big scene.

He went on. "So Abigail has found peace at least, and the tears we cry, we cry for ourselves. We lost a fine woman, a true pioneer, tough as winter beef jerky, but sweet as spring wine." His voice broke down completely and tears coursed down his cheeks. "She was the finest woman I have ever known." And dang me, but if he didn't smirk and say, "And as many of you know, I've known my fair share of women, so that is saying something."

Sharlotte let out a hiss, loud enough for everyone to hear. My mouth dropped open. Last night he seemed so sad with Betsy, and today he was making a joke out of it in front of everyone, including Betsy. Right then, I thought maybe Sharlotte was right about Pilate.

He smiled brightly up at the sky. "Say hello to heaven for us, Abigail, or so the old song goes. Now, let's get out of this goddamn wind." Even after blaspheming, he crossed himself, as we all did—in the name of the Father, the Son, and the Holy Spirit.

Breeze, Keys, and Aunt Bea did the final work, covering Mama's coffin with dirt. The rest of us went inside, and it wasn't long before the circus started. I got all the answers I could ever want about the cattle drive. It wasn't Sharlotte's plan, no way. It was Mama's.

And what a plan it was.

CHAPTER TEN

There has been talk that the greatest battle women still have to fight is the battle against drugs and alcohol. I don't think it's the government's job to teach temperance. I believe that such lessons should be learned in the home. However, from what I've seen, AA also makes for a wonderful classroom.

—Sally Browne Burke
On the 120th Anniversary of Alcoholics Anonymous
June 10, 2055

(i)

e packed ourselves into the house, and you couldn't walk anywhere without stepping on someone. The Garcias took off to get spare tables and lanterns for the barn, so it was like we were throwing two parties at once. I didn't get out there, but the Garcias would be good hosts.

I pressed myself into our huge kitchen, made tiny and hot by the ovens, bodies, and steaming platters of food on banquet tables. Everyone was touching me, saying sorry, and I found myself crying again from the kindness.

All my elementary school classmates showed up, the twenty-some girls and the three boys. Those boys looked like they always did: wind-blown from all the attention. People murmured it was a shame they weren't viable—couldn't talk about a boy without talking about that.

Speaking of which, Raymond Hitchcock held both his wife Malvina and their eleventh baby. He was viable and went to the ARK in Hays—got paid real well to do it, far more than he did for ranching.

Other than the Hitchcocks, everyone else had worked for Mama at one point or another. She'd hire on temporary help for big jobs, and then let them go right away. Mama believed in a small payroll, and those that did work for us steady were the best of the best. Except for Crete. The blonde girl's smile had softened Mama's heart.

At the end of one long buffet table, I grabbed a plate and started loading up. There was Aunt Bea's tortillas and her pork green chili, two kinds, Juniper hot and Yankee mild, and a beef-macaroni casserole and big slabs of honey BBQ ribs along with big thick potato rolls that were like eating sweet, half-baked flour. Darla Patil brought her spicy Indian lentils and put it beside the Nayar family's chickpea curries, aloo palak, and Tandoori naan bread that I have to say I liked as much as the potato rolls or Aunt Bea's tortillas.

For dessert, a wide stretch of dark chocolate cake tempted us, and if you could say no to that, you couldn't escape the pies, creamy and fruity, or the vanilla ice cream, fresh off the rock salt.

Back in Cleveland, I ate vegetarian, partly 'cause of the health benefits, partly 'cause I could never be sure where the meat came from. But for this meal, I went for it all.

I came out of the kitchen to see Pilate holding court in the parlor. He had hurried through the food to get to his cigar, one the size of my forearm. He loved his cigars and the coffee he'd sip from a stainless-steel travel mug he got from a Starbucks outside of the Vatican in Rome.

Wren stood behind his shoulder, also smoking a cigar. Sharlotte had propped open the window behind them, but it was still smoky. Folks braved the smog to listen to Pilate tell stories and flirt. I watched him get all kissy, wearing that priest collar like it didn't mean a thing.

Still he made me smile, and I was doing my best to hate him.

Of course, everyone asked Pilate the questions he loved to not answer. "Is Pilate your real name?"

"Maybe. Just don't call me Pontius."

"What's your first name, Pilate?"

He smiled all smart-alecky. "Don't have one. Got it shot off in the Sino."

"Should we call you Father?"

"Only if you have daddy issues." Pilate winked and blew smoke rings.

People guffawed at that, including Sketchy, who laughed harder than all of us. Tech had left after the funeral and took Peeperz with her. Also, Petal was nowhere to be seen.

Annabeth Burton, our newest employee, sat down at the piano. Long, braided hair fell from a hard face, creased and wrinkled. You'd think she'd never smiled a day in her life. And yet, when her weathered fingers started pounding out an old-timey song, "Don't Stop Believin'," her whole face lit up like fireworks, exploding all pretty.

The singing started, and more people came over. Someone pushed a drink in my hand, a beer in a colorful ceramic mug. I was about to put it aside when I noticed Wren's black eyes on me like magnets on gunmetal.

She sipped from her own mug, daring me to drink the beer.

Food filled my belly, so a little beer couldn't hurt. I took a sip. The taste brought me back to when Daddy was still alive, before he got sick. When he'd score a beer in an aluminum can, he'd cherish it. Of course, Mama, being New Morality, didn't approve of any sort of liquor, and Daddy had to sneak it, but he'd share it with me.

"Only a little," he'd say. "A little beer and a little wine is good for you. Too much, not so much."

I didn't like the taste then, and I didn't like it at Mama's funeral, but with Wren looking at me, I took hold of my *shakti* and drank the whole thing. I would show her that while I couldn't fight like her, I could drink like she did.

I wandered over to Pilate and asked, "Where's Petal?"

He talked around his cigar. "She wasn't feeling well, so I gave her some medicine and she's resting up in Wren's room."

Still didn't know what kind of medicine it was.

Wren found me without a drink and gave me a cup of hard cider just as Annabeth started playing an old country song, about callin' someone darlin', darlin'. It was funny, especially the part about her mama getting out of prison. The way Annabeth sang it, she made it even more funny and twangy. I never would've thought that tough old bird could be so lively.

Well, the cider tasted far better than the beer, and whenever my cup was empty, Wren was always around to fill it. Outside, dark and cold ruled the night, but inside, it was all lightness and happiness and sparkle.

We were halfway through one of Debra Alan Walker's songs when Sharlotte came busting through, waving her hand. "Okay, Pilate, time for you and your wretched cigar to leave."

"No, it's not." Wren's voice came out low and smoldering.

I was drinking sweet Irish coffee, and by that time, my head was spinning around as fast as the tires on a steam truck. A blur later, I found myself on my feet. Kind of. I swayed, and Pilate righted me. Dang, if only he would've shushed me as well. "No, Sharlotte," I said, "this is a party for Mama, and even though he might be a dog, Mama loved Pilate and she let him smoke in the house."

Sharlotte's jaws clamped shut like a bolt screwed down tight enough to strip. "I can't believe you're drinking, Cavvy. What would Mama say?"

I knew what Mama would say 'cause Sharlotte was saying it. I felt my scalp itch out of shame, and I turned red. I went to put my cup on the table, and I misjudged the distance. My Irish coffee hit the floor and made a big, brown puddle right on our good parlor carpet.

Sharlotte didn't yell at me. She turned on Wren. "This is your fault. All of this is your fault."

Wren waved a hand like she was batting away mosquitoes. "Aw, Shar, have you ever been anywhere where you didn't ruin everyone's good time? You're like a party killer. Wanna break up a party? Don't call Sheriff Lily. Call Sharlotte Weller." She slurred every word.

"I'll leave, Sharlotte," Pilate went to sit up, but Wren pushed him back down, then turned on Sharlotte.

My sisters were locked in a death-match-combat-battle stare down.

"Tell these good folks your plan," Wren said. "Mama's buried. Now, to the business. You've wanted to keep it all a big, jackin' secret, but I say it's time everyone knew about the suicide you've planned for us."

Sharlotte scowled. "This is not the time nor the place."

"She's right. Don't do this," Pilate added, but did that stop my sister? Hardly.

Wren swung into the middle of the room. Slutty-tight jeans hugged her skin, and her big sixteen-centimeter Colt Terminators were tied down in gunslinger holsters. Her blouse clung to her body, leaving nothing to the imagination. She was so strong, so sure of herself, so sexy. Right then, I wanted to be in jeans. I wanted to be that strong and confident.

Every eye fell on her, and Wren drank up the attention. "Sharlotte ain't gonna take our headcount to Hays. She's gonna take off for Wendover, Nevada, using a dirigible to re-supply and scout."

The whole room tilted. I turned my head. The tilt worsened. I wasn't sure I had understood all the words.

Malvina Hitchcock's mouth fell open. "You can't take your cattle west. You'll die. All your headcount will die. The deserts alone—"

Sharlotte let out a yell, a gasp, some sort of noise. "Yeah, my Mama had the idea, and yeah, it's gonna be a long shot, but all of you are livin' with your heads buried in the sand. I talked with Dob Howerter himself, and he isn't gonna let us sell our cattle for a fair price. He owns the market in Hays and all up and down the border. Mavis has her own buyer in the Buzzkill market or he'd own her too. Yankee lawmakers don't care 'cause we're only Juniper folk. So, we either sell our beefsteaks at prices that'll starve us in the end, or we think outside the box."

Betsy McNamara, matronly in her little bonnet, nodded. "Everything she's sayin' is the truth. Dob is done playin' nice. He offered me a bid on my ranch. I ain't got the hands to work what I have...." Her eyes flickered over to Pilate, then dropped. "So, I'm pretty sure I'm gonna sign on with the CTRA."

Other ranchers who'd joined Howerter's association dropped their eyes. Yeah, we'd let them come to Mama's funeral 'cause in a small town, you have to be friendly even to people who are spitting in your cobbler. Best revenge against them was gossiping anyway, which is another small-town tradition.

I tried to make sense out of it all, but I couldn't. My stomach churned. Should've taken it as a warning.

"You give Dob a drumstick, he'll take the whole chicken," Sharlotte said, then stopped herself. Raised up her hands to do it. Wren had roped her good, but Sharlotte was all about controlling herself and as much of the world as she could. "But that doesn't matter. We're gonna run our cattle to Nevada. Mama got paper from some Sysco executive who'll give us two dollars and seventy-eight cents per half-kilo."

The gasp at the price point made Sharlotte pause for a minute.

She continued. "Even if you're a member of Howerter's ranching association you wouldn't get that. So you keep selling your unqualified beef for eighty-six cents a half-kilo if you want. As for us, we're gonna go for it. You're all invited to throw in any headcount you want, and you'll get better than fair-market prices. You have my word."

Someone laughed meanly. "Hard to collect on all that money when you're dead. You won't make it halfway."

"Prolly not," Sharlotte whispered. "Gonna leave in a month. First of April."

The way she said it, there wasn't a single drop of enthusiasm or determination in her voice. Sounded like she was whispering bad news to herself.

Well, now I knew why she rushed the funeral and wanted us to get home so quick. We'd need to leave soon if things went wrong, so we wouldn't get caught trying to cross the Rocky Mountains when autumn hit. It was thirteen hundred kilometers from Burlington to Wendover. If we were lucky, we'd hit Nevada in time for Fourth of July Fireworks. If we got unlucky, we'd never make it.

Now it was clear why the *Moby Dick* carried so much water. Cattle get thirsty trying to cross deserts. Even with all her barrels full, it wouldn't be enough to satisfy all our cattle not even for a day, but then I imagined they had pumps, so they could find more water, and our headcount could drink in cycles.

Finally, it made sense that Sharlotte wanted to keep the drive west a secret. She knew we'd be the talk of the Colorado territory, and she had not wanted all of that sharp-tongued gossip at our good mother's funeral.

Wren sure ruined that.

People were yelling now, about Dob Howerter, about Betsy being one more ranch to join the CTRA, and then about our mama's crazy ideas.

"What about June Mai Angel?"

"What about a spring snowstorm? You'll die!"

"What about the Wind River people? Goshdarn Union Pacific won't run their trains through Wyoming on account of those savages."

"Big deserts up North. Nothing to drink or eat for kilometers and kilometers. You'll lose half your headcount. Naw, you'll lose 'em all!"

"Ain't no way I'd give you even a single yearling. No one will."

"And even if you get your headcount to the SLC, the market is in Wendover. You'd have to drive them across the Salt Flats. Ain't no way that can be done."

"Like the gal said, you won't make it halfway."

Sharlotte was snarling mad.

Wren smiled, showing her pearly whites, loving what she had caused.

Wren's smile had the same effect on Sharlotte that it had on me in Mrs. Justice's office back at the Academy. Before anyone could stop her, Sharlotte grabbed a handful of Wren's hair, and they were socking it out. Wren was too drunk to really make a go of it, and Sharlotte was so angry she could have beaten June Mai Angel's army using nothing but the serving spoons out of Aunt Bea's chili.

I went to stop them, I swear I did, but then I found myself on my knees. Everything I'd eaten came barfing out of me like a fountain.

Suffice to say, if our mama hadn't already passed on, her funeral party surely would've killed her dead.

(ii)

I don't remember getting from the parlor to the bathroom upstairs, but suddenly, I was there, leaning over the toilet. Someone was holding my hair back while I dry heaved into the bowl.

Nice to have indoor plumbing. Nice that it had nothing to do with electricity.

I glanced over my shoulder and died of embarrassment.

"Sorry, Pilate." My stomach cramped and I made horrible, puking noises right in front of a priest. Well, as much of a priest as Pilate was. I wanted to hate him for what he did with Betsy McNamara and for what he'd said at Mama's funeral, but I couldn't.

I coughed and spit. "Is this why you don't drink, Pilate?"

"No, I never minded getting sick. You took it as a place to stop, and that's a good sign. Me? Puking was merely a caesura before more drinking. When I drink, I drink until I've burned down the barn, shot the dog, and flushed the family Bible down the toilet. Or was it burn the barn, flush the dog, and shoot up the Bible? I can never remember. That's the problem with blackout drinking. You lose your priorities."

"Is that why you stopped?" I chanced a look back at him.

Pilate closed his eyes. "I hit bottom. Let's just leave it at that."

Slumped next to the bathtub, I put my cheek on the cold porcelain. Who knew a bathroom floor could be so comfortable? Then all the shame came flooding in. "Don't look at me. I've disgraced Mama, and I know Sharlotte will never forgive me."

Pilate sat down and before I knew it, my head was on his chest, and he was holding me close, petting my hair, real gentle. His arms felt so strong around me, like my father's had before the cancer took him. Now both him and Mama were gone. I was an orphan, like in Dickens.

I cried for a little bit 'cause unlike my sisters, I couldn't stop crying. Girly 'strogen. But then I thought of Sketchy and what she said. What was girly 'strogen about showing emotion? Better than being soulless like Wren.

When I found a break in my weeping, I peeked at Pilate. "That damn Wren. This is all her fault. Excuse my language."

"Poor Wren. Her worst fears always seem to come true."

I remembered how afraid she had been of coming home, but I still didn't understand how Pilate could pity her. She had caused all the trouble, bringing in booze, getting me drunk, and then starting a fight with Sharlotte in front of the whole town. "Wren should've just left. She doesn't belong here."

"Wren can't help herself. She tries, but she can't go anywhere without bringing her own chaos with her. That's why she was afraid to come home. That and the memories. It seems even if we can be saints to everyone else, we save our worst sins for our family."

Had Wren really been afraid of causing chaos? I didn't know. I thought about a story Mama told about Wren. Since Mama was always so busy with ranching, she put Sharlotte in charge of Wren's and my hygiene—bathing, hair-combing, teeth-brushing, that kind of thing. Wren must've been around eight years old, and she liked her hair princess-long, but didn't like anyone combing it. Sharlotte had to wrestle her down to brush out the tangles, and Wren would shriek and shriek.

After one such episode, Wren took Sharlotte's Betty knife out of her room, went into the bathroom, and used it to cut off all her hair. Down to the scalp. Mama said blood and hair covered the bathroom, and there was Wren, grinning, bald and bleeding. She'd rather scalp herself than let Sharlotte comb out her tangles.

I'd never be able to figure Wren out, so I decided I'd work on the Sharlotte puzzle for a while. "Pilate, is Sharlotte serious? Is she gonna try to take our headcount west?"

"Yeah, I guess she is. I talked with your mom about her finances a year ago. She was hawking everything, borrowing money, maybe paying too much for your schooling 'cause she was so certain the electricity would come back to the Juniper, and soon. You know how she could get."

Mama had dreams of power coming back on in Denver. She took them as prophetic—the lights of skyscrapers flickering on, powered by electricity. She wanted her family ready for such a miracle, which is why she sent me to Cleveland. People thought she was crazy. She hadn't cared.

Pilate continued. "So the situation was bad even before Dob Howerter started fixing prices, and then things got worse. She needed a way to beat Howerter, but at the time, she didn't see a way out. Well, she found one. Your Mom started writing letters to some woman, Mandi Petersen, a vice president at Sysco Foods who handles high-end Las Vegas and Reno restaurants. Both those women came up with a story because Ms. Petersen knew, like your mom did, Juniper steak is just dead cow-muscle, but the story behind it? Priceless. I guess you know how popular that Juniper family drama is, *Lonesome Moon?*"

"*Lonely Moon*," I corrected him.

"Yes, that's the one. Your mom and Ms. Petersen came up with a story to match it. A cattle drive across the Juniper. A fortune in dollars waiting on the other side of hell."

I did the math real quick, and the money made me dizzy. If we could get two dollars and seventy-eight cents per half-kilo and the average weight of any given beefsteak was six hundred kilograms, sell three thousand cows and that would be around ten million dollars.

"What about driving the cattle down south to where we could take a train through Texas on to Arizona?" I asked.

"Not as good a story," Pilate said. "And Howerter has contacts in the Union Pacific. I can guarantee you he'd make it difficult. No, the deal was to drive the beef to Nevada."

"How do you know so much?" I asked.

"Your mother hired me on for security before she passed. Me and Petal. So I got all the details, and I tried to talk her out of it, but you know how your mother was."

I took in a big, shuddery breath. "We gotta stop this. Sharlotte can't do it. Mama could've, maybe, but even then, driving our headcount west is just plain crazy no matter how much money we'd make."

Pilate's chest moved under my head as he spoke. "Sharlotte's going to do it, and Wren is going to help me run security, which should scare us—"

I cut him off. "What do you mean Wren is going?" I moved back to look at him. "Wren doesn't care about saving the ranch. I figured she'd run back to Amarillo the first chance she got."

Pilate's lips curved into a smile. "Wren loves you and Sharlotte, though it kills her and she can't figure out how to show it. She told me tonight she wanted to see this through, and you know Wren, any chance she has for a fight she'll take. Petal and I will be there to make sure your sister doesn't kill everyone we meet. And we'll hire some more hands and more guns. You met Sketchy, Tech, and Peeperz. With a zeppelin, we'll be able to scout ahead and get re-supplied if we need it. We'll just hope for the best."

"Why would you risk your life for us, Pilate?"

"With your mother gone, you Weller girls definitely need adult supervision." He smirked, but his face turned serious, spoiling the joke. "Besides, Sharlotte is going to need all the help she can get."

"Not from me," I whispered. "I can't go. I shouldn't go."

"Really?" Pilate asked.

That made me mad. "What the heck, Pilate? Shouldn't you be sayin' I'm too young and this is too dangerous?"

Pilate's face turned serious. "You don't get to be young, Cavatica. You reloaded for your mother when Queenie attacked, however questionable that parenting decision might've been. Regardless, no child could've done that. You were born forty years old and battle weary already. You're a Weller, like it or not. Would you really stay behind while the rest of your family goes off?"

"Yes!" My head was spinning, but I reckoned I was done throwing up. I had puked up everything but my toenails, and they were pretty well connected.

"Surprising." I felt Pilate sigh. "I thought for sure you'd be dying to come along. Well, that was a poor choice of words."

I sorted through my options, and none of them were good. I couldn't go back to school, since we were out of money. My Territory ID was back in Cleveland. No way to get it. Applying for a new one could take months or never. Which meant the United States was beyond my reach. Besides, after Wren's gunplay, I was prolly a wanted woman.

If I stayed in the Juniper I'd have to find work, which meant I'd end up either working for Howerter or Mavis. With my name, I could get on, but then I'd be living in barracks with other hands, starting at the very bottom of the rung.

Could I stay in Burlington? I couldn't really imagine it, not with my whole family taking off. If I didn't go, they'd have to hire another hand to replace me. I was free labor.

No good choice remained for me.

Still, I wanted to argue. "If I went, what can I do? I can't shoot anyone, not face to face. I proved that when our zeppelin got attacked. And yeah, I can run cattle, but it's been a long time, and I'd be real green at it."

Pilate touched my face. "Cavatica, the truth is, we don't know what your story is going to be. And if I know one thing for sure, anyone can be a warrior. The Sino taught me that. As for running cattle, it's like riding a bicycle, only a lot more smelly."

"I can't go." I repeated. "I just can't. You understand, right?"

He smiled sadly. "I understand. But do you know what kind of life you are choosing?"

"What kind?"

"A lonely one. Sometimes safety is a lie. And sometimes the only real heroes are the unexpected ones."

It was my turn to sigh.

Pilate helped me to my room where he tucked me into bed fully clothed. He joked, "If you sleep in your clothes, well then, you know you've been to a party."

In my bed, in my room, I watched the light and shadows mix across the familiar corners and edges of my nightstand, my dresser, the walls, the wainscoting. "Pilate, if y'all go and make it, we'll have enough money to send me back to school. Sharlotte can stay on the ranch, and Wren can go back to Amarillo. You guys don't need me."

"You're probably right." Now he was just being nice so I would go to sleep.

"Do you think you have a chance to make it that far, Pilate? All the way to Nevada?"

The answer was plain on his face. No, they wouldn't make it. And I'd be alone.

But Pilate lied to me, kind of. "If we make it through and sell them beefsteaks, what a story it will be. A ten million-dollar story to be exact. And if we all die, well, then we can work for your mother up in heaven. I'm sure she'll have started her own business."

He went to leave, but I was feeling young and scared. "Pilate, can you wait 'til I'm asleep?"

"Sure, Cavatica, sure thing." He took a seat in the rocking chair by the window, looking out. The moonlight showed his wrinkles. His smirky, smart-aleck smile was all gone. Only the troubled and weary was left—sad, like he had been with Betsy. I had the idea that even though he joked about it, sleeping around hurt him somehow.

"Halfway," I whispered. "Really, if you could make it halfway, get through Denver, you should be able to make it all the way."

"We can't go through Denver," Pilate said. "No way that can be done. We were going to cut up north at the very edge of it, but you shouldn't worry about all that."

I drifted off, looking at that sad face, safe in my house, warm in my bed, comfortable with my thick mattress and pillow.

I'd made up my mind. I would stay on at the ranch, take care of it while they were gone. I could make money by fixing things for our neighbors, since I'd always been good at steam engine repairs.

I'd let Wren and Pilate have their gunfights, and Sharlotte could order around all her employees, and I'd stay in the house, sleep in my bed, and let them all be heroes.

(iii)

The next day, we went into town to hear Pilate preach again at Mass, first Sunday of Lent. Most of the town Catholics were hung over from the night before 'cause of our party. I know I was. But we soldiered through.

We got home, but I didn't want to really be with anyone. I hadn't told Sharlotte I wasn't going, and I knew it would be a fight even though I was so young.

I saddled up Bob D, who'd only been a foal when I'd left for the Academy. Now he was a full-grown stallion, a gorgeous pinto tobiano, white with brown like spilled paint all across him, even his nose. He'd remained uncut, but he was still mellow and eerie smart. Like he could see right through me and into my heart.

Right then, though, he'd have to squint 'cause my heart was a shadowy place full of doubt.

Being home, going to Mass in Burlington, suddenly I was a young girl again, small under a wide blue sky. Yet having an animal under me, I found myself feeling powerful, his muscles like my muscles, his body like my own, my boots hooked in the stirrups, a saddle creaking, and the reins in my leather-gloved hands. The smell of the horse, while not exactly pleasant, was powerful and right, somehow. Horses should smell like horses.

I galloped that wonderful stallion off to the edge of our property. It wasn't marked with fences, just a gully we called the south ditch. There I reined Bob D around to look at the blue house rising up from a plain of yellow. An easy wind mussed the winter grasses. Sometimes even in February, we'd have nice breezes, simmered warm by a gentle sun. That Sunday was such a day.

My friend Anju would be taking communion in Cleveland. Billy Finn would be with her. They'd be singing hymns. Becca would be off somewhere nursing her broken nose.

Becca had called me names, made fun of me for growing up Juniper, and yet I'd always been proud of my heritage. My mama had literally bled for our home. She'd fought for it, over and over. And finally she'd died there, buried not thirty meters from the front door.

I rode the perimeter of our property, scaring up cows that watched me carefully, chewing their cud, spit drooling from their working jaws.

Their eyes sized up me and Bob D. It was like they were asking me, *Are you really going to stay? Are you really going to abandon your family?*

Every millimeter of our property brought back memories. Playing catch with my dad using salvaged baseball mitts and a ball shedding horsehide. Wren tagging me "it" during a blizzard and me tumbling through the snow trying to catch her. Sharlotte, Mama, and me helping a big heifer give birth to Betty Butter out by the south ditch. The calf's body steamed in the cold.

I drove the horse across the grass and through the memories until we stopped in front of the graves of the baby girls and my daddy and my mama.

If we lost the ranch, what would happen to the graves? What would happen to our sacred home, made sacred by the blood spilled there, by the bodies buried there?

It would be gone, all gone, and everything Mama had worked for would be chaff before the flame.

I dismounted and stood there before the graves of my ancestors. Bob D nestled his head under my arm, and I petted him while he nickered softly.

He didn't bend to eat. It was like he could feel the power in the moment.

As could Sharlotte.

She strode over in her New Morality dress, her hat low on her forehead, and her boots churning up dirt. She stopped beside me on the other side of the grave markers.

"Pilate told me you ain't going."

I nodded. Shame dug into my chest. Standing before the dead, it felt like a betrayal to everything Mama had held precious—work, duty, family, and the entrepreneurial adventures she'd dedicated her life to.

Sharlotte cleared her throat and spoke. "Mama borrowed from Howerter, borrowed three million dollars. No one knows it but me. She put up the farm, our land, our headcount, all as collateral. Used it to keep us going and to finance this drive west. Also, a fair chunk of that money went for your schooling. College and such. You know how much your tuition and board were each year?"

More shame. I didn't.

"A hundred thousand dollars. So she spent nearly a half a million dollars already on you, Cavvy, and was going to spend a bunch more. Not that I blame her."

That was a laugh.

Sharlotte's voice bristled with bitterness. "Mama went all in betting on this cattle drive, and on you, Cavvy. That's a poker term. You remember?"

I nodded. The amount of money choked me. In Cleveland, I never had money for anything extra other than school. I felt poor, and yet me going there had marked me as rich and privileged even though I hadn't felt like it.

Now I knew why Wren had tried to strong-arm Ms. Justice. There had been fifty thousand dollars left on the table.

It'd been quite a wager, but then Mama had loved Texas Hold 'Em and could bluff anyone to throw away full houses and flushes—throw them down in disgust onto the green felt of our poker table. Even Pilate. Only Wren would ever stand up to Mama, and my sister would lose just as often as she won. 'Cause Mama was so good, reckless, but always so lucky.

"That old poker table still in the basement?" I asked.

Sharlotte nodded.

What would happen to the poker table if we lost the ranch? Gone. Salvaged. Sold off to Dob Howerter and his evil Colorado Territory Ranching Association.

"If we sold every one of our beefsteaks in Hays, we'd get around three million dollars. Just enough to pay off the loan, but then we'd be broke. I asked Howerter about letting us stay on our ranch if we let him buy us out. He said we'd missed our chance to join the CTRA, and he wouldn't let us keep our house even if we begged. He said to the victor go the spoils. And you remember, he was real mad that Mama didn't join his association when he started it, but then why would she? Mama wasn't about to give Howerter any of her profits, just so she could get his dumb seal of quality. Stupid, it's all so stupid, but this is his revenge."

I couldn't believe how vile the man was, but then I could. The scuttlebutt claimed that Howerter had gone sterile, and it never sat right with him. Since he couldn't have babies, he wanted the rest of the world instead. Mama had children. Mavis Meetchum had children. And Howerter had the Colorado Territory Ranching Association.

"So we have no choice," I said with a sigh.

"None that I can see."

"What about leaving the Juniper?" I asked. It was a question loaded with dynamite.

"To do what?" Sharlotte asked right back. "I don't know computers. And the way I hear it, after the SISBI laws, immigrating to the U.S. would be harder than getting our headcount to Nevada. No, I was born here. I'll die here. Your story might be different, but then after Wren's gunfighting in Cleveland, it might not be."

I swallowed hard and harnessed my *shakti*. "Are you ordering me to go, Shar?"

Surprise, surprise, but Sharlotte softened. "Not hardly. I can't order you to die with us. 'Cause you know as well as I do, this is a suicide."

"Then why do it at all?"

Sharlotte pointed to the graves. "'Cause Mama loved a long shot. She would've done it, could've done it. Us together, our family, even Wren, we have a chance. It's a bad chance, but remember how Mama went all in that one Christmas Eve? She had nothing but off-suited low cards, but she won with bad cards, and we can, too. We have to. If we can get a ten million-dollar payday, we could pay off Howerter, re-invest in a new herd, heck, we might even make this a regular thing. We'd be flush. You could go back to school. Wren could go back to hell. I might even consider other options. If we can make it through."

The memories came on strong—Mama at the table, laughing, clutching her cards to her chest, betting high on every hand, and winning, always winning.

She'd taken out impossible loans from her worst enemy to send me to school, all to save a ranch she loved in a land she'd chosen above the U.S. I felt the guilt and obligation keenly.

"I have to go," I whispered.

Bob D nudged me as if to agree.

I talked on. "We have to save our ranch and show Dob Howerter he picked the wrong family to mess with. We have to be heroes."

"Whether we want to be or not." Sharlotte tacked on those last words, gazing down on Mama's grave. A fire burned in her eyes. Anger. Not at me, but at Mama.

It was raw *shakti*, but right then it didn't feel like a creative, powerful female energy.

To borrow from the Hindu myths, it was Kali's fury in her eyes. And what did Kali's fury do?

It destroyed the world.

Well, let the world die. I was going to save the ranch even if at the end of things, it was the only dirt left in the universe.

It was our land, where our parents and baby sisters were buried. It would be ours, forever and ever, amen.

You don't let go of sacred ground. You fight to the death for it.

(iv)

A month passed. Sharlotte had rushed the funeral, rushed to get me home, all so we could prepare for this cattle drive. Going west.

A month of work, of fretting and fighting and preparing our headcount—a round-up, branding, medicine for the sick, and bullets for the terminal.

We left on Monday, April 1, 2058. Most of the same people were there from Mama's funeral to help us with the final pack. More cooking. Aunt Bea's churros, two henhouses of eggs, and enough coffee that even Pilate couldn't have drunk it all. Everyone laughed we were leaving on April Fool's Day, but hoped for the best, predicted the worst, being neighbors, friends, enemies, and consultants, as people are wont to do.

The *Moby Dick* floated over our heads all loaded up. Before dawn, we had bucked bales out of our hay sheds and into the *Moby's* cargo hold. Sketchy said we needed the calm of the morning 'cause around 9 AM the wind would pick up, and the *Moby* didn't like wind that close to the ground.

She was right about the weather. Down to about five minutes.

Aunt Bea took off first in our Chevy Workhorse II, steam-powered, pulling the two-axle supply trailer. We called the whole rig our chuck wagon. Then our employees and new hires led Charles Goodnight, our best steer, and Betty Butter, our best cow, to amble after the chuck wagon. Both were really smart, but Betty, a scarred-up and snotty Holstein, had the temperament of a shaken wasp's nest. Ask the two coyotes who'd gone after Betty one night. We'd found her bleeding but alive the next morning, a hundred meters away from the mangled corpses of the coyotes.

Sharlotte, on her horse Prince, trotted into the herd moving west. She'd sheathed Mama's M16 in a leather scabbard next to her thigh. We'd named Mama's gun Tina Machinegun, partly 'cause as kids we confused sixteen with Tina, partly 'cause Mama had loved Tina Turner. Seeing the assault rifle put a tremor in my belly. Bad memories.

The dogs barked around Sharlotte and Prince, happy to be working and moving, but dodging the falling steps of the cows around them.

Wren galloped ahead to look for trouble. She'd found her old traveling clothes—worn chaps, a leather vest, and a dark green wool poncho. The poncho, woven rough, swirled around her in the breeze of her speed.

Pilate and Petal rode tail, which was the worst place to be on account of the dust raised by the hooves of our headcount.

On my favorite horse, Bob D, I turned around one last time to look at our blue house. It was a cloudy day, a little windy, but all in all, it felt like spring was knocking on the front door with her sister summer waiting to kiss us on the porch. My favorite New Morality dress, gray as the sage, was enough to keep me warm, though I had thick leggings and my Mortex parka stuffed into my saddlebags for when the weather turned chilly.

The doors were locked, the barns and sheds empty, and the whole ranch was closed down tight. We sold off our extra animals to neighbors, who gave us too much for them. Out of pity. They'd keep an eye on the ranch. We didn't leave any cattle behind 'cause with the price point the Sysco executive was offering, it would've been foolish. Like Sharlotte had said, if we could get that ten million-dollar paycheck, we could come back and buy a new herd and undercut Howerter's prices. Ha. That would show him.

Yeah, and if June Mai Angel came and burned it all down, well, what we did wouldn't matter. All our drama and fear wouldn't be worth a gutter-dirty dollar bill.

Well, if that did happen, we'd fight to get our cattle to Nevada and then we'd fight June Mai Angel. Might as well fight two wars if you're going to fight one.

Turning back, the cattle spread out before me as far as I could see. We mostly had Herefords, and their glossy red bodies looked dark as dried blood against the yellow grass of the open plains. Their white faces looked like snow banks against the grass.

I guided Bob D and the rest of our ponies into the mix. That was my job, the remuda, thirty-six horses, two for each of the hands.

Interstate 70, going west. My desire to fight had waned over the weeks since I'd stood before Mama's fresh grave. Now, a fear settled in at the impossible thing we were trying to do.

The first attack came twelve days later, the day after Good Friday, in what used to be Strasburg, Colorado. I didn't know who hit us, not right away.

All I knew for sure was that a gorgeous, viable boy fell out of the sky and right into my lap.

CHAPTER ELEVEN

It's clear that during the twentieth century we forgot history's most important lessons. So as a society, let's take our education from those strong women who built this country hundreds of years ago. Let's turn our calendars back to when women were chaste, strong, and ever obedient to an ever-loving God. Our greatest lessons lie in our past, not in the present, and certainly not in an unknowable future.

—Reverend Kip Parson
From the Eighth Annual International
New Morality Conference
June 21, 2057

(i)

Dusk outside of Strasburg, Colorado; the wind blew a bone-kissing chill down my parka. We were setting up camp by the ruins of a gas station complex, which at one time would have had pumps, a convenience store, a Taco Bell Express, and showers for the truckers. Now, a few minivan carcasses lay slumped on weed-split concrete. No more gas for the engines. Too electric to work.

I was building our temporary corral for our remuda of horses—we only needed a few aluminum poles and rope to keep our ponies together 'cause they were so well trained. We'd sold our brood mares along with our nags and colts too weak to make the trip.

Our regular employees and new hired hands pitched tents, Aunt Bea had her cooking fire going, and I was pounding the aluminum poles into the ground with a three-kilogram sledge. It had been real warm, so the ground wasn't completely frozen. After threading the rope through eyeholes in the aluminum poles, I commenced to picking Bob D's hooves. He nickered softly and closed his eyes against the wind. I'd gotten used to his strong horse smell, so much so, it felt like home now, as much as the infinite plain around us.

I kept glancing up at the cold sky, expecting to see the *Moby Dick*. Sketchy would scout ahead and come back every couple days, just in case we needed the hay and water in the *Moby Dick*.

I'd been right about the water. An average cow needs at least seventy-five liters of water daily, and the Moby couldn't carry enough for our entire headcount. However, she had pumps, so the plan was, she could water down half the herd, float off, reload, and then come back to water the other half.

Pretty clever. Mama and Sketchy had planned it down to the liter.

The history of those first twelve days on the trail was etched on my hands. Dry skin whitened my knuckles. Cuts, scrapes, and scratches cut a roadmap across the backs of my hands. My fingernails remained black and grimy even after I washed them. At the Sally Browne Burke Academy for the Moral and Literate, my hands had been pink and soft, and I wasn't even girly 'strogen enough to use lotion. But back in the World, my job was to think, and you don't need tough hands for that.

Cattle meandered around us—three thousand cows managed by thirteen people. Pilate kept saying we needed someone named Bilbo Baggins to make us an even fourteen, since thirteen was unlucky, though I had no idea what he was talking about. Besides, if you included Sketchy, Tech, and Peeperz, we had sixteen.

I was brushing Bob D down when we heard the first boom. I felt the wrongness of it, though my mind was trying to trick me into thinking one of the cowgirls had fired by accident. My heart knew the truth. That echoing explosion promised violence and killing.

"What in God's name was that?" Sharlotte called out from the other side of the gas station.

"That was something big, like anti-aircraft artillery." Pilate held his coffee in one hand, and a short slender cigar in the other. He cut them into thirds to make them last.

Petal stood next to him. She cradled her long sniper rifle to her chest—first time the gun had been out of its case. It was bigger than she was.

Bella barked her warning bark. Edward and Jacob woofed after her.

Another explosion. Then another. In the distance, something burned in the twilight sky, burning and falling. The dogs took to howling.

A zeppelin. Had June Mai Angel hit the *Moby Dick*?

"Prepare for incoming!" Pilate yelled over the dogs. "Get out every gun we have!"

I didn't have a gun, only my combs, brushes, and hoof picks. Before I could ask anyone what I should do, a little Jimmy airship dropped from the gray sky. The zeppelin was half on fire, the flames melting the Neofiber as it fell in slow motion to hit the ground in a rain of dirt, bashing through sagebrush and scattering burning plastic. The air washed over me in a wave of hellish heat.

My horses screamed and before I could do anything, they tore out of my temporary corral to streak away across the plains.

Thank God, it wasn't the *Moby Dick*. Definitely a Jimmy-class dirigible, not a Jonesy.

Something whistled past my ear. A bullet. I couldn't hear the gunfire 'cause of the crash's fire not fifty meters away.

Another bullet whizzed by me. I watched as something emerged out of the fiery light spilling across the prairie. A boy. My age. Tall and lean. Running.

"Cavvy! Get over here!"

I heard the words, but I couldn't take my eyes off the boy speeding toward me, his face smudged, his shirt flapping behind him, his boots kicking up dust. He was being chased but who was after him? Prolly whoever had shot his Jimmy out of the air. Prolly June Mai Angel.

"For the love of God, Cavvy, get over here!" Sharlotte yelled.

And I should've listened, I really should've, but I couldn't. That boy needed my help.

Instead of freezing up scared, instead of turning and retreating, which I should've done, I gathered up the skirt of my New Morality dress and launched myself after the boy to save him. That was what went through my mind—*Gotta save that boy from those outlaws. They'll sell him for sure.*

I dashed up, grabbed his hand, and pulled him over to a derelict minivan. I hauled open the back door and we both leapt inside onto the rotted flooring, brittle plastic, and rusted metal. He reached back and slammed the door shut, then fell right on top of me.

Bullets peppered the sides of the minivan. *Ping, ping, pang, pang, pang.* Above us, a hole punched open showing flickering firelight. My mouth ached with a taste I always got when being shot at. Which was far too often for a nice girl like me.

I looked up. My eyes stretched wide. He wasn't just a boy—he was a beautiful boy. Brownish-blonde hair, fashionably long, fell to his eyes, blue eyes, above nice, kissable lips. He lay right on top of me. Right between my legs. All that New Morality stuff went right out the window.

It was like an archangel was ravishing me. His breath puffed out hard. I was clutching him, my head against his chest, hearing his heart beat, smelling him, so powerful, but so good. I should've been all embarrassed and shy for being so close to a boy, but all I could think of was I didn't want to die without kissing him. Strange for me to think that—strange and completely sinful.

The shooting stopped for a minute. Then yelling, more gunshots, and explosions so big they lit up the inside of the minivan. The boy lifted his head.

"What do you see?" I asked.

He glanced down at me. Oh, he was handsome. But more than that, he smiled at me kindly, shyly, and there was some kind of twinkle in his eyes, some kind of bright intelligence. "Sorry to be, um, on you. I'm Muh … Muh … Micaiah."

Stutterer. That was all right. He wouldn't have to talk to kiss me.

"I'm Cavatica. Where'd you come from?"

"A zeppelin, they shot us down. Well, tried to hook us first, but then …" His voice faded. His eyes had locked onto something, intensely.

Horse hooves thundered on the ground.

Then a gunshot. The horse screamed, then galloped away. Not one of mine, I could tell.

Pilate's voice rang out in the distance, "I can guarantee you won't reach them. I'd recommend finding easier prey."

Right next to us, a response. "Omega nine. Execute."

Sino talk. Just like in the *Moby Dick*. These were June Mai Angel's girls. I shivered, thinking about how brutal they had been on the *Moby Dick* and those hellish words—*you let us in, or we'll eat you, feet first, so you can watch us do it.*

I hooked a hand around his head and pushed him down. My lips pressed against his ear. "Did you see ninja-type women out there?"

"Yeah." His breath tickled my skin. I could feel every square centimeter of him, every bit, every part.

I couldn't breathe. It took everything in me to gather enough wind to whisper. "What else did you see?"

"I think your people are in the gas station. The outlaws have us all surrounded. They want me. I'm sure of it. They know I'm a boy."

And of course, the next question *are you viable?* That was just what you asked. *Oh, you're a boy. Oh, are you viable?* Not that I cared, but if he was, the outlaws could sell him for bank.

Still didn't know how he had survived the crash, but my logic wasn't working so well at that point. I just wanted to rub up against him and kiss him long, wet, and hard. I was out of my mind. Jesus, forgive me.

"Kiss me." I didn't say it.

Only I did say it.

Only I never should've said it.

Only I did.

He raised his head, looking at me like I was crazy, and I was, but I wasn't, but I was.

His hair melted into my fingers even as his sweat dripped on me. "If we're gonna die, I gotta kiss you first." I pulled his lips to mine and I ate him up, rubbing against him, and him rubbing against me, and we were trying to moan through our kissing and trying to breathe through our moaning, and it was the end of the world, and it was heaven on earth, and it was all so right and all so wrong.

The doors were yanked open to reveal Wren, her Colt Terminators unholstered, her face bloody in the crash's firelight.

An outlaw lay on the ground next to her, shot through the head. Out of heaven—thrust into hell.

Wren spun and fired, yelled, "Run. For the gas station. Go!"

Didn't have to tell me twice. Hand in hand, Micaiah and I sprinted the twenty-five meters into the gas station. Half of it was full of disintegrating cardboard boxes. Sharlotte, Pilate, and Petal were inside, but Wren had stayed by the minivan. Didn't know where everyone else was.

Petal knelt by a front window, the glass long since busted out. Her long rifle rested on the built-in Neofiber bipod, which she balanced on the sill. The weapon was a Mauser Trip 6 Redux, best sniper rifle in the world. The polymer stock looked skeletal, full of holes to make it lightweight. The fluted muzzle break was as long as my forearm. A ten-round magazine hung down, loaded with .338 Ostrobothnia magnums. Moving at twelve hundred meters per second, that bullet could go through six layers of Kevlar at a thousand meters. Petal gazed through her rifle's Zeiss Real 18 scope.

Pilate had told us stories about Petal using bullets to drive nails with Mickey Mauser. That was the name of her rifle.

Pilate stood next to Petal with his Sino binocs covering his face. Petal murmured a rhyme, distracted with aiming.

Hickory Dickory dead,
the kids have holes in their head.
The clock struck one,
and they kissed a nun,
hickory dickory done.

She abruptly stopped talking, let out a long breath, and pulled the trigger. Dust shook down from the ceiling to swirl in the air. The noise in that little gas station slapped me, like stickpins shoved in my eardrums.

Sharlotte threw the boy and me behind her. "Get out of the way."

I could barely understand her words through the ringing. Sharlotte tromped through cardboard boxes to get to a window,

Mama's Tina Machinegun in her hands.

Pilate directed her. "Don't fire, Shar, unless they're right on top of us. Let Petal get them." He adjusted his binocs. "Eleven o'clock, baby."

Petal rhymed in a scratch of a voice.

Mary had a little lamb,
she also had a gun.
She killed the moon,
she killed the stars,
she even killed the sun.

Long breath out, she fired.

"Three o'clock," Pilate said.

A brief adjustment. Another rhyme.

Pussy cat, pussy cat,
where have you been?
I've been to London
to shoot the queen.

More thunder.

Micaiah had his hands over his ears, but he was looking at me with those clever blue eyes. And suddenly, I realized what I'd done. I'd seduced a boy I didn't know and got all sexy with him. I wanted to feel bad, but my body tingled, thinking about it. His eyes on me didn't help that any.

Petal's abrasive whisper finished the rhyme.

Pussycat, pussycat,
what did you there?
I pushed a pretty princess
right down the stairs.

She worked the action on her Mauser. Her next words came out lifeless. "She's dead, Pilate. I killed her. I've killed a lot of them today."

"Jesus will forgive you," Pilate said.

Wren climbed on top of the minivan, stood right out in the open. Her long dark hair fell across her wool poncho. "Come on, you dirty skanks. I'm all re-loaded and ready to dance. Come on out."

"Ten and two," Pilate called out.
Petal aimed, shot, aimed, shot.

Little girl green,
come blow your mean,
Charlie's in the grass,
and the girl's got no ass.

Gunfire behind us, a howl of grief, our dogs barked in a fury. My heart died in my chest. Those were our people. Those were their screams. A door smashed open in the back of the gas station. Light spilled into the darkness of the dying day. Soldier girls, heads silhouetted, charged in. A lot of them.

Pilate spun. He jerked his sawed-off Beijing Homewrecker out of its holster in a blur. Yelling "Matthew!" he lobbed a 20mm grenade into the middle of them. The gas station filled with fire, dust and death. Tina Machinegun's rattle followed.

I nearly tumbled to my knees, I was coughing so hard. Somehow I kept on my feet.

Pilate had yelled Matthew. Why?

"Out, now!" he shouted. "Sharlotte, that means you, too!"

I went to run, do as he said, but then I realized Micaiah knelt on the floor, his eyes white with wild fear, his hands over his ears.

Again, I had to save him. I grabbed him by his hair, like Wren had grabbed me during the gunfight at the Academy. He came, of course he did, but slapped my hand away once we came bursting out of the gas station with Sharlotte and Petal behind us.

"Mark!" Pilate hollered another boy's name from inside the gas station.

And another Homewrecker blast thundered from Pilate's Mossberg quad cannon. He'd be killed by his own shrapnel. Then what would we do?

Sharlotte, Micaiah, Petal, and me, we all staggered back to the minivan. Wren stood on top, a target no one could touch.

We heard, "Luke!" Another grenade exploded inside the gas station. A wall collapsed, sending a cloud of dust across the broken asphalt and weeds.

An outlaw scampered out of the hole left behind. Wren gunned her down, reaching and firing one Colt Terminator, then the other.

From roiling smoke, Pilate strode, smirking face and long hair gray with dust. Several loops of the bandolier slung over his shoulder were now empty. He stopped and yelled at an outlaw on the other side of the gas station. "Run away, soldier girl. I have John left. I always liked John. 'For God so loved the world, that He gave His only begotten Son, that whosoever believeth in Him should not perish, but have everlasting life.' You believeth, soldier girl? If you run, you just might make it."

Spurred on by his words, that last outlaw sprinted through the shadowy twilight.

"Take her down, Petal," Pilate said in an easy voice.

Petal's rifle was too big for her to fire free hand, but in a second she was balancing that beast on its shooting sticks.

Soldier girl, Soldier girl,
where have you been?
I've been to purgatory
counting out sheep.

The gun boomed, the muzzle flashed, and the fleeing outlaw tumbled down into the sagebrush.

But she was still alive. In the waning flicker of the crash, I watched her try to crawl away. I felt sick. Such violence. Such horror.

A hush fell. A little wind. The crackle of fire. And then Petal's whisper.

Soldier girl, Soldier girl,
what did you there?
I killed the lamb of God
under Satan's chair.

A final shot and the outlaw lay still.

Pilate came over to me. "You okay?"

Sick stuck in back of my throat. "You tricked that woman, Pilate, tricked her into running by quoting scripture. How could you do such a thing? How can you be so hard?"

He met my eyes. "You want to know what's hard? Hard is watching your friends die because you showed some soulless outlaw mercy. You kill everyone who comes after you, everyone, or more will come. Psalm 18, verse 37, 'I have pursued mine enemies, and overtaken them. Neither did I turn again till they were consumed.' And we still don't know if we devoured them all or not. If one slipped by us to get reinforcements, we'll have plenty to eat."

He turned around and marched back to the convenience store.

Well, let him quote scripture. He wasn't a priest. Pilate was a trickster killer, a womanizer, and a dog.

Still, he had saved us. Without his Beijing Homewrecker, those outlaws would've finished us off in the gas station. I winced my eyes shut. This was why I hadn't wanted to come home. Back in Cleveland, no war, no moral dilemmas, just my slate, Anju, and the only violence we saw was on episodes of *Lonely Moon*.

Wren, still on the minivan, scanned the horizon with her spotting scope. Pilate climbed up on what was left of the store, and did the same with his Sino binocs.

I chanced a look at Micaiah. "Sorry for grabbing you by your hair."

He shrugged. "Sorry I froze. You saved me. Twice now. I won't forget it."

I got embarrassed and looked away.

Pilate finally called out, "Looks like we made it. Nothing's moving, but we'll secure the perimeter."

Sharlotte let out a long breath. "How am I gonna gather up our headcount and secure a perimeter?"

"And what about our people?" I asked. No one had talked about the scream. Our dogs whined, an awful, heart-broke sound.

Sharlotte must've heard it, but she showed no emotion. Instead, she looked wearily at the boy. "What's your name?"

"Micaiah." No stuttering this time.

Sharlotte looked at him with a peculiar mixture of exhaustion and vexation. Then she said, "Limon is eighty kilometers that way. I'd get walkin'. There's water there. And your way out of the Juniper."

He didn't protest. Just nodded. I wanted to protest. Didn't get the chance.

Aunt Bea stumbled out from behind the gas station. Even at a distance, with only the leftovers of twilight in the sky, I saw the tears trickling down her face.

"Sharlotte, come quick. You have to see." And then that big Mexican woman broke down completely. "Oh, Sharlotte, we lost somebody. We did, we did, we did."

Arctic wind swept down and froze the tears in my eyes. It was our first casualty, but not our last. Certainly not our last.

CHAPTER TWELVE

I know that Sally Browne Burke thinks romance is God's divine plan to save our species, but I don't believe in love. I believe in neurochemistry. I did meet Miss Burke. We're almost the same age, but still, she kissed my cheek like I was her granddaughter. Personally, I like her.

—Maggie Jankowski
informal comments
February 14, 2058

(i)

We all stood around the body. Annabeth Burton lay on the ground, shot through the chest. Her mother's curse was final—with Annabeth gone, the Widow Burton had outlived every single one of her children.

Breeze held Annabeth's head on her lap. Keys held one hand, and Bella, Annabeth's favorite dog, nuzzled the cold skin of the other. Jacob and Edward circled them all, whining something awful.

I recalled how pretty Annabeth had played the piano at Mama's funeral party, how her smile had cracked open wide from her love of music. Up in heaven, I could see Annabeth and Mama singing some old-timey songs together, or maybe LeAnna Wright or Iris Heller. But on this earth, their voices had been silenced forevermore.

Pilate hustled over. "Wren's going out to look for other survivors from the crash and to make sure more outlaws aren't on their way. I'd love to get my hands on the anti-aircraft artillery they used to blow up that Jimmy, and I bet they also had a Cargador." He turned on Micaiah. "What did you see up there before the crash? Were you hit by grappling hooks?"

My breath caught, recalling the *chunk, chunk, chunk* of the *Moby Dick* getting snagged.

"I didn't see a thing," Micaiah said, "I think they were trying to force us down with rockets so they could hook us, but they accidentally hit our zeppelin. That's what the captain said, but she's dead now."

Pilate didn't respond to that. He just went on. "We have to get out of here. Put Annabeth in the chuck wagon. We can bury her once we get away from June Mai Angel and her cutthroats. We confirmed that's who attacked us. We found IDs on the bodies. IDs for a band of marauding criminals. Never thought an Outlaw Warlord would be so organized." His voice dropped as his thoughts took away his talk.

Sharlotte didn't move. The moonlight couldn't get to her face under her hat, but I could guess what she was thinking—how do you sneak away in the night with three-thousand cattle spread about from hell to breakfast?

Sharlotte didn't complain or cry, but started serving out orders. "Breeze, Keys, put Annabeth in the chuck wagon's trailer like Pilate said. Then go out and find the rest of our people, the hires and Crete. I told them to take off once the shooting started. If I only would've had you all go ..." She had to swallow hard. But of course, she kept her voice even. "Go and find them, and please, Lord Jesus, let them be safe. Aunt Bea and I will start packing it up. Gonna have to move our headcount in the dark. Three quarter moon is helpful, but I'd have preferred a full one. Cavvy, try and get our remuda back together. With the fighting over, the horses'll come looking for you. Lucky for us, those ponies love you."

For a minute no one moved. Annabeth was dead. Moving cattle at night was slow, impossible work. In the darkness, we might lose as many as fifty cows to coyotes, prairie dog holes, and general stubbornness. That'd be 1.6% of our total headcount. Rounding up, two percent less money.

I figured we'd only do it that one night, but still, it would hurt our total profits.

Sharlotte continued to throw orders like Mama would've done. "Get Charles Goodnight moving out front. Get his bell ringing. The herd'll follow. Go slow. Be careful."

Our hands got to work. I expected Sharlotte to leave with them, but she didn't. She raised her head to address the boy, but her face was still lost in the night. "So, Micaiah, you're gonna get on out of here, right?"

"If that's what you want." Micaiah shuffled his trendy faux-alligator skin cowboy boots in the white dirt. Those boots were meant for nightclubs and big cities, like the rest of his clothes—French fashion jeans and a nice, blue silk shirt. Knew it was silk. I'd nearly torn it off him. Got all hot again, thinking about how his shirt and skin felt. I prayed to Jesus for a minute, for strength and forgiveness.

"It's what I want," Sharlotte said, "and I'm in charge of this operation."

"I know," the boy said. "I could tell that right away. You're a natural leader."

Sharlotte fell silent. Quite the compliment.

"Shar, we can't send him away," I said. "He'll die of cold."

"You got a coat?" Sharlotte asked him.

"I did." He pointed in the general direction of the Jimmy crash.

"Please, Sharlotte," I pleaded.

My sister ignored me and addressed the boy. "I'll get you a blanket and a canteen, and you can get on out of here." She stomped away, which left us standing there alone. Just the two of us.

Yikes.

I couldn't talk to him, just couldn't. I'd kissed him and done more. Nope. Better to get back to work. While waiting for my horses to return, I could pack up my aluminum pole corral.

I followed the paths of white dirt between clumps of dark sagebrush. To my surprise, Micaiah trailed me.

I found my rope and started coiling it up. He stood watching until a question bubbled up out of me. "So, Micaiah, is that a Bible name?"

"I guess," he said. "What kind of a name is Cavatica?"

"It's from my mama's favorite book, *Charlotte's Web*, only she just passed, so it's hard to talk about and I'd rather not." I shouldn't have started the conversation in the first place.

I jiggled the poles to loosen the dirt. The boy helped, and we piled the poles by the rope. My parka warmed me despite the chill. He stood there shivering. I knew a way to heat him up.

Ugh. I shook my head at myself. I never knew the depth of my desire, and I couldn't keep the lustful thoughts out of my mind. My only recourse was prayer, but that felt like trying to stop a prairie fire with a bottle of Coke.

Eons of awkward silence later, Sharlotte came back and threw Micaiah a wool blanket, army green and itchy, but warm. "Couldn't find a canteen. Good luck." She pointed east. "Like I said, Limon is that way. You'll find water there, and your way out of the Juniper."

"I can't go back that way," he said in a low voice.

That surprised me. I figured he was on his way out of the Juniper, but then I thought about it—his Jimmy had been going west, toward the mountains, which didn't make sense. Everyone knew you couldn't fly through central Colorado, not with June Mai Angel and her Cargadors.

Sharlotte didn't seem to care about the mystery. And all his good looks seemed completely lost on her. "Not our problem sorry to say. Goodbye."

He didn't move. "Maybe if I stayed with you, I could make it worth your while. I have some money—"

Sharlotte cut him off. "We don't need your money. We have enough worries. We can't take you on."

Once more, I had to save him. He'd die on the plains if we cut him loose. And I needed his touch in some hungry way I couldn't explain. "Sharlotte, we can't send him away. It's not Christian. He's not prepared to travel."

"It's either him or us," Sharlotte said in a bleak voice. "Traveling with boys is too dangerous, especially if June Mai Angel is looking for him."

"That's nonsense," I said. "We have Pilate. He's a boy and he's along for the ride. We knew we'd run into Outlaw Warlords. Especially June Mai. She's been stealing zeppelins out of the sky, so she has air reconnaissance. Only a matter of time before she sees us. And you know she's heard about our grand cattle drive as well. Thank you, Juniper gossip."

The boy cocked his head to listen to me, but it seemed his eyes were on Sharlotte, gauging her reaction. She was in charge, after all.

"We can't help him," Sharlotte replied. "Yeah, it's wrong, but once again, we don't have a choice."

Wren galloped up on Mick, a sorrel gelding. Mick was a calm pony, but none too bright.

"Y'all talkin' about the boy?" Wren asked, holding up a sapropel lamp to see us better. She swung off the saddle, and set the lamp down in the middle between her, Sharlotte, Micaiah, and me.

"What are you doing with the light on?" Sharlotte demanded.

"Please," Wren said, "we have three-thousand cattle. We're not exactly inconspicuous. And if them outlaws do come? Good. More for me to kill. We searched the wreck and the boy was the only survivor. Pilate found their Cargador and their horses. He and Petal are going to drive it out a-ways, confuse them when more come lookin'. Don't worry, I told him to scavenge the fuel and weaponry for us." She held up an MG21. "Get more like this one. He'll load up a couple horses, but not all. With that big truck and all the horses, it will make a better false path for June Mai to follow."

"Not if they have zeppelins," I said.

"Better than us stealing it all and leading them right to us."

I felt my jaw go tight. How on earth could we sneak away without June Mai finding us?

The light was definitely a bad idea. However, now I could see Micaiah's face. He was looking hard at all three of us. We were about to decide his fate, and he was smart enough to keep quiet.

Sharlotte stood in her duster and hat, tall, like the statue of Justice at the Cleveland courthouse. "He can't come with us."

"The hell he can't," Wren said. "Now that June Mai Angel might know we're out here, we best turn the hell around and head back to Burlington. Rest up the headcount, then take 'em to Hays. Sell the cattle, sell the boy, divide up the money. That's the only plan that makes any sense."

My mouth dropped open. Dang. I thought it was awkward before. The lamp seemed to hiss louder. Micaiah shifted a little under his blanket.

"You're serious." Sharlotte's eyes were hidden by the brim of her hat.

Wren nodded violently. "Yeah, I am. This cattle drive is to save the ranch, right? A viable boy is goin' for hundreds of thousands of dollars. I bet we could get a million for this particular johnson. They milk 'em and sell it on Craigslist. Tibbs Hoyt and his ARK sure hate it, but they can't stop it. So, if we can get the johnson out of the Juniper, we could find a buyer for him. We all win. We pay back Howerter, you save the ranch, I get to go back to Amarillo, and Cavvy can go back to school. The end."

"What happened to you, Wren?" Sharlotte asked. "We all came from the same mama, but it's like you're devil spawn or somethin'." Her hand went into her pocket. She had something there, but I didn't know what it was. At the time, I thought it might be a pistol. It wasn't. A gun would've caused far less trouble.

"Come off it, Shar," Wren spat. "I heard you and Cavvy. You were gonna send him away to die. At least with my plan, he'll live."

"Sending him off is one thing, selling him is another." Sharlotte's hands were out of her pockets and curled into fists.

And still it wouldn't be enough. We needed more than a million dollars. A lot more.

"Seems my way is kinder," Wren shot back. "Someone is gonna make a fortune off him, and I say it should be us. Besides, June Mai Angel knows we're out here now. This cattle drive is over."

"No, it's not," Sharlotte growled and took a step toward Wren. "We knew we'd have to fight through June Mai Angel, or somehow pay her off. Either way, we wait and see if she comes at us. In the meantime, we'll just have to move quick. Push our headcount fifty kilometers a day. Yeah, some'll die. But we can make it. Having a boy makes our situation worse, can't you see that? June Mai makes her money by peddling drugs and boys, and if she sniffs out we have not one, but two viable males, she'll come at us hard."

My two sisters, once again, about to go to blows. And me, standing there watching. It was re-run video of my childhood.

In the sizzling quiet, Micaiah asked a question. "How do you know I'm viable?"

Wren chuckled. "Ain't you?"

He swallowed hard. "Yeah."

A sneer spread slowly across Wren's face. "Good-lookin' guy like you, figures you'd be viable. And who are you anyway? That was a nice Jimmy and you got nice clothes. Born rich, viable, and alive after that wreck? Well don't Jesus just love you?"

"I'm Micaiah Carlson. From St. Louis. My mom works in biomedical technologies. She's in Vegas, and she can—"

"Who cares, Johnson. You're just money to me." Wren cut him off, then winked at me, proving she had caught us sweaty and kissing. The teasing was going to be brutal.

Ashamed and angry, I still weighed in. "He's a human being, Wren. We need to take care of him. If we send him alone to walk back to the World, he won't make it a day. And we can't sell him. That's just plain evil. And we all know Mama wouldn't turn around at the first sign of trouble. So, it's settled. He comes with us."

Both of my sisters finally proved they were sisters and said the same thing, at the same time, in the same way. "Ain't no way that's gonna happen."

Dang me, but if Wren didn't smile. "Jinx. You owe me a Coke, Shar."

Sharlotte didn't crack a grin. "We're going west, and he's going east. Period."

"But he said he can't go back that way," I said.

All our eyes fell on the boy. He nodded. "Yeah, I'm going west, to Las Vegas, to see my mom."

Those words didn't make a lick a sense. There were a million better ways to get to Vegas than crossing the Juniper.

Wren also had trouble with his story. "Come again?"

"I need to get across the Juniper," he said, "to get to my mom. People are looking for me. My aunts ... they're ..." He dropped his head.

We waited for him to finish. My heart hurt for him, the way he held himself, so dejected. He never mentioned his father, but then again, most likely his daddy had come out of a vial from some ARK clinic.

"My aunts are rich," he said slowly, "they're powerful, and they're looking for me."

Wren's eyes blazed with greed. "Why's that?"

"That's my business," Micaiah whispered. He turned to Sharlotte. "Please. Help me. I just want to see my mom again. One more time before they find me."

The way he talked, it sounded like his aunts were bent on killing him. It seemed we held his life in our hands.

Sharlotte lifted her head so the light gleamed on her face. Her dark-lashed eyes rested softly on the boy for a moment—maybe something about the way he talked about his mother touched her. But the emotions were eclipsed by Sharlotte's business sense. "You can walk with us tonight. Tomorrow, we'll give you some supplies, maybe one of the horses we took from June Mai Angel, but then you're on your own. I'm sorry. Traveling with a boy in tow is just too dangerous out here."

"Okay," he murmured. "Thank you."

"Don't thank me for sending you off to die," Sharlotte said. She stared Wren and me down, making sure we understood her decision was final. Then she strutted off, not sexy like Wren, but queenly, like Mama used to walk.

Wren picked up her lantern, stepped in the stirrup and hoisted herself onto the saddle. "Well, Johnson," she said with a mean laugh. "How's it feel to be unlucky for once, you lucky bastard?"

She didn't wait for an answer, but took off trotting on Mick with the MG21 across her shoulder. Looking for a fight.

"I'm pretty much jacked," Micaiah muttered.

Once again, he and I were alone in the dark.

He had cursed, said the word "jacked" right in front of me, which wasn't very gentlemanly. I tried to ignore the fact by trying to piece together his story. "If you really need to get across the Juniper, then you prolly should come with us. But why didn't you just fly to Vegas? Not over the Juniper, but around it, or suborbital?"

"My aunts have spies everywhere outside of the Juniper," he said. "With the identity laws, people are easy to find."

I remembered the eye-scanners back at the Cleveland bus station.

Micaiah took a step closer. "Thank you for trying to save me a third time." His voice came out so warm and smiley, I forgot about my questions.

"Yeah, well," I said, getting uncomfortable. He was near enough I could feel his heat. Then I realized what he was trying to do. He was trying to seduce me.

Well, I'd show him. "Okay, Micaiah, let's get one thing straight. I want you to know, right now, what kind of girl I am."

"You want to talk about the kiss?"

"Yeah, that's right." I scowled. How had he known what I was thinking?

"Okay, what about the kiss?" he asked.

Suddenly I didn't have a single word in my head that made any sense.

(ii)

Standing there in the dark, I couldn't forget the cute blue of his clever eyes, or how he tasted on my lips. Help me, Lord.

Okay, I'd start with the Lord. "Listen up. I was raised with good Christian ethics, and I am a firm supporter of Sally Browne Burke and the New Morality. I truly believe that the future of all humanity rests on the virtue and intelligence of women everywhere, starting with me."

Once I got going, it felt like I was preaching from a pulpit, not standing among sagebrush under a cold, starry sky, so I really poured on the rhetoric. "As a guardian of our species, my conduct must be beyond reproach. What happened in the minivan was a mistake brought on by fear and extreme circumstances. I am now in firm control of my passions, and there won't be a repeat of the said incident." I had to inhale real deep after my speech.

I couldn't see his face. Dang Juniper and no light. But I could see him nod. "So, you're a firm member of the New Morality movement?"

"Very firm."

"Very firm," he echoed.

"We've established that." I said. I wasn't sure if he was making fun of me, and I was in too deep to retreat. "I'm sure you noticed my dress."

"Yes, very gray, very New Morality. However, Miss Burke does say that when two people have a deep attraction for each other, that such a union is blessed by God, and that love, in the end, will give us the next generation just like it has done for millennia." Now that he was making a speech of his own, his voice was Yankee crisp, accent neutral, as bright and shiny as a new silver dollar.

But I could tell he was trying to argue me into a corner. "Yeah, she did say all those things. And normally, well, I guess, you and me ..." My words failed me. Every syllable died right there.

That boy took up where I left off, not joking any more. "Cavatica, I'm in trouble. Real trouble. If your sisters get their way, I'll either be dead in a week or sold into slavery. I need your help. What we had, well, it was powerful, unexpected, incredible, but I understand what you're getting at. However good it was, we can't be together under these circumstances."

Now I wanted to protest, 'cause, dang it, I wanted to kiss him again. "I'll convince my sisters. You're with us 'til the end. In Wendover, you'll be able to catch a bus easy to Vegas, or a plane. And maybe you and I ..."

More dead syllables, scattered all around.

Maybe you and I could go to Vegas together. Didn't say it, only thought it—fell into a little fantasy, right there. He and I in a hotel suite, him respecting my decision to be chaste, and me wanting him more than I should. Sparkling cider in crystal glasses and a big tub full of bubble bath. No, had to stop myself.

"I understand." He put out a hand.

I shook it, still Yankee soft. Which gave me an idea. "You know, if they see you can do stuff, it'll go a long ways in convincing them to let you stay. Sharlotte loves free labor. You know anything about cows?"

"Nothing. I'm actually a raw food vegan."

I sighed. "Don't tell anyone that. Just follow me and act like you know more than you do."

"I'll try," he said.

Walking next to him felt like floating. Maybe he was telling the truth about his vicious aunts and a mama in Vegas. I prayed to God he was.

(iii)

First thing we did was take my temporary corral and head over to the steam truck and our supply trailer. We had an old Chevy

Workhorse II, fitted with an ASI attachment in the bed. With all the vehicles left behind in the Juniper, American Steam Ingenuity, or ASI came up with attachments you could link into the drive train of large rigs, like trucks and vans.

Mama had found the Chevy abandoned in a ditch west of our ranch and used horses to tow it back to our barn. We cut a hole in the bed and hooked up the ASI attachment. Ran piping for the pressure gauges under the body and up through the floor of the cab. Modified the brakes. Modified the pedals.

Mama and I worked on it together, well, with a lot of help from Paula Borland, a mechanic in town. I can still remember how I loved to read the ASI 5.3 Ultra install manual like some people remember their first Harry Potter book.

Over the last two weeks, every time I fiddled with the ASI on the Chevy, I'd get choked up, thinking about Mama and me, working long days together to figure everything out.

The ASI's steam engine ran on what had fueled fires for millennia on the Great Plains—poop. In our case, cow patties, but we'd add wood when we found it, and we had a small supply of Old Growth coal. We could make asphalt coal if we found any left.

Mama and I had removed the engine block, sold it for scrap, and then used the space to carry fuel. We also welded a big rack on top of the rig to use as storage and to dry manure. Lots of room in, on, and around that rig. The Chevy Workhorse II was the largest non-commercial truck any American company had ever built.

Micaiah and I dropped my temporary corral parts into the supply trailer. Aunt Bea had paused from working to lay her hand on Annabeth's body, wrapped in an old horse blanket.

She glanced up, then hugged me. "We'll get through this, *mija*. We will."

I swallowed my tears. "Yeah, we will."

Aunt Bea pulled away, then seemed to notice Micaiah for the first time. "Pleased to meet you, Micaiah. I hear you're going to be with us tonight."

The boy dropped his head. "Looks like it."

"Well, we'll see if we survive it," Aunt Bea said. "Cavvy, can you check and make sure the Chevy's engine is ready?"

"On my way, Bea." I walked over and stepped up onto the bed of the Chevy.

Again, Micaiah was full of surprises. He climbed up next to me. "That's an ASI 5.3. Ancient. It still works?"

"How did you know it was a five?"

He gestured at the piping. "The angle. The 7.1s are so much more efficient. The fives were so buggy."

"Not as awful as the three series," I said. "How come you know so much about ASI engines? I mean, you're a Yankee boy, and I'd figured you'd have pictures of frictionless cars on the walls of your bedroom."

"The ASI technology is fascinating. You have engines from the very start of the industrial revolution, re-vamped, re-engineered to be as efficient as possible. That they can run on cattle dung is amazing. I'm surprised you have such a crappyjack version."

"Watch your language," I said, feeling defensive. "We had to make do with what we had. And this old truck has taken us back and forth to Hays for years and years. Some of us ain't rich."

"You're not just a little family ranch," he replied. "Maybe you're not rich, but I would imagine you're doing okay."

"You don't know a thing, Mr. Fancy Pants." He had some gall, assuming we were wealthy when we were suffering from such money problems. For a minute, I was too mad to talk, so I focused on work. I filled the water tubes from a twenty-liter bucket and added some kindling to the firebox, still warm from burning all day. Micaiah crept in closer and put out his hands, to thaw them out. One thing about steam engines, they kept you warm.

I slid off the bed of the truck just as Crete came over. "Hey, Cavvy, we found some ponies looking for you." She had Puff Daddy, Katy, Taylor Quick, Delia, and some others. Crete's eyes had found Micaiah, and even in the moonlight she appreciated his handsome. "Why, Cavvy, introduce me to our guest." She didn't wait, though. She got down off her horse and curtsied. "I'm Lucretia Macaby, but my friends call me Crete. You can call me Crete."

He bounced off the truck and bowed. "I'm Micaiah Carlsbad."

I didn't like how quick he had moved, or how he smiled at Crete. Something bothered me more though. He got his name wrong. Micaiah Carlson, that was what he had said before. Then I remembered how he had stuttered in the minivan. After his iffy story about wicked aunts, the name mix-up deepened my doubts. Who was he really? Why were his aunts chasing him? He didn't have anything other than the clothes on his back.

While I sifted through my doubts, Crete continued to flirt. "Why, Micaiah, it's awful that your zeppelin got shot down. I can't believe you could survive something like that. How did you—"

"Yeah, Crete, awful," I said to stop her pathetic flirting. "But I'm sure you have things to do."

She frowned at me. Let her.

I was mad at the boy, suspicious as well, so I gave him the reins to Puff Daddy while I took the rest of the horses. Puff Daddy was a chestnut stallion with more attitude than wit, though he had plenty of that as well.

"Okay, Mr. Carlsbad," I said, "let's get to work."

"Nice meeting you, Crete," Micaiah said over his shoulder.

Puff Daddy knew he was dealing with a Yankee and wasn't acting very polite. It was fun watching the rich boy struggle for a moment, until I stepped in to give Micaiah a little ranching advice. "You might know about steam engines, but you have a lot to learn about horses. You gotta be firm, gentle, but firm, like you're so in charge of 'em you can be nice. Got it?"

"Yes, firm. Very firm," he said. "Like your firm convictions."

Now I knew he was making fun of me, and I swore I'd never say the word "firm" around him again. "Come on, Johnson."

We guided the horses over to a copse of cottonwoods. I loved the winter smell of their bark and the gentle sway of their limbs, heavy with buds. I tied the horses to the trees while we assembled the rest of the horses of my remuda.

Our people would come by to drop off horses and say how heartsick they were over Annabeth. No one batted an eye at him. It seemed only Crete and I were affected.

Our hires came in, one after another, chatty with nervousness. First came Kasey Romero, leading Elvis, a paint who was mostly white, but with a brown face. Kasey shook her head. "Folks say those June Mai outlaws are mutants from the Knockout. That they ain't human. I don't know about all that, but I sure don't wanna run into a whole army of 'em."

I figured Kasey was *gillian*, though it was wrong to stereotype her, and I had zero gaydar. Her hair was shaved short, but even if it were girly 'strogen long, her dirty brown Cartwright overalls would've made her look *gillian*. Kasey was an old hand, who had worked years and years for Dob Howerter in Lamar. I didn't know why she was with us, or why Sharlotte would've hired her. My big sister was full-on New Morality, when it came to their stance on homosexuality. Me? I wanted to be, but I just didn't know. The ARK had done some research on the genetic component of homosexuality. Their findings weren't rock-solid, but they made me wonder, and I couldn't be intolerant of someone 'cause of their biology. That simply wasn't fair. But was it biological? The New Morality's Kip Parson certainly didn't think so.

Next came Allie Chambers, holding the reins to Christina Pink, Mary B, and Beck. Allie spoke in a hushed voice. "Until tonight, I've never heard of anyone seeing one of June Mai's girls dead. I thought they'd be Chinese. But only one was. Whites and blacks, the others."

Allie Chambers had also worked down with Howerter in Lamar. She had left 'cause of problems, though I wasn't sure what they were. Allie had fire-red Irish hair, and after being sunburned so much, she was freckled completely brown and pink. She had a singing voice that broke your heart. Any song. Every time.

Kasey and Allie were new to me, but not Dolly Day Cornpone. She was legendary.

Living Juniper rough had aged Dolly Day—in her forties, she had an eighty-year-old woman's face, blasted by sun, burned by wind, froze by snow, as lined and lumpy as pemmican. While her whiskey lasted, she'd take sips out of a little metal flask, which was prolly the most expensive thing she owned. Though she had done cattle drives for decades, she never stuck with the same outfit. I figured she'd drove headcount with every operation in the Colorado territory.

"I can work a rifle if I have to," Dolly Day said in a rush. "When I was with Howerter, we got jumped by Mama Cass' rustlers. We drove 'em back. I ain't scared of no woman on this earth, not white, brown, black, or Chinese, but I'll tell you what—them Wind River savages in Wyoming ain't human. I believe they're devil spawn, all of them."

"You can't say that, Dolly," I said. "That's racist. The Wind River people are people like us."

"Ah, you're young and liberal, but I could tell you stories, Cavatica Weller, that would curl your hair. Believe you me, if we run into them savages, we'll all die, scalped, with our livers eaten out while we watch." She left, guzzling water from her three-liter Ultra Gulp, another prize possession she had found in some derelict Gas N Sip on her travels.

I glanced at Micaiah, to gauge what he thought of our hired hands.

"Colorful women," he said with a smile. Coaxed a smile out of me as well.

Before long, we found all of our horses and gathered up as much of our headcount as we could. With our chuck wagon chugging out front, we got Charles Goodnight moving to follow it. He wasn't happy, but he was smart enough to know we meant business. We attached a sapropel lantern to the back of the trailer, so our tired, frightened herd could follow the light along with Charles Goodnight's bell.

Fear dogged our every step. What if June Mai Angel saw us moving down the highway? She'd send in her outlaws, steal the boy, and kill us all.

At least I would die having kissed Micaiah. Problem was, not kissing him again might kill me as well.

CHAPTER THIRTEEN

It is the responsibility of everyone in this room to have themselves, their sons, husbands, brothers, and friends tested for viability. And continue to have them tested. And continue to encourage everyone to donate to the ARK. If we do not catalog and preserve Male Product, we are welcoming the extinction of our species.

Tiberius "Tibbs" Hoyt
Blackpoole Biomedical Shareholders Meeting
November 5, 2032

(i)

I layered on every bit of clothing I owned, but still the midnight air chilled me. Fear of June Mai Angel deepened the cold.

Micaiah rode behind me, and though he only had a blanket, he never complained once. He adjusted himself frequently, and I knew what he was feeling—stiff back, aching hips, chafed thighs. Long hours in the saddle does that to a body.

I thought maybe we'd do Midnight Mass since we were up anyway. But no, we were on the run. Easter would have to wait.

The beefsteaks fought us, thinking it was time to chew cud and sleep, but we kept them moving by focusing on their natural leaders—Charles Goodnight and Betty Butter. If you could get them hoofing along, thousands of their brothers, sisters, and cousins would follow behind.

As for my horses, they looked to Puff Daddy, who thought he knew everything, but I'd schooled him to know better. As long as I kept Puff Daddy trotting, the other horses fell into line. Still, my ponies kept giving me these long looks, like they were begging me for mercy. "Sorry, boys and girls," I said, "but if you wanna keep with Christian folk, you'll have to keep on keepin' on."

Despite our good animals, it was rough going. Lucky we had a three-quarter moon for most of the night as well as a road—the weedy cracks of I-70's hastily poured patchwork of concrete, gravel, and ground-up plastic.

I could tell we were getting closer to Denver, more signs of decayed civilization, haunted strip malls, and holes where houses had been. Even the studs were gone, burned in an ASI attachment for some salvage monkey.

The moonlight's glow made the landscape ghostly, but when the moon fell behind the mountains, it got so storm-cellar dark, we finally had to stop.

Not sure if Aunt Bea served up an early breakfast or late dinner, but in the wee morning hours, we were eating cold beans when Wren, Pilate, and Petal rode up. Their eyes were like dead coals in their faces.

Pilate had his big stormy-colored Arabian stallion, Windshadow, a king's horse if there ever was one. Petal rode Lambchop, a gentle-eyed palomino quarter. She was a golden-coated princess's pony, complete with a mane and tail the color of fresh snow. Wren was still on Mick, who clicked his teeth on his bit, wanting to rest and hating the night.

Our people left to go round up stragglers. Sharlotte stayed with Micaiah and me, to see what our security crew had to say.

Only no one said anything for a long time. Not even Pilate. He sipped from his Starbuck's mug and munched on a cheap, unlit cigar. Petal's chin was on her chest—she wasn't sleeping, but something was wrong with her. What was her sickness anyway? Narcolepsy?

Wren crouched on the ground, messing with her sapropel lamp so we wouldn't have to talk in the dark.

"Come on. Out with it," Sharlotte prompted.

Wren stood. "We got bad news."

"Not a surprise." Sharlotte sighed. "How bad?"

Pilate took a deep breath before he spoke. "Actually, we have all sorts of news. We have bad news, good news, better news, and evil news. Which flavor do you want first?"

"No games, Pilate. Just tell us." I wasn't in the mood for Pilate's wit. My brain was rusted from no sleep and charred from fear.

He took the cigar out of his mouth to spit tobacco bits. "June Mai Angel has an army. It's bivouacked about five klicks east. We got there just as the zeppelins showed up, which thank God, hadn't been there before or they'd have seen all the explosions. Long story short, I think she's going to take Burlington."

"What do you mean, take?" Sharlotte asked.

"Take, as in conquer, as in eighth grade social studies. Genghis Khan took Peking. The Visigoths took Rome. The kind of army she has, well, it's beyond anything I've ever seen in the Juniper. Explains the IDs. Really, it's like something straight out of the Sino." His voice got stuck, and he had to clear his throat.

My head seemed to float off my shoulders as I thought about my bedroom back in Burlington. I could imagine ninja outlaw girls fingering through my blue ribbons and stealing my candles.

"Is that the evil news?" Sharlotte asked.

"Well." Pilate smiled. "That's actually the good news."

Wren weighed in. "And the better news is that we think we killed every outlaw they sent to get Micaiah's zeppelin. So at this stage, June Mai Angel might not know we're out here."

Pilate took over. "But we have to keep moving. Come morning, June Mai'll send a unit to look for their Cargador and horses. If we're lucky, they'll follow the false path we made for them. If we're not, they'll see the mess your headcount made of the ground, figure out someone else is out here, and follow the cattle tracks right to us. Wren would just love to fight the whole army, but I'm not going to unleash her on them like that. I have some ethics left."

Wren grunted. "Still say we should sell the boy." She gave Micaiah a toothy grin so malicious I had to step in front of it.

"Okay, so what about Micaiah?" I asked. "What does this mean for him? We're not going to sell him."

"Ah, the evil news," Pilate said wearily. "The boy from the sky comes with us."

"How is that the evil news?" I asked.

Micaiah answered. "They can use me as a bargaining chip with June Mai Angel or any other Outlaw Warlord. Don't take our cattle because here's a viable boy. A rich, viable boy."

"Damn, Johnson, you're pretty smart," Wren laughed. "I think I might love him as much as Cavvy does."

"Shut up, Wren!" I said in a huff.

Pilate took out his torch lighter, clicked it on, and held it to his cigar. "I heard your story, Micaiah. I was never much for Vegas. All that sin in one place. Sin should be spread around. What's your last name?"

"Carlsbad."

At least he got his fake name correct twice in a row.

Pilate got biblical. "Micaiah, son of Imlah, and I quote, 'As the Lord liveth, what the Lord saith unto me, that will I speak.' Book of Kings. Four-hundred false prophets and only Micaiah spoke the truth. What truth do you have for us?"

"If you can get me to Nevada, I can make it worth your while. My mom can offer a substantial reward, more than you'd get for selling me." The boy shivered under the blanket draped across his shoulders, eyes bright on Pilate.

"How much?" Wren asked.

Micaiah let all our attention fix on him before he answered. It was like he was used to the stage. Was he an actor?

Finally, he spoke. "So on a good day in Hays, you'd get about two thousand dollars for one of your Herefords. An average cow weighs about six hundred kilograms. CRTA qualified beef is going for a dollar and sixty-six cents per half-kilo, that about right?"

No, he wasn't any kind of actor I'd ever heard of 'cause no actor would know about Hays cattle prices.

"How many head of cattle do you have?" he asked no one in particular.

Wren answered. "Well, before we got shot up, we had three thousand. Of various shapes and sizes."

"For a total of six million dollars. My mom could cover that," Micaiah said.

"Talk about a false prophet." Wren rolled her eyes. "This kid is telling us stories, none of them very true. Well, maybe June Mai'll listen."

Sharlotte stood motionless, silent, face hidden like always by her hat.

Was Micaiah telling us lies about such money? I didn't know, but I couldn't believe any boy was worth that much money.

I breathed in—the smell of the Pilate's cheap cherry-flavored cigar mixed with the cold wind on the sagebrush. I wanted to either rush home to stop June Mai Angel or run away to Nevada with Micaiah. He wasn't being completely honest with us, but my soul knew it was God's will for us to help him. Maybe we'd be rewarded in the process.

"Money or not, we won't give him to Outlaw Warlords," I said. "I won't allow it."

I was ignored.

"Tell us the rest if there's more to tell," Sharlotte demanded.

They all went on like I hadn't said a word. Made me madder.

Pilate exhaled smoke, then bent and drew a square in the ground with a stick. Etched a star right in the middle. "That's Denver, corporate headquarters of June Mai Angel and her conquering army. We simply can't go through her capital city." Next he drew a bad outline of an airplane north of the star. "That's DIA, the old airport." Then a bad stick-figure cow to the east of the star. He tapped the cow. "That's us. Our original plan was to avoid Denver and cut up past the airport and head north. Well, June Mai Angel has units camped around DIA. And she has units camped behind us, to the east. That's where the zeppelins are. Can't go west. Can't go east. So we either go south and skirt the Denver suburbs, which would add a week or more to our itinerary, or we turn north and try and sneak past her. Should be easy. We'll just put a couple hundred cattle under each of our coats and pretend we gained weight over the holidays."

Sharlotte exploded. "Can't you be serious for five seconds, Pilate?"

"How come no one wants to sell the boy?" Wren asked in a huff. "Y'all don't get it. Let June Mai have the ranch! I wouldn't bet on any rich mama in Vegas, but hell, we could live like queens if we sold him to some people I know in Amarillo."

The bickering and fighting started, but I knew what we needed to do.

"We should continue on west," I murmured, studying Pilate's drawings. "Go right down I-70 all the way to the mountains."

I figured I'd be ignored again, but Pilate shushed the others. "Wait, Cavatica said something. You want us to go through Denver? Really? It's been years since anyone has walked down Colfax and made it out alive. A few people tried a Denver colony after Pretty Myra disappeared, but then June Mai showed up on the scene."

All eyes fell on me. My words came out shaky. "Well, I reckon our only hope is to do what June Mai Angel won't never expect. No way would anyone walk their headcount down I-70 through her capital city in broad daylight. You'd have to be suicidal. Or so she'd think."

A wide smile spread across Pilate's face. "Cavvy has a point. June Mai is busy now with Burlington. Maybe Denver is empty. Even if it's not, I bet she wouldn't want to fight her war on two fronts. And there will be a war. Burlington's militia doesn't stand a chance, but when Howerter hears that his ranches are in trouble, he'll hire every gun in the territories and send them in as reinforcements."

Sharlotte, of course, was there to put me down. "Dang it, Cavvy, quit joking around. I've heard what you've all had to say, and now I'm going to tell you what we're going to do."

Sharlotte stood like she always did, arms across her chest, back straight, legs shoulder-width apart, hat low to cover her eyes. Her duster covered everything else. When she stood like that, she looked unmovable, like God Himself would have to walk around her. Even though she was only twenty-four years old, she talked like she was fifty and governor. "We are going to rest up for a couple hours, then go north on 470 past the airport. Head toward Wyoming as fast as we can. The plains are wide. We'll be fine. As for the boy, it seems he can come with us. For now. If we did kill all of June Mai's girls, then no one knows he's with us. Let's keep it that way. That's the plan."

Pilate's eyes narrowed. "I was kidding before, about putting the cows under our coats, right? We can't sneak by anyone with all these Herefords, especially not outlaws in the sky riding around in stolen zeppelins. But this isn't about logic or strategy or our collective safety. Your mother is dead, and you think you need to call all the shots, so we don't see how hurt you are. Or how scared."

Wren smirked. "Yeah, Sharlotte, you have what they call control issues."

"You think I chose to be in charge?" Sharlotte growled. "You think I chose to do any of this?"

We were back to fighting. Well, that wasn't going to do anyone any good.

"Stop," I said. This time when I spoke, my voice came out stronger. "We're already in June Mai Angel's house, standing right here on her front porch. Might as well go lickety-split into her living room, up the steps, and crawl into her bed. Hopefully it'll be empty. My only fear is that Sketchy, Tech, and Peeperz might not find us again. They'll be looking north, and we'll be going west." I didn't mention that air pirates might have already captured the *Moby Dick*.

"Sketchy will find us," Pilate said. "She's loyal to a fault, that woman, and three thousand cattle would be kind of hard to miss. I'm with Cavatica on this. What about you, Wren?"

"Hell, yeah," Wren said. "I love a plan that's crazy. Best kind and they always work."

Petal was asleep on her horse. She didn't vote.

Micaiah lifted a tentative hand and spoke. "I know I don't get a say, but I don't think June Mai Angel cares about you or your cattle drive. If she's going for Burlington, she'll have all the beef she wants. And if she comes for me, she won't attack you directly, not after what Petal, Pilate, and Wren did to her forces back at the gas station. No, she'll wait until I'm alone and snatch me away."

Every word he said made sense. Like Petal when she was shooting, a rhyme came into my head. *So smart, so fine, I wanna make him mine.*

"Okay, so I'm outvoted. Good!" Sharlotte snapped. "I got two things to say. First, if we all die, Cavvy, it's on your head. Can you live with that?"

The idea snatched my breath away.

"How very dramatic." Pilate shook his head and smirked.

"Sharlotte just hates any idea that's not hers," Wren taunted.

My big sister fixed her glare on Pilate and didn't let it waver. "Second, if we're killed, Pilate, I'll ride on the backs of angels down into hell to shoot you again and again for all eternity."

Pilate laughed at that. "Aw, Sharlotte, you and I will be playing poker with Jesus in heaven, all of us will be. But I gotta warn you, I'll still cheat that jackerdan for every goddamn penny he's got."

"Pilate, you can't cuss like that," I said. Last thing in the world we needed was any part of the Holy Trinity mad at us for blasphemy. Especially not on Easter.

(ii)

It was only a couple of hours until dawn and we needed to rest. Cows and horses ain't machines but living animals, and we'd pushed them far and hard. Like I figured, we'd lost at least a dozen beefsteaks already. We'd heard a cougar scream, and that explained at least one. Not sure about the others, but every cow we lost cut into our profits.

Though I was skeptical about Micaiah's story, I still felt responsible for him. I made sure he had a sleeping bag and a good spot on the Chevy's bed next to the steam engine. He needed the heat after our cold night of riding.

The tough cattle hands, like Breeze and Keys, would sleep in the saddle, surrounded by the cows. Sharlotte told me I had to get some rest, since I was only sixteen and still growing. I hated it when she mothered me—she'd been doing it all my life.

I put my bedroll against a long, broken concrete wall off the freeway to block the wind. Ten meters away, my ponies were tied off to rebar sticking out of the cement, so I could cut 'em free quick if we got attacked.

I used my saddle for a pillow and wormed my way down into the sleeping bag. Finally warm, I still couldn't sleep. What if an outlaw came up and slit my throat while I slept?

My horses would scream me awake. They loved me. Yet the "what if" wouldn't go away. The dogs, Bella, Edward, and Jacob, came over and slumped down in a pile around me, which made me feel a whole lot better—their warmth and their company.

The puppies were only the first of my visitors. Guess who wandered up and put his stuff next to me? The cute, viable boy creature we'd picked up.

"Do you mind, Cavatica?" he asked.

I could smell him, his scent, mixed with the smoke from the crash. My heart quickened. Of course I minded. Sally Browne Burke would mind. Sharlotte would mind. If Mama were alive, she'd take a switch to him, getting so close to one of her daughters.

"I guess it's okay, though you'd be safer on the chuck wagon," I said. "Just don't talk. We gotta sleep some. Tomorrow we'll prolly die, but I don't wanna die tired."

Who was I kidding? My eyes were owl-wide open. I lay with my back to him so he couldn't see.

"Good night, Cavatica," he said. God, I wished he wouldn't say my name. My hand went over my heart, and I felt it beat there, thudding hard.

I listened as he shuffled down into his own sleeping bag. I could picture us together in a tent, a fire going in the stove, and maybe I would get on a cot with him, and in that warm tent, we'd kiss.

Every millimeter of my body tingled. Guess there was some electricity in the Juniper after all. I used a few Hail Marys and Our Fathers to stop the lust.

"I can't stay with you," he said. "What if June Mai Angel does know I'm with you? What if my aunts send people into the Juniper looking for me? They're worse than any Outlaw Warlord, believe me." He paused. The only sound was the wind tousling the sagebrush, the horses shifting their feet, weary cows lowing themselves to sleep. Way out in the distance, coyotes chattered like insane idiots. We'd lose more headcount to them.

Micaiah sighed. "It's too dangerous for all of you. Tomorrow, I'll leave."

Fear shocked me. Fear that someone worse than June Mai Angel would attack us. Fear that he'd leave and I'd never see him again. Fear that my first kiss would be my last.

Right then, I knew he was telling us the truth. Not about everything, some of his story, like his name, was a lie, but the rest of it, like being hunted by his aunts, was real. And I swore to myself I'd protect him.

"No, Micaiah, you're with us 'til the end," I said. "Pilate and Petal are Sino veterans and Wren is bloodthirsty. They'll keep us safe."

"Are you serious?" he asked. "If I have your blessing to stay, well, then I'll stay."

"You have it," I said.

"And if they try and give me away to an Outlaw Warlord?"

"It'll never happen," I said. "Not as long as I'm around. And I'll pray to St. Jude, 'cause if there was ever an impossible cause, it's this cattle drive."

"Catholic," he said, kind of laughy. "Surprising. I thought the Catholics didn't really believe in the New Morality."

Those were fighting words.

I swung around to see him with his head pillowed on his hands, gazing at the stars. Bella looked at me with bright eyes, wondering why I was upset. Edward and Jacob were snoring away oblivious. Such boys.

I kept my response brief, though I had a whole diatribe on the subject. "There was an ecumenical council in Baltimore where the American Catholic archbishops met with Sally Browne Burke and Reverend Kip Parson. There is common ground."

"Tell that to the people vandalizing Catholic churches."

He was right. While the New Morality accepted the work the ARK did, the Catholics came down hard against Tibbs Hoyt and any sort of fertilization outside of the marriage bed, which in our day and age, well, was real controversial. Still, I was Catholic, and Catholics didn't believe in artificial insemination if the man wasn't married to the woman.

Okay, fine, but what if a woman couldn't find a husband? It was either the ARK or men like Pilate.

Before I could say anything, Micaiah spoke. "I know, I know, good night a third time. Thanks again, Cavatica. You saved me again and again."

My top half froze, being out of my bag, but I didn't care. He had me all riled up. I couldn't get Pilate and Betsy out of mind—a priest forced to break his vows to help a woman who needed children to work her ranch.

"It's wrong, Micaiah."

"What's wrong?"

"All of it." I winced. I couldn't get my words clear. Every time I was with him, I got all jumbled up.

He chuckled. "Well, I'm glad we cleared that up. Once again I am in awe of your keen debating skills."

More teasing. Well, the anger made me talk fast. "It's wrong for people to be defacing Catholic churches, and it's wrong that we don't have enough boys and that we need the ARK, but it's really a crime that Tibbs Hoyt is making a fortune off of women's misery."

No smart-aleck response. Bella woofed, but I shushed her.

"Tibbs Hoyt is a villain, Cavatica, and what he is doing is the very worst of crimes." Micaiah's voice came out soft, hurt somehow. It was clear that Hoyt and his ARK had wounded Micaiah in some way.

"I'm sorry," I said, meaning it.

"Don't apologize for sins that aren't yours." He chuckled. "That's something Pilate might've said. I can't believe I met him."

"You know about Pilate?" I asked, surprised.

"I was in Chicago, and I heard an ARK district manager make a joke— if you can't afford the ARK, there's always Father Pilate in the Juniper. Good night, Cavatica."

But good night was a long time away and almost over anyway. People knew about Pilate in the World? What else did they know about him? And how could Micaiah have overheard an ARK district manager making the joke?

"Who are you really?" I asked. "You said before that your aunts were looking for you 'cause you had something. Like what? Couldn't be those boots, so what else do you have on you?"

He didn't reply. Kept his head on his hands. Kept his eyes on the stars.

"It's 'cause you're viable, ain't it?" I asked.

"That's it." He let out a long breath. "And I don't like to talk about it. Good night, Cavvy. That's your cue to go to sleep—the good night part."

I frowned and curled up against Bella and her boys. Thinking about our conversation, I realized I'd answered the question before he could. Most boys were uncomfortable talking about their viability, but it seemed to me he seemed relieved to have escaped without having to say more.

Great. Now he had me lying for him.

However, if he was being hunted for being viable, it would make sense for him to hate Tibbs Hoyt. If the ARK gave Male Product away, well, his life might be very different.

I didn't know what to believe. Like with Pilate, I wanted to push Micaiah away, but I just couldn't find it in me. He was so beautiful, so smart, so kind—even when he teased me, which I didn't like, but somehow wanted.

I was falling in love with him.

Which made the next day's hurt all the more hard to bear.

CHAPTER FOURTEEN

I'm pretty sure it was Crush Jones who started the nickname. We both had watched those old Bonanza *videos online growing up. We couldn't call it the Ponderosa—not a lot of big trees on the Great Plains, but we have Juniper. Grows like a weed. Smells like money.*

—Dob Howerter
Colorado Courier Interview
August 4, 2034

(i)

Only a couple of hours of sleep and we were back moving the cattle down I-70 at first light on Easter Sunday morning. The highway widened to six lanes running through clusters of buildings, siding peeling off like sunburned skin. The skeletons of old hotels slumped like dinosaurs, all their flesh rotted away.

At least the sky was blue and the wind was warm. Might've been a nice spring morning if not for the fact we were heading straight into June Mai Angel's capital city.

My ponies tripped along, exhausted. Felt bad, but I had to keep them going. I encouraged, prodded, and sometimes got real stern. Despite being busy, I noticed right away when Micaiah rode over to Sharlotte. On her horse, she rose above a sea of white-faced Herefords. Their red hides glistened in the sunlight.

My sister and my boy looked like they were deep in conversation. What could they be talking about so intensely? Jealousy rose up inside of me. Sharlotte knew he was mine, didn't she?

I watched them close after that, and they never left each other's side.

Wren rode tail, making sure our flank was covered. Petal and Pilate scouted ahead.

Aunt Bea drove the chuck wagon way out front, guiding Charles Goodnight, who in turn led our whole drive. I was a little nervous about the *chugga-chugga* of the truck drawing attention. The smoke rising up from the steam engine worried me less. Thank God for Colorado wind.

Bella, Jacob, and Edward lounged in the cab next to Bea. They were good cattle dogs, but we worried that a cranky beefsteak might kick them if they got too close.

Tenisha Keys drifted next to me. "Hi, Cavvy." In her saddle, she kept one eye on the cattle, the other focused on weaving long pieces of plastic and several strands of colored wire together.

"Hi, Miss Keys," I said. "Did you and Nikki get any sleep last night?"

"Nope," she said. "Spent all night gathering strays."

She wasn't complaining, but I wanted to, since I was so sleep-deprived and scared. I tried to forget about my discomfort by asking, "What're you making there, Miss Keys?"

"Just weavin' some," Keys said. "If my fingers are busy, it keeps my mind from wandering. The minute I think about June Mai Angel, I fall apart. So, yeah, busy fingers, focused mind. Don't know how we're gonna get out of this one. I keep telling myself ... halfway. Just gotta make it halfway."

I nodded. "Yeah, that's what we're all thinking I guess. Too hard to think about all the kilometers ahead."

"You think we'll make it through Denver?"

I turned away, to keep my gaze on Sharlotte and Micaiah.

When I didn't respond, Keys moseyed on ahead.

I got upset with myself for being so rude. I should've tried to comfort her. Like the prayer of St. Francis of Assisi—better to comfort than to be comforted. I prayed to be less selfish.

It didn't work.

I glanced up just in time to see my sister, Sharlotte-work-yourself-to-death-Weller smiling at Micaiah. Oh, the smile she gave him—it was full of roses and wedding gowns. You'd think we were at an ice cream social rather than trying to run cattle through enemy territory.

Couldn't believe it came from Sharlotte. Even though she was twenty-four, it seemed like she'd been born an old spinster and was determined to stay the course.

She smiled at him.

He smiled back.

For a minute, I wondered if someone else had joined our cattle drive. Couldn't be my sister. My eyes got dry, I stared so hard.

A voice wailed up inside of me. *No, he's mine. I kissed him. He's mine!* Had to swallow and swallow, but the hurt stayed stuck in my throat.

I thought I would've had to fight Wren or Crete for the boy. Wasn't fair for my big sister to be the competition. Maybe Sharlotte had been faking wanting to send Micaiah away.

No. I closed my eyes and remembered family was more important than romantic love. If Sharlotte wanted him, well, who was I to stop her? I had to side with Sharlotte. Maybe I was imagining things. Maybe the smiles were more friendly than full of love.

Watching the two together, however, didn't put me at ease. I went back through every conversation I'd had with Micaiah and catalogued my mistakes. I should've been nicer to him. I should've tried to believe his story more. I should've been less suspicious. I'd blown my chance. Now Sharlotte would run off and get married, and I'd be alone forever. My fantasies of finding love seemed so empty.

Even so, the day passed in a hard blur. When Sharlotte gave the signal to stop, I forgot about my anguish and obsessing long enough to be glad. I hadn't known if Sharlotte wanted us to do another night of cattle driving.

My eyelids felt sandy—I was so drained. Twilight chased away the warmth, and a cold night slammed down like a lid closing on a freezer.

I had my remuda chores to do, but next up on the agenda was a long conversation with Sharlotte about Micaiah.

Not sure what I was going to say, but I had to say something.

(ii)

Cast-off car parts and plastic-trash scatter lined the highway and the shoulder. Rotted King Soopers bags melted into the dirt next to brittle water bottles. Junk mail, thirty years old, lay half-buried or blew like leaves across the concrete. We found some grass, but our headcount and horses weren't too interested in eating. They wanted to stop, rest, sleep.

Aunt Bea told me Pilate planned the camp for maximum safety, and I needed to build my temporary corral west of her chuck wagon. I got the sledgehammer and pounded the aluminum poles into the ground. When the cowgirls brought in their horses, I took care of them. Both the horses and the cowgirls were sullen and scared, even Crete.

Allie Chambers, Kasey Romero, and Dolly Day Cornpone turned in their horses and stomped off, talking about food and maybe sleep, if Sharlotte would let them. All three had MG21s strapped across their shoulders and 9mm pistols in holsters at their hips.

Keys and Breeze arrived next, but they dropped off their horses only to take two more out. It was clear they were going to work through the night again. Those women were iron-nail tough.

Lastly, Sharlotte rode in on Prince, holding the reins to Katy, the horse Micaiah had been on all day. He was by the chuck wagon, talking to Crete. Her sullen hadn't lasted long. She spun her hair around a finger and giggled all flirty.

I wanted to growl. Instead, I grabbed Sharlotte in a glare and asked, "What are you and the boy talking about? You two sure are smiley."

The way my voice sounded, I might as well have said, *Hey Shar, let's me and you fight over Micaiah 'cause we both love him.*

My sister went dead-eyed. Her mouth crept away into a scowl. "We're running for our lives, Cavvy. Or haven't you noticed?"

"Do you still want to send Micaiah away?"

It was like she hadn't heard me. Sharlotte shifted Tina Machinegun on her shoulder and pointed at her horse's right front hoof. "Katy's limp is getting a whole lot worse. Check for a hoof abscess, but I hope to God it's just bits of asphalt in her frog. If she goes lame we'll have to put her down, and I'd hate to do that. And while you're at it, pick Prince carefully as well. He's favoring his front left. I hate all the crap covering the highway. Those bits of plastic are bound to get into their hooves and make a world of mischief. I wish we were on dirt and on our way to Hays."

Just business. Like always.

"You never mind about the boy," she said abruptly. "We need to focus on getting our headcount to Nevada. It's stupid for that Petersen woman from Sysco to give us so much money, like our beef was special, even though you and I both know it tastes the same—Colorado beef, Mormon beef, all the same. I still think your plan of going through Denver is foolish, but I was outvoted. I keep kicking myself, letting y'all bully me. Mama always said this family wasn't a democracy."

"Mama's gone," I said forcefully, "and now it is a democracy. You got outvoted. So deal with it." Not sleeping had filled my mind and mouth with venom. And I'd spent the day scared we'd get killed and it'd be my fault. Top it all off, watching her and my boy get all cozy had made me crazy.

Sharlotte took a step toward me. She wasn't quite in my face, but that step was to prove who was in charge. "I have been dealing with it. You haven't. Mama let Howerter into our pockets, so you could go off and have fun at your school for the past four years. And Wren left right after to have fun of her own. Me? I've been here, dealing with it, but that doesn't matter." Then she got sarcastic. "As we all know, nothing matters, except our headcount and saving the ranch 'cause Mama left us with no other option."

Her tone silenced me. What was going on with her? I thought the ranch meant everything to her.

She turned away. "Dang it, Cavvy, I just wish. Oh, how I wish ..." Her voice came out chipped, soft, hurting.

I waited for her to finish, but she didn't. She didn't walk away, either. She stood there, one hand balancing Tina Machinegun on her shoulder, the other in her pocket, fiddling with whatever was inside.

Couldn't quite believe Sharlotte was wishing for things. I figured that part of her heart had been turned off.

"What do you wish for?" I asked.

She sighed. "If wishes were diesel, how the Juniper would roar." She turned around to face me. "I wish we didn't have to do this. I wish I hadn't let you come. If anything happened to you, I'd take it hard. But it seems to me you're a part of this, whether we like it or not. You have to promise though, if any shooting starts, you run and hide, okay? You stay safe. I know you disobeyed me to go and save Micaiah, but you can't risk yourself again for him, okay?"

But I love him. How I wanted to say those words so she'd know the truth.

Good thing I didn't 'cause not a second later Sharlotte came as close as she dared to proclaiming her own love. "I'll watch out for Micaiah. He's a good guy, handsome, bright as a sparkle, and polite. Even though it's risky, I'm glad he's with us. You were right. It was the Christian thing to do."

I stood there awkwardly. She'd said we needed to focus on the cattle drive, and ended up talking about Micaiah. It seemed she was as conflicted as I was.

Not sure how she took my silence, but her eyes fell on me, and for once, they weren't hard or angry or focused on the next task to do. They took me in, fully, and I remembered the times Sharlotte would read to me from our copy of *The Lives of the Saints*. After showers in the evening, we'd light sapropel lanterns, and she'd curl up in my bed and we'd read until she thought I was asleep. Only I wouldn't let myself drift off completely until Mama came in and prayed over me before kissing me goodnight.

"I had to come, Sharlotte," I whispered. "I couldn't stay behind. If we all die, I want us to die together."

Sharlotte shrugged, hat covering her eyes. "Well, you may get your wish. Sketchy is going to be looking north for us, so we might never see the *Moby Dick* again. As for Wren, she and I had words. She still wants to sell Micaiah. She took off when I told her I'd rather die than give him up."

Sharlotte colored. Told more of the truth than she'd wanted. The blush on her face meant only one thing—she was falling for Micaiah. I had my answer.

She went on, a hard edge to her voice. "If Wren did leave for good, oh well. All I know for sure is we gotta keep going. Even dead, Mama always gets what Mama wants. Good night, Cavvy."

Sharlotte marched off. The way she kept saying Mama, it sounded like a curse word. But how could that be? Sharlotte loved Mama. Didn't she?

I'd wept over our mother, but Sharlotte hadn't, not that I'd seen. And sometimes uncried tears can be a poison. But something was changing in her. Micaiah might be the cause.

If he could help my sister change for the better, I was right to step aside. If I kept on pining for him, I would change for the worse.

(iii)

Aunt Bea brought around a cold dinner—carrots going limp, beef jerky, cracker biscuits. I ate alone, working my remuda, combing down coats and picking hooves. If we had to take off in the middle of the night, I didn't want any of my horses running with debris stuck in their shoes or burrs under their saddles.

In the rope corral, my ponies seemed okay. Thirsty, jumpy, but okay. They'd sleep some, then wake up to nose through the spring grass.

Sun was gone, but a gray light spread over the horizon, turning the sky into a star-filled midnight blue.

That evening, Pilate did double-duty—Easter Mass and Annabeth's funeral. He kept it fairly short and sweet and didn't say anything outlandish. We stood for the whole thing.

During the communal "Our Father," I noticed Micaiah didn't know the prayer, but he was watching Sharlotte's lips.

Sharlotte caught him looking at her, and she smiled shyly. She looked my age, not like a worn-out spinster, not heartsick and troubled, just young and in love.

Sharlotte's words echoed around in my head. She was right. I had gotten to leave, while she was stuck at home, dealing with Mama, who never made things easy. Who was never satisfied. Who never stopped to give a compliment or a word of encouragement. Who never stopped. Period.

My better nature whispered to me. *Let Sharlotte have the boy. Let Sharlotte win for once.*

As Saint Francis said in his prayer—it is better to love, than to be loved.

I would love Sharlotte. And I would let Sharlotte love Micaiah. Losing him would be a death, but like Easter promised, I would be resurrected from the darkness. I just had to have faith, and right then, I did.

Peace filled my heart when I got in line to get communion from Pilate, the round hosts in a cracked Tupperware container and wine from a small, wooden chalice.

We sang "On Eagle's Wings" and then Allie Chambers sang "Amazing Grace" which brought tears to all our eyes. That girl sang so well even the angels were jealous. We wiped our eyes, hugged each other, and got back to work.

While the cattle hands divided up the nighttime duties, I took my sleeping bag and found a place by a gold Chevy Camaro. The wheels were gone, and the body was rusting away into the soil, but it would protect me from the wind.

My horses slept in their corral. I slept alone, no dogs, no boy, just me and my ponies near. It felt like enough.

Coffee and crumble-butter biscuits for breakfast and we were moving again. Dawn wasn't even blue.

We'd only been riding an hour or two when the freeway rose up on bridges. Not just a simple overpass, but kilometers and kilometers of elevated highway. All the way through Denver, quick but dangerous. The two walls of concrete on either side created a perfect channel for a stampede.

Made me swallow hard. If the cattle stampeded, we'd have nowhere to run, and twelve-thousand hooves might pound us into pulp.

I was worrying about that, and Wren leaving, and the *Moby Dick*, when I got my first glimpse of downtown Denver. The buildings towered over the ruins like the thrones of hell, and though we thought the streets would be empty, they could be filled with June Mai's girls, waiting to slaughter us.

Sharlotte would die with her boy close, and I'd meet Saint Peter with a clear conscience. There were worse ways to go.

CHAPTER FIFTEEN

I was in Brooklyn. I had a little scrap metal business. I was watching the news after the Yellowstone Knockout. I watched all those refugees pouring out of the Juniper. I remember seeing that black sky on the video. Everyone was crying. I kept thinking, what about all the copper in the houses? What about the wiring? What about the highway guardrails? That's kilometers of galvanized steel. No, that's kilometers of money. I didn't feel bad about the refugees. Maybe I should've. The government said they could go back in and get their belongings. But I knew no one would.

—Calvin "Crush" Jones
60 Minutes Interview
April 27, 2037

(i)

The next day passed. Up before dawn, moving headcount until after dusk, barely sleeping in between. Twilight and morning light swirled together until it was like we'd walked all day in our sleep.

No *Moby Dick*. No Wren. But no attack either.

That next night, Sharlotte decided to set up one tent, a place where a few of us could sleep, while everyone else kept watch or slept on the ground.

Our expedition tent measured eight meters long and five meters wide, big enough for most of our crew, but we didn't want to work to throw that monster up. Instead, we set up one of our round all-weather four-women yurts. The smell of the waterproof canvas brought back a world of memories of cattle drives to Hays. We slid the stovepipe through a hole in the top of the tent and into the stove inside. With two bunkable cots, the tent could sleep four easily.

Sharlotte insisted I join Breeze and Keys for a good, solid night's sleep. I didn't protest all that much. Too tired.

Inside the tent, I noticed Breeze wore the little plastic and wire bracelet Keys had woven. I watched them closely. They never touched, but never strayed far from one another. Every glance was like a gentle caress.

They were *gillian*. No doubt. I debated telling Sharlotte, but we didn't need that kind of drama with everything else going on. And they were being discreet.

Watching Breeze and Keys, petite and pretty, loving each other, wordlessly, deeply, made me even more confused. How could that love be bad? If only I had someone to look at me like they were looking at each other.

Longing for Micaiah hit me. Only for a second, and then I laughed at myself. I hoped Sharlotte enjoyed such glances. I bet she was all a-flutter inside, despite her best efforts to remain cool and business-like.

I was pretty proud of myself when I went to sleep that night. Letting go of Micaiah was going to be a process, but I felt well on my way.

(ii)

Another night. Another day.

A nasty breeze blew off the Rockies, which were white where they weren't bruised blue like our sleepless faces. Interstate 70 ran penny-nail straight toward the mountains on crumbling bridges of concrete and asphalt. The salvage monkeys were smart enough not to burn the asphalt on the bridges, thank God. Below us slouched the ruins of Denver, deserted, or so it seemed.

To keep the fear out of my head, I played a little game of derelict-fast-food-building bingo. I started with "B" for Burger King. All the red was rubbed off the sign, so it was hard to read. "I" for Jack-In-The-Box. I loved their Oreo cookie milkshakes. "N" for Wendy's. The wind and sun had wiped clean the freckles on the smiling little girl. "G" for Good Times, and back in Cleveland, Anju and I used to go there for their frozen custard. "O" for Taco Bell. The bell on the sign was bashed in. Broken glass twinkled in the morning sunlight on bare ground, all the asphalt long gone.

We spent the afternoon in a hush, hurrying past downtown Denver to the south. One of the kings of the Juniper salvage industry, Crush Jones, swore he'd scavenge the buildings down to their sub-basements, but in the end it had turned out to be too much work. He started at the top but gave up, so what was left of the towers looked like broken teeth.

We passed the old Purina rendering plant. The shattered windows stared at us with moaning ghost eyes. Funny, we also passed the old National Western Stock Show grounds, which Annabeth's mother, the Widow Burton, talked about. Ours were prolly the first cows to go past there in thirty years. For generations, the National Western had been the biggest stock show in the country, if not the world, and you'd get a million people strolling through there, looking and buying a million farm animals and eating funnel cakes and watching rodeo. The National Western allowed city folks to enjoy the ranching life without getting their shoes dirty. After the Yellowstone Knockout, they moved the stock show to Hays, Kansas.

I remembered how Widow Burton talked about the old National Western with a sizzle in her eye—all the flirting and dancing and kissing.

My mind couldn't quite imagine it. A dozen boys for every girl, all of them exchanging smiles. Wow. If I had lived in such a world, giving up on Micaiah would've been easier.

I could've walked down five steps and found an even better one. But would I? I had a feeling even when boys were plenty, Micaiah would've stood out.

We set up the tent again that night, put in the same four bunkable cots, and lit a fire in the stove to keep them warm. Pilate, Petal, and Micaiah would get a turn in the tent. The rest of us would camp out on the highway and keep watch or stay with the headcount, divided equally behind us and in front of us.

My remuda lay between the tent and the first of the cattle. Like the cows, my ponies stamped restlessly and shook themselves, signs of stress. They wanted off the ramp. I couldn't blame them a bit, but I was getting annoyed. Just when I got comfortable, Puff Daddy raised a stink, and I shucked myself out of my sleeping bag to go and get him under control. It was chilly, but pretty. Stars milked up the sky, while the moon rose from the horizon, spilling a silver glow over the elevated highway and the dead city beneath.

I was trying to soothe my ponies, when Christina Pink ambled over, her reins tied to the horn of her empty saddle. She was Wren's horse, a piebald Gypsy Vanner mare and one of our biggest horses with the endurance of a tractor. Wren liked her 'cause they were both snake-bit mean. Christina Pink loved to fight with my sister, but loved to fight Puff Daddy more. Had to keep those two separate.

Which I did. But if Christina Pink had come back riderless, either Wren had fallen off or my sister had re-joined our crew in secret.

I looked about and that's when I saw Wren duck into the tent.

Wren hadn't left us! She was alive! My first thought was to go after her, talk to her about what she'd been doing.

I took two steps toward the tent and stopped. The silhouettes of Wren and Pilate closed in an embrace. Just the two of them. Only saw them together for a minute. Wren turned off the sapropel lantern and the tent went dark.

Petal was in there with them, but knowing her, she would be out cold, so it was like the two were really alone.

And where was Micaiah? Not in that tent.

My stomach turned, thinking about what Pilate and Wren might be doing. It wasn't right. Wren didn't want no baby, which meant Pilate really was a dog.

Sure explained why Petal hated Wren. Explained that perfectly.

I backed away, claws of disgust tore up my insides. Then I saw something that added poison to the claws.

Sharlotte and Micaiah sat on the bones of a sofa, looking up at the stars. He put his arm around her, and she took his other hand in hers. They were all snuggled up and romantic like in one of my fantasies.

Wanting them to be together and happy was a lot different than seeing them together and happy. I backed away, silently, and swallowed the hurt.

I'd been the third wheel before, with Anju and Billy Finn, but that had been a whole different story. Billy Finn was fine, but not a boy for me.

Micaiah?

He was my first kiss, the first boy I'd ever held, or really talked to. He was smart, so smart, knowing about the steam engine and even guessing the cost of our headcount though it was clear he wasn't any kind of rancher.

His eyes. Those bright blue eyes. Bright as a sparkle. Like Sharlotte said.

I let my horses lull me back into my right mind. Puff Daddy even settled down, and that was a great kindness.

If only there were more boys, I kept thinking. If only I had more boys to choose from. If only.

I knew the truth, though, deep down. I'd been lucky to kiss a boy like Micaiah. Sharlotte was even luckier.

The next morning, Christina Pink was gone. So was Wren.

(iii)

Our cattle stopped moving on the early morning of the fourth day since the attack. They all stopped square in the middle of the freeway and wouldn't move. Tongues drooped from open mouths and eyes were dull. They needed water and they needed it right away. Their bodies packed in tighter and tighter as more cows caught up to the traffic jam.

The stink of them hit me like a hammer—the plop and spray of them relieving themselves. Quite a noise, smelly and disgusting.

Charles Goodnight had been walking slower and slower, so he'd been pushed to the back to walk near Aunt Bea and the chuck wagon. Betty Butter had taken over the front. She had simply stopped and apparently every one of the beefsteaks agreed with her decision.

She glared at us. Snot leaked from her nose to drip onto the pavement. Others around her let up cries of complaint, wails of frustration. Betty stayed quiet and vexed.

We'd made it to the western suburbs of Denver, near some major interchange. The buildings and houses around us were silent, eerily so.

I didn't know the name of the streets 'cause all the signs had been salvaged. My ponies and I were shoved to the left side, next to the concrete wall with Crete.

Micaiah rode on the far right side with Sharlotte, both stuck there by the motionless cattle.

Dolly Day called from the front of the herd. "Hey, boss lady, now what? Looks like these girls are done, and to tell you the truth, so am I!"

Sharlotte didn't answer. Tina Machinegun lay across her lap, and she had her head down. What was she doing? She couldn't let Dolly Day talk to her like that.

I yelled back. "Hey, Dolly, give us a minute." I wanted to go and confer with Sharlotte, but the cattle jammed the freeway. Luckily, I'd saddled up Puff Daddy that morning. He was big enough to push through the beef, but his temper ran hot.

The cries of the cattle grew louder. Thirsty, hungry, tired, some bashed each other, and others bashed back. A stampede on the highway might just kill us all. Or at the very least, we'd lose millions of dollars in beef left on the pavement to rot.

"What are we going to do, Cavatica?" Crete asked.

I had no answer, but I didn't want my horses hurt. "Don't know, but take my remuda back to Aunt Bea. Go slow. These beefsteaks are on a hair-trigger."

She didn't argue and left with my ponies.

Sharlotte tilted her head to talk to Micaiah as if she didn't have a care in the world. Well, I did. I had a ranch to save, and I couldn't do it stuck on a highway in enemy territory.

I patted Puff Daddy and whispered into his ear, "Okay, Puff, we're going to go slow and easy, yeah?"

He snorted. Answer enough. I got my lariat ready, took in a deep breath to gather my *shakti*, and then maneuvered the stallion into the cows. They squealed at us, bawled, pushed away, pushed back, and their big, swaying, sweaty bodies pinched my legs.

The day was warm, which didn't help any, and dry, so dry.

"Cavatica Jeanne, you okay?" Sharlotte called out.

I wasn't going to raise my voice to answer. Not when I was shoving my way through kilotons of horns, hooves, and hate.

I reached Betty Butter. She stared at me like she'd love to stomp my head to mush. Her ear flicked, she snotted and sneezed, then returned to giving me the evil eye.

I tossed my lariat around her. "Listen, Betty, I've known you your entire life. I was there, right there, when you were born in the south ditch. Now, we need you to move 'cause you are a natural leader. When you move, all your friends'll move, even Bluto. I know you know Bluto 'cause you two like each other, well, like each other when you aren't hating each other. You get me?"

Too bad that big, nasty cow couldn't tell me in English what she was planning to do.

I turned my back on her, in complete trust, and stepped Puff Daddy forward. I would've dragged Betty behind him, but I didn't need to. The minute the rope grew taunt Betty followed.

And the herd moved with her.

I trotted on past Dolly Day, who had her toothless maw open, laughing, and congratulating me. "Well, dang, Cavvy, ain't you something. You got her going, and without too much fuss. And we all thought that fancy school might have schooled the cattle-drivin' out of you."

My hands were shaking, sweat leaked down from my hat, and my heart banged about in my chest. "No, Dolly, not hardly. But you and I know we got lucky. Another bad day on this highway and we might find ourselves in the middle of a worser mess."

"We'll just put you in charge," she said back.

"Not hardly," I repeated. "I'm way too young."

I stood up on my saddle and caught sight of Sharlotte and Micaiah. My sister gave me a thumbs up. I'd been useful, and being useful meant a lot to a woman like her.

Again, the debt I owed my family lessened a bit.

Wendover, Nevada never felt closer.

Something in the sky caught my attention. A zeppelin zoomed toward us. Machineguns on top. Machineguns on the bottom.

Coming in fast.

CHAPTER SIXTEEN

Someday there won't be anything left to salvage. Do you know what I predict? Ranchers, farmers, communities of strong people will come to work the soil and tend animals. If I'm lucky, I'll see the day, and the Juniper will be a magical place.

—Mavis Meetchum
Colorado Courier Interview
August 4, 2032

(i)

The zeppelin chugging into sight was a Jonesy, but I couldn't see her name. Smoke belched thick from her steam engine.

Then she turned, just enough for us to let out a happy yell. It was the *Moby Dick*, finding us right when we needed her. I'm pretty sure angels fly around heaven in dirigibles.

Sketchy maneuvered the zeppelin down onto the highway, behind our bawling headcount, complaining, not knowing that they were about to be served a take-out dinner.

We tied the zeppelin downwind from the cattle 'cause if they smelled the water and hay on the *Moby Dick*, they'd take off after it, and there would be chaos.

Sketchy and Tech climbed down the rope ladder, and Tech hugged me hard. "Oh, Cavatica, we were so worried."

Sketchy then blasted out the story. "We saw the army of that goddamn June Mai Angel, and they took shots at us, and we had to fly up north, but we couldn't find you, which is kinda funny, losing a big ol' herd of cows. I kept bein' mean to poor Peeperz, but I was just so scared. And then Tech thought maybe you'd keep on I-70, but that would be crazy, and then she said that you Weller girls are crazy, and we headed west. Which is good we did. But it's dang strange. Denver is empty. I guess all the soldiers are out on the plains, which meant y'all picked the absolute best time to run west. It's so great seeing you, and Pilate, and all your people again."

She didn't ask about Wren, and I was glad. Thinking about him and Wren together hurt my heart.

Tech gave me a final squeeze then took off to help Sharlotte and Micaiah secure the mooring lines.

The boy's nose was sunburned 'cause he didn't have a hat. Made him cuter. Not that I cared any more.

"Who'd you guys pick up?" Sketchy asked. "Or are they growing handsome boys in Denver now that June Mai is gone?"

I told her the little we knew about him, and Sketchy put on a pout. "That damn outlaw and her Cargadors and grappling hooks. It's a shame."

"Do you think he was headed to Vegas?" I asked.

Sketchy shook her head. "Maybe, but such a trip would be a bundle of money and twice the cash. Folks would just as soon go suborbital across the Juniper for the same price."

I slapped my thigh. "That's what I thought."

Micaiah asked Sharlotte something, which elicited a bright smile from my sister.

"Well lookey there." The *Moby Dick's* captain breathed out.

"Yeah, I know," I said, feeling pretty calm about the whole situation.

"Dang, but he looks familiar. Hey, boy!" Sketchy called out. "You spend time in the ZZK?"

He looked confused. And more than a little worried.

"She means Buzzkill, Nebraska," I explained.

Micaiah wandered over and shook Sketchy's hand. "No, ma'am," Micaiah said. "I've not spent much time in the Juniper at all."

Sketchy studied him for a long time. "You famous? Like in Hollywood video? I like video, but I never get to watch any, only when we venture out into the World, which isn't often. Not sure if Cavvy told you, but we got a Kung Pao Eterna battery, which means we got the fastest Jonesy in the world. Pretty sure. Pretty sure."

"A Kung Pao?" His eyebrow perked. "Wow, I'd like to see that but not right now. Sharlotte wanted me up front, to keep stragglers in check." With that he was off.

Our boy, famous? Maybe that was why he had escaped into the Juniper. Got tired of the paparazzi. I did recall how he handled being the center of attention. Then again, he was a boy, and boys either got used to the instant fame or turned dreadfully shy, like Billy Finn.

Sharlotte saw me idle, and she had a fix for that. "Hey, Cavvy, go help Micaiah at the front. The herd is getting restless."

That was an understatement. Our headcount was thirsty, hungry, mad for being run hard for days on end, and even madder for being crammed onto a freeway. The whining, piping, and moaning of the cows got worse and worse, while our team pulled long, blue collapsible troughs out of the *Moby Dick's* rear bay doors. The Neofiber troughs could be set up in a second, and Tech had julie-rigged a system of hoses to deliver the water. Soon those beefsteaks would be happy enough.

I threw a leg over Puff Daddy and pushed through to the front of the herd.

A cloud covered the sun for a moment. My nose warned me of the snow.

Micaiah spun around on Mick. Standing his stirrups, he scanned the remnants of houses.

We were still elevated, but ahead of us, the road dropped down a gradual incline to where an off ramp led to the dirt of an old street and the tangled brush of a river glen. If the cattle caught the scent of the water, we wouldn't be able to stop them.

"What is it?" I asked.

He opened his mouth to answer.

A gunshot answered for him.

(ii)

The report of an MG21 echoed across the landscape. Betty Butter let out a bellow that started in her butt and threw itself out of her mouth.

She wasn't going to wait for us to unload the *Moby Dick*. The gunshot frightened her, and she took off, and then I watched her eyes go down to the water in the glen. She'd smelled it. She was going there for a drink, and God help anything that stood in her way.

She drove forward, and in that minute, Micaiah and I were staring down a carpet of seething, horned fury, coming right at us. Hundreds and hundreds of cattle. Thousands of hooves. Megatons of moving meat.

The earth-cracking noise of their hooves on the pavement eclipsed any other bullets, any other shouts of alarm, everything else.

It was a stampede. And stampedes mean death.

Puff Daddy ignited on instinct and took off running down the freeway, away from them, as did Mick. Micaiah clung to his horse, face pale. Neither of our ponies was fast—Mick didn't have the heart for it, and Puff swayed with too much bulk.

Snorting, hot breath, the rage of wet stink from the cattle stifled us as we fled on working legs and pounding hooves.

We needed off the highway. Right then. Or die.

Puff and Mick streaked in a full sprint, shoes striking sparks. I had to direct the escape, but I had to be careful or Puff might freak out completely. A subtle pull on the reins, leaning in the saddle, and Puff knew I needed him to go right. He followed my lead, driving Mick nearer to the concrete wall.

That boy, however green, did the exact thing I needed, like he could read my mind. Or like we'd been rehearsing a suicidal circus act.

He unhooked his left foot from the stirrup, lifted himself on his right, and then offered me his hand.

My *shakti* focused me. I didn't pause a second. I caught his hand in a steel grip, stepped off Puff Daddy and hurled myself onto Mick for a minute, until I yanked both Micaiah and myself off the saddle and over the concrete wall.

It was ten meters down to the bottom of the glen.

A fall like that could shatter a leg or kill you outright. But then I hit a tree branch, heavy with buds, and another one, and another, until I threw my arm around cottonwood limb, but I was going too fast.

The limb was jerked out of my arms. I fell, again, crashing through more branches. I landed on my belly in a carpet of dry leaves, several seasons worth, cushioning that last plummet.

Micaiah lay next to me, mouth open, but I couldn't hear his groan, or anything else.

The stampede and gunfire drowned out everything else. The ground shook, and for a second I thought it was from the cattle on the highway, but then I realized it was from horses in front of us.

Women on horseback galloped through the glen. They were dressed in the same half-army, half-cowgirl outfits I'd seen before on the air pirates. June Mai's soldier girls. So Denver wasn't deserted after all.

Ironic, but the *Moby Dick* had prolly led the soldiers right to us.

The troop drove their horses under the bridge, wheeled around, then splashed through the river and charged away. They hadn't seen us, but were they there for the cattle, or were they there for Micaiah?

The boy carefully raised his head and glanced around. He turned to me. "What now?"

Yeah, that certainly was the question.

(iii)

Before I could answer, I had to say a prayer for Mick and Puff Daddy. Our little circus trick had helped us over the edge of the highway, but it might've meant the death of them and maybe half of our headcount.

If we were down that much money, Micaiah might be our only way to save the ranch. Six million dollars. He'd said he could match what we'd get in Hays if we got fair-market prices for our beef.

"We have to get you to safety," I said. "Then I have to go back and help my sisters." But what could I do? I wasn't even armed. Not even a pistol.

Micaiah didn't argue. We picked ourselves up and crossed the river, jumping from rock to rock to rock to avoid the freezing water. A culvert on the other side took us under another highway.

We paused at the mouth of the tunnel for a minute. Heavy machinegun fire mixed with the explosion of grenades. It sounded like a war on the freeway.

Across the street from us sat an old strip-mall complex, mostly split concrete and yellow-weeded dirt.

We ran through an intersection and across the blasted earth of the parking lot toward a huge building. Glass doors leaned empty— no windows, just tall concrete walls.

I recognized the building as an old Costco. So close to I-70, it would be picked clean.

We could speed through it, come out the other side, and then sweep around to get back to our people.

The broken glass of the doors scratched beneath our boots. Darkness swallowed us. From our vantage point, we couldn't see much of the highway, but we could still hear the remnants of the stampede. And of course, more weapons' fire.

"Should we—"

Micaiah silenced me with a raised hand.

There, in the intersection, five of June Mai's soldiers sat tall on horseback. Fully armed. Scanning around, searching.

We moved further into the darkness. Only dust remained on the floor and some drywall litter. Our shifting feet seemed horribly loud. They weren't, but keyed up, on the run, it sure seemed like the outlaws would hear us.

It got so midnight dark in there that Micaiah finally took my hand. I was glad he did. Not for any romantic reason, but so we'd stay together. My other hand reached and searched so I wouldn't bang into a shelf or box left behind. Finally, we found a wall.

We stopped and waited. Sweat dripped from my nose while we listened. Nothing.

I led Micaiah down the wall. It hooked around into more blackness. We pushed through doors into the rear automotive garage. The bay doors were gone, leaving an open mouth, facing north. I blinked sight back into my eyes and let out a breath.

Micaiah stood at the opening, already looking for more outlaws.

"So do we stay here?" he asked in a whisper. "Or do we try and make a run for it? Maybe circle around to get back to your sisters and the cattle. Or maybe the *Moby Dick* might come looking for us and we can hitch a ride with Sketchy. I hope your people weren't captured."

"Not likely," I said. "Wren would die before she ever surrendered. And you saw how Pilate and Petal were in a fight. I just hope the rest of our crew is okay."

Horses clopped in the distance, women yelled, but their calls faded away, going south. It was prolly the five soldiers we saw out front.

We seemed safe for a minute.

"So what do we do?" he asked.

I did a quick check of my knowledge of local geography and recalled all the planning we'd done. We'd wanted to get across Denver then head north in the valley between the hogsback and the foothills of the Rockies. The way would take us up through the ghost towns of Golden, Boulder, Longmont, and Fort Collins. Rivers ran down from the mountains, so there would be water, and it was pretty remote, so we thought we wouldn't come across any more outlaws.

"We should head for Golden," I said. "If we try and find our people now, we're just as likely to get caught by June Mai's soldiers. If Sharlotte and the others survived, Golden is the most logical rendezvous point."

"If I gave myself up to the soldiers, maybe they would let you go. I mean, that was the plan." His eyes dropped. His chest rose and fell rapidly. He was scared, and not just a little.

"That was Pilate's evil plan," I whispered back. "Not mine."

"What's your plan?" he asked, and he wasn't teasing, not then.

"Can you really pay us six million dollars to get you to Nevada?" I asked.

He nodded.

"Then you are my plan." I said it wrong, like in a romantic way, and I blushed as much as he did, though he didn't turn away. In fact, he got closer.

I stopped him with a hand. Now my own breath was coming fast. "But you're keeping stuff from us. If I bet on you, I need all our cards on the table."

He stiffened and retreated. "You know about the Tree of the Knowledge of Good and Evil from the Book of Genesis, right?"

I nodded. Didn't anticipate Bible study at a time like that.

"Who I am, the fruit I bear, it's the apple, Cavatica. If you know the truth about me, if you eat the apple, you will know things, and that knowledge is poisonous." He swallowed hard. "I won't murder you and your family by telling you the truth. I know it sounds crazy, I know it does, but you'll have to trust me."

He raised his eyes, and I looked into them. I wasn't shy, and I wasn't hateful, and I wasn't even lustful for him. No, a great compassion welled up in my chest. I did trust him.

"So you're telling me you're the apple and not the snake," I whispered. "What about the Tree of Life?"

He closed his eyes. "It's all about the Tree of Life. We have to protect it."

"What if I don't care about staying in Eden?" I asked. "What if I want to eat from the Tree of Knowledge of Good and Evil?"

"I can't do that to you. I can't be the Satan that kills you."

A frown weighed down my face. "All right, Micaiah, okay, but what's gonna happen between you and Sharlotte once we get you to safety? Are you going to tell her the truth?"

"Yes." He said. "But Cavatica, me and Sharlotte, you understand how it is, right?" His eyes said everything else. I closed mine 'cause I couldn't bear to hear what his next words might be. They'd either break my heart or Sharlotte's or maybe both at once.

I moved far away to the other side of the bay. "Let's go. So we run north for a bit, then in Arvada, we can cut over west. We can salvage food, though it won't be easy. This place has been picked over. But Mama taught me a thing or two about finding food tucked away in trash."

My mind shook me back and forth, going over every one of a million scenarios in great bloody detail. All of our headcount dead in the stampede or stolen by June Mai Angel to feed her troops. All of my family and the crew dead. Or maybe Wren, Pilate, and Petal had defeated the outlaws and were worried sick about me and Micaiah. They'd have to track us.

At every bit of leftover wood, I carved "AW" with the "A" and the "W" sharing the "A's" right-side line. It was our brand and

Mama's initials, Abigail Weller, and if Wren were searching for our spoor, she'd see it. Only, what if she were dead?

Or Sharlotte, what if she'd died in the attack?

I'd be left alone with her boy—such a danger to my uncertain heart.

(iv)

That night, Micaiah and I found a suburban ranch-style house, a packrat's nest of paper, so much paper, and a variety of other crapjack not worth a dime. Mama said a hoarder's nest held goodies if you could scrape off the litter. Most salvage monkeys kept right on going to cleaner, easier pickings.

Mama, though, Mama knew.

We shoved our way through the front door and crawled over stacks of old newspapers and magazines. Plastic crap covered the floor where the paper grew thin. Several old sleds, a rack of bins full of junk-drawer leavings, and stacks of old CDs, DVDs, Blu-Rays, and some old-school VHS tapes.

Digging through the mess, the hoarder's nest revealed its treasures. Candles. A tray of canned peaches and several can openers to open them. Spam, which was awful, but it was protein, sealed tight in tin.

I didn't want the candles to give us away, so we made a little space in the basement amid all the trash, and found sleeping bags that weren't too gross. They'd keep us warm at any rate.

I found myself all chatty with him, nervous. Me. Him. Alone.

"We can't go looking for them," I blabbered, "'cause if we go looking for them, June Mai's soldiers are already looking for us, or our people, or our cows, and I guess we knew we'd run into outlaws, but then we thought they'd all be in Burlington, attacking my home. Dang, but won't Howerter be upset if he comes to collect on his loan and all that's left is a smoking hole in the earth. Not that I want my home destroyed, no, and I wouldn't think it would come to that. But I don't know. I keep praying for my family and our team and I just hope we're all going to be okay."

I went on and on while I opened cans of peaches and spam and got our dinner ready. I had iodine tablets in my emergency wallet, and I used them to clean brackish water I found in a ditch behind the house. The candles flickered in our little nest, making it more romantic than I had really wanted, making me even more nervous.

I finally stopped talking and sighed. "I'm sorry. I sound like Sketchy. I'm just afraid of losing my family."

"I understand," he said quietly. "Not that I've ever had a family. Not really."

I leapt on this little bit of information. "You have your Mom and your aunts, right?"

"They grew up fighting," he said. "And my father ..." He shook his head. "He's a real jackerdan. I never, ever, ever, want to see him again."

"I'm sorry about that," I said. "Having a daddy in this world nowadays is rare, and to hate him so much, it's kind of ironic. Kind of sad. But let me tell you, sometimes family doesn't seem like it's worth the trouble. It's like—"

He watched me closely. His intense stare stopped me in my tracks.

"It's like what?" he asked eagerly.

"You know ..." I said, trying to get him to stop staring at me like I had the answers to the universe. I set peaches in front of him and a slice of Spam on a sheet of paper with grids and graphs on it. Some kind of financial report from before the Yellowstone Knockout.

"I don't know," he said. "What's a family like?"

"Well, you have people who've seen you at your worst, and they can tease you forever about it. Like what Wren does. And then you have people who've seen you at your youngest, and they'll never let you forget they changed your diapers. Like Sharlotte. So in all that history, there is so much ammunition, that if you wanted to, you could blast the people you're supposed to love all to pieces."

I flashed back to the bombs I'd dropped on Wren after she told me our Mama was dead in Ms. Justice's office.

"So the history makes it hard to love them?" Micaiah asked, leaving his food untouched.

"And it makes them easier to love. Like one Christmas, Wren got this really fancy saddle, and she never hugged anyone, but she hugged Mama. Mama's face nearly cracked from her smile. Wren was impossible to please, but Mama knew Wren enough to know she loved horses and riding fast and nice things, and that saddle was nice, new in fact. A new saddle, not salvaged, it was quite a present."

Soon after, Wren got in trouble for not cleaning her room. Sharlotte beat her, and Christmas turned into another fight. Love and hate, hate and love, that was at the heart of a family. Sharlotte had prolly been jealous of Wren's new saddle, and took it out on her while trying to mother her. Which is why sisters raising sisters isn't such a good idea.

Sharlotte kept a tally on Mama's love all right, who got what, and how much. What kind of damage had my school tuition caused Sharlotte?

I grinned at Micaiah. He was Sharlotte's present. I'd only used him a little, so he was in fact a hand-me-down, but us Weller girls were used to salvage. Made me grin more.

He raised an eyebrow at me. "What?"

I shrugged and ate a peach. It was sweet and good and a little cold. Just right. "You gonna eat?"

"Yes, but I can't believe you found canned peaches." He picked one up. "Peaches. Such a treat."

"I was vegan for a while in Cleveland," I said. "You get used to the phytonutrients."

"Nice word."

I felt comfortable enough to joke. "For white trash. I know, I know. I don't talk like it, but I'm pretty educated, and I know about the benefits of proper nutrition."

"Yeah, but food is more than that," he said quietly. He stared at the peach in his hand before slowly placing it in his mouth, like it was communion. Eyes closed, he chewed it carefully. When he opened his eyes, they were puddled with tears. "Growing up, they would give me peaches out of a can. Like these. It was better than the other food, much better, so sweet, so sweet. I was always so little, always growing so fast, and always so hungry." His voice went away. The tears trickled down his cheeks, catching the candlelight. He dropped his head.

I ain't never seen a boy my age cry. Heck, I'd rarely seen boys at all. I didn't know how to react.

I needed to comfort him, but any kind of touch seemed to be tempting fate. I wasn't sure what might happen if I felt his skin again.

Risking it, I leaned forward and put my hand on his bare arm. "It's okay to cry in front of me. I don't think it's girly 'strogen."

He laughed at that. "No, I'm certainly a boy. Viable. How could I ever forget it? And I want to feel my feelings. You have no idea how important my feelings are to me."

"And I won't have an idea for a long time, huh?" I asked. "The apple."

"From the Tree of Knowledge," he said, a smile on his lips, a tender expression in his eyes, and tears on his cheeks. He covered my hand with his own.

The electricity of his touch zinged through every part of me. I wanted more. I needed more. The shock of the desire sent me to my feet. I fought to clear my throat. "I'm going to go out and scout around for a minute. I want to see if I can see anything, you know, from the roof. I have to go."

Before he could stop me, I escaped up the steps. I left my coat and gear below and went out in my dress and boots. The night, thank goodness, wasn't frigid, but it was far from warm. I was sweating so much, so churned up inside, I was grateful for the chill.

Okay, it was clear—I couldn't touch him or let him touch me. No way. However, I'd kept my chastity. I hadn't gone for him. But he was putting out signals, and I know for a rich, viable boy, dating sisters or a whole gaggle of girls at the same time might be fine with him, but not for me, not for Sharlotte, not for any good Catholic girl.

I climbed a fence and boosted myself onto the roof, which still had most of its shingles, but not all of them.

Clouds filled up the sky and I smelled the wet smell again. Snow was on its way. Once again, I went through worrying over the cattle drive, my family, our crew.

But Micaiah's Tree of Knowledge mystery joined in. And how he had talked about the peaches, and the pronouns he used— "they" gave them to him. They. It sounded like he hadn't grown up in a family, but more like in some kind of institution setting. He hated his dad, but what about his aunts and his mom?

Secrets. The apple kept safely on the tree lest it poison me, or so he said.

I took in deep breaths, the touch of him, the smell of him, his eyes on me, his hand covering mine.

I couldn't fight my heart anymore, so I let my fantasies have free reign. I pictured us traveling the world on his money—London, Paris, Rome, India, Thailand, Australia. We'd get separate rooms in the hotels 'cause of my high moral standards, and he could afford it. Once we were married, we'd come back to Burlington, to live in the ranch house, 'cause he'd paid Howerter back in full.

Sharlotte was conveniently left out. It was wrong of me, but the thought of Micaiah and me together felt so good that it was easy to forget about reality.

I was so lost in my own little world I jumped when he called up to me in a quiet voice. "Cavatica, are you there?"

"Yeah."

"We should get some sleep. I don't think you need to keep watch."

I went back inside with him and didn't sleep a wink all night.

I listened to Micaiah's breathing and the shuffle of his movements. He was a noisy sleeper, but he never said a word.

His dreams, like his secrets, he kept to himself.

(v)

I woke up to light filtering down through the window wells of the basement. Took me only a second to see Micaiah was gone.

I leaned back into the mound of *Rocky Mountain News* bundles, figuring he'd gone out to relieve himself, and that he would be back.

Hooves clopped above on the back patio's concrete, a horse whinnied loudly, and wild shapes threw shadows across the basement windows.

Something wasn't right. I could feel it.

In a flash, I climbed up stacks of papers and boxes until I could heave myself up to the window. Spider webs clung to my fingers. Spiders scattered.

I ignored them. My eyes were fixed on Micaiah's familiar boots, his jeans. In less than a second, he was scooped up by figures on horseback. All I could see was the gray-colored camouflage pants they wore and the black combat boots on their feet, stuck in stirrups.

Before I could do a thing, the riders stormed away.

Taking Micaiah with them.

CHAPTER SEVENTEEN

During the salvaging days, there were men bandits, but they weren't organized. Queenie was organized. Women know how to come together. I just wish it was for a better purpose than to steal. As for June Mai Angel, I'm not sure she exists. The stories I've heard, well, no Outlaw Warlord could have that many followers and be that organized. June Mai Angel is just Juniper gossip gone bad.

—Abigail Weller
Colorado Courier Interview
June 6, 2057

(i)

I bent and touched the tracks in the dirt of the road. Clouds swirled cold in the early morning sky. The ruins of the suburbs spread out to infinity, and I was a lone girl, standing there with a choice to make. Go north and follow the riders. Or go west to try and find my people in Golden.

I wondered at how capricious the Juniper could be. One minute the boy and I were eating peaches and he's crying, and the next, he's stolen away.

The scales inside of me tipped into balance—the weight of my love for him, Sharlotte's love, and his promise of six million dollars versus my family, my cattle, and the drive.

But how many beefsteaks had survived the stampede? Would there be any left to sell? Or would we lose the ranch to Howerter?

Back and forth, back and forth—my head couldn't make a decision. My boots finally made the decision, my boots connected to my heart by invisible strings of desire and destiny.

Full of *shakti*, I ran north. I still left the AW mark, but I did it hastily, not wanting to lose the spoor of the riders who'd taken the boy.

I hadn't gone a kilometer when Pilate, Petal, and Wren found me.

(ii)

I recognized the ponies first, then the riders. Windshadow came galloping up ridden by Pilate, Lampchop carrying Petal, and Wren fighting to keep control of Christina Pink. The horse's muscles flexed tensely, her eyes slits—that fiery mare wanted to run the Devil down.

Mary B trailed them on long reins. Tina Machinegun was sheathed next to the saddlebags.

"Is Sharlotte okay?" I asked. "Did Mick and Puff Daddy make it?"

"Glad you asked about a human first, then horses," Wren said. "Everyone made it. We dealt with June Mai's girls. Not sure what all them scary stories are about. Got through 'em easy." My sister smiled, showing her perfect teeth, bright and recently flossed, knowing her. In the chill, she wore both her Mortex parka and the wool poncho—both a dark green, I wouldn't have thought the colors would match, but on Wren they did.

Pilate dismounted and threw his arms around me. "Thank God you left a trail for us to follow."

I bristled at his touch and stepped away. The dog. "Yeah, I'm brilliant. But what happened?"

They told me how June Mai's girls had hit our crew, but they had missed Wren, who had been riding separate from the herd, which had been her plan all along. It explained why she drifted around alone, only coming in at night to visit Pilate.

Once the shooting started, Wren gunned down the outlaws from the back while Pilate and Petal hit them from the front.

The outlaws soon gave up on the attack and dragged the fallen beef off the freeway.

Wren smirked. "Yeah, we let those skanks have our roadkill."

Petal, who seemed half asleep on Lambchop, leaned close to Pilate. "We killed all the Jacquelines and Jills, but we're done shooting for a little while, aren't we? I don't want to shoot anyone for a while. And can I have more medicine?"

"Soon, Petal," Pilate said. "And I agree. I think we should avoid any shooting we can."

"How many of the headcount did we lose?" I asked.

"We think about two hundred, but they were still counting them when we took off to find you," Pilate said. He seemed to care, but not Wren nor Petal.

My sister whirled Christina Pink around and around, going forward, looking at the tracks, frowning in concentration, letting the hoof prints in the dirt tell their story. "Did you see who took your boy?" she asked.

I hadn't, not really, but now that I had a posse, I was keen to get him back. I told them everything I knew and finished up by saying, "We're going after him."

Pilate shook his head slowly and firmly. "No, we're not. Micaiah broke off from the herd, and June Mai's bandits leapt on him like coyotes on a calf. Yes, Wren has bested June Mai's soldiers three times now, but if I were throwing dice in Vegas, I would gratefully take my money off the table and get some pie. I love pie."

I had to take a deep breath. If I lost it to crying and screaming, Pilate would throw me over Mary B's saddle and carry me back to Sharlotte. No, I had to be logical and persuasive. "When we lost those two hundred beefsteaks on the freeway, we also lost nearly a half-million dollars. We have a long way to Nevada and we're bound to lose more. The boy is our insurance policy. I won't give up on the ranch, Pilate. I won't."

Petal let out a long, annoyed sigh.

Wren chortled. "Now you're thinking straight, Cavvy. That boy is our meal ticket. Even if he's full of crapjack about his Mama and his money."

"Enough," Pilate snapped harshly. "All of your thinking has been skewed ever since the boy joined our operation. Sharlotte is blind in love, Wren's greed is staggering, and Cavatica is divided right down the middle."

"I just want to save the ranch," I muttered. I didn't meet his eyes. Dumb man had called it all perfectly.

Wren flung me Mary B's reins. "Saddle up, and let's get after them."

"No," Pilate said. "I won't risk our lives for a boy we don't know a thing about, with a story as thin as a communion wafer."

I raised myself up straight, squared my shoulders, and I found the courage to look him in the eye. "I order you to help us get Micaiah back."

"How old are you again?" Pilate smirked.

"I'm Abigail's daughter. I'm family. Wren agrees with me. You, Father Pilate, are an employee of the Weller ranch. And you are outvoted. We go after him."

Pilate opened his mouth.

I knew what he was going to say, so I cut him off. "I won't fight. I'll stay out of harm's way. And I'm sure you'd rather keep an eye on me than send me off alone with June Mai's soldiers still around."

Pilate closed his mouth.

"Are you going to ask me to shoot more?" Petal asked.

He nodded.

"I will," she said. "But first my medicine."

Another nod from Pilate. Sad. But resigned.

(iii)

I didn't see what medicine Pilate gave Petal 'cause I had to get Mary B ready to run. I went through her saddlebags, inventorying the extra clips and grenades, checked her hooves, and then stepped up into her stirrups.

I slid Tina Machinegun out of the sheath. But could I really use her?

A sudden breeze tumbled snowflakes out of the sky, just a few. It'd been threatening bad weather for a while now, and there was no way to tell if all we'd get was spits of snow, or if we'd be buried in a blizzard. The cold air bit any bare skin.

I fixed my cattling goggles into place, then rode off with my posse through the snowfall and under clouds that stretched from horizon to horizon. The houses around us had been salvaged down hard. Some only had their foundations left. Others leaned in tatters, but the whole place felt more like open prairie now than a suburb. No asphalt anywhere, but weeds, grass, and cactus instead.

We rode hard until Pilate told us to stop at the bottom of a hillock. Off our horses, we crept up a hill like mice, slipping some in the slush and mud. Spring snow blasted down wet, cold, and blowing. Grasses shivered in that wind. My Mortex parka kept me dry on top, but my leggings and dress were soon soaked.

At the crest, we dropped to the ground. Petal peered through the Zeiss lens on her rifle, Pilate had his Sino binocs, and Wren used her spotting scope.

Below us sat an abandoned office complex—four buildings, three stories, all connected with bridges on the second stories. In the middle, cottonwoods rose above the rooftops.

Fifty meters away sat a derelict Ford Excelsior with an ASI attachment in the bed—most likely abandoned 'cause the technology of those early steam engines had always been real iffy.

Pilate whispered to Wren, "In those office buildings."

"Prolly waiting to meet up with a larger force. But why did they bring the boy north? June Mai's girls were south."

"No idea," Pilate answered. "They're inside the office, though, lots of places to hide. Very defendable."

"Yeah, if they're lookin', they'll see us comin'."

"Not if we hurry. They're just getting set up. If we go quick, the blowing snow should hide us. We'll sneak in from the north."

Pilate moved his head to look at me. His eyes were colder than the ground we were lying on. "You ordered me here, insisted on coming, and all that's fine. But now I'm taking over. Our first order of business? Father Pilate's ten-second boot camp. You don't know nothin' about nothin'. Not even about your own pimpled butt. You will do as you are told. Arguing means you are choosing to kill us all. If you are shot, it doesn't mean you'll die. You'll continue to fight, no matter what. Which goes back to what I said first. You don't know nothin'. You will die if, and only if, I say it's okay to die. Do you understand?"

I nodded. His words and that mad-dog stare wiped every thought from my mind, including fear.

He went on. "Those are not people down there in that office building. They do not eat, they do not sleep, they do not love their babies. They are killers, and when you're sleeping, they're awake, making plans on the best way to BBQ our horses and deep-fry us. God did not create the women down there. Satan did. And it's our job to rid the world of them. Understood?"

"Yeah," I said.

"Good. Now is not the time to be a Christian. This will go quick. For good or bad. You'll be able to go back to Christianing in a minute."

Pilate and Wren returned to planning, and my job wasn't planning. My job was to do what I was told.

We slid back down the hill, mounted up, and rode quickly around to the north, then back south, through the ever-thickening snow. It covered us, our ponies, everything, in a cold layer of white. Thank you, Lord.

The office park was in good condition, comparatively speaking. A roof covered it, and some of the windows remained intact. The computers would be all gone, of course, and most everything else.

We rode quickly to the west side of the structure. We were out of sight from the windowed bridge connecting the north building to the west. A good place to hide.

My sister had her back against the building and used a little Hello Kitty compact mirror to look into the courtyard behind her. She held up one finger. Did some other signs. I didn't get a thing from them.

Pilate did. He nodded quick. He pointed up.

She nodded back.

All that without talking, and they had a plan. I was clueless.

Pilate tried the door by us. Locked. An unbroken window hung above us.

Pilate bent down to whisper quietly in my ear. I could barely hear it, with the snow pattering on my parka. "You stay here with the horses. But be ready. We think they're in this building, or the one down from us. Okay?"

I nodded.

Pilate climbed up on Windshadow, and I held the reins. Up at the window, Pilate peeked through. He unholstered his Beijing

Homewrecker and waited. The wind gusted, blew snow, then soothed back down.

Next gust, Pilate smashed through the glass, cleared the edges, and hauled himself up.

Petal handed her Mickey Mauser up next. Then followed him. Wren stuffed her coat and poncho into Christina Pink's saddlebags and up she went.

They would go and fight. I would wait.

After tying the horses to a bike rack next to the building, I positioned myself right next to that locked door. The horses were skittish, nosing through the snow to get to the grass, but only to worry at it. They weren't really interested in eating. They could feel it coming. The gunfire, the bloodshed, the death.

I felt like puking. Tina Machinegun's cold metal froze my fingers through my Secondskin gloves.

For a nanosecond, I considered crawling up Windshadow and going into the building, but then decided against it. Pilate would slap the heck out of me. If not him, Wren.

Nope. My job was the horses. And waiting. I tried to pray a little of the fear out of me, even as I prayed for all our safety.

Once again, God had other plans.

An outlaw came around the side of the building, armed with an Armalite AZ3, military issue, brand new. Quite a weapon, it had self-correcting laser targeting, tactical readout, including ammunition count, and water-cooled barrels. Of course the electronics didn't work, but it was still an amazing weapon.

There was nothing Juniper about that rifle or her. Sagebrush camo covered her, everything matched, like she herself was military issued. A holster held a huge pistol under her arm. Short hair boxed in a square, Slavic jaw. She walked with an oily precision, as if she was calculating the energy it took to make even the simplest of movements.

Something was wrong about her. Even from a distance, something was very wrong.

The sight of her froze me to the ground. She wasn't one of June Mai Angel's girls. Who were we fighting? Micaiah's aunts? He'd said they were worse than any Outlaw Warlord. Part of me hadn't believed him.

Right then I did.

That horrible soldier woman threw the fear of God into me and took away every gram of *shakti* I had.

She looked right through those horses and caught me up in a dead stare, no surprise, no emotion—a computer clicking through code. *If, then, else.*

Execute.

She raised her rifle and fired.

(iv)

When the Devil rises up with a machinegun, you don't get to choose how you act unless you are trained. I was a civilian, through and through, and I went on instinct. Unfortunately, all my instincts ran fearful.

Bullets buzzed my face. One clipped my ear.

First thing I did was drop Tina Machinegun.

The woman was bad. Whoever she was, that woman radiated evil.

Before I realized what I was doing, I grabbed Mary B and put her between me and the soldier. 'Cause she wouldn't murder Mary B, right? People don't kill horses in cold blood, right?

Without pausing, she gunned Mary B down right under my hand. The pounding of bullets reverberated through her flesh. The AZ3 fired 7.62 cartridges, which were big and nasty bullets, Teflon-coated, maybe. My pretty pony, my dapple gray, swayed and stumbled, making awful noises. She toppled to lay still in the snow.

I fled behind Lambchop and the soldier shot her, too. Blood flecked my face. The palomino reared then slumped down onto her side. Bloodied. Bloodied something awful.

Hooves hammered the ground around my feet. The two remaining horses kicked and yanked against the bike rack. The metal clanged and squealed, like the horses were squealing. Slaughterhouse shrieks.

The soldier would murder all the horses to get to me. Every single one of them. Well, not if I could help it. I plucked Tina Machinegun off the ground and charged her.

"Don't you kill no more of my ponies!" I yelled. "Kill me, but don't kill any more of my horses!"

She fired, full auto. I took two bullets, the first in my left arm, the next in my upper chest, near my shoulder.

Until Petal, with her Mickey Mauser, shot that soldier girl through the heart. I watched the soldier's head loll back. Blood misted in the air around her.

We both sank to our knees at the same time.

The pain made me gasp—felt like hot coals in my body, and someone was blowing on them to fan the flame.

Above me in the bridge, Petal peered through the scope of her rifle. Pilate and Wren stood next to her.

Through the haze of agony, a plan crept into my head. I heard footsteps running toward me. Good. Let them come and kill me, then my posse could gun them down. They'd escape with Micaiah and save the ranch, and bury me next to Mama, Daddy, and the babies.

Blood dripped down my arm and dribbled down my chest. I figured I'd bleed out, but not before I drew the rest of those soldiers right to me.

The bike rack behind me finally gave way. Christina Pink and Windshadow ran free. Too bad I'd been so cowardly and Mary B and Lambchop had died. Just like I'd done all my life, I'd messed up during a gunfight. Shame on me.

Well, I'd try and make up for my mistake.

I stood and triggered the M320 grenade launcher underneath Tina Machinegun's gun barrel. An MX2 shell floated through the air. It hit the westernmost building and blew a chunk out of the wall.

It was loud, but I wanted to be louder. "Hey, you skanks!" I screamed. "Come and get me!" Dang, but I was so Wren at that moment.

Soldiers charged around the building, armed and firing. All were dressed in the same uniform.

Bullets splashed all around me, but I dove behind Mary B's body, still warm, her flanks smelling like sagebrush. I fished more grenades out of her saddlebags. My fingers were slippery with blood, but I managed to slip a grenade into Tina.

I launched another shell out behind me and another explosion rumbled the ground.

My blood warmed me in my parka, and I grinned. Least I wouldn't die cold.

Pilate, Petal, and Wren opened fire. I prayed to God my plan worked, that they'd get rid of the soldiers and get to Micaiah.

Never seeing Micaiah again made my heart weak. But Sharlotte would. I'd done the right thing. I had to ignore that, so I could reload Tina. I fumbled with a grenade, but my left arm failed me. I dropped the shell. My head was fogging up.

The wind howled sorrow.

More gunfire.

Snow on wet ground.

I could smell Queenie's brains.

I whispered, "Sorry, Mama. Sorry I ain't better in a fight."

Darkness snatched me away.

(v)

I woke to being carried through halls of the office by the scruff of my parka and my feet. Cotton-headed and cotton-mouthed, they must've given me something 'cause the pain felt distant and my mind moved slow, sluggishly dreamy. Snow fell on my face, only it wasn't snow, but flecks of rotted-out ceiling tiles.

Funny, maybe it was the drugs, but I wasn't scared, not right then. Remembering my ponies, though, shot so I could live, I got weepy.

"Don't cry, Cavatica." Pilate's voice broke through muffled and wavering. "You saved us. *Divide et impera*. Divided them up so we could cut them down. Those soldier girls went right for you. Good work."

"But I ran behind Mary B and Lambchop to save myself," I said, "and I dropped Tina Machinegun first thing. I should've been better, but I didn't ... I didn't ..."

"But you did. You're alive. And Mary B adored you, Cavvy. She would've wanted to sacrifice herself to save you. But we have to focus now. I have something important for you to do."

"I'm shot up, Pilate. What can I do?" I asked weakly.

"Don't die. And that's an order."

They carried me across a big room. Collapsed cubicle walls were stacked in the corners. On them lay the bodies of soldier girls, the leftovers of the soldiers who'd grabbed Micaiah. Pilate and

Petal stuck me in the next room, a corner office on bare concrete. Rolled-up carpet lay in one corner leaving the floor covered in fluffy backing like yellow mold. Coils of CAT-6 wire snaked around in a loop near the window.

Stupid salvage monkeys, they'd left behind cabling like they left their Ford out front. Either they'd been lazy or they'd gotten unlucky.

Through broken windows, we had a clear view east into the courtyard and south into the snowstorm blowing.

They put me down into Micaiah's arms. I could tell right away by the hair on his arms and his thick, male fingers. The power of Micaiah's touch made me weepy all over again.

"Hey, Cavatica." Tears thickened his voice. "I heard about how you insisted on coming to get me—how you were going to save me, no matter what."

"No matter what," I said.

"No matter what."

His touch and those words sealed up our love inside them, our treasure chest of a poem only three words long.

Petal peeled off my parka and ripped down my dress top. For a scared second, I thought she'd pull off my brassiere as well. But she didn't. Micaiah could see my underwear though, and my cleavage. I should've been shocked, but it felt so good just to be close to him again.

Petal whispered, "Keep pressure on her shoulder, boy. *Little Jack Horner, sat in a corner, bleeding down his thighs.*"

"I will," he said. He bent down and whispered into my ear, "We're going to get out of this, Cavatica. When we do, things will be different between you and me. I promise."

I closed my eyes at those words and sighed at my need for him. All my desire had been re-ignited by his touch. Then I realized we were missing someone. "Where's Wren?"

Pilate knelt by the east window. "We think more soldiers are coming. If so, she'll flank them like she did in Strasburg and on I-70. Wren's good at that. Shooting people in the back."

"*Besharam besiya,*" Petal spit.

"Love you, too," I murmured. Oh, I was drunk, drugged, sorrowful for losing my horses, in love with the boy nearly standing on my shoulder. Poor Sharlotte. Poor me.

"Cavatica got lucky, Pilate. Her wounds are really nice." Petal's voice scratched out.

"Why's that?"

"Two shots, clean through. Arm's only a flesh wound. The one in her upper chest, the bullet glanced off her clavicle, but didn't break it. She'll live." She ripped open a package of U.S. military-grade instant sutures and pressed them into my skin.

I had nice wounds. I found that funny. I laughed.

"Can she fight?" Pilate asked.

"Yes. I have something to help her."

I stopped laughing.

A heartbeat later, a woman's voice called from the courtyard through the wind, whistling across the broken glass. "To our enemy in the office building!"

Pilate jerked himself back from the window. "Reinforcements," he said in a hiss.

"We know you are in there! We know you have the boy!" The voice cut cleanly, sharpened by a precise, Yankee accent.

We fell silent in our corner office. Of course we weren't going to give away our position by answering. Micaiah and me were up against the western wall, the full spread of windows before us. Pilate and Petal were crouched against the north wall.

I swallowed against my fear, then whispered, "Pilate, those aren't June Mai Angel's girls. They ain't dressed right, and they have AZ3s, brand new by the look of 'em. Do you know who they are?"

"No," Pilate said, "and I hate being shot at by people I don't know."

"Micaiah, were those women sent by your aunts?" I asked.

Before he could answer, the woman's voice lashed out again. "We have one of your people. We will shoot her in the head if you do not answer."

Wren. They'd captured Wren.

Pilate spun on Micaiah. "What do you know?"

Micaiah met his gaze. "You have to be careful. They can fight better than anyone you've ever met. And aim for the head."

"Why is that exactly?" Pilate's mouth twitched like he was holding in a snarl. "Dammit, kid, you should've been straight with us from the beginning. If we die, I'm going to beat the truth out of you." Pilate paused, grinned. "Wait, no, I'll beat you before we die. It'll work better that way."

The voice from below. "You will give us the boy. You have sixty seconds to bring him out, or we will kill your woman."

Not just a woman. My sister.

"I'll deal with you later," Pilate said to Micaiah. Then to Petal, "Okay?"

Petal nodded. And suddenly, they had a plan. I guess if you spend years fighting wars together, you too can have such telepathy.

Pilate took off out of the office, Petal came over and started wrapping a bandage around me. Where did she get a bandage? She wrapped it tight, quickly and well. "Cavvy, you and your boy, you'll have to shoot from this office. I'm going to find another place. *Maybe in London, to see the queen.* Don't let them see you in here. Don't fire until you hear me. You'll hear Mickey Mauser. *Hickory dickory dock. Mickey shot up the clock.*" Petal leaned in close. She reeked. "We took the AZ3s off the soldier girls, and we have a bundle here, so don't re-load. Just grab the next one. Quicker. Make sure the safety is off. Aim lower than you think. The kick will buck the barrel. Buck the barrel. That's fun to say. Buck the barrel." Then she fell into a rhyme.

Oh little soldier
come play with me
and bring your bullets three
Climb up my rifle
Slide into your grave
You're dead if you're a sally
You're dead if you're a dave

Petal pressed a strip of EMAT against my neck. EMAT stood for Emergency Medical Absorption Tape, and it was a way of delivering drugs to someone in a combat situation. My skin would absorb the drugs. Petal whispered, "A little pick you up and up and up. *To the sky, smiling. But the sky is falling, the sky is falling, the sky is falling down.*"

Not sure what chemical was on the adhesive, but my heart thudded up, kickstarted, and suddenly I could see everything around me in crystalline detail.

Petal left the room lugging Mickey Mauser and murmuring rhymes about Chicken Little.

Micaiah crawled over and pulled an AZ3 out of a pile. I slid over up against the north wall with Tina Machinegun pressed against my good shoulder. Out the south window, I could see the horses of the soldier girls, tied to the handrail of the southernmost building. The horses sure were pretty in the snow.

I blinked and found myself staring at Micaiah. He was sweaty, pale, my blood crusting on his hands. I felt embarrassed by that. Not sure why. My blood on his hands. It felt so intimate.

"Looks like your forbidden fruit might get us killed even though you've kept the apple in your pocket," I said.

"I'm sorry." He winced.

"It's okay." It wasn't, but now was not the time for any sort of deep discussion. I gripped Tina Machinegun, and slowly inched myself to my left until I could see out into the courtyard.

Two dozen soldier girls in sagebrush camo stood ready to fight. There were so many. How could we fight them all? We needed to get out of there, run away like Chicken Little 'cause it certainly felt like the sky was falling down.

Two soldiers restrained Wren. One of the soldiers pressed my sister's own Colt Terminator against her head, hair frosty with snowflakes. Her hands were bound behind her back.

Next to them stood the leader. It was the same woman who had killed the horses to get to me—the very same woman that Petal shot. But how could she still be standing? I could see the bloodstains on her chest. Even if Kevlar covered her chest, Petal's bullet had hit her.

Aim for the head. Micaiah's words. A shiver tickled my neck.

"You are out of time," the leader woman shouted.

Pilate's voice boomed from under us. "Hello ladies, I'm Father Pilate. If you kill me, well, first of all, that's a sin. Sixth commandment I believe. Or is that the one about coveting thy neighbor's manservant? I can never remember." A pause. "Kill me, we kill your rich, viable boy."

"He's just bluffing," I whispered to Micaiah. He nodded, all nervous. I was too drugged for nervous.

Pilate ambled into view, his bandolier of ammo crossing his chest and his Homewrecker dangling in his hand. "I'm Father Pilate. And who may I ask am I fighting today?"

The leader woman didn't answer. "All we want is the boy. Give him to us and you will live. Refuse us and you will all die." She chose each word precisely, without a hint of emotion.

Pilate laughed. "Shy about who you are? Well, I see you certainly are well armed. And you all have very similar fashion sense. Very military. Answer me this, though. How do we know you won't harm the boy? Some of us like him. I don't, personally, but I can't just give him to you."

The woman opened her mouth.

Before she could make a sound, Pilate spoke five words as casually as you please.

"Mary had a little lamb."

CHAPTER EIGHTEEN

We made good money recycling brass, nickel, and aluminum from shell casings. Sure were a lot of bullets lying around in the Juniper.

—Calvin "Crush" Jones
60 Minutes Interview
April 27, 2037

(i)

ary had a little lamb
She also had a gun.

That was how Petal had started the nursery rhyme before.

Not sure where she was or how she finished it this time, but she failed to make the headshot. The leader woman took the bullet in the neck and wheeled backwards.

Next to me in the corner office, Micaiah opened up on his AZ3, and the noise made my head explode. Gunfire in a tight room is like having your eardrums plucked out of your head, hit with a hammer, and then stuffed back into your ear canal with an ice pick.

Since my left arm was iffy, I rested Tina Machinegun on my knee and took aim at the soldiers in the courtyard. I pressed the trigger, but it wouldn't press.

"Dammit." Forgot the safety.

The horses of the soldier girls screamed, trying to get away, but they were tied down. Well, not for long. I took aim and fired burst after burst until a bullet snapped through the braided rope tied to the handrail and the horses disappeared into the storm. Good.

I turned back to the courtyard battle.

Wren head-bashed one of the soldiers near her, then drove a knee into another. The soldiers scattered as Petal's Mickey Mauser tore them apart. Pilate yelled, "Matthew! Mark! Luke! John!" as he took 'em out in groups.

"Gospel writers," I said. That was how Pilate kept track of his ammunition.

More soldiers were pouring in—or running away—it was hard to tell. I fired twice before the action on Tina Machinegun snapped open. My clip was empty. I'd used all my bullets to free the horses.

Bullets pocked the walls of our hideout.

I dropped Tina and grabbed an AZ3, following Petal's orders. Back against the north wall, I looked out.

Wren stood with her hands over her head, handcuffed. She'd wriggled herself through her own arms, to get the cuffs in front of her. Then again, handcuffs on Wren were like Hello Kitty charm bracelets on most girls.

She held her hands over her head, but only for a second. The chain melted—Petal aiming true. Wren was thrown back. Either ducking or shot. I aimed at anything around her that moved.

My gun clicked dry, and I slammed in another clip.

"Cavvy!" Pilate shouted. "Petal! Get out of the offices! Now! Get out now!"

"What the …" Micaiah started, but I wouldn't let him cuss.

I cradled Tina Machinegun in my bad arm and used my good arm to shove him out of the room.

A second later, I found myself on the floor, face first, blinking away concrete dust, ceiling tile snowflakes, general explosion debris. They'd hit the corner office with some sort of artillery shell.

Micaiah helped me up. I leaned on him, and we hurried through the big main room, toward the stairs.

I couldn't swallow. Dust coated my throat. My left hand on Tina Machinegun was tacky with blood, from my wounds bleeding again. Didn't feel the pain and my thoughts were still moving slippery quick from the patch on my neck.

Micaiah and I shuffled down the steps and out into the courtyard. Petal didn't join us. Wren was also gone. I prayed both were okay.

Pilate and the leader woman stood there, guns in their hands, both staring each other down before they reloaded, feeling each other out to see who might be quicker.

The torn flesh of the leader woman's neck wound made me wince. What was she? Surely not human. If we hadn't been in the Juniper, I would've sworn she was some cyborg thing, but robotics like that would need electricity.

She held a speedloader for her revolver, a Desert Messiah. Pretty much a hand-cannon packing huge bullets with a diameter base of 13.9 millimeters. Blow a woman's head clean off.

Pilate held another shell for his Homewrecker.

Of course, Pilate started chatting.

"Nice trick, coming back from the dead," he said with a smart-aleck grin on his face. "Zombie much?"

The woman answered as if she were following a script even though her voice gurgled horrifically. "If you do not give up the boy, you will die. Others assets will come for him."

Pilate laughed. "Assets. Aren't you just so black-ops? I have to know who you are. Actually, a better question is *what* are you? And why do you want Micaiah enough to come back from the dead to get him?"

The leader woman was sweating. Good. At least she was human enough to sweat. Her eyes flickered over Micaiah and me in the doorway of the building. She sure wasn't acting like he was her nephew.

"Stay there, Cavatica," Pilate said. "I'll get her. Or I might not have to. She should be about to drop any minute from her wounds."

Didn't look like it to me. Her color was good, like she'd been dancing at a party and spilled fruit punch down her chest.

Pistol shots. Wren's Colt Terminators pocked from the other side of the buildings.

"Pilate," Micaiah said. "Aim for the head. The other women can't heal as well as my aunts can."

I felt my eyes go wide. "Is that one of your aunts?"

He nodded. Lines of sweat etched through the dust on his skin.

The woman kept her eyes on Pilate. "We have severely underestimated you, and so I will attempt to negotiate. You said you did not like the boy. If you give him to us, you will be rewarded even after this confrontation. We could give you millions. More money than you could spend in a lifetime."

"Who are you?" Pilate asked.

The leader opened her mouth to answer, but didn't get a word out. Wren came sauntering from the south, all hips and strutting. Her Colt Terminators filled her hands. Blood dripped off her boots, making rusty footprints in the snow. "Hey you. I killed all your skanks, and now I'm gonna kill you."

Pilate yelled out, "Wait, Wren!"

Words weren't gonna stop my psycho sister. She raised her Colts. Pilate shoved a shell into his open quad cannon. The leader woman was quicker than both of them. She was blurry fast. Reload, click, snap, and her Desert Messiah fired three times and hit Pilate twice. One bullet grazed his head. Another pierced his chest. He fell back, coughing wetly, firing, but poorly. The Homewrecker shell whirled up over the leader woman's head and hit the south building, blowing out a chunk of concrete.

Pilate fell to his knees. He was working to get another shell out, but his hands were shaking too bad. Blood gushed from his scalp and dribbled from his mouth.

It was all happening faster than I could move. Same for Micaiah.

Wren ducked to the snow to avoid the gunfire from the leader woman, but my sister was up in a minute, firing. The .45 slugs thumped into the leader's chest. Didn't stop her at all. She charged Wren. Both women struck each other like freight trains derailed and heading for destruction.

Wren took a swing, but the leader woman dodged it, took her Desert Messiah, and smacked Wren right in the face. Dropped my sister like a bad habit. That sparked me. I raised Tina Machinegun.

Pilate's Homewrecker clicked shut, he'd reloaded.

The leader woman snatched Wren up by her hair, threw an arm around her throat, and put her revolver right to my sister's temple.

"The boy! Now!"

"Goddammit, Cavvy!" Wren screeched. "You blow this *kutia's* head off right now or I'm gonna beat your ass. Kill her! Kill me if you have to! Just get her!"

I looked down Tina's sights, but couldn't shoot. I couldn't make that shot on a sunny day, let alone wounded, in snow, adrenaline roaring in my ears.

The leader woman locked eyes with me. I felt like I was having a staring contest with a rattlesnake. "You cannot kill me," she started, "I am—"

Wren jammed her Betty knife through the leader woman's thigh, snatched the Desert Messiah out of her grip, and shot the woman through the head. Didn't stop until her skull was a smudge in the snow.

I expected some funny quip from Pilate, but he was on his knees. His Homewrecker quivered in his hand before it fell from his hand.

He tumbled over. His chest wound wheezed, like a whistle in meat. He'd been shot in the lung with a large caliber weapon.

A wound like that, without a doctor, he'd die.

(ii)

Wren screamed and cursed.

I thought she was upset about Pilate or my failure at not taking the shot, but then I made out some words. "Skank knocked out my teeth. Knocked out my good front ones. Goddammit. Goddammit."

She started to weep.

She tripped over to me, big fat tears mixing with the blood on her face, her eyes wounded and vulnerable. Nice to see human eyes after dealing with the demon soldiers we'd been fighting. But still, Wren crying? I wasn't quite sure it was real.

"How bad did she get me, Cavvy?" she asked. "How ugly am I now?"

My mind spun with what I might say but nothing came out. The drugs in my system coated my every thought in grease. Too much going on—Pilate dying next to me, Petal missing, and Wren finally showing some emotion. Not about people, but her own vanity. It made me want to cry myself. My strong, gunfighter sister, weepy over her lost beauty.

She slumped to her knees in front of me and took my hands. "I need my pretty, Cavvy. I need my pretty!"

She opened her mouth. Both of her front teeth were gone, the bottom ones cracked jagged. "How bad is it?"

Broken nose, broken teeth, even healed, she'd look like a Juniper hard luck story, a hillbilly, like Dolly Day Cornpone.

Didn't have the heart to tell her that. And we had other problems. Pilate continued to bleed. "Micaiah, can you help him?" I asked.

Micaiah looked pale even under the layer of dust coating him. He shook his head.

Wren noticed Pilate for the first time, and she darted over to him. "Petal! Petal, we need you! Petal!" Panic raged in her voice.

I didn't know how a sniper could help us.

A dusty Petal stumbled out of the building at last. She limped on her right leg, gashed up bad. She leaned Mickey Mauser carefully against a wall, then bent over Pilate and put her ear to his chest.

Didn't need to do that. His chest whistled loud despite the wind. Collapsed lung. Might as well get the shovels out.

Petal sprang to her feet. "Take him into the office building. Hurry. I'll get my bag of tricks." She limped off, half-running.

"What can she do?" I asked.

"Petal's a doctor. She'll help." Wren slammed a fresh clip into an AZ3 and slid the strap over her shoulder. "I'll find more skanks to kill for making me ugly. I'll kill 'em, kill 'em all. But first Pilate. God, I don't know what I'll do if he goes."

He couldn't die. We wouldn't let him. But how could Petal be both a doctor and a sniper?

Wren and Micaiah carried Pilate into the office building. Inside, wires trailed down the scratched-up walls. Drywall scraps dusted over bare concrete, but we found a swatch of carpet and laid Pilate on top of it. Outside the western window, snow drifted up the glass.

Petal came back with a black bag, a bottle of Pains whiskey, and more bandages. She and Wren stripped Pilate, revealing his hairy, muscled torso. A little red hole puckered the white skin of his chest. Blood foamed around the edges.

Dead for sure. Pilate dead. Hard thought to hold in my head.

"Cavvy," Wren barked, making me jump. "Go find our horses. Petal needs me, and you don't want to see all this blood."

I went to protest, but Wren wouldn't have it. She shoved the AZ3 into my hands. "Shoot to kill, little sister. These *kutias* deserve every bit of hurt we can give 'em."

I staggered outside, trembling, my mind still a mess from the drugs and violence. Wren was right, my job was the horses, and they'd come back to me if they'd come at all.

Snow fell in whipping tornados. My wet leggings and dress froze stiff. I put up a hand, squinted, and ran to where Lambchop and Mary B lay dead half buried under white drifts. The blizzard had scraped the ground clean of any tracks.

I circled the northern section. Then I saw one of the horses, out of the wind and protected by the eastern section. "Christina Pink!" I yelled. "Come over here, girl!"

For once, she listened and trotted over. I brushed some snow off her and petted her nose. "You seen Windshadow around? Can you help me?"

She reared and went to pull away. Such a foul-tempered horse. I figured she missed Wren, since birds of a feather flock together.

I got her settled enough to slip a boot into the stirrup. On horseback, I was higher, but still couldn't see a thing, not even a couple meters.

I circled around to the southern building, to where the enemy horses had been tied. Those ponies were long gone, but stacked next to the wall were five twenty-liter geri fuel cans. They were lined up in a row like green upright soldiers. My heart shivered in my chest. I got off Christina Pink and walked over.

"Can't be," I whispered.

I flipped open the container and took a whiff. The rank smell of diesel greeted me. The geri cans were not from the salvaging days, no way. So the mysterious soldiers who grabbed Micaiah didn't have just horses, they had other vehicles, diesel-powered. Had to be diesel 'cause straight-up gasoline engines needed continuous electricity to work. Some engineers had worked on a flint-and-steel type of ignition system for gas engines, but there hadn't been a market for it. Not a lot of gas left in the world, and what was around was a ton of money. Diesel was just as expensive. How could Micaiah's aunts afford it all?

I didn't know. But those geri cans meant soldiers were coming back. Another round for us to fight, and we were all so wounded. We had to get out of there and quick.

I gave up on trying to find Windshadow. If Pilate lived, he'd be heartbroken. He loved that horse.

CHAPTER NINETEEN

You think the Sino was about Taiwan? Please. A hundred years ago China invaded Tibet and only actors and poets seemed to mind. No, the Sino-American War wasn't about invasion. It was about a half-a-trillion dollar trade deficit. That's a whole lotta of Hayao tablets, made in China and shipped to the U.S. And all we gave them was blue jeans and cheeseburgers.

—Former President Jack Kanton
48th President of the United States
Unconfirmed comments from a private conversation
August, 2057

(i)

I led Christina Pink into the western section of the office complex and twisted her reins around a rail in the hallway. She shook to stamp the snow off. Her hooves on the cement sounded like pistol shots. I was already on edge when I heard Wren howl.

I sped into the main room and right into a horror movie. Wren was bent over next to the window in nothing but her jeans and a brassiere. She clutched the bottle of Pains whiskey in a fist. Petal knelt next to her. Our sniper turned doctor held forceps over Wren's bloody back. The forceps must've come from Petal's bag of tricks. Petal, a doctor, still couldn't quite believe it, but who was I to argue with such a miracle?

Micaiah cringed off to the side, looking terrified and miserable. He'd found a coat for himself, scavenged off one of the fallen soldiers. It was thick, looked real warm and nice with synthetic fibers and a compressed down lining. Prolly found gloves and a hat as well. But not better boots. Those alligator ones were still on his feet.

Wren straightened, took a long pull of the Pains whiskey that must've hurt like hell on her broken teeth. Way she was tipping that bottle, though, it looked like sobriety hurt more.

Petal screeched, "*Besharam besiya*, let me give you a shot!"

"No, gotta save the painkiller for Pilate and Cavvy," Wren wheezed back. After another hit from her bottle, she bent over again. "I got Pains whiskey. Pains for the pain just like in the newspaper advertisements. Come on, Petal. Here's your chance to hurt like you always wanted. You saved Pilate. Now save me."

Relief made me feel light. Pilate alive. He lay on his back, with some kind of little tent on his chest. His bandolier coiled in a pile beside him.

Petal dug into my sister's body, and she caterwauled until Petal withdrew.

Wren laughed jaggedly. "Oh, that was a good one, Rosie. Now, you're lovin' this, right? You did good with my nose. That's the important thing. Once we cash out in Nevada, I'll go and have everything put right. Find me a good plastic surgeon and a better cosmetic dentist. Now, Rosie, hit me again! Get on that jackerdan!"

Wren screamed worse than ever.

Petal removed her forceps from my sister's flesh and dropped the bullet to the floor. "Got it. *Little bug, little bug, fly away home. Your house is on fire and your children are all stoned.*"

I let us all get a breath in, and then I hit them with the bad news. I told them about the cans of diesel and what they meant.

Wren whistled. "Your boy must've grown up sleeping in gold-plated beds. Whoever has that kind of money, well, we should go through the pockets of those dead girls out there."

"No," I said. "We have to run."

Wren took a last gulp and then capped the bottle. She made no motion to cover up even though Micaiah could clearly see her cleavage. She gave me a close-mouthed grin. "Run? That involves me getting sweaty and not in the good way."

"Wren!" I wished she wouldn't say such things. And I wished she'd put on a shirt.

Petal finished cleaning Wren's wound and then applied instant sutures. "Now, Irene, this is important." Her words came out urgent, panicked. "I need my medicine. It will be in Pilate's saddlebags on Windshadow. I found Lambchop dead, found my bag of tricks, but I couldn't find Windshadow. Please, I need my medicine."

"I looked," I said, "but I only found Christina Pink. But really, we have to get out of here before more soldiers come."

The room fell quiet. Wind gusted against the window, shaking it. Snowflakes pecked the glass.

"No!" Petal wept, wringing her hands, face twisted with terror. "No, no, no. I need it. You don't understand."

Her whole demeanor changed, and it was like watching a demon possession in progress. Petal pushed her face into Wren's. "You lie, you jackering *kutia* skank. You lie! You have my medicine. You do."

Wren took a step back, "Easy, Rosie. Easy."

I also took a step back.

Petal shrieked her nonsense rhyming.

Jack and Jill killed the hill
and murdered each other beside her!

Micaiah approached Petal bravely. "It's okay. It's okay."

It wasn't. That strange woman seized him in a Judo hold, quick as spit. In seconds, she had her arms around his neck, squeezing the life out of him.

"Where's my medicine?" Petal howled. Her eyes were inky marbles in her face.

Little Jack Horner, sat in a corner,
eating my medicine pie!

Both Wren and I went for Petal, but Wren, even post-operation, was faster. She ripped Petal off Micaiah, and the two women squared off. I stayed back.

"You don't want to be doing this, Rosie," Wren said.

Petal didn't answer. Instead she whirled, plucked a Colt Terminator out of Wren's holster, and struck my sister across the forehead. "I want my medicine now! Now!"

My sister didn't fight back. Instead, she touched blood trickling down her eyebrow. "You patched me up not a minute ago, and now you're making more work for yourself. Cavvy would call that ironic."

I thought about going for Petal, but I knew I wouldn't be fast enough and I didn't want anyone to get shot.

Micaiah rose from the floor and moved in front of Petal. If she fired, he'd take the bullet in his chest. "First do no harm. Didn't you take that oath when you became a doctor?"

"First do no harm," Petal whispered. All the fight dribbled out of her.

"That's right. First do no harm." Micaiah eased the pistol out of her hands and gave it to Wren.

Petal went from fighting to pleading. "Micaiah, I need my medicine. Please."

*Jack and Jill swallowed a pill
and it made it all better forever.*

"I'll see what I can do," he said.

She leaned into him and whispered in a scratch, "I'll die without it."

*Little Miss Muffet,
dead on her tuffet,
meds eaten all away.*

"Petal, don't you have any in your bag of tricks?" Micaiah asked. "I mean, you had all this other stuff. I don't—"

"No!" Petal shouted. "Pilate kept me on a schedule because I liked it too much. I'm late for it now. I'm sick, Johnson, so sick."

Wren shouldered on her ivory-colored shirt and moved over to me. She didn't button up her shirt, and I found myself looking at her belly button. Ugh.

"I'm fixed, but how bad are you hurt, Cavvy?" she asked in a cloud of booze-breath.

"Not too bad," I lied.

"Don't believe that," Wren said. "Funny, but we're all bleeding except your boy. He's quite the Prince Charming, letting a bunch of girls save his skinny ass, and then keeping secrets from us." She sat with her back to the window. She took her whiskey bottle and splashed some on some extra bandages, then pushed them against her head.

I paced. "Please. We need to go." My head was still going a million kilometers an hour.

"Hold up, Cavvy." Wren said quietly. "Let's get Petal taken care of first."

It was hard to stay still, but I watched as my boy helped Petal.

First he laid her down next to Pilate on the floor. Then he took his coat, rolled it up, and put it under Petal's head. He then went to her leg, slashed up by shrapnel.

"I don't care about my leg," Petal said. "I need my medicine. How are you going to help me without my medicine?"

"I'm going to nurse the nurse," Micaiah said and ripped open a package of antibacterial wipes. He gently cleaned the wound.

"I wasn't a nurse," Petal murmured. "I was Dr. Rose Wilson, MD. I was a field surgeon. I didn't want to go to the Sino. I hated the war. I protested it. I occupied Washington DC, in fact. No more war. No more war."

The Sino really had turned her from a doctor into a sniper. Like it had turned Pilate into whatever he was. I crossed to the window to look out, but I couldn't see anything. Maybe the other soldiers were taking cover. The storm seemed bad enough to drive even inhuman zombie women to seek shelter.

Micaiah continued to carefully, mercifully, tend to Petal's wounds. "Yeah, the Sino was bad news. If you were so against it, how come you went?"

Petal sighed a little. "In the end, everyone went. The draft. Everyone I knew died. Everyone except for Pilate. I had to become a sniper. I had to. It all changed in the Hutongs."

The Battle of the Hutongs in Beijing. It was both a Gettysburg and an Iwo Jima. The body count and bloodshed made both of them battles look like schoolyard scuffles.

Petal's face changed. Each word became more agonized. The minute she said that word, Hutongs, she started to weep. "My medicine. I need my medicine. I can't talk about it. I can't get to the other side. Pilate said there wasn't another side for people like us. Don't make me talk about it. I'll die. I'll die, it hurts so bad."

Micaiah shushed her gently. "No, Petal, we're not going to talk about the Hutongs. We'll talk about me. You know, I wanted to be a doctor when I grew up."

I listened carefully. Micaiah was talking about his past.

"I guess it made sense," he said. "I was around all these doctors and scientists all the time, watching them. The human body is amazing, a miracle. Even more fascinating? The mind, our logic, our emotions."

Micaiah gently applied instant sutures, all the while talking and soothing her. She was relaxing, but she could mutate into a demonic harpy at any minute. What was her medicine? And where could we get some more? My sister was right. We had to help Petal before we could run.

The boy picked up her black bag and brought it over to the window, where Wren sat and I stood. We all crouched down so we could whisper.

"How much do you two know about what Pilate's been giving her?" Micaiah asked.

"Nothing," I said.

"None of my business," Wren said at first, but then sighed. "You and I both know what her medicine is, Johnson. So cut to the chase. Is there any in there?"

Micaiah rummaged through Petal's bag of tricks.

"How do you guys know what her medicine is?" I asked. "Or are you both doctors too?"

"Hush, Cavvy," Wren said, "and you better pray there's enough for both of you. Once that first round of drugs and your adrenaline wears off, you're going to be one hurtin' pup." When she talked, she kept her hand near her mouth—to hide her mouth now that her pretty smile was gone. It didn't do much to hide the stink of her drinking though.

"I think I found what we need." Micaiah pulled out a length of rubber tubing, a syringe still in its plastic, and a vial. "Diacetyl-morphinesextus. Otherwise known as Skye6."

Skye6 was a synthetic morphine, real easy to make, and real

cheap. One more miserable thing that the Sino gave to this weary world. I choked in a breath.

If Petal was a Skye6 addict, then Pilate had helped to keep her addicted. The son of a skank.

"How can he do it to her?" I asked. "How can he keep her hooked, and how can she believe it's medicine and not narcotics?"

Micaiah shook his head sorrowfully. "I don't know. But sometimes people can make themselves believe crazy things."

"Yes, they can," Wren muttered. "And what Petal and Pilate have is complicated. Suffice to say, we've seen Petal off her meds, so we'll give her what she needs."

Complicated. Like what Pilate and Wren had. Like, me, Micaiah, and Sharlotte. I sighed.

"How much do we give her?" Micaiah asked.

I held out a hand.

He gave me the vial. Words were scrawled across a white label in Sharpie marker—the name of the drug and two-hundred milligrams, a slash, and a twenty milliliters. I shook it in my right hand, my left hanging limp. There wasn't but a quarter left. "Feels like five milliliters left, which I bet is the dose. Four doses per vial. We got lucky."

"Dang, Cavvy," Wren said. "That's impressive."

"We have two more vials." Micaiah loaded up the syringe and removed the air inside like any doctor drama you ever saw. He'd loaded a rig before. Obviously. "Eight doses. When the time comes, Cavvy, I think I'll try and give you a half-dose. You won't have Petal's tolerance."

"No," I said. "I don't want that evil drug in me."

Wren shook the whiskey in her bottle. "I'll try and save some of this for you, but I can't promise anything. Hard for me to stop until I see the bottom of the bottle."

"No whiskey. No drugs. I'll be fine."

Wren laughed at that. "Whatever you say, Princess." Then she shook her head. "You guys are brilliant. Even you, Johnson. And I thought you only had your looks and your viability."

Micaiah moved away and talked in quiet whispers to Petal. She woke up long enough for him to tie the rubber tube around her arm and to slip a needle into her vein. To dope her up like Pilate had been doing.

I would never forgive Pilate for keeping her so enslaved. Never. Micaiah moved back. "We need to get out of here."

"Yes, we do," I said.

The wind died down, and that was when we all heard the roaring sound in the distance. It'd been a long time since I'd heard such a noise.

Internal combustion engines, a lot of them, coming toward us. Say what you will about diesel engines, but they do have a distinctive sound.

We'd waited too long.

(ii)

Wren buttoned up her shirt, threw on her leather vest, and retrieved an AZ3 from the floor. She snapped back the action. "Cavvy, you run with the boy. Pilate and Petal will be fine here while I take care of the new batch of skanks. I'm going to make them pay for bustin' out my teeth."

I'd watched Mama argue with Wren, then Sharlotte, and I'd even tried it myself. It was useless. I couldn't stand up to Wren, couldn't fight her, and reasoning with her even in the best of situations was an iffy proposition. Yet I'd have to try. We couldn't fight the reinforcements coming for the boy. Pilate was down and Petal was nodding.

The time for fighting was over. It was time for thinking. And for engineering. I knew exactly what we needed to do.

I took a deep breath, steadied myself, and spoke in a strong voice. "Fifty meters north of the office complex is a truck with an ASI attachment, prolly the 3.0.3—the very worst release ever to come out of Detroit. Most likely, some salvage monkey got fed up and left it for another vehicle. If I could get the truck up and running, we'd have our getaway."

Wren immediately listed off everything that was wrong with my plan. Might as well have been talking with Sharlotte. "That's crazy, Cavvy. We ain't got time for you to fiddle with no engine. And where would we get the wood? No, you take the horse. I'll stay and hold them off."

"Give me ten minutes to see if I can get the truck moving. Might be fine, just abandoned, but I won't know if I don't look at it. In the meantime, you get Pilate and Petal ready to move. Micaiah can search for wood."

Wren cut me off. "Ten minutes? Yeah, we both know that's twenty minutes in engineer talk. If not an hour. Even if you could get it working, they'll hear the ASI. Come right for it."

"With the wind blowing? Over them loud internal combustion engines? Not a chance. Come on, Wren. You can't fight 'em all."

She looked me dead in the eye. "I've spent my whole life looking for a fight I can't win. Why do you think I came on this cattle drive?"

"Don't kill us in the process. When it was time for fighting, you fought. You saved us. Now it's time to run. Let me be the hero. Let me save us."

"Save us?" Wren smirked. "You couldn't save me not an hour ago. You didn't take the shot. Again. Seems to me you ain't much of a hero."

"Maybe not with a gun," I said. I felt the heat in my face, ashamed, and I had to look away. I couldn't fight her, but maybe she'd take pity on me.

Micaiah shuffled a bit. Petal sighed. The wind sighed with her. With it blowing, we couldn't hear the diesel engines.

"Okay, Cavvy," Wren said. "I'm giving you ten minutes, not a second more. I'll gather up the troops. You get going, Princess."

"Not princess. Engineer," I said with a nervous smile. I scooped up Tina Machinegun and sped out of the room.

The snow dropped down in swirling walls of white and cold and I thought about Petal's rhyme. The sky was falling, Chicken Little, but I wasn't going to let the world end.

I kicked my way through thirty centimeters of snow and got to the truck, a Ford Excelsior, with fat, deep-treaded snow tires. Lucky us. Thank God, His Son, and all the angels and saints in Heaven for the blizzard. It would hide our escape.

But what about Sharlotte and our headcount? Would they survive the storm? Or had the soldiers in the vehicles already found them and killed them all? Couldn't think about that.

Couldn't think about Sharlotte at all right then.

(iii)

I opened the driver's side door and a skeleton in rags tumbled out causing me to curse and shiver. Didn't calm my racing brain any. My thoughts were like skipped stones across a stormy pond.

Maybe the engine was just fine, I reasoned, and the poor salvage monkey just got unlucky. No time to check for cause of death.

I stepped over the bones and set Tina Machinegun on the passenger seat. The Ford was junked up, pipes and debris scattered around. Had the dead salvager been killed while trying to fix the thing? Seemed like it. Even if there was something seriously wrong, all I needed was steering and propulsion. I turned the steering wheel. The over-sized tires twisted in the snow.

The wind whistled like the Devil in church. After a mighty gust, it died down enough for me to hear the diesel engines again. How far away? Impossible to tell. The wind might be carrying the sound.

Dry kindling, split logs, and round trunks of wood lay heaped in the back of the cab. Greasy, disintegrating rags filled the cracks. We had fuel for the engine. Thank God.

I rushed out and around to the bed and swept snow off the ASI attachment. I could check components later. I needed a fire. I was a little afraid even with the wind blowing, the oncoming soldiers might see the smoke. Then again, God hid heroes in the Bible all the time.

Running to the cab, I threw open the back suicide door, grabbed the oily rags and saw a box of FireForge on the floor. The red lettering of the box promised "a quick fire, hot and immediate!" Better still, they had a bottle of Fast Boil. I still remembered the song the traveling saleswoman had sung to us.

In a hurry?
Don't toil!
Use Fast Boil.
It never spoils!

I was going to put that last part to the test. I grabbed an armload of supplies and sped back to the bed and plunked down the packages. First the FireForge. I ripped it open and fluffed the ultra-flammable material. I snatched a waterproof match out of my pocket and lit it up.

The wind killed that one dead as well as the next couple. Hands trembling, I dropped two more. Had to get a match to the igniter. Had to get a fire started to heat the water. Had to. Please, Lord Jesus.

The chemical smells of the FireForge soured my nose. I bent closer. I got a match going and touched it to the cottony accelerant. The tinder flashed into flames. I tossed in the oily rags and dry wood. The explosion of heat had me sweating. Good.

I emptied my canteen into the tank. Didn't have water-tubes, another limitation to the 3.0.3. We were going to need more water, a lot more, but I could get what we did have boiling. The Fast Boil came in powdered form, and I sprinkled the chemicals in the water to loosen the molecules so they'd turn from liquid into steam quicker.

I stuffed snow down the top of the tank, added more wood to the firebox, and then started looking for why the salvage monkeys had abandoned the truck in the first place. I was dangerously close to my ten-minute mark, but I also knew Wren would give me a few extra minutes. She was right. Engineering time differed from normal time.

Scurrying on to the bed, I cleared snow away from the hole where the ASI pistons interfaced with the drive train. If there was a problem there, I'd have to grab Tina Machinegun and fight Micaiah's aunts to the death. But no, the big pieces of the engine looked fine.

Must be a problem with the ASI itself. Heat from the fire was clearing away snow around the boiler, which gave me a clear view.

I saw the problem. All four of the pipes leading to the compression chamber had holes in them. Without sealed pipes, the steam couldn't get enough pressure to pump the pistons. The salvage monkey had most likely died before he could fix the problem.

So the fix was easy. Sure. Got any auxiliary ASI 3.0.3 piping on you? I didn't.

The FireForge burned like hellfire, the old logs burned like paper, and I kept having to refill the firebox.

Back in the cab, I rummaged through the debris, praying full novenas, before I found the piping tape, a whole roll, but how old? Ten years gone? Fifteen?

From under the seat, I dug out an ASI toolbox with pipe wrenches and two spare pipes. I needed four, but well, you know—beggars, choosers, all that.

I sprinted back to the pipes and jacked loose the bolts tightened by years of rust. God gave me strength and I got the two new pipes in. I taped up the other two with tape that wasn't sticky at all.

Just had to hope it was heat-activated shrink tape.

I stuffed more snow into the tank. I had a fire. I had sealed pipes, hopefully. Now I just needed steam.

The diesel engines seemed like they were on top of us.

Please, God, help me.

In the driver's seat, I checked the homemade gauges covering the electric displays. My pressure was bad. Prolly wouldn't spin a bicycle tire.

Still. I clutched in. Geared in.

The Excelsior shuddered like a cow lurching out of March mud. Growled, spun, growled some more, then stopped moving. Not enough pressure. I threw her in neutral to wait for the needle to creep into the green on the gauge.

Every minute punched me in the belly. I didn't want to pick up the rifle and fail fighting again. I wanted this to work, to be the unexpected hero, and come through in my own engineering way, just as Wren had always come through with her guns.

The wind died for an instant, the snow cleared, and in the distance, a dozen black all-terrain ATV's barreled through the snow, coming right at us.

Now. It had to be now. Work.

Begging heaven, my bloody hands wet on the gear shifter, I threw her in gear again and drove the gas pedal to the floor.

The Ford wrestled forward, churning through the snow.

Not a second to lose.

I rocketed over to the apartment and tore into the courtyard. The ATVs hadn't found us yet, but we only had seconds.

Micaiah and Wren got Pilate in the back. Petal climbed in, doped up, but moving. Wren threw a leg over Christina Pink. Micaiah slid into the cab next to me.

We raced out of the courtyard and headed north, into the wind, the snow, the storm. Wren galloped after us, her green poncho fluttering darkly against the white landscape.

We'd done it. We'd escaped. But we weren't safe yet.

We still had some fighting to do amongst ourselves.

CHAPTER TWENTY

Sexual ethics, the sanctity of human life, God, the Holy Roman Catholic Church—you cannot pull them apart. They are bound together by fate, history, and divine will. While we respect the work of the New Morality, we cannot tolerate their support of the ARK. God will save our species, not Tiberius Hoyt nor his Satanic research.

—Archbishop Jeremy Corfu
The Ecumenical Council on Ethics and Procreation
Baltimore, Maryland
October 7, 2057

(i)

A while later, the steering wheel was sticky from my blood. Dang gunshot wounds. Running for your life will do that to a girl. The second I remembered about the wounds, a rockslide of agony covered me. Left me breathless. Wren had warned me that once the drugs and adrenaline cleared my system I'd feel the full effects of being shot twice. Even so, I kept us going.

"You okay, Cavatica?" Micaiah asked.

I nodded. My brain had slowed down. Finally. "We'll need you to take everyone's water and get it into the tank and any snow that's in the bed. And there's a bottle of Fast Boil back there."

"Does that stuff actually work?"

I swallowed, croaked out the jingle, and somehow managed a smile.

We stopped so Micaiah could take care of the engine and Petal could get Pilate into the cab. We cleared out the backseat and burned everything that could be burned. The wood was termited and dry, so it burned like paper and the ASI 3.0.3s were horribly inefficient. Like driving around a hungry brick fireplace.

Petal, gone to nodding town on Skye6, slept holding Pilate. His chest rose and fell, thank God. Petal's Mauser lay on the floor, carelessly thrown there.

Wren rode up on Christina Pink, worrying over Pilate. My sister's face colored gray going pasty.

"You okay?" I asked her.

She spit as if disgusted by the question, reined Christina Pink back and moved away, keeping her eyes to the south. Nothing but snow followed us. We'd left tracks heading out of the office complex, but the force and fierceness of the driving snow would soon wipe away our trail.

We drove until we found an old suburban neighborhood. Might've been North Arvada or Boulder, not sure, only that we found ourselves in the middle of a graveyard of houses, entombed in white. Most didn't look salvaged at all, which made them seem even more creepy and silent in the blizzard.

Night was coming, and we needed more wood and fast. Also, I'd need something from Petal's bag of tricks 'cause the pain buried me. Hopefully she had more medical adhesive without Skye6.

I chose a driveway at random and pulled in. The windows of the house were as black as the inside of a coffin.

Micaiah jumped off the bed and came around with Tina Machinegun slung across his shoulder.

I banged out of the truck and my knees nearly came unhinged. My head spun woozy from blood loss, thirst, hunger, full of agony. I should've stayed in the cab, but with Pilate down and Petal sleeping, I wanted to help the boy get fuel for the steam engine. Wren, as usual, wasn't around.

I washed my hands off in the snow and swore I'd force myself to be okay. I was shot. No big deal. I was tough.

Micaiah and I walked right through the front door of the house. Sad to think about that unlocked door. In what kind of panic had the people left? The sky would've been black from the Yellowstone Knockout, ash covering everything, people throwing their possessions into whatever vehicle they had only to jam up the freeways. Others prolly didn't even try and died in their homes.

Sure the houses in the Juniper were haunted. Standing in the kitchen, I could feel the sadness of the ghosts around me.

Micaiah took hold of a cabinet door and ripped it from its hinges. I tried to do the same, but ended up falling against the wall, eyes squeezed closed.

He moved over to me. Close enough to feel his heat. "I know you're trying to be strong, but you can't go on this. I need to give you a half-dose of the Skye6."

I gritted my teeth. "No, we have to find Sharlotte and our headcount. We have to know if they're safe. If the rest of your aunts found them, and if they started asking questions—"

Micaiah didn't let me finish. "Sharlotte wouldn't be able to tell them a thing. She doesn't know who I am, what I have, or anything. Just a vague description of a boy wandering around the Juniper. My aunts would leave them alone."

"Are you sure?" I asked.

"I'm not positive, but what would they gain? Nothing. Because I've kept the apple to myself. It's been hard, but you and Sharlotte are safe. At least in some ways."

Hearing my sister's name stung my soul. Sharlotte. Poor Sharlotte. The honesty in his touch, our *no matter what*, made it clear he wanted me, not her. Or did he think he could have us both?

What did I want? I wouldn't share him. Sharlotte deserved him. I wanted to do the right thing, which was to side with my family, but I wanted him more than my next breath.

His gaze on me was soft. "If I left, you'd be even safer."

An icy anxiety stabbed me at the idea of never seeing him again. "Do you want to leave?"

"Dammit ..." he started in frustration. My head whirled as the dizziness got to me, and I fell against him. We tumbled to the ground with me on top. Perfect for kissing.

Even through all the clothes and jackets, I felt his warmth, his hot breath on my face, and all my parts wanting him. I was betraying my sister, but I couldn't help it. I lost all my resolve in his touch.

Dizzy, so dizzy. Suddenly I was kissing him. But it wasn't like before, that frenzy and moaning. This time I went slow, exploring his mouth, nipping his lips, all instinct and sexy hotness.

Before long, I had his taste in my mouth, and we were both gasping for breath and my heart played an orchestra of lust in my chest. I drew back. Looked him in the eye.

"Don't cuss," I said.

His eyes widened. "I didn't cuss."

"You said 'dammit.'" It was dumb, but I wasn't thinking clearly. It took all my strength to pull back and sit back against the cabinets. "You and I can't do this. 'Cause of Sharlotte. You and I ... it's so good ... but we can't ..." I stuttered and stammered myself into silence. Then I started to cry. "This is wrong. Why can't I stop myself?"

He sat where the refrigerator would've been. "Cavatica."

That one word. My name. It sounded like a song on his lips. I cried harder.

"Cavatica, it's okay. It's natural. Why can't you let yourself be with me?"

Dumb boy, I could give him a list. My sister was in love with him. The kisses were just a gateway drug to the sex. And it wasn't the right time for any kind of romance. I was bleeding and dying. Pilate was bleeding and dying. I'd watched Petal pull a bullet out of Wren. The headcount might've survived the stampede only to be killed by a blizzard. And where were Sharlotte and the rest of our people?

Lastly, and maybe most important, Micaiah was a liar. Lies of omission were just as hateful in the eyes of God as lies of commission.

I took in a big breath, all the wind I could get in me. "If you can't be honest with me, I can't be with you."

He looked away, all emotion disappearing from his face. "Fine." The word came out flat, resigned. "It's better this way. I know what you would do if you knew the truth."

"What would I do?" I asked, troubled he wasn't fighting to keep me.

"You would join me on my quest and you'd call it sacred and you would kill yourself and sacrifice your family to see it all through. Like what you're doing to save your ranch. Please. Please, just let this drop." He begged so hard, I felt a lump grow in my throat.

He knew all about my Catholic determination to do the right thing no matter how heavy the cross on my shoulder.

He knew me, but I didn't know him. It felt unfair and sad. I dropped my head and let myself cry and cry—I cried out all the hardness and sorrow and violence of that long, hard, bad day.

He waited with me while I wept. He didn't try to touch me, and I was glad. Don't know what I would've done. Let him have me. Or punch him in his liar mouth.

I sniffled away the last of my tears. "You said you weren't the snake, fine, but what about Sharlotte? What about what you're doing with the both of us? Which one of us do you want? 'Cause you can't have us both."

"You," he said quickly. "You, Cavatica Jeanne Weller, you. No matter what."

His words stole my breath away. But I just had to ask, "Then why did you go after my sister?"

There was a split second where I could breathe, but the silence felt like a horse hoof on my chest.

"Yeah, Sharlotte, about that." Another long, long pause. "I had to get her on my side. You know I didn't have any other choice, right? She was going to send me away. I had to get close to her." The damn boy blushed. Right there in front of me.

That got my *shakti* going. I stood up and got hateful on him. "You know what, Johnson? We all have choices. You tricking my sister makes you low, no matter how holy your quest is. I'll be out in the truck. Bring those cabinet doors and anything else we can burn. Since you're the only one who ain't bleeding, you might as well be useful for once in your goddamn life."

I'd blasphemed, but I was mad. He had come out and said he'd tricked my sister into loving him, which was a foul thing to do when there were so many women and so few men. I turned to walk away.

"Stop!" It was the first time I'd ever heard him raise his voice. "I'm sorry for what I did to Sharlotte. I'm sorry for dragging you and your family into this. But who I am, what I have, I will do anything to escape the Vixx sisters. Anything. I *am* on a quest, and it *is* sacred, and it's made me do awful things, but I have to protect the Tree of Life. I don't have a choice."

His mouth trembled. His eyes closed. And it was his turn to cry. I crossed back to him. He really was like a storybook knight, sent to do some great, impossible task. And he was right about me. I couldn't say no to a sacred quest.

Like I couldn't say no to him, even though he'd played my sister and might be playing me.

I held him as he sobbed.

It all came down to choices. He didn't think he had a choice. As for me?

I was going to choose, free and clear, to believe him, to believe in him, even though I didn't have the truth. He was torn up, that was clear, about what he had done and the things he might have to do. Like keeping secrets from me. Like wanting to leave to protect us but unable to walk away.

Couldn't blame him. Having to choose between love and saving the world is an impossible situation—choosing one will destroy the other.

CHAPTER TWENTY-ONE

Without the money and science the ARK provided, the Mayo Clinic could not have cured cancer. America turned itself into a factory to create the atomic bomb during World War II. Likewise, it took the nation and another war to find the key to reversing the DNA mutations that cause cancer. Thank you, Tibbs Hoyt.

—Dr. Kristinn Poper
Executive VP of Research,
Mayo Clinic
July 2, 2043

(i)

The front door opened and closed. Wren and Petal shuffled in followed by the sound of a body being dragged.

Micaiah wiped his face, and I gave him a kiss on the cheek. We then moved into the living room. Pilate lay next to the fireplace on a dusty carpet. The furniture was long gone, but old clothes and blankets lay stacked on the hearth next to framed pictures of families and the relatives of strangers. Happy faces smiled at us. Happy or not, it wasn't good salvage. The blankets weren't either, but they were good for us. It was going to be a long, cold night out looking for Sharlotte and our headcount. The sky was already black—the storm had stolen the twilight.

Petal adjusted some bandages on Pilate, and then sank down beside him and fell back asleep. If you could call being high as a kite sleeping.

Micaiah left and came back with an armload of splintered cabinetry. He'd also found a little cache of canned tomato soup. Another bit of luck. We'd eat and get going.

Wren had other ideas. "We're going to stop here for the night." She sat on the window seat. In her hand was the bottle of Pains whiskey, which she'd had before. She took a slurp from it and wiped her mouth with the back of her hand.

"No," I said. "We have to find our people and make sure our headcount is safe."

"Not in the dark, Cavvy." Wren looked at me disgusted, then guzzled more whiskey. "Use your head."

"What about Sharlotte?" I asked.

"We'll find her in the morning. She was going to push our beefsteaks up the old highway through Golden toward Boulder. We'll look for her there."

Wren was calling the shots, but how clear was her head?

"So you're going to get drunk tonight? What if we get attacked?"

She shrugged.

"I hate watching you drink, Wren."

"Then don't watch."

Micaiah unsnapped a frame, crumpled up the picture, and jammed it into the fireplace. I felt bad about him using the pictures as kindling, but then again, every one of those people were prolly dead.

He broke sticks and placed them in a pattern over the torn photographs. He struck a match and soon we had a fire going. The darkness and storm would hide the smoke and the fifty-kilometer-an-hour wind would dissipate the smell.

Not sure if the boy knew how to make a fire before our little adventure, but watching him now, he was doing a good job. He jammed an old pot full of snow next to the flames to melt.

I was feeling faint from my wounds, troubled by Wren's drinking, and so I picked up Petal's bag of tricks and looked for more EMAT, or any adhesive that might help me with the pain. I found the spool, but it was empty. Dang. I sat on the hearth with Tina Machinegun on my lap.

Micaiah watched his fire burn. We were all quiet for several long moments.

Wren drained the last of the bottle and stood up. "Okay, pretty boy. You need to dose Cavvy with Skye6, and then you and I are gonna have us a real long conversation, and every time you get cute about the truth I'm going to smack you."

"No," I said. I used Tina Machinegun to push myself to my feet. I wanted no part of that evil drug, and I sure as heck wasn't going to let Wren intimidate my boy into spilling his secrets. "You leave him alone, Wren."

My sister shook her head and grinned at me. "Love has made you stupid."

She was wrong. Dead wrong.

Love had made me brave.

(ii)

Wren threw a chair leg into the fireplace. The chemical stink of varnish burning blasted out. The living room was downright hot, but dark, like a back alley in the pits of hell.

"Sit down, Cavvy," Wren said in a slur of words. "This is between the boy and me." She walked up to him. "Who grabbed you? Those gals weren't Outlaw Warlords. Too armed and trained and nasty. Was Miss Desert Messiah really your long lost auntie?"

Micaiah didn't say a word. He moved away from her, looking both wary and worried.

"You're going to tell me who you are," Wren growled. "Don't make me beat it out of you."

My sister was determined to pluck the apple off the Tree of Knowledge and eat the whole thing. She pierced him with her drunken gaze. He stood, turned and pierced her right back.

I was off to the side, trying not to fall down, wondering how I could stop Wren.

"I'm not going to tell you who I am," he said. "Not until we're out of the Juniper, and I can give you the reward money for saving me. I will tell you a few things though."

I held my breath, hoping for the truth, but afraid of the Pandora's Box we might be opening.

Wren swayed a little and gestured for him to continue.

"The woman you faced was one of my aunts, Renee Vixx. They can heal almost any wound except for brain trauma or spinal cord injuries. There are now three left ... Rebecca, Ronnie, and Rachel. The last of the identical quadruplets. The other soldiers are called the Cuius Regios. You can think of them as foot soldiers. They will follow any order my aunts give them, but the Regios can't heal like the Vixxes. Now, that's all you need to know. That, and if you get me out of the Juniper, you'll be six million dollars richer."

My mouth went dry. I couldn't believe it. Identical quadruplets, all nearly bulletproof? What he was talking about sounded like cloning and genetic engineering. But that was strictly illegal and highly unlikely—something you might see on the sci-fi show *Altered*, but not in real life. Had to be another explanation.

"You really think I believe you'll give us that kind of money?" Wren asked. "And I ain't buying your fairytale about killer aunts. How can they heal so well, or are they not human?"

Micaiah shrugged.

Wren huffed out a laugh. "You know, but won't say. That won't cut it. You're gonna tell me everything. If we're going to get your jacked-up ass to Nevada, you're going to tell me exactly what kind of hell you've brought down upon us."

Micaiah shook his head, slowly, firmly.

"I could make you talk," Wren said.

"No, you can't."

Wren jerked the Colt Terminator on her right hip out of its holster, dropped the magazine, but caught it with her left hand. She then tossed it up, ejected the shell in the chamber, snatched it from the air like she'd done in Mrs. Justice's office, while at the same time catching the falling magazine and slamming it back into the butt of her pistol.

Quite the juggling act. The whiskey hardly slowed her down.

She tossed him the extra bullet, which he caught on instinct, and then she leveled her Colt at his forehead.

Wren hadn't snapped back the action to load another bullet into the chamber. If she pulled the trigger, it would dry fire.

Micaiah didn't know that. To him, she was pointing a loaded gun at his face.

"Talk. Now." Wren whispered. "Pilate's life is hanging on by a string. My little sister got shot up saving you. And you're playing with Sharlotte's heart as sure as I'm standing here. You don't care about nothing except for your own worthless skin. I want to know why you and your superhero aunties think that skin is so important."

Micaiah's voice quavered. "I won't tell you. So shoot me."

Wren stepped forward in a flash, gun in his face, and drove a fist into his stomach. Micaiah's legs crumbled beneath him. She'd knocked the wind out of him. The bullet he'd caught dropped from his hand and clattered to the floor.

"Talk. Now." Wren repeated.

A sick horror clenched my stomach. She'd hit him. She'd actually hit him.

"No." Micaiah gasped.

"Don't make me do this." Wren cocked her head, blinked, and breathed deep. "Who are you?"

The boy didn't answer.

She lifted a boot to kick him, but I shoved her back.

And lowered Tina Machinegun's barrel at my own sister's chest.

"Get back." I filled those two words with venom and a quiet rage. "You're drunk, and I won't watch you beat the truth out of him. To get to Micaiah, you'll have to kill me. If I don't kill you first."

Wren's sneer crashed off her face—surprise, shock, and finally, a sadness washed through her eyes and sobered her up. She could've taken me easily even if I wasn't suffering and weak. But me pointing a gun at her broke something inside her.

"Cavvy, what are you doing?"

"Leave him alone."

"But we're family. He's just some stupid johnson. What are you doing?" she asked again. She'd lost her swagger and her voice fell weak from her lips.

I had my finger on the trigger of the machine gun. I stared her down. Her gun wasn't loaded. Mine was. "Sharlotte and I love him. We trust him. We're going to help him get to Nevada. His secrets are safe as long as I'm around. End of story."

Micaiah looked on from the floor. As I fought for him. As I stood up to the sister who had terrorized me growing up, who had ignored me, who had beat on me, who had hated me. For the first time in my life, I was going to fight her and I was going to win.

Wren stiffened and, yeah, she'd lost her swagger for a minute but wasn't a second later and she found her smirk. "End of the story? For me it is. For you, it's just the beginning. Fine, Cavvy, you want to play house with this johnson, okay, but when Sharlotte gets wind of this, she is going to come after you. Shame, but I won't be around to see you two fight over some lying sack of boy."

She snapped the action back on the Colt and slammed it into her holster. "We'll just see how y'all do without me. Won't be no marriages on this trip, I don't reckon, but a whole lotta funerals instead." She strutted to the door.

"Where are you going?" I asked. I wasn't aiming the rifle at her anymore, and I felt the shame of what I'd done keenly. You don't aim a gun at anything you don't want to destroy. It's the first rule of gun safety. Still, I couldn't have stood by and watched her hurt Micaiah. Never.

She turned and looked me dead in the eye, swallowed hard, and said in a sorrowful fury, "Before, on the *Moby Dick*, you said you couldn't take that shot 'cause you couldn't risk me. That you loved me. And earlier today, when that Vixx skank had me, you couldn't take that shot either. Now, though, now I bet you could. Wouldn't even aim. Wouldn't even care if you killed me."

"Wait." My head was swirling again, the adrenaline of the confrontation getting to me.

She didn't. She took off into the blizzard.

I wanted to go after her, but I couldn't. I fell.

Again, Micaiah caught me.

"I need something for the pain," I said in a long breath. I felt deflated, torn, horrible for pointing our family's M16 at my sister.

"God," I whispered, "what have I done?"

CHAPTER TWENTY-TWO

War is no big deal. We've been killing each other since Cain and Abel. What's important is how we choose to live once the bullets stop flying. Once the bloodshed is over, what kind of people do we want to be?

—Former President Jack Kanton
48th President of the United States
On the 29th Anniversary of the start of the
Sino-American War
July 28, 2057

(i)

Though I hated the idea of doing drugs, Micaiah gave me a half-dose of the Skye6, 2.5 milliliters. The half-dose was enough to push most of the pain away, but not all. I was left hurting, but still feeling floaty, while I sat on the hearth next to the popping fireplace.

"You're good at giving people shots," I murmured. "You've done it before, haven't you?"

A sad smile painted his face. "I could lie to you and say my mother has Type 1 diabetes and I grew up giving her shots. That would be a really good lie, wouldn't it?"

"It would. But what's the truth?"

"The truth is that I've already let too much slip by because I hate lying to you, Cavatica. I hate it."

"Okay," I said softly. "Tell me why you knew so much about the Hays beef market back on that first night. You knew how much our herd was worth. How?"

"By listening." He winked at me. "You guys were constantly talking about Howerter, the CRTA, and the price of beef. I can do a lot of things well, but the thing I do best? I listen. And draw connections."

We ate hot tomato soup from the old cans. It had a tinny, acidic taste to it, and we had to share the one spoon I carried around with me. Juniper folks always carried spoons. Forks were a luxury, we used our Betty knives mostly, but spoons were a necessity.

Both Pilate and Petal were laid out on the floor by the fireplace, and it was hard to tell who was the patient and who was the doctor. I hated Pilate, but I couldn't imagine a world where he wasn't walking around, smirking, and saving us. I needed him, and not just for security. He was the closest thing to a father I had, and yet, what a miserable excuse for a man he was. In some ways, he even made Wren look sane.

Wren. My poor sister. I picked up the bullet she'd thrown at Micaiah and put it in my pocket.

After eating, Micaiah and I moved to the cushioned window seat where he'd fashioned a musty-smelling nest of moth-eaten blankets. My dress and leggings had dried, and I was glad for their warmth. The living room glowed red from the coals in the fireplace, while the corners were as shadowy as the abyss. The window showed us the unbroken windy-white of the storm.

I relaxed into his arms, my back feeling the hard muscles of his chest. I'd said I couldn't be with him romantically, not with how things were, but I couldn't help but let him hold me and comfort me. However wrong, it felt really good. I needed the comforting.

We hadn't heard Wren ride away on Christina Pink. I figured she'd hide out in another house, get her own fire burning, and bring Christina Pink into the living room to keep her warm. She'd take care of my pony, but I didn't imagine I'd see her or the horse again.

"She'll be back," Micaiah said as if reading my worried mind. "She won't just abandon you all."

"You have a lot to learn about family," I said. "Wren's always been a stranger in our home. From the very beginning."

"I'm sorry I got between you. Can you forgive me?"

I nodded. Didn't want to talk. The way I was feeling, if I talked, I might cry, and I was tired of crying in front of him. Tired of crying. Period.

He seemed to understand. He kept his hand in mine and spoke over my shoulder, his breath warm and soft on my cheek. "Tomorrow, everything will be better. Pilate will wake up. Wren'll come back, and we'll find Sharlotte and the cattle. Headcount, that's what you call all your cattle, isn't that right?"

Another nod from me.

"With the storm, the Vixx sisters and their Regios won't be able to really search for us, not like they could in nice weather. But I want you to know, I'm going to leave. I can't keep risking you or your family."

"No," I choked out the word. "If Wren is really gone, we'll need you."

"You don't know how powerful they are," he said softly. "Or what they'll do to get me."

"I won't let them hurt you. I'll fight them. Whatever they are."

He fell silent. He wasn't going to reveal anything else.

I shivered, then felt a pinch in my arm and I realized a goathead thorn was stuck there in the folds of my dress. We also called those burrs devil's thorn, from some weed brought over by Europeans. Not sure where it had come from, but I pinched it off my skin and held it there.

"What's that?" Micaiah asked.

"A thorn. They come from the flowers of weeds."

We didn't say anything for a long time. I'd been such a flower in Cleveland, a weed maybe, according to Becca Olson. But now? That flower was gone. Was I destined to become a thorn like Wren? Or just tough like Sharlotte?

I threw the devil's thorn away and relaxed into Micaiah's arms.

"Are we halfway?" Micaiah asked.

Even if we were in Boulder, heck, even if we were in Fort Collins, we were still hundreds of kilometers short.

"No," I murmured. Pilate shot, Petal uncertain, Wren prolly gone forever, and Sharlotte and our headcount lost, it felt like certain failure.

We hadn't made it halfway. And I felt the defeat keenly.

"You can't leave." I yawned, getting sleepy. "I fought Wren so you could keep your secrets and stay with us. You'll stay, right?"

Again, he got quiet, but at the same time, he held me tighter.

Being human is hard. Our hearts hold a million desires, each fighting the others and all complaining. Micaiah wanted to stay. He wanted to tell me the truth, but at the same time, he wanted to keep me safe.

Problem was, safety never stayed around long in the Juniper.

(ii)

In the early morning hours, I woke to the sound of internal combustion engines roaring down the street outside. The window was a sheet of ice from the condensation of our breathing and the cold. The fire was long dead, so they wouldn't see or smell the smoke. Micaiah kept my body warm, but my heart froze in my chest at the sound of the ATVs.

We didn't say a word—just listened as the sound of the engines faded away to the north. The blizzard had covered our tracks. My plan had worked, and I felt proud for a minute. I'd gotten us out of trouble and no one had been killed in the process. The bad guys had missed us.

I hoped they also missed Wren, wherever she was.

(iii)

Later that morning, Micaiah ran recon and confirmed the ATVs hadn't stopped anywhere near us. We were safe.

The storm still raged, giving us cover to find Sharlotte, our people, our cattle.

Before I knew it, I was back in the Ford Excelsior, riding shotgun. Micaiah drove 'cause I was in too much pain to do anything but keep my eyes squeezed shut, trying not to hate Petal. She gave herself full doses while I had to settle for half, half-alive and half-dead.

Even full doses weren't enough for Petal. She was chewing on her thumbnail like it was a dog's squeaky toy. The black pits of her eyes ate up her pale face—it seemed she was about five seconds from losing it and murdering us all.

She caught me gazing at her. "I know what my medicine is now. I know it's just Skye6. You think I'm some addict, but I'm not. I'm going to quit once this cattle drive is over."

"Why wait?" I murmured.

Her voice broke out nasty. "If you want me to keep killing for you, Cavvy, I need to be high to do it."

Ouch.

I turned away to watch the wind blasting around the snowflakes while I worried. If she got clean, she couldn't shoot, and if Wren was gone, we were left with only one gunslinger, Pilate, who was currently unconscious.

Without security, we'd have to turn east. We'd have to go to Mavis, sell all of our beef for pennies, and hope she took pity on us enough to help us pay back Howerter.

No. I grit my teeth. We'd find Sharlotte and our cows, and we'd go on, even if I had to shoot every outlaw skank in the Juniper myself. Which was a joke 'cause I was terrible under fire.

That thought killed my hope and determination—both were already under attack from the general agony of my gunshot wounds. Every pitch and bump of the Ford in the snow made my teeth clench and my heart shrivel. I longed to be unconscious.

I was about to beg someone to hit me over the head when the wind had one last tear about the sky and dropped to nothing. The snow ceased like someone had unplugged it. We came up onto a ridge and Micaiah stopped the truck.

"What is it?" I asked miserably.

"Down there. I think I saw something." Micaiah threw open the door, threw more scrap wood into the firebox, then banged back into the truck.

We chugged down an incline toward a huge building, standing above ruins like a castle. I figured it had been an old government building, but it was hard to tell 'cause only concrete and a little roofing remained.

Then I knew. From her years of salvage, Mama taught us how to figure out the purpose of a building just by looking at the leftovers. Kind of like figuring out how some old lady might have looked at her junior prom.

The building had been a shopping mall, now scrapped out and demolished, rooftops sunk under snow.

Micaiah turned off the engine. Petal was zombified, chewing on her fingernails. Pilate was comatosing.

When Micaiah got out, I followed him, though moving sent icy needles of pain through my arm and shoulder. My head joined in the fun by aching something awful, and I thought I might be running a fever.

Then I heard the lowing of cattle, inside the shopping mall. Relief flooded through me. We'd found our cattle, and I just knew, our people were close by.

Micaiah helped me push through the snow, waist deep in some places, and we stepped through the outlines of shattered glass doors and into the mall's wide corridor. Everything had been stripped and carted off, no merchandise, no gates—nothing but cracked tiles, concrete and cinderblocks remained.

The smell of beefsteak hit us strong, and I knew instantly what Sharlotte had done. That girl, real clever. She'd found shelter from the storm. A sanctuary.

A pretty cow came nosing out of a shop like she was looking for a Cinnabon. I chuckled. Micaiah joined me.

We edged past the cow and what might have been a Macy's or a Nordstrom's. The glass counters, the display racks, even the guts of the escalators were gone. Instead, our headcount packed the open space. Some of the beefsteaks bawled, some wrestled around ornery, some stood content. All they needed was something to eat and a few free samples from the perfume counter.

Micaiah and I were gazing at the cows when I heard a familiar voice. "The food court's gone, but Aunt Bea is preparing us an early dinner. Ten bucks a plate. We'll charge you the family rate. Eleven dollars and fifty cents."

It was Sharlotte, making the rare joke. She and Dolly Day Cornpone stood in the main corridor, MG21 rifles over their shoulders. Dolly Day let out a triumphant yell, and soon everyone had gathered around us.

I was hugged over and over by our hires and hands. I watched Sharlotte forget herself and throw her arms around Micaiah, nearly in tears, she was so happy to see him.

The acid of my guilt burned my belly.

When Sharlotte approached me, I shifted my feet uncomfortably. She didn't hug me, only put out a hand. I took it, but I couldn't look her in the eyes, so I glanced around, forcing a grin. "Dang, Sharlotte, what an idea, bringing the cows in here."

She shrugged. "It was the only thing that made sense. You okay? You look pale."

"I'm okay," I whispered.

"Where's everyone else?" Sharlotte asked. "What happened?"

I didn't say a thing. I couldn't tell the full story in front of our employees. If they found out I'd driven Wren away, or that we'd been chased by soldiers, nearly impossible to kill, riding through Juniper on diesel-powered engines, all to get Micaiah, well, morale would be a problem. Right then, it was best they thought it was more June Mai Angel evilness.

Micaiah took over. He spoke with joy and relief in his voice, once again showing how easily he could spin things in a way that encouraged people to believe exactly what he wanted them to. Who was he? And how could he lie so easily?

Micaiah didn't mention his aunts, nor did he talk about how close we'd come to dying. He simply said we'd rescued him, Pilate and Petal were in the truck, and Wren was out scouting. In the end, that boy made it sound more like a church picnic than a vicious gunfight.

I'd chosen to trust Micaiah, had even pointed a gun at my sister, but now doubt crept into me. If he could lie so easily about our adventures since the stampede, could he also be lying to me about his quest? He said he hated keeping secrets from me, but of course he would say that if he was a manipulative snake.

Folks were sent out to bring Pilate and Petal into the shopping mall. Aunt Bea served up *tacos al carbón* and *horchata*, and it was a party. Even though Pilate was wounded, he was still alive, and we were safe for the moment. Everyone laughed and hugged, so glad we were all back together. The dogs curled around our legs, barking, tails wagging, as happy as everyone else.

I sipped a little of the sweet milk, nibbled a taco, but I wasn't hungry or thirsty. Or maybe I was, but too troubled to know it. I felt stifled.

I went outside for some fresh air, but there was no place to sit, so I went to sit on the bed of the Excelsior. I was done in, exhausted, guilt-ridden.

Sharlotte came up and sat beside me.

"You're hurt bad," Sharlotte said. "And something else is going on. Tell me."

I found some words to say, none of them good. "Wasn't June Mai Angel. It was other soldiers, well-armed, well-trained, and we were lucky to get away. They're bad, Shar, worst we ever fought. And they want Micaiah. They'll do anything to get him, and we don't have a clue who he really is."

"Micaiah is good. We can trust him."

"I want to. I think I do. But you saw his performance back there. He's a really good liar."

And so was I. Sharlotte didn't seem a bit suspicious. Of course she'd trust him. She was in love with him.

The sun broke through the clouds, throwing down light and heat. The world seemed to sigh.

A *V* of Canadian geese drifted overhead. I recalled my time at Sally Browne Burke Academy for the Moral and Literate and my own migration.

I missed the wood of the classrooms, the video screens on the walls, even the simple drama of Becca Olson, fighting with my best friend Anju over Billy Finn. Cleveland and the World never felt farther.

"We aren't even halfway," I murmured.

"Yes, we are," Sharlotte said evenly. "Not in kilometers, but in effort. We got out of Burlington. We made it through Denver and only lost three hundred head doing it. Your plan was good. You have a good head on your shoulders, and I don't appreciate you enough. Who knows? Maybe if you and I work together, we might make it to Nevada."

We stared at each other for a long time. She'd said nice things about me, talked about us working together, and somehow she seemed different, more human. Was she still under the influence of Micaiah's spell, or was something else going on?

"You think we can make it?" I asked.

"Maybe. Yes. No. I don't know." Sharlotte let a grin creep across her lips. "We have those dry Wyoming deserts ahead of us. The Rocky Mountains. The Great Salt Flats. We made it through June Mai Angel's territory, but we still have to make it through the Psycho Princess. And now we have new enemies gunning for us. This cattle drive was doomed to fail from the start, but I would imagine when you risk everything on a long shot, it always feels like that."

"Like Mama playing poker," I said.

Sharlotte turned sour. "Like Mama."

"Mama was only thinking outside the box," I said gently. "Howerter's greed and revenge forced us into this. We didn't have a choice."

"We always have a choice," Sharlotte said. "I'm seeing that more and more." Her hand was in her pocket, worrying over what was inside.

I didn't have the strength to ask about it. Instead, I let myself be young. I inched over and leaned against her. Instead of getting up and going back to work, Sharlotte held me as we watched the sun sparkling on the snow. The noise of the geese disappeared and only silence remained.

I pushed a hand into the pocket of my dress and felt the bullet I'd picked up off the floor. "Wren's gone. I chased her off."

"She'll come back," Sharlotte said. "Irene likes to make a big show of things, but in the end, she can't stay away 'cause we're connected, a cluster of thorns stuck in God's heel, forever vexing Him, forever reminding Him about us and all our troubles."

Her words were pretty. Another surprise, such poetry coming from my big sister.

I thought about what she had said about being halfway. Despite all the danger ahead of us, Micaiah's secrets, our wounds, Wren leaving, I couldn't help but feel we'd make it to the stockyards of Wendover.

There we'd sell our headcount, make a fortune, and finally learn the truth about Micaiah.

But would Sharlotte be willing to hold me like her sister when she discovered my love for Micaiah and his love for me? Or would it tear our family apart?

The pain, the guilt, the sorrow overwhelmed me. I'd been praying to be unconscious all day. Finally, God found pity on me. I closed my eyes and slipped into the darkness, even as the sun shined down—on us, on the Vixxes, on all of the Juniper—the just and the unjust alike.

MEMORARE

Remember, O most gracious Virgin Mary,
that never was it known that anyone who fled to your protection,
implored your help, or sought your intercession,
was left unaided.

—Traditional Roman Catholic Prayer

(i)

ama used to whisper the Memorare every night over us before we went to sleep. As if we needed the Virgin Mary's intercession during our dreams. Really, we should've said it before breakfast 'cause our days were generally far more troubled than our nights.

The Virgin Mary was working overtime during our cattle drive, which was how we all came together in the big shopping mall full of cows. All of us except for Wren.

After passing out beside Sharlotte, what felt like an instant later, I jerked awake to find myself lying in a bed, in a nice bedroom, not salvaged, but lived in, smelling like home. Someone had taken me there. Thank you, Mary, Mother of God.

For a second, I thought I was in my old room, and I had dreamed those last few horrible weeks of our doomed cattle drive. Nice idea, but it was a lie. My room was blue—this one glowed yellow. Gold curtains, trimmed in lace, covered the window. On top of a polished dresser sat a little ceramic vase full of plastic daisies.

I had no idea where I was, or how long I'd been there.

My life had changed again it seemed, as quickly as it had when Wren came traipsing into my principal's office with her 9mm pistol and a wicked smile.

I pulled myself, wincing at the fiery pain in my left arm and shoulder. It made me never want to move again, though that was just wishful thinking.

A cotton nightgown dotted with little pink flowers covered me. Other than the bandages on my shoulder, I was naked underneath. Someone had washed and dressed me, which was just plain embarrassing. Medical supplies lay in an orbit around me— sponges, rags, bandages. I checked, and yeah, under the bedding was a rubber sheet covering the mattress. Which made me even more embarrassed. I'd been a real chore for someone.

I put my bare feet on the floor and noticed my toenails needed to be clipped. Hadn't really looked at my feet for a long time. For weeks they'd been in boots.

Standing, I teetered for a minute, and then the dizziness sent me down onto my butt. I slumped over, my cheek resting on the floor, my body curled up in agony. I said the Memorare until the pain subsided, then opened my eyes.

Under the bed lay a magazine in the dust. Something made me grab it. Something deep inside.

Sliding it out, I got upright, my back against the bed.

Ads for *Lonely Moon* merchandise filled the back cover— perfume, accessories, shirts and hoodies, that kind of thing. They even had a genuine *Lonely Moon* duster as worn by the cast of the show and you could order it by express mail.

I remembered how much Anju loved each episode. How comfortable we'd been watching the Juniper drama in our dorm room, so safe and protected.

I flipped the magazine over to look at the front cover. It was the Christmas issue of *Modern Society* magazine, December, 2057, an actual paper copy, printed for the Juniper since everyone in the World would read it on their electric slates.

A handsome young man flashed a breathtaking smile at me from the cover. Hair, sandy brownish blond, a little long, half-covered his bright blue eyes, just enough to be the very essence of fashion even with the red and white Santa cap on his head.

I recognized the face instantly. My heart took off in a sprint.

I read the caption—*Micah Hoyt. What do you get the boy who has everything?*

Micaiah was actually Micah Hoyt, the son of Tiberius "Tibbs" Hoyt, president and CEO of the American Reproduction Knowledge Initiative. The richest, most powerful man in the United States of America. No. He was more than that. Tibbs Hoyt was king of the world.

And my sister and I had fallen soul-deep in love with his son, a true prince if there ever was one.

To be continued ...

Cavatica Weller will return in *Killdeer Winds*,
book two of the Juniper Wars series.

Glossary of Historical Figures, Slang, and Technology

Angel, June Mai—The most powerful of the outlaw warlords and the most organized. Her past is a mystery, but her soldiers are fierce. She controls the Denver area, from Colorado Springs to Fort Collins.

ASI Attachment—A steam engine that can interface with the drivetrains of larger vehicles such as trucks or minivans. Manufactured by the American Steam Ingenuity Company.

ARK—The American Reproduction Knowledge Initiative—A publicly funded corporation researching the Sterility Epidemic and running insemination clinics across the world.

AZ3—The next generation of assault rifle manufactured by Armalite Industries. Includes self-correcting laser targeting, tactical readout/ammunition count, and water-cooled barrels.

Beefsteaks—Cattle

Besharam—Shameless (from the Hindi word)

Besiya—Prostitute (from the Hindi word)

Burke, Sally Browne—Co-founder of the New Morality movement

Chalkdrive—Removable computer storage devices

Cargador—A large steam-powered vehicle used in the Juniper for salvaging operations and later as military vehicles.

Colton, Anna—Professor of Sociology, Princeton University, and a firm supporter of women's rights outside of religious or domestic roles.

Corfu, Archbishop Jeremy—An archbishop of the Roman Catholic Church in the U.S. and highly critical of the ARK and any artificial insemination outside of marriage.

CTRA—The Colorado Territory Ranching Association—An organization created by Robert "Dob" Howerter, presumably to ensure high quality beef and ethical ranching practices, but in reality was used to fix prices and drive other ranchers out of business.

EMAT—Emergency Medication Absorption Tape—A delivery system for medication during combat situations.

Eterna Batteries—A perfectly clean power source created by General Electric. Named after Chinese food, the most powerful and efficient is the Kung Pao. A weaker version is the Egg Drop.

Frictionless Automobiles—The next generation in automotive engineering, frictionless cars float thirty centimeters off the ground.

Gillian—Lesbian (from the Mandarin phrase *tong xing lian*)

Girly 'strogen—Excessively feminine ('strogen is short for estrogen)

Headcount—The number of cattle owned by a ranch

Howerter, Robert "Dob"—Founder of the Colorado Territory Ranching Association and the largest cattle baron in the Juniper

Hoyt, Tiberius "Tibbs"—President and CEO of the American Reproduction Knowledge Initiative

Jankowski, Maggie—Lead engineer on the Eterna battery project funded by General Electric

Johnson—A derogatory term for a male

Jones, Calvin "Crush"—Founder of the Old Glory Salvage and Renewal Company and the first to become what was later known as the Juniper Millionaires

Juniper—1,438,577 square kilometers in the middle of the United States of America comprising what once was Colorado, New Mexico, Utah, Wyoming, Montana, and sections of surrounding states. Due to the Yellowstone Knockout and the subsequent flood basalt, electrical current does not function in this area.

Kanton, Jack Anthony—48th President of the United States of America and the second president to hold four terms in office.

Kutia—Female dog (from the Hindi word)

MG21—Standard issue assault rifle in the Sino-American War.

Male Product—The male reproductive cell.

Masterson-Wayne Act—Signed into law by President Jack Kanton in 2033, this act of Congress relegated the five states affected by the Yellowstone Knockout back to being territories.

Meetchum, Mavis—Second largest cattle operator in the Colorado territory. Located in Sterling, she has established treaties with the Wind River people and is a strong advocate for Native American rights. She introduced buffalo back into Wyoming in the mid-2030s during a critical time for the Wind River people.

MRE—Meal, Ready-to-Eat.

Neofiber—A variant of carbon fiber but stronger and lighter

New Morality—A religious movement with socio-political connections that encouraged women to remain chaste, dress appropriately, and behave in a conservative manner.

New Morality Dress—A dress of a neutral color (usually gray, brown, or cream-colored) that covers as much of a woman's body as possible to comply with New Morality etiquette.

Old Growth—A synthetic coal created from wood taken from old-growth forests

Parson, Reverend Kip—Co-founder of the New Morality movement

RSD—Reality Simulator Displays—Video screens with near-perfect resolution

Sapropel—A weak fuel used for heating and lighting in the Juniper. Chemically manufactured by using remnants of oil shale.

Shakti—Raw female power (from the Hindi word)

SISBI—The Security, Identity, and Special Borders Injunction (SISBI) is a set of laws enacted by a special executive order that requires all U.S. citizens to register eye-scans with the government. It also allows for border fences around the Juniper and military units to secure the perimeter of the territories.

Skye6—Diacetylmorphinesextus (a synthetic morphine)

Slate—Tablet computer

Sterility Epidemic—First cases discovered in January of 2030. One in ten births are male. Of males born, 90% are sterile.

Thelium—Theta-helium—Synthetic helium manufactured to give zeppelins greater lift.

Thor Stunner—Eterna-powered electrical non-lethal weapon

Viable—Non-sterile (refers to males)

Weller, Abigail—Growing up in the family business (The Buckeye Urban Recycling and Reclamation Company), Abigail Weller chose to enter the Juniper to run salvage for Crush Jones. After the Salvage Era, she operated the third largest ranch in the Colorado territory until her death in the winter of 2058. She had three daughters: Sharlotte, Wren, and Cavatica.

Wind River People—The general term for all Native American tribes living in the Wyoming and Montana territories.

Yellowstone Knockout—A term used to describe China's missile attack on the Yellowstone caldera and the subsequent flood basalt.

Zeppelins—Four classes of airships: Jonesies, Jimmies, Johnnies, and Bobbies. All manufactured by Boeing for use in the Juniper. Jimmies are engineered for maximum speed and Johnnies for maximum cargo hold. Bobbies are a mid-size zeppelin. Lastly, Jonesies are the most customizable. Also known as dirigibles or blimps, the airships have rigid skeletons of Neofiber covered with next-generation lightweight Kevlar. The superstructure contains air-cells filled with thelium.

Zeus 2 Charge Gun—Eterna-powered electric rifle for short-range lethal combat and area-of-attack demolition.

IF YOU LIKED ...

If you liked *Dandelion Iron*, you might also enjoy:

Oshenerth
Alan Dean Foster

Blood Ties
Quincy J. Allen

Crystal Doors
Rebecca Moesta and Kevin J. Anderson

ABOUT THE AUTHOR

Aaron Michael Ritchey is the author of *The Never Prayer*, *Long Live the Suicide King*, and *Elizabeth's Midnight*. He was born on a cold and snowy September day in Denver, Colorado, and while he's lived and traveled all over the world, he's a child of the American West. Sagebrush makes him homesick. While he pines for Paris, he still lives in Colorado with his cactus flower of a wife and two stormy daughters.

A NOTE FROM THE AUTHOR

I hoped you enjoyed reading *Dandelion Iron*. The second book, *Killdeer Winds*, will be available in the coming months.

A prequel novella based in the world of the *Juniper Wars* series is available now. *Armageddon Dimes* takes place five years before the events of *Dandelion Iron* and follows the adventures of a returning Sino-American War veteran, Mariposa Hernandez. Bored of civilian life, haunted by the war, Mariposa is invited by a long lost friend on a treasure hunt into the wastelands of Denver. Can Mariposa reclaim a fortune in abandoned dimes before the ghosts of her past consume her?

Another prequel story is available for free on www.Wattpad.com. *Trapdoor Boy* is about Robert, a rare, viable boy, who carries a secret that is crushing him.

I have invited other writers to write short stories in the world of *The Juniper Wars*, and I'm excited to share their work with you. I'll be making them available to my newsletter subscribers and to anyone who is interested in the series. For more about me, my books, and *The Juniper Wars*, visit my website at:

www.aaronmritchey.com.

OTHER WORDFIRE PRESS TITLES

Our list of other WordFire Press authors and titles is always growing. To find out more and to see our selection of titles, visit us at:

wordfirepress.com

Made in the USA
Charleston, SC
08 May 2016